The albinos were an Umibozu l
tially more potent than that o
his sword. Unlike Katou's, his wa
late Tokugawa period. The Umibozu
with tridents, but the specimens he had trained responded just as well to his sword. He pointed the blade at the disgraced captain who stared resolutely into those white eyestalks.

"Kurikka," he said, the best translation he could come up with for what the Umibozu themselves called the creatures, "strike!"

The Kurikka obediently charged, its claws working into a frenzy. It caught Katou in its grasp and held him tight before its tail flashed forward and stabbed the general through the chest. Blood erupted from Katou's mouth and his teeth were gritted tight, but all present could hear the pained wheezing escaping from his throat. His flesh turned a bright shade of orange. Ota had seen this happen before on test subjects.

Katou's flesh rippled, then the skin began to slide away, wet piles melted to the floor. Ota watched with special pride as the general didn't so much as open his mouth to scream, as was fitting during seppuku.

Nor did he scream when his eyes melted and rolled out of their sockets. Truly the man was a credit to the Japanese fighting man, and Hanshiro regretted his loss.

The Kurikka feasted, white claws scooping up puddles of flesh and shoveling them into its mouth. Ota stood before it without fear, looking at each of Katou's men in the eyes, their faces filled with terror. No. Not Katou's men any longer. They were his now, welly and truly.

ISBN 978-1-63789-807-9

For information address Crossroad Press at 141 Brayden Dr., Hertford, NC 27944
A Macabre Ink Production -Macabre Ink is an imprint of Crossroad Press.
www.crossroadpress.com

First Trade Edition

CLICKERS NEVER DIE

STEPHEN KOZENIEWSKI
AND WILE E. YOUNG

This book is dedicated to the memory of Mark Williams and J.F. Gonzalez.

A NOTE FROM THE AUTHORS

If you've identified a factual or historical discrepancy in this book, please bear in mind that the seeming error was deliberate on our part. We wished to signal to those truly "in the know" that this novel takes place in a reality somewhat different from our own. Subtle differences such as PT boats appearing at Guadalcanal three months early, or a military head of Los Alamos rather than civilian, are meant to hint at the deeper secrets hiding in this tragic timeline. That, or a wizard did it.

- Kozeniewski and Young

A NOTE FROM THE ESTATE OF J.F. GONZALEZ

This work is a reboot of the *Clickers* franchise, and should be considered separate and removed from the previous continuity found in the novels *Clickers, Clickers II: The Next Wave, Clickers III: Dagon Rising,* and *Clickers vs. Zombies,* the *Clickers Forever* anthology, or the various short stories they've appeared in. In other words, these are not your parents' Clickers. These are Clickers for a new generation. Because Clickers never die…

- Brian Keene

"Old Clickers never die, they simply…argh! It got me in the eyes! It got me in the eyes!"

- Douglas MacArthur, last words

CLICKERS: THE NEXT GENERATION

AN INTRODUCTION BY BRIAN KEENE

In 1993, J.F. (Jesus) Gonzalez and Mark Williams began working together on a novel called Wave of Terror. It was meant to be tribute to the horror and science fiction B movies of the 1950s, Guy N. Smith's Crabs series, and other "munch-out" novels such as James Herbert's Rats series and Sean Huston's Slugs saga. It was also meant to have elements of both extreme horror and something akin to H.P. Lovecraft's mythos. In talking about Wave of Terror, Jesus said: "We were more interested in appealing to readers who were into H.P. Lovecraft's Cthulhu or Richard Laymon's The Cellar and The Beast House…Mark and I grew up with the monsters in the cinema and between the covers of magazines like Famous Monsters of Filmland and books like The Rats by James Herbert, and this is the book we intended to write. We had no use for flowery purple prose, obscure metaphors, or politically-correct statements or themes. We wanted monsters, blood and guts, violence, naked women, and some humor. In short, a Roger Corman movie on paper."

Jesus once told me that he figured it actually took them about six months to write Wave of Terror, but that actual process was spread out over a period of three years, due to their other commitments. Jesus was editing two horror magazines at the time—Iniquities and Phantasm—and Mark was shopping several screenplays, and doing artwork for films like The Fly and the Alien franchise). Horror fiction, as a publishing category, was healthy when they started collaborating on the book, but by the time they had finished it, the genre was undergoing a now historic collapse. Again, in Jesus's own words: "I loved the book…was having a great time writing it. But during its initial composition I was learning from friends and colleagues that the entire market for horror novels was collapsing. So how did Mark and I react? We ignored what was going on in publishing and continued writing the book anyway. How's that for throwing caution to the wind?"

Here is an excerpt from Jesus's journals, about the creation of the novel: "Set in the fictional town of Phillipsport, Maine, this is the straightforward story of a young author who relocates to the small town to get away from the big city. Coincidentally, upon his arrival, the town is besieged by hundreds of giant crabs which go on a killing spree in the town, reminiscent of Guy N. Smith's Crab series, of which Mark was influenced by and who provided the initial seed of inspiration for this work. The crabs are also equipped with scorpion like appendages and highly toxic venom which acts as a corrosive on flesh. After joining the town in fighting the creatures off, Rick, along with the town physician, get the impression the creatures aren't so much as invading the town, but are trying to escape something from the ocean. And the next day, with all the creatures dead, something from the ocean does come. Giant, man-like amphibian creatures who hunt the crab things for food, that display human like intelligence. More slaughter occurs, and in the end Rick manages to escape with one of the people he met earlier in town, a waitress named Melissa, but not without seeing a woman he has come to fall in love with and her son be brutally killed by what he has come to call The Dark Ones. With Melissa, he escapes government detection as the government has covered up the truth about what happened, and plans a dossier that will unravel the truth and expose the secret of the life that exists in the deepest part of the ocean.

This novel was originally conceived by Mark in '91, and in '93 we talked about collaborating on it together. We started the novel in late '93, and in early '94 showed a portion to Pat LoBrutto at Zebra, who was interested and wanted to see the rest of it. Midway through the year, Pat left Zebra, and both myself and Mark became involved in outside projects (films with Don Jackson for Mark, Phantasm Magazine for me). In late '95, I resumed writing the book with the help and input of Mark and finished it in Spring of '96. Its pulpiness, reminiscent of the British "Nasties" which it was intended as an homage to, has made it a difficult sell. It was almost bought in '98 by Canadian Publisher Commonwealth Publishers, but the deal was nixed by me due to a bad contract. The novel will inevitably see print in some form, either serialized in a small press magazine, or on the web."

It is also worth noting that Kensington had also expressed renewed interest in publishing the book in paperback, but by then, the horror market had completely collapsed.

Time passed.

And then so did Mark, who died in 1998.

Jesus wanted to honor his friend. He saw Wave of Terror as Mark's legacy, and he was determined that the rest of the world see it, as well. And so, even with the pressures and responsibilities of having just become a father to a newborn daughter, he continued to shop the manuscript. Eventually, he sold the electronic rights to Hard Shell Word Factory and the print rights to DarkTales Publications, both in 2000. The title was changed from Wave of Terror to Clickers. Through Hard Shell, it was released (as were Jesus's novels Conversion and Shapeshifter) as one of the very first e-books—a then unheard of and untested concept. If only for that reason alone, Clickers deserves a place in publishing history, particularly. But Clickers was also one of the first bona fide hits of our generation of horror writers. Its success earned Jesus a devoted readership. It has since gone through countless printings in many different languages and has become a genuine cult classic, viewed by many critics and academics as a seminal work of pulp horror.

It also went on to spawn three book-length sequels—Clickers II: The Next Wave, Clickers III: Dagon Rising, and Clickers vs. Zombies, (all co-written with me), a tribute anthology called Clickers Forever, and several short stories. And the Clickers themselves have since guest-starred or made cameo appearances in works by other authors in the genre, all with Jesus's blessing.

Fair to say that Jesus honored Mark's legacy, and then some.

Since we were already good friends, and knowing that I was a fan of the first novel, when Jesus decided to continue the franchise, he asked me to collaborate with him on the first sequel, rather than writing it by himself. I said yes, because I wanted to help out my friend, and because I thought it would be fun to play with the Clickers and the Dark Ones (and Colonel Livingston, whom I had a fondness for). We started writing, and soon found out that we worked very well together, with both of us able to end in the middle of a sentence and pick up where the other person left off without thinking about it. Our styles meshed. Our imaginations meshed. And our love of the horror genre—and of all of the things that inspired the first Clickers—meshed. I've been lucky enough to collaborate with a number of our peers over the years, and enjoyed every one of those efforts, but with Jesus, it was often like I was writing with myself. He used to say the same thing.

The books became popular. Not bestsellers—but reliable, steady sellers. Critics called the series "a cult hit" and in this case, they were right. Even in the worst months, when nothing we'd written seemed to be selling, Jesus and I could always count on receiving royalty checks for the Clickers books. That's one of the reasons we kept writing them—for the money. Why lie about it? We made a lot of money from these ridiculous crab-scorpion-lobster monsters over the year. And since both of us had families to care for and support, that was always something that factored into our decisions. But we also kept writing them because it was just so much goddamned fun. We had a blast doing these together, and the only thing better than that camaraderie was how much fun our fans had reading the books. That was always important to both of us. If people weren't having fun, we'd have stopped.

We had plans for two more Clickers books. They would have been called High Plains Clickers and Southern Fried Clickers. The first one would have been set in the past, during the era of the American Old West. It is Southern Fried Clickers that summons one of my happiest memories of Jesus. And I have hundreds of happy memories regarding him, but this one is one of my absolute favorites. We were on a long drive and were bullshitting back and forth, and somehow, we got on the idea for Southern Fried Clickers, which would take place in Mississippi and Louisiana. We were brainstorming plot points and scenes and lines of dialogue, and Jesus came up with the idea of the Clickers attacking a Ku Klux Klan rally, and somebody hollering, "That's the biggest damn crawdad I ever done seen!" This caused us both to double over with laughter, because it was ludicrous, and we were exhausted, and punch-drunk, and his southern accent was atrocious. We were laughing so hard that we had to pull over to the side of the road because neither of us could drive. And for nearly twenty-minutes we sat there, laughing. Every time one of us stopped, the other would repeat the line, and we'd start giggling again. By the end, our stomachs hurt and both our faces were streaked with tears.

Unfortunately, we never got a chance to write them. The month Jesus got sick, we were just finishing up a short story collection together, and had planned on starting High Plains Clickers next. On a Wednesday, we were supposed to give publisher Larry Roberts some art suggestions for our short story collection. Jesus called me that morning and asked me if I could go over it with Larry by myself. He had to go to the doctor because "he'd woken up yellow". Turned out that an unknown tumor had blocked off his bile duct and was messing with his liver. He was diagnosed with cancer later that day. A little over a month later, he was gone.

When Jesus died, I originally thought that the Clickers franchise should rest with him. After all, these weren't my creations. He and Mark created them. All I did was help keep the franchise going, and introduce a few new facets. It had been fun while it lasted, but in the aftermath of his death, it seemed like all the fun in my life had died, as well. But about a year after his death, his wife, Cathy, mentioned to me that she'd like to see the franchise live on, given its enduring popularity with readers. As the executor of Jesus's literary estate, it's my job to honor his wishes, and those of Cathy and their daughter. She pointed out that Jesus had asked me to collaborate on a second

Clickers novel with him as a way to honor his friend Mark. If I figured out a way for the series to continue, I'd be honoring the memories of Jesus and Mark both.

So, I went about figuring out how to let the Clickers live on.

I didn't want to be involved in the writing process. Of that, I was certain. No matter who I collaborated with, I'd be constantly reminded of collaborating with Jesus—and my writing partner would feel the weight of that. It was unfair to whomever was saddled with me. So instead, I proposed to Cathy that we use writing teams composed of fans of the series. We'd do four new books—one to match each of the novels in the original series. It would be a reboot, so that the new writers weren't beholden to the continuity of the previous books if they didn't want to be. She enthusiastically agreed. And I knew right away who I wanted for the first team.

Stephen Kozeniewski and Wile E. Young are two younger authors whom I have a great deal of fondness and admiration for. Admiration because they're talented. Fondness because they remind me of Jesus and myself. Stephen has Jesus's personality, and Wile E. has mine at that age. The two are dear friends, as Jesus and I were, and they've collaborated together before (on the exquisite The Perfectly Fine House). Both were fans of the original series. And I knew they could both write within the franchise, as they'd both contributed stories to the aforementioned Clickers Forever anthology. The question was…would they want to do it? Well, luckily, they said yes. I gave them the parameters (of which there weren't many) and set them loose.

And this is the result.

When I received the manuscript from them, I set it aside for the evening, and then, after some trepidation on my part, started reading it the next day. My nervousness vanished by the end of the first chapter. By the end of the second, I was engrossed. By the middle of the book, I was laughing and cheering. And by the end, I cried. I was so happy with the results. As a fan of the original novel, they'd made me a fan all over again. I loved it. More importantly, Jesus and Mark would have loved it, as well. Thank you, Stephen and Wile E., for being the first to breathe new life into this franchise, and help me honor its original creators.

It's perfect, really. A new generation of writers rebooting a popular horror franchise for a new generation of readers.

Clickers never die, indeed…

—Brian Keene
Somewhere along the Susquehanna River
September 2021

PROLOGUE

PRIMETIME PROGRAM LISTING

Staff
Guide For Television
September 17, 1999
Friday
9:00 pm
Channel 3—UNDERSEA WORLDS – Documentary

Yawn. Tune in (or don't) for the premiere of the once-vaunted series. Cameron Custer, once the toast of public broadcasting, is as long in the tooth as the sharks he swims with. Possibly a cheap alternative to sleeping pills. (60 min.)

WHEN WESTWORLDS COLLIDE

Duke Thorn, interviewer
Transcript, Guest of Honor interview, Saddlecon VII
May 18, 2013
Duke Thorn: Howdy, pardners!
<raucous applause>
DT: Boy, that is good to hear. But I know you're not here for me. I'm just a dumbass actor. Let's meet the real star. Dudes and dudettes, I give you the head writer, executive producer, and showrunner of *Unashamed, Black Fang, The Kudos Kid,* and, of course, *Reboot Hill*...Ms. Christine Morgan.
<raucous applause>

Christine Morgan: Wow! What a reception.
DT: Well deserved, well deserved.
CM: Well, thank you, Duke.
DT: Let's cut to the chase. You made my career. I owe you everything. And really, how many people can you say have changed the entire course of pop culture?
CM: Oh, come on!
DT: No, I'm serious. If you'd told me ten years ago that even elementary school kids could rattle off all the old cowboy characters of the '50s and '60s, I'd have called you crazy. But here we are!
CM: Well, it was a group effort…
DT: A group effort started by you.
CM: No, no. There's love there. The fans, they have this immense love for the Western as a genre. That never went away. They just stopped making the movies.
DT: Well, that's interesting. Westerns were famously movies. Why did you say, "Let's take it to the small screen?"
CM: The TV execs were the ones who were willing to hear me out.
<chuckling>
DT: How did that go, exactly?
CM: Well, first I pitched *Unashamed,* you know, and I had to sell that as a continuation, where it was the kids of the original characters, and the original actors would show up in their original roles and everybody claps like a seal, which is fine, you know, as far as that goes, but a bit exhausting. But then that one blew up, so they asked me to do more and then once I had three shows I knew it was time to bring them all together for *Reboot Hill.*
<raucous applause>
DT: So, you said *Unashamed* was a continuation, but *Reboot Hill* is a reboot, obviously. What exactly is the difference?
CM: Well, the main difference is that in a continuation you have to respect everything that was established beforehand. The history, the character attributes, everything. In a reboot, just imagine it's a different world. Like, imagine our world except instead of Westerns being brought back to television, I don't know, comics were brought to the movie screen.

<chuckling>
DT: So our world is like a reboot of somebody else's universe?
CM: You could look at it that way. In a reboot, it's a whole other world, things are different, history went differently, don't worry about continuity, just enjoy the ride and…yeah.
DT: Yeah, indeed.

PREHISTORIC PERIL? OR PASSIONATE PROPAGANDA?

Katie Trivilino
International Geographic
June 4, 2018

What lurks under the ice? That's the question explorers have been asking themselves ever since the discovery of our world's two poles. Buried under miles and miles of frozen tundra, the far north and south are nature's "no-man's land". But that hasn't stopped man from arriving, or at least the effects of man.

As populations around the world continue to increase, carbon emissions are becoming trapped at an increasing rate, and while scientists and activists have leaned on the "climate change" and "global warming" horn for years, it has seen very little if any traction in changing political or cultural positions on the subject. But now scientists say a new threat lurks beneath the ice. That of a prehistoric variety.

"Prehistoric viruses trapped in the ice could run rampant, solving the overpopulation crisis in barely a fortnight," leading Brazilian climatologist Dr. Sebastio Romas stated, striking quite a figure with his windchilled rosy cheeks, a melting piece of glacier chipped off in his hand.

With the current global pandemic, people seem to be taking the thought of a Jurassic Plague more seriously. But Dr. Romas believes that pre-Cambrian super-flus are just the tip of the melting iceberg.

"Worms frozen in permafrost after 42,000 years have come back to life. Who is to say other, more deadly creatures aren't frozen and waiting for the right time?" Dr. Romas says.

Dr. Romas's threat has yet to emerge, and though plenty of dead and frozen animals have been pulled from melting permafrost, other than worms, the icy wastes are quiet. But as the world heats up, this reporter watches each new melting glacier with new and dreadful curiosity.

I THOUGHT I WAS DONE WITH SEX UNTIL I DISCOVERED MY MONSTER KINK

"Uncie Wesley"
UK Today
January 29, 2019

I Thought I Was Done with Sex Until I Discovered My Monster Kink

Dear Uncie Wesley,

I didn't know how to describe my situation until I saw somebody on Facebook use the term "bed death." I didn't have to Google it. I immediately knew what it meant. And that my husband and I had been suffering from it for years.

We hadn't fallen out of love. He was still my best friend. We still cuddled up on the couch together and watched cartoons and cable news every night. Our children were raised in a loving environment. The only thing that was missing was, well, sex.

Then it happened.

I'd never been much for monster movies. Maybe I remembered watching a "Godzilla" movie or two on Saturday afternoons when I was a kid. But, one day, flipping through channels, I happened to settle on that old black-and-white movie "Creature from the Black Lagoon." And then I couldn't stop myself. Seeing that…thing climb out of the water and slither away with the blonde bimbo just made me tingle. For the first time in years I jumped my husband's bones.

We discussed what had happened, of course, because it had been so long. But I couldn't bear to tell him the truth: I was in lust with a weird reptile man. What the hell was wrong with me?

So, what is wrong with me? What do I do? Tell my husband the truth? Or just close my eyes and dream of my amphibious lover?

- Generally In Lust Maiden At Nebraska

Dear GILMAN,
Let me tell you about a community called the Furries. I hope you've got some money in your savings account…

OZARK MYSTERY, MOONSHINE MONSTER?

Kyle Parish
Arkansas Times
April 26, 2020

There is an unspoken rule when going in the backwoods: know where you're going and never go exploring.

Time has brought a sense of legality to the old Ozarks: illegal growing operations evolving into legitimized farms for cannabis, old moonshiners grabbing licenses to sell their wares. But there are still places that locals warn tourists to avoid.

Nowhere is this truer than the remote mountain rivers. Though hundreds of float trips make their way down the Spring Creek, Buffalo, and White Rivers every year, the list of missing persons increase with every season.

Detective Oswald King states that the most likely cause is drowning. Flash floods are a recurring danger to canoers traversing remote river systems. But he admits that other, more sinister elements could be at play. Namely, the New Testament of Hemah, originally a tent congregation who fled into the backwoods due to their extreme religious beliefs. With converts rare, this sect has taken to a new form of revenue: moonshine.

Reverend Argent Payne, two-time felon and leader of this religious sect is not seen in town, nor are their activities spoken about, though many in the communities surrounding these rivers suspect their involvement in a number of mysterious deaths. So little is known about the congregation and its leader that the only source of information comes from a member who was found at the Woolum access point, half dead and bearing serious burns across his entire body.

Thomas Woolf sits in a hospital, his blind eyes staring at the ceiling, his skin alabaster pale, a far cry from the powerful Wall Street investor who once ruled the speculative trading scene (readers will remember his fall from grace in 2015). When questioned, Mr. Woolf stated that he had not been tormented or tortured into his lowly state, but baptized in the blood of the angel.

"Brother Payne took us to the mound when I was ready to receive the bowl of anger, my turn to be made worthy. All the faithful know the mound, like a tower. The angel lives there. Brother Payne called forth and it came clicking up from the mound, member waving above its head. Its dark eyes locked into mine as Brother Payne milked it, letting its issue into the tub. I bathed in it and it closed my eyes to this world, opening my eyes to the next."

And while Mr. Woolf is under heavy anti-psychotics, locals believe there might be something to his "angel" and the Hemahite moonshine spreading through the community.

"Pappy used to put a little rattlesnake venom in his morning coffee. Gave it a tang!" said local resident, Jeff Johnson.

1. AUGUST, 2020

Dr. Cameron Custer clutched the railing of the *Claverhouse,* trying to assert control over the queasy fire in his stomach before his dinner splattered across the freighter's iron sides.

"Keep it bent over nice and steady, Doc. The deckhands have enough work already without having to clean up your carrots and mash."

That was Remo, the captain of the ship and an all-around bastard. Cam thought that his face looked scrunched up like a bulldog's, bobbing along with the roll of the ship against the waves.

This wasn't the first time Cam had ridden along on the *Claverhouse.* Some of the places that the seedy vessel had ferried the good doctor to in the past hadn't been the safest or sanest, but this time wasn't going to be quite as extreme. Not even top ten, probably. Guadalcanal was no Haiti or Vietnam. Still, the thought of sailing with a stockpile of illegal weapons in the hull made him almost as sick as whatever cookie had put in his meal. One stop by a respectable nation's patrol and Cam could kiss his already faltering career goodbye.

The island before him was set against the black sheet of night. Lights shone from the shore to let ships of all kinds know that there was safe harbor in the town here. He stared into the black sea, mentally charting the metal hulks lining the bottom of this channel. The Ironbottom Sound, that's what they called it. Cam knew all the ships resting beneath him, some fifty-plus, had been sunk during the Battle of Guadalcanal. That had been nearly eighty years ago, almost to the day.

The date of Remo's journey had been a coincidence, and

not a welcome one. The *Claverhouse* had to be in and out before whatever United States destroyer had drawn the duty to sail through here in remembrance arrived. It would be just Cam's luck to get picked up for illegal arms trade by a ship on a ceremonial mission.

Cam wiped his mouth with his handkerchief. He'd never thought of himself as a handkerchief guy before, but here he was. He paused, taken by the uncanny sense of eyes on him. He turned, slowly, and spotted two swabbies sticking their elbows in each other's sides and snickering.

"Yeah, it's him, man!"

They were talking about him and not even trying to hide it. Rolling his eyes, he turned back to his contemplation of Ironbottom Sound. Tentatively, he nudged some of his puke over the side with the side of his shoe.

The two swabbies were now humming the theme music from his show.

"Do *you* believe in undersea worlds?" one of them said mockingly.

His old catchphrase. He had opened a dozen Ivy League commencement speeches with it. Then, slowly, only state schools were interested in inviting him anymore. His honoraria had declined precipitously as his reputation. He thought he'd reached the bottom of the barrel when he started getting invited to supermarket grand openings - but then he stopped even getting invites to those.

He was, in a phrase, washed up. And he would be damned if he was going to help the swabbies reminding him of that fact clean up his vomit anymore. Christ, the time was he never would have gotten sick on a boat as a matter of pride, not in a monsoon, and certainly not just bobbing off the coast of an island. He walked away, leaving them to it.

Remo followed him through the maze of shipping containers that held more than cheap car parts and luxuries. Cam wished that he could've had a moment to ensure that the habitat for his specimen was up to speed, but he understood entertaining the captain who loved to pester his famous passenger was part of the dance.

Cam could smell the earthy scent of Remo digging into a can of tobacco even over the spray of the sea.

"They're just giving you a little ribbing, Doc. You know how sailors are. Chew?" Cam shook his head. Remo's voice reminded him of crackling paper. Everything about the tobacco-stained seaman was repulsive to the core, but he'd never let Cam down yet. "So, this thing you're looking for is like an extinct lobster?"

Cam drummed his fingers against the metal crates as they passed, as though physically tamping down his annoyance. "In a manner of speaking, Captain. Consider it my ticket back into the greater scientific community."

His greatest living rival, Dr. Rosamilia of Jacksonville University, had insisted that the animal simply didn't exist. Edler in Princeton had been somewhat kinder, asserting only that the fossil fragments were contradictory. Even his most trusted friend, Jay Wilburn out of Coastal Carolina, had granted him only that it was just another species of Eurypterid. Cam had heard all the arguments, then the accusations, and then the laughter that had drummed him out of serious academia.

"Any money in it?" Remo asked, spitting onto the deck.

Cam did everything to keep his lips from curling back in disgust. "As a matter of fact, there very well might be. It's proof of a prehistoric specimen and if the other artifacts they've recovered match—"

Remo waved a hand. "Yeah, yeah, yeah, benefit to society and all that. Let's talk figures, Doc. This is the first time you've paid me in advance with a song and a dance instead of cold, hard ducats. Those *Undersea Worlds* royalties coming a bit slim these days?"

Cam wanted to tell him that if this roll of the dice didn't land a natural then he'd be lucky to get a teaching job at some underfunded public school district. Although VHS sales of his show had been all right in the '90s, no production company had even been able to justify a DVD re-release. These days even the free streaming services didn't want his dated old show anymore. His royalty checks had gone the way of the silver trout, and what was left of his dwindling savings would be there soon, too.

Instead, Cam gave a warm smile, the same one that had captivated tens of thousands. "The sudden appearance of the specimen on the market made for a quick trip. You'll get paid, same as always."

Remo stood, contemplating for a moment. Cam hoped that he couldn't see through his line of bullshit. The captain shrugged and stuck out his hand. "You've never disappointed me before, Doc. Can I tell you a secret?"

Cam worried that the artery in his head would explode but somehow he just smiled and nodded. Remo leaned in so close that his chaw breath threatened to make Cam vomit for a second time.

"I was always a fan." To be fair, Cam was taken aback. But a moment later Remo straightened up, ever the salty sailor again. "I'll send Morrison and Southard to the launch. I figure you'll need some help transporting your dinosaur lobster.

Get what you need. We weigh anchor in six hours."

Cam nodded and took the hatch into the lower levels of the *Claverhouse* where he'd been given a berth on the Fiesta Deck. He'd done his best to keep his research and materials neat and orderly, but somehow they'd exploded across the space like his university room.

He had statements from fishermen, cargo ship captains, islanders, anyone, really, who had a connection to the sea and a story. Some tales were, understandably, taller than others. There were hypotheses on potential care, reports on the proper salinity in water, everything needed for proper care and feeding. And alongside all of the charts and forms were drawings, rough sketches of what the animals were supposed to look like. His favorite was almost cartoonlike, and dated from the '40s, supposedly the work of an American castaway.

But all this flotsam and jetsam was no more convincing than a grainy photo of Bigfoot. The holy grail had come from one of Remo's less savory contacts. It had almost seemed a dream come true when Cam received the call.

"My name's Bonifaco. I caught a Clicker."

Cam felt the sea spray on his face and tried to hold the edge of the launch tight as they rolled over the water. Morrison had a handle on the rudder and Southard reached out a steady hand to keep the good doctor from pitching over the side as they motored over a speedboat's wake.

"Easy there, Dr. Custer. You're not a fat seal, but the sea dogs would jump clear out for a morsel like you."

Cam knew that the swabbie meant well, but years of amateurs trying to prove they knew more about sea life than him had frayed his patience. Still, he had to tolerate it. They had no way of knowing they were on the cusp of a scientific breakthrough, that *he* was on the verge of newfound waves of fame.

His thoughts drifted to the classics, the black-and white-film that had awakened his desire to go exploring and see the world. *King Kong* had sailors who hadn't been interested in their prehistoric discovery either.

At least until it was staring them in the face.

Morrison angled the rudder and the launch shifted, heading into a small inlet with a smattering of docks and dilapidated warehouses. Cam noted the boarded-up windows and weeds growing from the roads. This area was little used.

A flashlight blinked once, twice. Southard pulled a similar one from the launch's compartment and mimicked the signal. Morrison killed the motor and the launch drifted to the end of a long dock.

Cam had traveled to his fair share of dangerous locales, but in all that time he and his film crew had never been through a real violent altercation. He was an academic at heart and the sight of three men bearing rifles made his heart beat rapidly. These men reminded him of a Moray eel he'd seen once coiled in a round ball of coral on the edge of a reef near Cozumel: at ease, but dangerous.

"Dr. Custer?" the lead man asked, his accent making it sound more like *cos-stare*. Cam raised his hand. "We spoke over the phone. Do you have the money?"

Cam heard Morrison shift behind him. Remo's swabbies were always armed, but Bonifaco and his men clearly had the drop on them. If this came to violence, they would end up floating, chum for the crabs and sharks.

He fished around in his coat and retrieved the fat wad of bills, almost the last bit of money to his name. Bonifaco snatched the cash as soon as it was within reach, flipping through the stack of bills like a dealer on poker night.

Now they're going to shoot you.

The thought came unbidden, too many of Remo's horror stories about deals gone bad playing through his mind. Cam shook those thoughts from his mind. He had come all this way and to start giving into fear now was not an option.

"Alright, doctor, undersea wonders await." Bonifaco and his men laughed, and Cam affected a smile.

The Filipino mercenary offered him a hand ashore and Cam took it, grateful for the feeling of something other than a boat under his legs. The tension died away just as fast as it had come, replaced by excitement.

"We found it lurking out on one of the reefs in the sound. Couldn't believe my fucking eyes!"

Bonifaco chattered away. Longtime fans always had a way babbling on about their favorite moments from the show or asking him more questions than he could possibly answer. He'd always nodded pleasantly, waiting for them to run out of gas. But this time he was hanging on every word.

The mercenaries led Cam and his companions to the nearest building. It was a dark, crumbling edifice with boards nailed everywhere proclaiming, *No Trespassing* and *Keep Out*.

The doors of the warehouse slid back, revealing thrumming overhead lights and a veritable indoor bazaar. It was a small building, maybe only a few hundred feet across but Cam could make out tables with disassembled weapons, sunglasses, hats, wallets, even kilos of cocaine just laying out for all to see. Shady fuckers who looked like they had come from everywhere from Hong Kong to Hawaii sifted through it all. Cam's attention was instantly drawn to one thing and one thing only: a massive saltwater tank in the center of the room.

"Reinforced steel structure and nearly a foot of plastic all around. This thing killed two of my guys before we figured out a way to keep it from removing any more arms." Bonifaco was launching into his story like Cam hadn't already handed over ten thousand dollars, like this was just another sales pitch to some street kid hesitant to try their first dollop of pearl.

The good doctor pressed himself to the glass and whispered under his breath, "Hello, beautiful. Aren't you gorgeous?"

And in Cameron Custer's mind, it was the most beautiful thing he'd ever seen. The specimen was about the size of a St. Bernard. The tank was just big enough for the animal to swim and turn from one end to the other. He'd seen blurry photographs, drawings based on fossils, but none of it compared to the real thing. It looked like a massive lobster, its beady black eyes on the ends of its stalks seemed to focus on him. Was it just his imagination or did the animal turn around in its tank to follow him?

But the color…

His studies had shown that the creatures' carapaces were supposed to be bright red, like a crab left in boiling water. This one was solid white.

Well, solid white except for the large, smiling cartoon face that had been drawn on its back.

Cam's eyes trailed up to the tail, expecting to see the creature's magnificent signature stinger. He realized that the tail was nothing but a deformed stump at the same time the Clicker rushed the glass.

Cam screamed and fell ass-over-end to get away as the tank barely rattled. Bonifaco and his men lost all sense of decorum, pointing and laughing like it was damn grade school. Cam flushed. He picked himself up from the floor and tried to regain the air of dignity he'd always comported himself with.

Bonifaco tapped the glass, "Aggressive little bastard, isn't he, Doctor?"

Cam had to agree with the mercenary. The tank had barely rattled but the thing was still trying to get its pincers through the plastic. He could faintly hear a telltale *click-click.*

He felt frustration build, anger. It wasn't supposed to be like this. This was supposed to be his moment of triumph. He supposed that it still was. He had a live Clicker, he could prove his theories, prove their existence. But it was maimed and his hopes of testing the effects of the venom vanished. "What caused its injury?"

At this, Bonifaco smiled. "That's the thing, Doc. You didn't pay just for the *sugpo.* It comes with party favors."

The mercenary waved two fingers and Bonifaco's men produced a chest from the depths of the warehouse. Cam felt the weight reverberate in his chest as it thudded to the floor. He immediately recognized the object. World War II footlockers were common in old surplus stores. His trained eye scanned over it, noting the rusted metal and faded words stamped in black across the lid: CLASSIFIED: MAJESTIC 13. The side was similarly stamped, this time in white: WEBB, ARTHUR: GySgt, 1ST MARINES.

"Found that out in the wrecks at the bottom of the sound, not too far from where we found that big fucker. Should be quite the prize for you, Dr. Custer."

Cam covered his nose and threw back the lid. The smell of mildew, dead fish, and old seawater came spilling out in to the warehouse. Cam was momentarily confused by what he saw; the ocean had done its work and plenty of items inside were ruined, but the rest were strange.

This doesn't look like a World War II soldier's kit.

There were necklaces of teeth and hand-carved symbols. Each side of the trunk bore a carving that Cam didn't recognize and small mason jars full of dirt and other materials that he didn't even want to guess about were strewn across the bottom. But sitting on top of it all was a small leather-bound book, sealed tight in a waterproof bag. The bag was from the right era, but it had recently been opened.

Cam looked up at Bonifaco. "You've read it?"

The other man smiled deep and produced a cigarette from the pocket of his cargo shorts, "It's a hell of story."

Gingerly, Cam picked up the book, whispering to himself as he read the words scrawled in faded pencil across the interior.

Property of Alcide Robichaude

2. JUNE, 1942

"Dammit!"

Christopher "Doodles" Enterline angrily tossed his stick as far out into the ocean as he could, which, frankly, wasn't very far these days. The stick bobbed away on the waves.

Doodles was pissed because he was eight apostles into his sand recreation of "The Last Supper" and the tide was coming in. The salt water nibbled away at the bottom of Jesus's table. Wait, had Jesus been the host? He'd have to remember that question if he ever saw Chaplain Broaddus again.

"When," Doodles corrected himself out loud. He had to stay positive, right?

Sighing, he stood up and wandered into the brush to find another stick. By the time he found one long and sturdy enough for drawing in the sand, his entire masterwork had been washed away. Retreating further up the beach he drew a circle, added two eyes and a smile. Then a nose, hands, and the whole rest of the body. He couldn't help himself. He could never just stop with a simple drawing.

"Wish I had my damn sketch pad back."

Doodles sank to a crouch, cradling his head in his hands. He should have been happy, he knew. And he had been at first. Some people saved up their whole lives to retire to a tropical paradise, and most never made it. For his first few days on the island he had avoided panicking, happily wading into the bathwater-warm ocean, climbing trees, pretending his halved coconuts were tropical island drinks. And at first there'd been no reason to panic.

He'd had managed to salvage half the galley supplies from

the *Lexington* when it had gone down in early May. He'd been working below, peeling potatoes, when explosions had started to rock the ship. At first he hadn't thought much of it. That part of sailing wasn't really his concern. He just had to keep the bellies of the people who had to worry about that stuff full. But when the fires had started Doodles had immediately begun a furious rush to pack up pots, pans, and produce into his packs.

Other men might have tried to save their personal goods—and a lot of men whose ships went down did, he supposed, and he didn't blame them. But for Doodles the galley was his home. His tea kettle was like a picture of his kids, his pantries like his foot locker. His only regret was that he hadn't saved his sketchbook, the only thing he ever used in off hours (not that he had many off hours, feeding a crew of nearly 3000. It was also the reason he was called Doodles instead of Cookie, like almost every other cook in the Navy.

He'd made his way off the *Lady Lex*, aboard a lifeboat with a dozen other sailors. And all had seemed well at first until a swell had pushed them out of earshot of the salvage boats. When no amount of rowing could set them right, the men had all left the boat and started swimming back to safety at Ensign Mangum's orders. All except one: Doodles Enterline, who had never learned to swim. That, and he had been reluctant to leave behind the pack of kitchen supplies he'd managed to salvage. They were like his kids.

Mangum had given him a compass, map, flares, and extensive directions on how to meet up with the salvage boats, but it had been nearly a day before he had finally reached land, making any instructions pointless. They had probably looked for him for a while, but he could hardly blame them for giving up. The ocean was a vast place.

So, washing ashore, he'd at first had food aplenty, and, turning the lifeboat over, shelter enough. He'd spent his first few days on the island trying to catch crabs with an increasingly comic series of traps before finally learning that they weren't really all that smart. A large enough rock, dropped shortly in front of their path of flight, would both kill them and finish half the business of shelling them. He'd started gathering coconuts and lemon grass, and all manner of edible forageables, a skill that combined his experience as a youth on the farms of rural Lancaster County, Pennsylvania and his years since as a Navy cook. Food just made sense to him, and he had no trouble finding it.

As the days had stretched into weeks, he'd started weaving a fishing net out of some of the local fibrous plants. And that had been his worst mistake. In a way, though, he'd been lucky. He'd wandered off into the brush to see a man about a horse and then, returning, found a gaggle of uniformed Japanese tugging his fishing net in from the ocean, and turning over his lifeboat-cum-hut.

Well, "gaggle" was too strong. There had probably been three of them. Honestly, though, he'd never seen an enemy combatant before in his life, and had really never expected to. Things would've had to go to all hell and gone before they stuck a cook on one of the guns. Down in the galley he could've easily passed the whole war without even seeing a Japanese vessel. That fateful day, though, his hands still reeking of his own shit, hastily cleaned in the dirt, he was not more than fifty yards from an armed trio of them.

And they looked…well, pretty normal honestly. Somehow, probably through the cartoons they played before picture shows if he had to guess, he'd gotten the impression that Tojos would look like monkeys or rats, with huge hanging buckteeth, tiny pinprick eyes, and glasses the size of half their face. Instead they'd been three pretty ordinary looking guys, pawing through all his worldly possessions. Still, he'd been terrified.

He'd stood stock still, like a rabbit caught in a car's head beams, and then he'd carefully slunk away in to the underbrush. As soon as he'd been sure he was out of earshot, he'd taken off like a bolt and never gone near his temporary campground again.

That'd been months ago. Since then he'd survived like a real pioneer. Mostly, he'd figured out where the Japanese base was, and figured out their patrols, and then avoided them. Living largely in fear of people, and surviving in no small part off their castoffs, he liked to think he'd learned a lot about them.

Besides, spying on the Japanese base was the closest he got to a radio show around here. He couldn't read any Japanese, but he'd picked up a few words, and thought he'd figured out the names of the ones who commonly got sent on patrol and some of the bigwigs at the base.

Private Yotashi was a skittish sort, and one of the few who always paid attention on patrol. Sergeant Ohno was fat, somehow, and lazy, and more likely to wander far enough from base not to be noticed and then take a nap rather than completing his rounds. Still, Doodles had never felt inclined to attack Ohno, although it would have been easy enough. Better not to draw attention was always his outlook. As far as he was concerned, if the Japanese went on for the rest of the war never noticing he was there, all the better.

But then there was General Katou. He'd developed a grudging respect for the man. Neither quiet nor overly loud, the man was clearly in charge. His men loved him to the extent that any enlisted man could love an officer. In the last few weeks, though, a gaunt storm cloud of a man, Colonel Hanshiro, who had always been busy and invisible had started undermining the general at every turn. Doodles didn't know much, but he knew a mutiny brewing when he saw one.

Doodles rose as the waves began to eat up his cartoon. Maybe it was time to go spy on the Japanese base a bit. He glanced back at the beach, seeing his figure reduced to nothing more than a nose and face peeking over what could've been a wall, before it was washed away entirely. Hmm, he kind of liked how that looked. He'd have to remember it.

Moving with a noiseless grace, he found himself not much later within spitting distance of the Japanese camp, his belly full of wild taro. Sergeant Ohno was snoozing happily in a glen nearby, rather than leading a patrol, so Doodles was confident he could watch in peace.

Now, here was something strange. The general wasn't wearing his usual uniform. In fact, he was wearing what looked like a white dress. Doodles was so put off by this funny appearance, that he was startled into laughing. Normally he never broke his silence this close to base. Even Ohno might get suspicious, and he was not one who went looking for trouble, or even woke from his naps normally. But Doodles couldn't help himself. The general, looking as dour as possible, wearing a fancy dress, was just a sight he couldn't unsee.

But Doodles shut up real quick when he heard what sounded like the bolt of a gun locking.

Click-click.

Doodles's heart sank into his stomach. Since the day his makeshift camp had been discovered, he hadn't had so much as a close call. Luck had always been on his side, he knew, but maybe God had been, too, and maybe, just maybe, he'd developed a certain skill for skulking around. It wasn't one he'd ever expected. Drawing, sure. Maybe he'd get hired by Warner Brothers to make pictures one day. Cooking, eh, he wasn't going to be a chef at a fancy French restaurant, but maybe he could make some dough as a short order cook someday. He wasn't sure what could be done with sneaking and spying, aside from maybe being a secret agent, but he didn't plan on ever getting into that line of work.

But all of those options were gone now and his number was up. He raised his hands about halfway, enough that he could claim he was surrendering if necessary, or maybe jump the guy if he was alone. Slowly he turned around.

But it wasn't Private Yotashi facing him. And it sure as shit wasn't Sergeant Ohno, who was still sawing wood, or any of the other Japanese soldiers for that matter. He found himself staring smack dab into the maw of some horrifying, massive crab-type creature. And the thing looked pissed.

3. AUGUST, 1942

Alcide Robichaude muttered prayers as the ships behind him hurled thunderous cannonade. He could smell the spray of the sea and the sweat of the men in front of him. They made a fat target stuck in as tight as they were.

There were thirty or so men tucked in with him. A few slickers and the boys from the landlocked states weren't handling it so well. Vomit joined the seawater swirling around his boots, vibrating along with the motor from the landing craft as they maneuvered toward the island dominating their view.

Alcide had barely paid attention while the colonel had been giving the briefing back on the ship. He'd been busy whispering protection for the men he'd spent the past months training and traveling with. All of them were going to meet what was waiting in this jungle thrust out from the middle of the sea.

He knew the island's name, Guadalcanal, and that the Tojos controlled it. He'd heard the scuttlebutt same as the rest of the guys. They'd be seeing combat today and despite his upbringing, his preparation, Alcide still fidgeted as the green on the horizon slowly overtook the blue of the sky.

Captain Palmer was shouting orders, screaming over the drone of the engine and the battleships turning whatever positions the Tojos were still trying to hold onto nothing but mud and dead brush. "As soon as we hit the beach, move up! Don't get caught in the open! Hear me, Marines?" Alcide shouted back that he heard him, just like every other man in the boat, then he went right back to muttering workings under his breath, and praying to whatever god could hear him that a bullet wouldn't find him today. Alcide heard the shout from behind him, the time until the ramp dropped and they'd be charging up the beach.

"Thirty seconds!"

He heard someone breathing sharp and quick. It was a kid they called Trick, on account that he always seemed to be coming ahead in their card games on the way over. Alcide wanted to pat him on the back, let him know that he'd watch over him, that he just had to remember his training like the rest of them. He couldn't reach the kid, though, so he continued to hyperventilate. And he wasn't the only one.

Planes flashed overhead, Corsairs by the looks of them. The coxswain shouted, "Ten seconds!"

"Here we go, Papa. Don't go looking for me to come calling at the crossroads just yet." He felt the boat grind into the shallow sand. There was a pause like the world taking a deep breath, then the ramp was falling.

He heard the skipper hollering, "Let's go, Devil Dogs! *Get your asses off the beach*!"

Alcide felt his breath hitch and he jogged forward. There was nowhere else to go as the men behind him jostled their way forward to get off the boat before some Tojo machine gun round tore through them.

His boots hit the water, immediately soaking through, and he struggled with his pack and weapon as he tried to leave the surf. Alcide expected war cries, chattering weapons, and screaming. But instead he only heard the splash of the surf, the thousands of motors from landing craft… and laughter?

The crowds thinned and Alcide noticed that he wasn't the only one staring. Marines lounged at the tree line, gear strewn about the place as they watched the arriving men.

One of them waved a cigarette, "Welcome to Guadalcanal!"

Alcide looked over at Trick and both of them began to laugh before they heard Gunnery Sergeant Arthur Webb begin barking orders. "Don't sit there with your pecker in your hand, Boudin. Get your ass up the beach!"

Boudin. They'd been calling him that since basic, on account of his Cajun accent. Alcide was just glad they hadn't cottoned to his practices yet.

Dutifully he responded, "Aye, Gunny," and began the jog toward the rest of his unit.

4. AUGUST, 1942

Captain Ezekiel Palmer rubbed the five-o'-clock shadow that had already started forming under his chin. This wasn't what he had been told, hadn't been what he'd expected. The colonel had made sure that all of them were aware of just how savage the resistance was going to be.

So where the hell was it?

The truth was he felt relieved. Annapolis and all the finer lessons on command seemed like a lifetime ago. A few years in the peacetime Corps shuffling papers around and overseeing base expansion had left him unsure of his capacity for combat. Ezekiel was untested and he knew that if he screwed up, his men would die.

Of course, some men were going to die anyway. That was the way of things, as his father who had fought in the Great War had told him. It was his job to get as many boys home as possible.

Your goddamned feelings don't matter, Marine. Move up, secure the objectives, and eradicate resistance. Those are your orders.

"What's the word, Skipper? Can we get back on the fucking boat? It's hot as shit and these mosquitoes have already bitten my ass enough that it's redder than my mama's fucking Sunday gravy!"

The curly-haired private chewing gum and holding his rifle in the air like he was posing for some news rag's war hero editorials was Allen Martino. Only a Brooklyn boy could get away with being such a smartass, but everyone in the company seemed to like him, Ezekiel, much to his chagrin, included.

"Well, Martino, today isn't your lucky day since we're

marching straight into that jungle to root out Tojo holdouts."

There were a flurry of groans and cursing. One of his other men, a big hick from somewhere close to Alabama named Basher asked, "What about the airfield, Skip? Don't know about the rest of you lugs, but I'd rather be hoofing it somewhere without monkeys and poison frogs and nonsense."

Gunny Webb, who would have quickly shut both men up if they had dared to sass Ezekiel in front of him, was just out of earshot, helping a man who had spilled half his kit. Webb hadn't been frocked yet, but since 1st Sgt Masterton was recovering from dysentery in Australia, Webb was filling the role in his place. Ezekiel knew Webb's absence was why the men were testing him and he had prepared for all manner of bad attitudes and disrespect. More importantly, he didn't want to just hide under any NCO's skirts.

Most of his boys were fresh out of boot. His two years filling out concrete requisition forms practically made him a veteran by comparison. And truth be told, he didn't want to be heading into those dark trees, either. But orders, he reminded himself, were goddamned orders. He opened his mouth to remind the men of that same fact when he stopped dead in his tracks.

About a hundred yards from them a dark wall of green gave way to darkness the deeper he looked. Tangles of limbs and brush on the side of the trail resembled a man.

Sniper.

Ezekiel's mind was screaming, but he kept his composure. But upon closer inspection there was nothing there. The enemy had retreated deeper than anywhere that his men could reach today.

He realized that he still needed to answer his man's question, but his Executive Officer jumped in before he could look like a fool spooked by the shadows.

"Why don't you stuff a rag in your cheesehole, Basher? Scared of frogs. You'd better be scared of Tojo instead. Now if the skipper doesn't have anything else, we're heading up into the hills."

Ezekiel and Jake Dempsey had graduated from Annapolis the same year, but hadn't really run in the same circles. A prodigious love of liquor and loose women had held Jake back from making captain, but it had suited him just fine. "Would rather follow your lead," he'd say when Ezekiel questioned him about his career goals.

He picked up the slack when Ezekiel was unsure of himself.

All eyes were on him again. Ezekiel nodded his head and motioned with one hand towards the jungle. "Said it all already. We've got our orders, so let's try not to fuck them up. Move out!"

Jake and Webb immediately took the lead on getting the men moving, hollering for them to get everything in gear as they marched resolutely towards that towering wall of green.

Ezekiel's breath hitched in his throat. He clutched his carbine tight and walked resolutely forward.

Please God, if you're listening, don't let me catch a bullet right here.

The excited chatter that each man had brought with him after they realized they weren't going to die on the beach had disappeared. All of them were staring at the green leaves that were mimicking the waves crashing against the shore. Each new gust of wind caused the limbs of emerald to jump like the crowd at a baseball game.

They reached the edge of the trees and Ezekiel held up a hand. The men stopped and immediately ducked into the tall grass. He scanned each edge of shadow, looking for any sign of movement, the glint of a rifle, the light breathing of a man waiting to kill.

"Better not kill me now, you bastards," Ezekiel muttered as he stepped into the woods sweeping his weapon back and forth.

But nothing moved and no bullet came. He sighed in relief and waved them on.

One by one, they went into the trees.

5. AUGUST, 1942

Deep beneath the green trees, in a cave carved under the dirt closer to the high hills of the island, a man prepared to die.

Colonel Ota Hanshiro was not that man. His hand was poised over a sheaf of rice paper. He had been trying to write a letter to his wife back home in Hokkaido for the past week. He'd been able to put together no more than two words at a time, though. Never in their thirty years together had he spoken a false word to her. Now, though, he could think of nothing, not about his mission, not about his feelings, not even about the weather that wouldn't be a lie.

A shadow loomed over him and he rolled his eyes. Captain Atagi, his aide-de-camp, was from a no-name town in rural Gifu prefecture. He was too polite to knock. Too polite for a lot of things, really, to make an effective aide-de-camp, though Ota, as a fellow country boy, respected his rural upbringing. So, instead of knocking, he loomed, loomed in doorways or, as now, the entrance to Hanshiro's cave.

"Yes?" Ota asked, after a pregnant enough pause to let Atagi know that he was doing him a favor by breaking the silence.

"It's time, Hanshiro-*sama*."

Ota nodded and packed away his calligraphy tools. He checked his uniform, making sure every button shined and every line was perfect. Ota had never enjoyed the harsh, disciplinary nature of his job, but he also understood that it was vital. For the Empire he would force down his normal, academic, pacifistic nature. For the Empire he would do anything.

Katou, the Imperial Japanese Army general in charge of the island's defenses, kneeled in the dirt, eyes staring resolutely forward, a frond of *sakaki* leaves before him. Katou wore a white kimono, rather than his uniform. Given the time they had, it was the appropriate dress for the ceremony. The dishes before him showed he'd eaten his last meal and drunk his *sake*, and Atagi would not have fetched him before the man had been given the chance to compose his final words.

That, though, would be the last of the traditional elements of today's ceremony.

"Your failure to hold the beach against the invaders has brought weakness and shame to our work here." Ota paced back and forth, forcing his voice to be stern, despite his overwhelming desire to comfort his fellow soldier.

Katou's most trusted officers surrounded him, including his second-in-command and apparent successor, Colonel Shinsato, ostensibly Ota's peer. Most knew Ota by sight from his long tenure on the island, but few knew the nature of his secretive work, leading the island's detachment of Unit 731 scientists and soldiers. And none of Katou's men knew that the IJA General Staff had sent orders for him to take over for their beloved leader.

Shinsato obviously suspected, and hated Ota's guts for it. That was all right. Ota had never had a shred of respect for Shinsato. He was a city boy, Kyoto born and bred. Unlike himself and Atagi, someone like Shinsato had no business being in the IJA. He should've joined the Navy, perhaps.

The engineers had designed their fortifications well, bunkers threaded with underground tunnels hollowed the highlands of the island jungle, but Ota had specifically asked for this fortification.

The one closest to the sea.

There were caves on the island, ancient entries underground that the IJA had made use of when they had first come to this green hell. It would have been perfect for holding out if the pools of water deep inside the mountains had been fresh. The ocean had seeped in and these dark pools were just passages to the vast darkness of the sea.

But things that Ota had never considered in his wildest dreams laid claim to these passages. He'd seen them after coming to see why a whole company had not emerged from the dark of one particular cavern. And what he and the rest of his unit had found there could change the course of the war.

Ota had been pleased with the initial results. The deep waters around the island had been brimming with specimens and his patrons the *Umibozu* had brought him fresh ones when his previous samples expired.

His subjects bred quickly, a fact that had proved invaluable in his experiments. He'd tested the creatures out on the natives of the island, all the worst sorts of traitors to the Greater East Asian Co-Prosperity Sphere. The successes were still serving His Imperial Majesty. The failures had been returned to the *Umibozu* and their pets as fodder or sport. So it went with traitors. Though Ota was a man of peace, he understood that in times of war men had to forge themselves into blades of steel, and he had no patience for treason. And as a man of science he was delighted. Even if his project was in the early stages of success, there was still so much to learn and so much to do.

But first, he had his duty.

"Bring me my sword," Katou said.

Shinsato, who was also Katou's second for the seppuku ceremony, was quick to comply, placing the weapon tenderly into his beloved leader's hands. Ota noted by the stamp that it was a *showato*, a modern-day knockoff rather than a family heirloom. That was like Katou. He was a pragmatist. The General Staff ordered officers to wear swords, so he wore one, but he placed his faith in rifles and modern tactics.

Still, here he was.

Katou proffered his sword to Ota. "I accept what is to come, I give my life in honor of myself, my comrades, and His Imperial Majesty."

Ota nodded, then stood behind the general. There were nearly two-dozen men here to witness Katou's death. They'd also be witnessing the first public display of their new commander's work.

"Are you ready, Katou-*sama*?" It was a small thing to address the dying man with honor. By this sacrifice he would retain it in the next world and for his family in this one.

Katou nodded his head and began the intricate, painful

process of self-vivisection. It was not much done these days, being a relic of a bygone age, but all the men present still understood the gravity of the situation. Ota also supposed that in those olden days a second would have allowed his master to go hours at this purifying self-torture before beheading him. Times had changed, though, and Shinsato, either out of love or respect, stepped forward after only about a minute to take Katou's head.

Ota held up a hand to stop him, eliciting horrified stares from all those assembled.

"Japan must modernize," Ota said loudly, "without forgetting our traditions. That has always been General Katou's philosophy, is it not so, Katou-*sama*?"

"Hai," Katou choked out, struggling to speak and hold his intestines in simultaneously.

Ota nodded. "It is in honor of that philosophy, I offer you this blending of the old world and the new."

Ota gestured at two of his men holding ropes attached to a metal grate that led deeper into the caverns. Both men looked pale as they pulled the ropes. The metal ground as it hit the rough edges of stone before locking in place with a piercing clang that echoed through the caves.

Katou stared into the dark cave, his face placid in a way that made Ota proud to be a member of the Imperial Army.

Water splashed around inside the dark hole, and then came another sound.

It sounded like a pistol cocking, or a rifle, a weapon now primed to take any of their lives. The soldiers surrounding their beloved leader shuddered, memories of the morning and other battles across the whole of the Pacific flashing through their minds.

The noise never stopped. *Click-click, click-click.* Katou himself strained to see whatever was crawling up from the dark sinkhole.

Ota watched with barely restrained excitement, but maintained complete decorum as the creature emerged. Two pincers the size of a man's chest clutched at the metal rails. A keening screech echoed through the cave as it scratched the metal. Two eyes as black as night on the end of stalks reflected Katou's no longer placid expression.

Eight legs dug into the dirt as the bone-white creature hesitantly stepped into the cave, claws clicking as it eyed each man in turn, segmented mouth parts opening and closing in anticipation.

The monstrous crustacean's tail arched up and small drops seeped from the sharp tip at its apex. The rock below steamed from the fallen venom, drilling tiny holes into the cave floor.

The albinos were an Umibozu breed, their venom exponentially more potent than that of a wild specimen. Ota drew his sword. Unlike Katou's, his was a family heirloom from the late Tokugawa period. The *Umibozu* trained these creatures with tridents, but the specimens he had trained responded just as well to his sword. He pointed the blade at the disgraced captain who stared resolutely into those white eyestalks.

"Kurikka," he said, the best translation he could come up with for what the *Umibozu* themselves called the creatures, "strike!"

The *Kurikka* obediently charged, its claws working into a frenzy. It caught Katou in its grasp and held him tight before its tail flashed forward and stabbed the general through the chest. Blood erupted from Katou's mouth and his teeth were gritted tight, but all present could hear the pained wheezing escaping from his throat. His flesh turned a bright shade of orange. Ota had seen this happen before on test subjects.

Katou's flesh rippled, then the skin began to slide away, wet piles melted to the floor. Ota watched with special pride as the general didn't so much as open his mouth to scream, as was fitting during *seppuku*.

Nor did he scream when his eyes melted and rolled out of their sockets. Truly the man was a credit to the Japanese fighting man, and Hanshiro regretted his loss.

The *Kurikka* feasted, white claws scooping up puddles of flesh and shoveling them into its mouth. Ota stood before it without fear, looking at each of Katou's men in the eyes, their faces filled with terror. No. Not Katou's men any longer. They were his now, welly and truly. Shinsato's look of terrified respect sealed the matter.

"Go now and do not speak of what you have learned here today. But know that with the work that you make possible with your unwavering defense of this island, and by the grace of His Imperial Majesty the Emperor we shall triumph over the foreign cowards who have come to our lands."

The men didn't cheer, as was customary after such a speech, but filed out as fast as they could, leaving Ota alone with thoughts of his wife and farm, and kinder times that had no need of monsters.

6. AUGUST, 1942

The going had been tense, the path strangely quiet but for the billowing breeze that brought smells of death. Alcide had spent plenty of time out on the bayou and he knew the scent of something left to rot. Pools of stagnant water coalesced in the low places, so still that they looked like deep pits in the island's rock before a leaf would land and send ripples across their dark surfaces.

But stagnant water wasn't the faint odor that came drifting. No, this was something putrid, something that had gasped its last breath in dark water. Back home in the bayous of Caddo, he'd once seen a deer that had fallen victim to a hunter's shot and plunged headlong into a bog. Alcide had been out appeasing the things that his family kept under their thrall when he'd found it, bloated eyes writhing with maggots and water bugs, its skin and fur a soggy mess swarming with flies feasting on the black rot oozing from the bullet wound and into the water.

So when Captain Palmer called for the unit to halt, Alcide had an idea of what they might discover. Everyone crouched low, sweeping weapons back and forth and eyeing the trees for any sign of movement. Trick just seemed to delight in finally being able to put down his "pig." Somehow the tiniest man in the unit had been saddled with carrying a massive .30 caliber Browning. No doubt the battle buddies would welcome the pig's protection come nightfall, though.

Trick licked his lips and nudged Alcide, nodding up the hill where the skipper and XO were discussing something between themselves.

"Think it's Tojo?"

Alcide pursed his lips and stared at a shadow under the trees that looked vaguely like a man. "If it is then we're crawdads roasting in a pot."

Alcide notice that the two hundred and fifty or so men were spread out in a raised copse of bamboo bordered on all sides by the low pools and the jungle. If the enemy was poised to attack they'd make suckers of them all.

"You two becoming sweethearts?" Gunny Webb hissed as he hustled down the line, making sure that each man had enough ammo.

"No, First Sergeant," Alcide and Trick said in near-unison.

Webb paused, his lower jaw sliding back and forth, seeming to decide whether to correct them or not. But 1st Sgt Masterton had been convalescing for a while now, and whether he liked it or not, Webb was the new top NCO in the company.

"Count the rockers, you numb nutses," he grunted.

"Sorry, Gunny," they both replied, again in infuriating sync.

They'd been marching for three hours and hadn't seen hide or hair of the Japanese. Occasionally a group of planes would fly overhead, but Alcide hadn't been able to tell if they were Zeroes or Corsairs. Didn't much matter; their problems were on the ground.

The tension was beginning to get to the men. Every time a twig snapped it was weapons at the ready. Alcide had tried to read the trees and land, relying on the same skills that helped him track game back home, but if the enemy had been there, they had covered their tracks a damn sight better than most living things. But that itch that they were being watched tickled the back of the Cajun's neck and it hadn't gone away since they'd entered the jungle.

The skipper signaled from the front of the line and the unit was moving again. Trick sighed. "Probably stopping to check the fucking map. The old man's greener than lime Jell-O."

Alcide liked Captain Palmer all right, but Trick was right that the man lacked confidence. He decided not to comment one way or the other, which was his usual decision about most things. When they reached the top of the hill, they saw that the skipper had not, in fact, been stopping to check the fucking map. Two marines had been tied to bamboo crosses, erected up to their calves in the brackish water. Both of them had been castrated and their midsections eviscerated, intestines spilling out of the gaping wound.

Alcide watched the blood drain from Trick's face, anger filling up the space that it had occupied. Then he whispered, "Bastards. Fucking bastards."

"Boudin! Trick!" Gunny Webb growled, looking around and spotting another pair. "Basher and Martino, too. Take care of those men. We'll bury them next time we stop."

Trick looked ghastly, but for once refrained from bitching. Alcide didn't much like drawing the short straw either, but knew he would want someone else to do it for him.

Alcide and Trick began to cut the bodies down while the other two began constructing makeshift litters. All four tried not to stare at one of the dead marines' heads as it floated in the dark pool at their feet.

A small crab dug its claw into the eye socket, a wet plop sounding as it lifted its prize in the air.

7. AUGUST, 1942

Ezekiel Palmer wiped the sweat from his eye, staring at the map which had soaked through with humidity. He thought about asking Boudin if this was what it was like back home in the bayou. The man barely looked like he was sweating.

He hadn't recognized the dead men (thank God for small favors), but they hadn't died clean. Maybe he should have directed the company so as to avoid the corpses, as he had initially intended, but Jake had convinced him it was only fair for his guys to witness the brutal truth.

The dignity of the dead men, Jake had argued, benefited no one. But the lesson they imparted might stiffen the resolve of those still living. Though squeamish about the matter, Ezekiel had acquiesced.

He'd been told to expect resistance on his route, but so far all he'd seen and heard was the deep green of the jungle and the distant gunfire from other units whose paths had been less fortunate. He was beginning to imagine Tojos behind every tree.

The sun began to set. They'd been on the Canal for most of the day after weeks at sea, and now their shadows under the jungle canopy were growing long and threatening to swallow them whole. This position wasn't defensible, and he could feel in his bones that something dreadful was coming with the onset of night.

Ezekiel decided that he didn't want to find out here. He made a circle in the air with his finger in Webb's direction. "Let's get a move on."

Arthur Webb nodded, his grizzled bulldog face twisting

into a snarl. "All right, Marines, let's go. Double time!"

Ezekiel watched as his men picked up the pace. Earlier they had been complaining about seasickness, empty stomachs, his leadership, and everything else under the sun. Now, after seeing the battle dead, they were unanimous in cursing the enemy under their breaths.

Good.

8. JUNE, 1942

Doodles scrambled haphazardly backward in the sand in what his schoolteachers had always called a "crabwalk." The thing standing before him—like a crab, yet not quite a crab—belied that notion as it scuttled toward him. He tried to struggle to his feet, but the sand was too soft and he just flailed. Louder than a bullet, a snapping sound ripped through the jungle as the crab-thing snapped its claw just shy of his crotch, catching a bit of his trousers.

"Oh, hell," Doodles shouted, "he's after my dingle-doodle!"

Doodles immediately flipped onto his belly, a decision he regretted as the creature's next snap ripped a bloody chunk out of his butt. He vigorously pulled himself through the sand with his forearms toward a palm tree. Glancing back to make sure he was staying out of the scuttling menace's reach he saw the long bloody slug trail he was leaving behind.

He yanked himself to his feet and began scooting up the tree like he'd seen lumberjacks do in cartoons. Without a lumberjack's strap, though, he pretty much just had to hug the trunk. The blood dripping from his derriere seemed to be driving the monster below into a frenzy of clicking and scuttling back and forth.

"You pinched my butt!" Doodles shouted.

Holding on to the trunk as best he could with one arm and nearly toppling to the ground not just once, not just twice, but four times, Doodles finally managed to finagle the boot off his right foot. The boot wasn't really what he wanted, but as long as he had it, he decided turnabout was fair play.

"Eh, maybe it's good we met, Pinchy. Tonight I can make a tasty bisque."

Doodles tossed his boot angrily down at the crab-thing, hoping to kill it or at least stun it. Instead, it didn't even react as the boot bounced off its white-hued carapace. Doodles grunted in annoyance, but when he nearly lost his grip on the tree trunk again, remembered why he'd taken his boot off in the first place. He tugged his sock off, sighing because socks were worth more than gold here in the South Pacific.

Nevertheless, he'd have to clean it later or try to scrounge another one from the Japanese base. He filled the hole in his butt (the new one, anyway) with the sock and held it in place until the blood seemed not to be flowing as much.

He glanced down at his unlikely captor. Pinchy was continuously clacking its claws together, making an annoying, rhythmic clicking noise. Its tail was also slashing forward.

Doodles had once seen a scorpion in a Tijuana brothel. Some of the other boys had been trying to make it fight a Gila monster, to little avail. But the scorpion had acted just like that, lashing out with its tail. In fact, the more Doodles looked at it, the more he thought Pinchy's tail looked like a scorpion's, except that the long stingy part was missing. Doodles was no animal expert, and hadn't even been much of a good attention payer in science class, but he would have sworn that the end of Pinchy's tail was wounded, as though it had once had possessed a stinger which had been broken off.

Doodles nearly swooned from blood loss, which was not helping him keep his grip. He had to get out of that tree but fast.

Reaching up, he wrapped his one free hand around a still-green coconut. Those things were as hard as rocks. With all of his might, he threw it down and hit Pinchy squarely in the... head. Or middle of its back. Whatever that part of a giant crab monster was. In any case, Pinchy seemed unfazed by the strike.

"Ah, stick it in your nose," Doodles muttered, grabbing a second, even greener coconut.

This time he tossed it down with even more force. Pinchy's left claw shot out with pinpoint accuracy and snatched the incoming fruity projectile out of the air. The creature barely seemed to exert any pressure at all and the green coconut exploded into a million shards under its grasp.

"Okay," he said, "no more Mr. Nice Guy. Coconuts are for kids and tropical drinks with umbrellas. Let me introduce you to my friend, Lieutenant Commander Rock."

His head still swimming from blood loss, Doodles grabbed another coconut and tossed it off into the surf. Pinchy turned to watch it go, giving Doodles just enough time to slide down the palm tree and take off running. He didn't even look back as a fusillade of clicks sounded closer and closer behind him as he ran.

He knew exactly where he was heading, because he had nearly died there not two weeks ago. He'd even made special note of it in case the Tojos had ever gotten wise to him and he needed a booby trap. He hadn't set it, exactly. It was nature's booby trap.

A small promontory composed of shale stacked in a just-barely stable arrangement loomed up ahead of him. He pounded up the incline, nimble as a mountain goat, locating just the perfect purchases in a pattern he had spent many whole afternoons practicing. By the time Pinchy, only a few seconds behind him, had reached the base of the outcropping, he was at the top. He kicked at the precarious rocks and the whole thing came tumbling down.

"And that's the end of that chapter," he said proudly, clapping his hands against each other.

Atop his personal little bear trap he sighed wistfully. He had really wanted to see Sergeant Ohno get crushed under the rockslide one day. He hated to waste it on an oversized decapodian, but there'd been no alternative. He figured it was better for someone to use their last shot than to be buried with a loaded gun.

He was truly wiped out from a combination of terror, blood loss, and running around.

He started to head back to his new camp. The Japanese had discovered his first camp, but they'd only taken some of his most basic cooking implements. He'd managed to recover most of the best stuff from his galley.

He rummaged through his gear, before finally finding a heavy metal mallet and a pair of nutcrackers. He stuffed them into a burlap sack and slung it over his back, then thought to rip off a piece of fabric to replace the now sodden sock in his million-dollar wound. Then he stopped dead.

There, on the ground, just outside his camp, was a long but unmistakable stinger. Just as he had suspected, Pinchy was an amputee. He grabbed the thing out of the sand, which at its base was as thick around as his fist. A long, wicked needle sprouted from the fist-like connecting base.

"So, this is how you found me. You tracked me from camp. But something got you first. A shark or a crocodile or…"

He shrugged. It could have been almost anything. These jungles were dangerous.

He turned the stinger over and over in his hands, at one point staring down the pointy end like a gun barrel. A few seconds later, as he fiddled with the fistula, he realized how close he had come to being blinded or even killed. He triggered something and a long, thin stream of liquid sprayed out of the needle and onto the sand. Whatever goo or venom he had just released ate up a gallon of sand like it was nothing.

"Holy craparooni!" Doodles exclaimed. "Well, now I'm glad you lost this."

He shoved the stinger into his pocket and turned around, only to be greeted by a leering, clicking lobster-crab monster. Pinchy had not only survived being crushed under half a ton of rubble, but it seemed no worse for wear, save for gray dust and chunks of gravel covering its normally bright white carapace.

Doodles immediately shifted on his feet to a boxing pose, although even at his athletic peak in high school he'd never been very good at the sweet science. Thinking he'd better find a weapon, he snatched a filleting knife out of his knife block.

Bobbing back and forth like Joe Louis, he looked for a spot to shove the knife into the monster. But, unfortunately, he couldn't see any obvious seams in its armor. He struck with the knife anyway, which immediately splintered.

"Holy shit," Doodles muttered, for once forgoing his trademark pseudo-profanity.

The creature was obviously incapable of giggling, but Doodles assumed it was doing the crabby equivalent as it lunged at him, massive claws clicking in gruesome delight. Squeaking like a mouse, he ran around the campsite, tossing pots, pans, and even some of the precious plates the Japanese had left him. Everything either dented or shattered against the creature's seemingly impenetrable shell.

"I got something for you," Doodles muttered, stopping his Three Stooges routine with the deadly creature just long enough to fish a massive, cast iron skillet out of his stores.

He stood back like Joe DiMaggio at the pitch, and when Pinchy lunged at him, swung away with all his might, straight into what he assumed to be the creature's face. He was disappointed, but, sadly, not shocked when the skillet came away dented into the shape of a Clicker's carapace.

That was it. His last bullet fired. Pinchy toppled him over like he weighed nothing. He felt the last of his strength ebbing away into the sand, bleeding out from his butt. That would be his epitaph: "He bled out from his butt while a sea monster ate him." Well, something like that anyway. He wasn't a poet.

The thing loomed large over him, much larger than its dog-like stature would have allowed in normal times. But, then, like manna from Heaven, his hand fumbled into something that would get him out of all of this.

Rubber bands.

The Navy didn't spring for lobster often. Usually on special occasions, like the *Lexington*'s birthday. But when they did, Doodles had kept the lobsters properly subdued with those little rubber bands. He'd always wondered why they came in so many different sizes. Surely lobsters didn't grow to greyhound-like stature. He'd even remembered laughing about it once with the other cooks. But, now, here he was, hands on two foot-long restraining bands.

As Pinchy's useless tail flicked, attempting, no doubt, to figure out how to dissolve and devour him without its stinger, Doodles fought with every last ounce of his might to slip the rubber bands over first the left, then the right claw. Pinchy reared back, angered by its sudden inability to grasp, slice, or even make its trademark intimidating clicking noise. Now, deprived of both its stinging tail and its shearing claws, it had been rendered essentially neutered, and collapsed in the sand.

"My, how the tides have turned," Doodles said, smiling happily. "How do you want to end up, as a Thermidor or a Newberg?"

Pinchy didn't respond. It simply cowered like a beaten dog. If a mindless crab monster was capable of looking morose, this one did.

"Aw, now, don't be like that, Pinchy. I won fair and square. You'd've eaten me if the shoe were on the other fist…claw…you know what I mean."

Pinchy simply hung its "head."

"Craptastic," Doodles muttered.

The immediate danger over, he remembered how famished he was. And despite his chest-thumping, he didn't have the heart to kill the defeated animal before him. Not yet, anyway.

He stood and set about putting together some porridge from the raw grain he'd managed to scrounge. Pinchy didn't move from the spot where it'd been banded, seemingly utterly despondent. When the porridge was finished, he plopped down next to it. The bowl was still steaming and, though it wasn't much, it was better than a kick in the face by a long shot.

"Now, look," Doodles said, scooping a warm and much-needed mouthful of mush into his waiting mouth, "this isn't a pardon. It's just a reprieve. I reserve the right to eat you, just as soon as I can figure out how to crack open that shell of yours."

Pinchy seemed to shrug in resignation.

"Ah, heckballs," Doodles said, and shoved the bowl in its direction. "You hungry?"

Sore, but not willing to pass up a meal, the monstrosity lurched forward and began scraping the mush into its mouth with its banded claws. Perhaps porridge had been a good choice. It didn't seem capable of eating anything much chunkier, which certainly explained the acid in its tail. Maybe it just sprayed any animal or plant it wanted to eat, then slurped it up.

Doodles rose and made himself a second bowl. Together they sat, slurping their porridge together noisily.

"You know, Pinchy, I think this might be the beginning of a beautiful friendship."

9. AUGUST, 1942

Night had fallen and the entire company had dug into their foxholes. Alcide and Trick had dug deep, and, as Alcide had expected earlier, no matter what a pain in the derriere it was to lug during the day both men were happy to be under the protection of the massive Browning come nightfall.

The memory of the dead Marines they'd found weighed heavily on everyone in the company. Basher and Martino were in the nearest foxhole, and both looked white. For his own part, he'd had to swallow the urge to vomit when burying the bodies. He'd tried to get the parts he needed then, but his three comrades had never given him a chance.

They were camped on a hillside overlooking the airfield and the ocean beyond it. The night was bright with sounds of distant cannons and screams. Ships burned in the strait, fire raging on their decks. Alcide thought it looked like the damn Fourth of July. Small drops of rain began to fall. Alcide could smell the storm on the air, a thick humidity that preceded the deluge.

"The squids must be giving Tojo Hell," Trick whispered beside him.

Alcide sighed and shook his head. "Admire that spirit, but I don't think we're the ones down there giving out the hits."

A ship went up in a massive explosion that echoed across the island hills. A wave of dirt fell into their foxhole and they were still trying to clean it back out when Basher appeared to pass along ammunition.

"Here's your .30 cal rounds, guys."

"Hey, hey, Betty Grable, you going to kiss and run?"

Basher sighed. He was carrying practically a foot locker's

worth of rounds on his wide shoulders.

"Give me a break, Trick. I've got twenty more foxholes to get to."

Trick held up a hand in mock surrender. "All right, all right. Just tell me if any of the great minds in this company know what that explosion just was."

Basher shrugged. "Had to be a Tojo ship!"

He disappeared back into the dark to complete his rounds. Alcide decided that he'd had enough of just sitting and waiting in the dirt. There were powerful ingredients he needed, and they were just waiting on the edge of camp. If it helped him and the rest get home, he'd risk leaving his position.

"I'm crawling outside the wire to take a piss."

Trick looked at him like he'd lost his mind. "Are you kidding me? Webb will have you by the gonads. Not to mention the Tojos will skin you alive if they're watching."

Alcide smiled and touched the red mojo bag that he'd hung around his neck. "Good thing I've got all sorts of things looking after me."

Trick didn't ask him what he meant, just shook his head and pointed at the dark tree line. "I'll cover for you as best I can, but if Webb comes I'm denying I ever met you. Better get going while everyone is enjoying the show."

Alcide grinned and crawled out of the foxhole, pressing himself into the dirt and feeling the soft coolness even through his shirt as he crawled through the overgrown grass.

A few men's heads popped up as he crawled past, and when his intentions became clear, whispered at him not to be an idiot and to get back in his foxhole. He ignored them, hell-bent on getting to the trees. Alcide hoped that any Tojos in the area were just as enthralled with the battle taking place in the strait as his comrades were.

He'd subtly encouraged the others to dig shallow graves earlier in anticipation of this moment. After just a few minutes with his e-tool, he'd uncovered the bodies.

The dead marines had that putrid smell common for things that had been left to stew in brackish water. It wasn't the first time he'd smelled a dead man, either. Carefully, he pulled back the first man's lips, easier when his head wasn't attached. His knife sliced through the gums, what little blood was left staining his hands as he collected the dead man's teeth.

If Gunny Webb or the skipper or…pretty much anyone saw him now, he'd be out on his ass and probably court martialed, but he had no choice. Human ingredients were necessary for his workings.

Alcide had moved on to the second body when he heard it. The river that ran through tree line wasn't deep, but it was deep enough that Gunny had warned them to watch for crocodiles before they'd crossed. This was different, though. He'd heard plenty of gators back in the bayou. But he was also familiar with this sound.

A flash of red came from the bushes. He saw the waving tail as it watched him from behind the high brush, its dark eyes, blacker than the night, barely visible. But it couldn't disguise the noise of those claws…*click-click click-click.*

Oddly enough, it reminded him of home, where the river ran deep and a colony of these creatures bred, summoned up by him and his kin only on rare occasions, and even then only in desperate need. But this wasn't one of the strain he was familiar with. This was a wild creature that to his knowledge shouldn't have been prowling around on land, much less a battlefield.

Alcide stared down the Clicker, keeping absolutely still as it emerged from the tree line, its claws wrapping around the corpse of the man that he hadn't begun to work on.

His mojo bag wouldn't protect him here. The animal could be summoned, but it couldn't be controlled.

Slowly, the dead Marine's teeth clutched tight in his hand, he backed away. The Clicker barely noticed, its claws digging into the bloated flesh and peeling it like wet paper, spilling putrid black blood into the grass.

He had managed to back off a good way when Goodrich, the sixteen-year-old from Vermont who'd lied about his age to join up, appeared. "Boudin, Trick said that you were out here taking a…Sweet Christ!"

The Clicker hissed and the young private swung his Springfield, taking a potshot that barely scraped the shell.

"Goodrich, don't..."

"*Incoming*!" someone yelled.

The night came alive with explosions, both tiny and large, until Boudin curled up into a ball, putting his hands over his head.

It seemed like an eternity before Webb's unmistakable voice rang out with, "*Hold your fire*!"

Slowly, the gunfire trickled away and then the calls came to sound off. Alcide opened his eyes and took in everything. The bodies of the dead men were gone, a trail of black blood and viscera disappearing into the brush. Pvt. Goodrich was ventilated, blood and chips of bone leaking into the brush.

His frozen face still looked afraid.

10. AUGUST, 2020

Cam couldn't get his top mop to sit right. He licked his hand and ran it through his hair, but that wasn't doing anything aside from making the secretary watching him nervous.

"Can I…get you anything, Dr. Custer?"

"Do you have a comb?" Cam asked, realizing even as he said it that he must have sounded like a hammy '90s movie villain.

"Uh…I meant, like coffee."

"Oh," Cam said, scowling. Then a thought struck him. "Oh, yes, then in that case, a fork."

The poor girl had a look in her eye like she had many follow-up questions but didn't want to deal with the lunatic any more. She stood, walked over to the mini-canteen co-located in the waiting room, and handed him a plastic spork.

"Thanks!"

Cam turned back to the not-quite-a-mirror he had been using to clean himself up and began running the spork through the trouble spot in his coif. It immediately bent backwards and broke off in his hair. He turned back to the secretary, holding the broken plastic handle toward her in what must have been a threatening way, judging by her terrified expression and the sudden rush of blood to her face.

"Have you got a metal one?"

A boisterous voice intoned, "Do *you* believe in undersea worlds?"

Cam whirled around. Marching towards him, finally, out of the main office, was the head of the National Oceanographic and

Atmospheric Administration. Cam flashed the most roguish smile he could muster.

"Mr. Under Secretary! I don't think I've seen you since that conference in, where was it…?"

The chief of NOAA wrapped Cam in a semi-dignified man-hug, which consisted mostly of back slapping.

"Good to see you, Dr. Custer! Ah, was it Rota?"

Cam smiled. They'd never met at a conference, and if they'd ever even attended one together, Cam wasn't aware of it. He was just that damn smooth.

"That must have been it."

"Well, come in, come in. I haven't got much time, but you've got my undivided attention while it lasts. Tammy, hold my calls for fifteen minutes, would you, lamb chop?"

When the under secretary's back was turned, Cam wrinkled his brow. He'd heard sexism was back in a big way in this administration, but even this seemed a bit extreme.

"Uh, fifteen minutes?"

"And all of them yours, Dr. Custer. Well, we're down to fourteen and a half now."

"Uh…of course."

Cam scrambled to wheel what looked like a hotel dinner service behind the under secretary as he followed him into his office. He nearly bashed into the man's back after an unexpected pause. He felt the water inside sloshing almost inexorably forward, and had to yank back with all his might to stop from running over the Under Secretary of Commerce for Oceans and Atmosphere's ankles.

"So, how are you liking Silver Springs?" the man asked after taking his seat, almost so slowly that he might have been deliberately wasting time to irk Cam.

"It's lovely, Jim. We should discuss more about it over lunch…"

"Nah, can't. I'm having lunch with the presidents of Exxon, Sunoco, and Shell today."

Shit. Things really were changing. He should have known that when he'd had so much trouble even getting this appointment. The name Cameron Custer had once carried great weight in these circles. Now it didn't so much open doors as crack them briefly before the occupant shooed him away like a door-to-door salesman.

"Well, then," Cam said, deciding not to waste any more of his limited time and switching directly into big top mode, "I want to talk to you today about something that I know is near and dear to your heart: climate change."

"Nope," the head of NOAA said.

Cam was caught up short. He hadn't expected to be interrupted so soon. He hadn't even given his opening yet, god damn it.

"What do you mean, 'nope?'"

"I mean do you want to get me fired? Do you want to get arrested? It's a federal crime to even say those two words in the same sentence in this building."

"You mean climate…"

The head of NOAA nearly leapt out of his seat, waving his arms wildly to shut Cam down.

"Yes," he hissed, "those two words. You get one pass and then it's Guantanamo Bay."

He pointed to a series of cameras positioned in the corners of the office which all, ominously, seemed to be zeroing in on Cam simultaneously like the scopes of sniper rifles.

"Uh…can I use a euphemism like global…"

"Nope. No euphemisms either. There's a whole list of shit we can't say."

The under secretary pulled out a mammoth tome called *Don't Sez What Donny Sez Doesn't Sez* and tossed it to the floor at Cam's feet. Cam struggled to lift it off the ground and began flipping through it. Apparently "pollution" could be called "job creation gas" and "fracking" was supposed to be referred to as "fun mining" but "climate change" and all of its variants were right out.

"Oh, Christ," Cam said.

"Oh, that you can say. In fact, it's strongly encouraged. We probably should have started this meeting with a prayer, in fact."

The head of NOAA seemed to be getting out of his chair and

down on his knees when Cam suddenly remembered how truly little time he had left.

"Ah, no wait, ah, Jim, praying is so…personal?"

Jim furrowed his brow. "But you do do it?"

"Yes, of course."

The under secretary wiped his hand across his forehead.

"Well, thank God for that. Goddy Goddy God." The cameras seemed somewhat mollified by that and returned to a less aggressive pose. "Yes. Would not have wanted to have to send you to Gitmo for that, either. I want you to know, Dr. Custer, that I am, generally speaking, against your extraordinary rendition."

"Well, thanks, Jim. Um… you know what, fuck it. We'll just jump to the meat of the demonstration. Due to…reasons unknown…many marine animals are…spontaneously… appearing in different habitats. And this little beauty is one of them."

Cam dramatically whipped the curtain away from his mobile aquarium. The bright white Clicker inside was sluggish and miserable. Partly that was due to being confined in a cage barely bigger than itself. But another serious component was the sedatives Cam had dosed the water with. Though the creature's stinger was missing, he didn't doubt that its claws were still dangerous enough to rip a human being limb from limb. So, bulletproof glass, a water refrigerator, and a fuckton of crab sedative had eaten up the last few droplets of his fortune before the trip here.

Cam smiled and waited to bask in his long-awaited moment of triumph.

"What's that, some kind of Muppet?"

"Muppet? Jim, you're a scientist for God's sake. At least you used to be before this administration got to you. Take a look. This is a previously undiscovered species. A modern-day coelacanth. It's a man-killer, too. And they're coming up on land in Guadalcanal. Some day in the not-too-distant future, due to climate…unknown reasons, people are going to worry about crocodiles, alligators, sharks, and Clickers."

The under secretary snorted. "People will never be scared of a thing named after a remote control."

"Custersaurus, then," Cam said with disgust.

"Ah. So we get down to it. You think I made this meeting because I wanted to help you get back in the limelight, Dr. Custer? I took this meeting because I might…might…get a headline or two in some obscure pop culture rag that still follows washed-up celebrities. Maybe a few hardcore ocean nuts on Twitter will chatter about us talking. And you may think NOAA has taken a NOAA-sedive since the heady days of the '80s or whatever, but we still have some fucking integrity here, Custer. I am not going to underwrite your last gasp at relevance by claiming this jackalope here is real."

"Jacka…you think this is a fake?"

Cam shook the aquarium, causing the Clicker to stagger drunkenly and snap its claws. It wasn't a very convincing display, considering how doped up the monster was, but it was certainly proof of life.

"I've seen better animatronics than this in a Reel Splatter movie. Sure, it's a little more convincing than sewing a fishtail to a monkey skeleton, but I know a carnival mermaid when I see one, Custer. Maybe you shouldn't have painted a cartoon on its back."

"It's real, you buffoon! I spent my entire fortune hunting this thing down. I've verified it, I've had DNA tests, the whole McGillicuddy. At least look at my damn research. You haven't even given me the dignity of hearing me out."

The phone rang. The under secretary deliberately and heavily pressed his meaty finger on the speaker button. "Yes, Tammy?"

"Sir, the oil company execs are here for your working lunch."

"I'm so sorry, Dr. Custer, I guess that's all the time we have. Will you please show him out, Tammy?"

The secretary appeared at the door with a smile and gestured for Cam to follow him.

"Oh, and Dr. Custer?"

Cam turned back, hope springing eternally on his face.

"You've got a broken fork or something in your hair."

Dejected, Cam reached up and pulled the spork head out of his hair. It had clearly been prominent the entire meeting. As he rolled his aquarium out, a squad of men in cowboy hats and snake leather boots strode past him.

"Well, would you look at that," one of them said with a whistle, "They must be remaking that Abbess movie."

"It's pro-nounct 'abyss,' yaidjit."

As Cam made his slow, dejected walk of shame, Tammy scurried in front of him to open doors so he wouldn't have to stop, open the door with his back, and pull the tank through after him. Probably she was more worried about him doing damage to any of the doors or walls than concerned for his dignity, though he did appreciate that at least someone in NOAA still acted like they cared about it.

As soon as they reached the parking lot, he jumped back in surprise as the woman leaned in to kiss him.

"What the hell?"

"Quiet," she whispered. "The bugs are all inside. Out here the cameras don't have audio."

"Oh," he said, weirdly upset at what suddenly felt like a romantic rejection, "I thought you were trying to kiss me."

She smiled. "Maybe when I was a teenager and had your poster on my wall. But I'm not a creeper, Dr. Custer. I…was the one who swung you this meeting."

"You did? I…well, thank you."

She nodded as though it were nothing.

"I can get you another one with people almost as high up as him, but that'll actually listen, that haven't swallowed the Kool-Aid yet. But there's a problem. People will always find a way to debunk a single specimen, even if it is real. And I believe you about this monstrosity and the danger it poses. Is there any way you can get a second one?"

Cam held up his hands and let them drop to the sides with two loud simultaneous slaps.

"It was my whole life to find this one."

"Is there anything else? Haven't you spent your whole career hunting down rumors?"

Cam's eyes suddenly lit up.

"Actually…there might be something else."

11. AUGUST, 1942

Ota stared out at the crashing waves and burning ships as his green flare shot into the sky. A breeze blew in over the sea carrying the sweet smell of the ocean and the distant screams of dying men. Nearby, Colonel Shinsato shivered despite the tropical heat, glancing at each rolling wave like it would reach out to drag him down into the depths. City boys were always terrified of nature. Ota found it all so relaxing. Still, Ota didn't begrudge the man his anxiety. It wasn't often that a man was able to stride between the worlds of flesh and spirit.

"Tell me something, Hanshiro-*san*."

Ota glanced at his ostensible peer, never losing his eye on the waves. Peers they were, technically, granting Shinsato tacit permission to address him as an equal. But Ota recognized it as a slight disguised as respect. Shinsato had not bought off on Ota's command. He'd undercut him at every turn since he'd taken over for Katou.

Ota preferred the path of least resistance, like the Abashiri River back home. He would simply pass over the rocks in his way. And tonight he would grant Shinsato an honor afforded to few before in the world. Frankly, he'd broken Atagi's heart choosing Shinsato to accompany him tonight, and both men knew it. Ota hoped that would quell any mutinous feelings Shinsato harbored permanently. If not, he would have to find other ways to secure his command.

"You may ask," he granted, after judging that he'd paused long enough.

"The creatures from…that night. Some of my patrols have

reported seeing something like that on the other side of the island."

Ota shook his head.

"Impossible. All of the *Kurikka* are accounted for."

Well...that wasn't strictly true, but there was no reason Shinsato had to know about Ota's lone error.

"Are there white ones? My men report it to be bright white, but otherwise similar to the one we saw...that night."

"A white one? How interesting."

A low buzz sounded through the sky and both men dove to the ground. As the plane passed, Ota prayed that they would not be spotted. Luckily, two men on a beach are not so easy to spot.

When they recovered their feet, Shinsato said, "The carrier *Saratoga* is near. The Americans will be flying patrols all night. Should we not wait in the forest to avoid being spotted?"

"Your fear is unfounded. Navy has done its job so that the *Umibozu* can come. There will be no planes tonight. They will dig in and make sure that we do not take the airfield."

He smiled to himself, thinking of his return to the farmstead. Despite his own dearth of letters, Haruki had written him recently with glorious news. She was with child, a product of their furious lovemaking during his last leave. He would return to the home islands not only the man who had bent the *Kami* themselves to the emperor's divine will, but as a new father.

Shinsato looked to protest again before a wave crashed. The man looked astonished and fearful as shapes appeared in the surf, standing tall, their large eyes reflecting the fire light of the sinking American fleet. Ota had to remind himself that while he had been through this, no matter how much he had tried to prepare Shinsato, his first time would still be world-shattering. Each of the creatures emerging from the surf carried tridents of various designs and lengths, each prong glinting, leveled at the two humans on the shore.

Ota bowed deep, his second belatedly mimicking the motion as the *Umibozu* came ashore. There were half a dozen, centered on one particular specimen who was larger than the rest by a good two feet.

The *Umibozu* chieftainess stood a good twelve feet tall, her head like bone. She had two rows of teeth that seemed to merge into her skull and muscles that rippled beneath green skin so dark that it almost was black. Nets adorned her chest, but the nations of origin Ota could not speculate, and fishhooks were buried deep in the creature's chest. He had studied the tribes of the Pacific and it reminded him of some kind of ritualistic scarring.

But the coral that grew on her seemed to speak to her age more than anything else. It scarred the left side of her face like a cancerous growth, each one suckling at her flesh. There was more of it than the last time Ota had seen the creature and the suspicion of sickness entered his mind, but it was not something he could dwell on or take advantage of, not with the rest of its kind standing so close.

"Rise, land-dweller," she spoke in her own language.

It had been torturous, learning the deep grunts and chirps of *Umibozu* speech, but Ota was nothing if not focused, and slowly the communication had become easier if not perfect.

"It is an honor to stand in your presence again," Ota remarked, rising from his bow.

The smaller specimens chirped in a way that Ota was sure was laughter, but the large one merely shot a glare with its one eye and the heckling died as each one cringed away from their leader.

Ota took pride in seeing that he would not be disrespected. Seeing Shinsato's hand drift to his service weapon on instinct, Ota cleared his throat, arresting the younger man's movement. The creatures did not respond well to even the subtlest hints of defiance. The dark black eye that wasn't covered in coral polyps focused on him, the primeval visage portraying a subtle sense of fury.

"Your kind fight. Our home is being destroyed. This is not what you promised us."

Ota nodded, taking his time to discern every syllable to make sure that he didn't mistranslate any of the sounds. "It is not our kind. It is an enemy tribe, and one we are honor-bound to destroy."

The creature's gills flapped on the side of her neck, her webbed hands gripping her ancient trident tighter. Ota's family sword was over a hundred years old. This creature's trident was likely thousands. Ota steadied himself, mentally reciting poetry from his family's old scrolls, the same ones that were read when a relative was put on their pyre, then read again when their ashes were spread into the sea.

One of the lesser *Umibozu* spoke something and the chieftainess growled something in return. Her eye focused back and she asked, "Will you kill them? Are they weak? Will you defeat them?"

Ota was no linguist, but he felt sure that the words had a more elegant history, but sounded now strangely primitive. It was a clear sign of a fallen civilization, reduced to barbarism.

"They are weaklings, yes, and cowards, but even a great warrior can be brought down by a horde of peasants.

"I see," the chieftainess replied, her intent opaque as always. "And what of your work for us?"

"I am close to perfecting what you have asked, along with other designs that will help our war effort. But if the enemy disrupts my research, I will have to start again."

Ota let the unspoken threat hang in the air, and while it was true that the American's invasion had been detrimental, it was also a perfect opportunity to field test what he and his assistants had managed to create.

The chieftainess let out a hiss and leveled the trident at Ota, its blades so long and wicked that it cut small tears into his uniform. "You have taken so much time. We have given you many specimens. If you have failed us, you will die."

"I haven't failed you."

Ota barked a command at Shinsato, who bowed and gestured to the men hiding in the trees. The small squad of Unit 731 men dragged a half-conscious islander between them.

All of the men looked away from the *Umibozu*. Ota had witnessed firsthand their phenomenal psychic potential and he did not need his secrets falling into their hands, not before the proper time. This partnership was built on the hope that Ota could replicate the knowledge they had lost when their empire had fallen, and Ota was confident he could keep them in line while extracting great advantages for his still-standing Empire.

The squad of his men deposited the wretch on the sand and departed just as quick. The creatures stared in curiosity as Ota stepped up next to his test subject, a man from one of the hundreds of islands they had conquered, clothed in a spare uniform from a dead soldier. The man shivered, his eyes staring blankly at the sand.

"This should be an effective demonstration," Ota said and then he commanded the man to stand. Slowly the man did, the waves from the surf crashing across his feet.

The man babbled something in his own barbaric tongue, his terror of the creatures standing in front of him naked. Ota ignored him. Traitors deserved nothing.

"The mainline species and the remnants from the specialized breeds were useful. This quick breeding of this particular strain allowed me to create something truly unique."

Ota reached over and unbuttoned the shirt concealing the man's chest. When the last button came free, Shinsato recoiled beside him. The *Umibozu*'s throats ululated in a low thrumming that Ota recognized as a sign of pleasure.

He stared at his work, giving voice to his thoughts."It is not perfect and does not do what the original specimens do. The host still has too much freedom and it lacks any ability to adapt. The enzymes are killing the host just like the primary specimens. As it stands, this man barely has a day to live. The poison is too strong, but they will be useful regardless."

The *Umibozu* looked among each other, grunting to each other too quickly for him to understand, though he sensed that the younger ones approved of this bastardization of their practices. Ota watched as the chieftainess held up her hand, silencing her compatriots and fixing the Japanese colonel with that dark eye that seemed to spiral away into the depths of infinity.

"I will take that back with me to convince my people that this alliance is yet valuable. I will also take a sacrifice of flesh from you, to prove that you are committed to your promise."

The creature's eye fell on Shinsato, who looked nervously

at Ota. Ota was gratified that his second couldn't understand the language they were speaking. He bowed deeply to the chieftainess once again. "Of course, mistress. I would not dare of cheating you out of what you deserve, not after what help you have given."

He took a deep breath, taking a gamble that would either result in the trident eviscerating him or great benefits for the Empire. "You have given so much, but if the Americans are successful in their conquest, I won't be able to provide what you have tasked me with."

The fish-man's gills undulated and Ota could feel the annoyance billowing off of the creature in a psychic wave that he was sure Shinsato could also feel. But just like the tide, it receded, draining away from the air and allowing Ota a moment to breathe again.

"You will have aid."

With those simple words she turned her back on Ota Hanshiro, striding back into the waves as the other *Umibozu* rushed forward and grabbed the diseased islander from where he stood.

The last *Umibozu* stuck his trident through Shinsato's chest. Ota heard the tear in his skin, the silent gasp and then pained coughing as his second-in-command tried to cling to life. He could hear the blood dripping into the sand and then the pleasured hissing as the creature opened its maw. There was a sickening crunch, more wet dripping, and then the *Umibozu* was walking past him, Shinsato's corpse held easily on the end of its weapon, the needle teeth chewing on his head.

One of the colonel's eyes came free from the side of his head, impaled on the dagger sharpness of the creature's jaws. It paused in its feast, swallowing the head, roaring at the waves and gesturing with his trident toward Ota. Then it departed, disappearing into the waves, but replaced by something just as deadly.

A symphony of claws sounded. *Click-click click-click.* All were red, the color of wild *Kurikka* Ota had encountered before. But one in particular stopped him in his tracks. He stared in awe at the shell as black as night, shining like polished obsidian.

He drew his sword from the sheath on his hip, raising it high so that the creatures could see it, trusting that they operated on the same principles as their albino cousins.

Eyestalks stared at the sword, swaying tails ceased their motion, and when Ota pointed at the jungle and the refuge within, segmented legs eagerly followed into the deep gloom.

He hoped Atagi would forgive him for choosing Shinsato to accompany him tonight.

12. AUGUST, 1942

Gunny Webb had an astonishing way of dismembering a man with just a stern tone. "You were taking a piss?"

Ezekiel hunkered in a corner of his foxhole, arms folded. The Cajun seemed to be staring right through Webb, his mouth forming a thin line, unmoved despite Webb practically shouting in his face. To Ezekiel's mind, it looked like Boudin's thoughts were a thousand miles away.

Ezekiel certainly had more important shit to deal with right now. The least Boudin could do was be mentally present for his own ass chewing.

"Goodrich is dead. Captain Palmer here is going to have to write a letter to that kid's mother. He wasn't even out of high school. What do you have to say to that, shit-for-brains?"

Alcide took a deep breath before he spoke. "I didn't mean for no one to get hurt, Gunnery Sergeant. Goodrich saved my life. He gunned down that Tojo, I mean, Japanese soldier what took a shot at me."

The sun was beginning to rise and the burial detail was just now finishing their work. Palmer had carefully noted the grid coordinates of all three graves and reported them to battalion, but knowing the Marine Corps he doubted the remains would make their way home any time this century. And now two of them had been dragged out of their graves.

Webb looked ready to launch into another verbal assault, but Ezekiel stepped in.

"Boudin, if I put Goodrich in for a posthumous Commendation Medal, I might need you to sign some paperwork. Would that be all right? Swearing that he saved your life?"

Boudin's pause was tiny, but perceptible. "Yes, sir."

"Good. Can you take me to where you saw the Japanese soldier? The one you swear Goodrich—sixteen-year-old Goodrich—died saving you from?"

Ezekiel was staring at the man intently, thinking that the young Marine's eyes looked far older than they had a right to be. It was a moment before he answered, "I didn't see any Japanese soldier, sir."

Ezekiel knew untruth when he heard it, and Alcide Robichaude wasn't lying. But the private must have seen *something*.

"What happened to those men's bodies, then, Robichaude?" Jake asked, stepping in.

Boudin hesitated, barely the blink of an eye, but Ezekiel saw the story forming in the man's head before he spoke. "Couldn't rightly say, First Lieutenant. Back in the bayou, gators come and snatch a man if they smell blood. Maybe that happened with the crocodiles that live here, yeah?"

Ezekiel wanted to spend the next six months grilling the man until he got the truth, but he didn't even have six hours.

"Private First Class Robichaude, you had better spend the time you have between now and the next break in the fighting trying to impress Gunnery Sergeant Webb. If he is not impressed, then I will send a report thicker than *Moby Dick* to battalion. Now get the hell out of here."

Boudin disappeared.

Ezekiel laid out his laminated map and tried to discern where best they could intercept the Tojos if they moved toward the airfield.

"Keep an eye on him, Gunny. And try to get the truth out of his buddies if you can. But otherwise we've got bigger fish to fry."

"Agreed, sir," Webb growled.

"Get the men prepared to move. We're going to make a push south of the airfield."

The older man nodded and left, shouting orders as he climbed up out of the foxhole, leaving Jake and Ezekiel alone. Jake glanced around for eavesdroppers before asking the obvious. "Why do you think he'd lie about seeing things? Tojo spy?"

Ezekiel sighed, rubbing his temples. "Unless the Japanese have infiltrated deep Louisiana, I doubt it. More likely, he was doing something he wasn't supposed to be doing."

"What would a man do with dead bodies? Cannibalism? Or…some kind of weird sex thing?"

Jake shuddered.

"He's not Jack the Ripper. He probably just stole the dead men's watches. Or lifted their wallets."

"He was on their burial detail, Zeke. He could've done that any time."

Ezekiel knew that. Of course he knew that. Something didn't add up.

"It doesn't matter really. We've got more important things to take care of today and he can shoot a gun same as any other man. If he bleeds with me today he can be my brother."

Ezekiel realized as he spoke that he was no longer feeling like some pretender.

Leave it to Jake to steal his thunder. His XO shivered in mock awe. "Well shucks, Captain Palmer, sir, if that didn't beat all. That the same speech you're going to give when they're handing you your Congressional Medal of Honor?"

Ezekiel smiled and went back to his map. "Just get someone to watch Boudin. If he's out doing wrong, we'll catch him."

13. AUGUST, 1942

A court martial was the last thing on Alcide's mind as he returned to his foxhole. Trick looked at him like some new convert would have stared at a god in the flesh. "I thought you were a goner for sure. What was it like when Goodrich bought it?"

Alcide shrugged, trying to avoid his friend's gaze. "I don't know nothing about that."

"Weren't you there?"

"He died right in front of me."

Trick's eyes were wide. "Was it... do you think it hurt?"

Alcide remembered the blood pooling out of the dead man's chest and the look of fear etched on his face. But most of all, he remembered the Clicker.

"Yeah, I think it hurt," he finally said, putting his back to the man. The early morning light revealed the Japanese fleet trolling the channel, with no sign of their ships.

Gunny Webb began to shout the order to move out. Men appeared from their foxholes, reaching down to retrieve their companions and amassing close to the tree line and the path towards the airfield.

Loose soil fell into Alcide's face as he packed up the Browning. Basher and Martino were standing above him and Trick, not acknowledging either one of them. They stared open-mouthed at the ships sitting in the channel, like fat gators sunning themselves.

"Where... where's the fleet?" Basher asked.

"Told you that you were being optimistic, thinking we were

winning down there," Alcide muttered, wiping a clod of dirt off of the ammo box.

Martino sniffed, the faint shadow of anger falling across his face. "Oh yeah, Boudin? Well at least we didn't go for a fucking piss that got a man killed."

Alcide froze, turning slowly. He saw Trick's eyes widen and heard him whisper frantically, no doubt trying to talk him out of confronting Martino. He ignored all of this and focused on Martino, fixing the man with the same glare that his family had been giving people who thought they were too big for their britches for years.

Silence reigned between the two of them. Even Webb's orders were just a faint echo. Something subtle moved through the air and the other men exiting their foxholes seemed to notice that violence was one ruptured temper away from happening.

"Go ahead, Boudin. Work your fucking voodoo on me. Don't think I haven't seen you praying over that fucking bag around your neck and drawing that shit all over the dirt in your foxhole." Martino whispered the words.

Alcide's eyes were drawn to the designs that he had drawn in the soil with his finger, absentminded little protections that would deter the eye if you meant to cause harm. "You're my friend, Martino. Don't want to go putting things on you that aren't so easy taking off again."

Martino looked like he was going to retort when a hand fell across his shoulder.

"Take a breather, both of you, before this gets worse." The voice was firm but sympathetic, which would have been one of the best ways to describe Corporal Willie Cantor.

He had come up in the Midwest and his frame still showed telltale signs of a time when food was scarcer during the height of the Depression, even if he had been living out in California when he had signed up.

Cantor had a smile that Alcide would have described as naïve, but his eyes had a world weariness that Alcide hadn't seen in many men, despite the corporal's twenty-five years of age. He carried a pocket bible with him, same as Alcide and others, loaded down with mementos of home, and a rosary like some of the other Catholic men did. But the difference was that he spoke on the benefits of the Good Lord every chance that he could get, saying things about tangible evil in the world, more monstrous than man. When there wasn't a proper chaplain around, he usually got some of the men together on Sundays for a prayer circle or Bible study. The men had taken to calling him Preach, and behind maybe Webb he was the most respected man in the unit. The fact that he could get Marines to give up some of their precious free time every Sunday was testament to that.

Martino snuck another look at Alcide and mumbled, "Sorry, Preach. Got a little fucking hotheaded is all."

Cantor smiled. "You got hotheaded because this place is a humid mosquito trap. It happens to the best of us. Now you and Basher get moving before Gunny notices."

Basher and Martino both did as instructed and vanished from the top of the foxhole. Cantor looked around at the other men who had just been hanging around gawking. "That goes for you, too!"

They did as they were told and when all was said and done, it was just Preach, Alcide, and Trick left.

"Thanks, Preach," Alcide said, trying to surreptitiously kick away his drawings. If the Tojos appropriated this hole, he didn't want them to benefit from his working.

"Is that devil worship?" Preach asked. Alcide thought that his eyes had a mad gleam to them, like he was barely containing some long-held fervor.

"Nah, nothing like that, Preach. You and I fear the same God. We just worship him different like. Ain't that the American way?"

Every word he'd said was true, though he still felt a bit like he was lying. He didn't dare use words like hoodoo around most folk, least of all a true believer like Preach Cantor.

But maybe he'd misjudged the guy. What Alcide had thought was a mad gleam was something else. He had seen the distinct fear in men over the years and there was only one reason that Preach would be afraid of what Alcide had drawn in the soil.

"You've seen something, haven't you, Preach?" Alcide asked,

curiosity flooding through him. The Clicker was prominent in his mind.

"Just get moving, Boudin," Preach replied, standing up abruptly and disappearing over the rim of the foxhole.

Alcide watched him go, then kicked the last remaining design, watching the dirt and roots fall into wetness and earth.

14. JULY, 1942

Doodles hadn't been excited to wake up since the night before Christmas when he was a kid.

No.

Wait.

That wasn't true. He did remember being excited to wake up the day he'd passed a mash note to Mary Anne Higgenbottom during school. So excited, in fact, that he'd stayed up half the night pacing his room.

Still, excepting a few occasions in his youth he rarely had trouble going to sleep and staying that way. In boot camp, sleep had been a blessed relief. On the *Lexington* he'd barely had a few moments to himself in any given day. Cooks had to get up at 0300 to start baking, and the day didn't end until 1900 at the earliest, and there were really nothing more than five minute breaks in between. Breakfast, lunch, dinner, and coffee for the officers really all rolled together into one long period in the galley.

All his life sleep had been something dearly to be desired. Now, though, for the first time, on this isolated island, sleep seemed like a necessary evil, keeping him from the joys of wakefulness.

When he woke up that morning, he had a full-on smile. An erection, too, but ever since Pinchy had come into his life, he just wasn't interested in tenderizing his own meat anymore. He sat up, unable to wipe the rictus grin off his face, and whistled shrilly three times in the air.

Click-click. Click! Click-click. Click!

With his claws bound by the lobster bands, Pinchy sounded

a bit more like he was thumping than clicking, but Doodles knew this particular rhythm well. Pinchy was excited.

Doodles whistled three more times. They were about as close to communicating with each other plainly as he imagined was possible between a man and an aquatic sea monster, but he found that whistles, clicks, and similar noises seemed to get his point across much better than words. Tone of voice was practically lost on the monstrosity altogether.

"What have you got there, boy?" he asked as Pinchy came bounding into camp, something long and furry in its grasp.

Pinchy had taken to scavenging for all sorts of things lately. After their first night together, Doodles had promised to show off his culinary skills to his new friend. He'd gathered together an armload of papayas, coconuts, shredded crabmeat, and even a quail he'd caught earlier that day, determined to figure out what Pinchy liked to eat.

He'd sat down and offered Pinchy the coconut, but the monster angrily batted that away, a clear no. Even though it might have been cannibalism, he'd then laid out some shredded crabmeat in a plate made of the former owner's own shell. Pinchy had seemed eager about that, even trying to scoop it into his mouth, but the crab meat kept falling out, uneaten. In an angry, almost human motion, Pinchy had slammed both of his claws down in the sand simultaneously, raising two tiny puffs of dust.

It had taken Doodles a little while to figure it out, but since the oatmeal had gone over so well, he had figured that Pinchy could only eat liquefied food. He'd then taken one of the papayas and mashed it up with the crabmeat into a near porridge.

Pinchy had seemed so eager at that point that Doodles had nearly fed him by hand, but realizing his mistake, had instead served the crab flesh and papaya mash in the crab shell. Pinchy had happily, greedily devoured it, then begged for more, which Doodles had been happy to provide.

Ever since, Pinchy had been hunting and scavenging all over the island, bringing new meals for Doodles to whip up into culinary masterpieces for him. Batwings, centipedes, strange ugly rodents, even mysteriously unbroken snake eggs had somehow all made it into Doodles's cooking pots. He liked having someone to "cook" for, strange though the circumstances may have been.

He was weirdly eager to see what Pinchy had brought today.

"Ah, shucks," Doodles said when Pinchy finally reached him and dropped the object he was carrying in front of his lap.

It was a leg. A Tojo leg, judging by the tuft of uniform still jammed in the boot. He felt a weird pang, hoping that it wasn't one of the men he knew by name, but knew that, for now, there was no way to tell whose leg it was.

"Where in the tarnation did you get this?" Doodles asked, waving the leg in Pinchy's face and then instantly regretting it as a wave of bile rose in the back of his throat.

Click-click-click-click…

"Slow down," Doodles said, holding out a hand to pantomime calming a kitty, "think before each click."

Click. Click click click. Click-click.

"Oh," Doodles said, seeming to apprehend, "the intersection just outside the base, huh? Well, how did you even do this?"

Pinchy's right claw began to quiver. Doodles narrowed his eyes as he watched. Slowly, grudgingly, the band around Pinchy's claw began to give way, more than the usual little bit that allowed him to still click, or, rather, thump. With what seemed to be an agonizing display of strength, Pinchy slowly opened his claw until the pincers were about an ankle's length apart. Then he stopped struggling and the pincers snapped back together.

Doodles narrowed his eyes.

"You'd better not do that to me."

Pinchy shook his head (or, body, rather) from side to side. Sighing, Doodles turned the leg over and over in his hand.

"I'm not baby birding this for you."

Pinchy nuzzled him. It wasn't a gesture of affection, but more a way of saying, "Just do it."

"I'm not. I said I'm not. I know we've done a lot of weird things on this island together - well, maybe the weirdest is a man becoming friends with a lobster monster - but I'm not going to chew up and regurgitate human flesh for you."

Pinchy nuzzled him again. "Pretty please?"

Laughing, Doodles rummaged around in his supplies before pulling out a breadfruit.

"You want a *pan'noki* instead?" He didn't actually know the English word for it, but that was what Yotashi always called them.

Pinchy sank, defeated. Doodles shoved him. "Oh, don't be that way."

He ran his fingers down his friend's carapace, as always not quite sure if the creature could even feel it.

Not for the first time his fingers traced, well, doodles, around Pinchy's white shell. It was such a remarkable color, and not one that he often saw in nature. Maybe as a larvae, Pinchy had been hurt, or exposed to a barnacle or algae or something. Or maybe Doodles was just overthinking it.

"Come on," he said, "let's go play fetch."

That seemed to brighten Pinchy up. He zipped into the undergrowth so fast he practically left a crab-monster-shaped cloud in the air behind him. Pinchy returned with a suitable length of wood, and Doodles had already taken a bite out of the breadfruit and started chewing it.

As they walked along the beach, the sun rising over the horizon, man and monster happily laughed and skittered, respectively. Doodles would toss the stick, sometimes short enough that Pinchy would overshoot the mark scuttling after it, sometimes long enough that it took him a while to get back.

With his claws rubber banded together, Pinchy couldn't exactly pick up the stick when Doodles tossed it. But he'd figured out a way to manhandle the hell out of it until he was able to return balancing it on his massive claws, like a waiter holding a platter.

Each time they stopped Doodles spit up about half of the masticated breadfruit pulp onto the sand and Pinchy eagerly slurped up the mess. Maybe their relationship was weird. Hell, Doodles knew it was weird, maybe even unique in human history. But he didn't care. He was just a man, finding love in a pet, as so many others had over the millennia. They could hang him for it when he got back to civilization if they wanted. If that was the case, though, he'd rather just stay here forever.

After about an hour he had to pee, and stopped to trace his signature guy with the nose poking over a wall in the sand. Pinchy muscled his legs aside. Doodles laughed as he practically sat astride his crabby friend.

"You like that, Pinchy? That's high art right there. That's why they call me Doodles."

Pinchy began to scratch at the sand. At first Doodles thought he might just be digging, but slowly, almost shockingly, patterns began to emerge in the scratching. It wasn't a recognizable picture, per se, but in the same way you might pick out patterns in the rutting of a deer on a tree, Doodles could see that Pinchy favored certain circular shapes and harsh, diagonal flourishes.

"Huh. An artistic crab. I knew there was a reason I liked you."

He petted Pinchy hard, and the monster thrilled at his touch, confirming that, yes, he could feel Doodles's caresses, even through the shell. Doodles nodded approvingly at the artwork. In fact, it reminded him of something he'd seen when the ship had put port in China.

"You know what you've done here, Pinch? This is called a mandala."

Pinchy seemed to shrug, then scattered forward, demolishing both of their masterpieces under his scuttling legs.

"Ah, well," Doodles mused, "easy come, easy go. Then again, maybe I could, ah…"

Doodles had made a pot of dark ink out of crushed flowers. With a horsetail brush he drew the cartoon face on Pinchy's back. He nodded at his own handiwork.

"Well, let's see how long that lasts."

Pinchy led him back to camp. Then he stood, wagging his broken tail like a metronome, before his earlier prey. Doodles sighed resignedly.

"You really want that?"

Click.

"All right, fine. Not like I had anything else going on today."

Doodles spent the rest of his day taking bites out of a human leg and chewing raw manflesh into puree for a demon from beneath the sea which had become his best friend.

15. AUGUST, 2020

Bullets chewed through the undergrowth, turning the paradise greens into unrecognizable heaps of mulch that mixed with the blood running from the dead.

Alcide's hands vibrated as the Browning fired, peppering the Tojos as they ran from the woods. Normally, since he had to carry it, Trick insisted on manning the .30 cal. Sometimes, though, like now, after he'd been behind the hot pig all afternoon, he handed it over to Alcide. Single-shot Arisaka rifles cracked into the Marine line and, every so often, caught a man unaware. The belt of ammunition ran dry.

Alcide screamed, *"Reload!"*

Trick went to work, pouring a cup of water over the gun to cool it down. Alcide twitched, Springfield at the ready and watched the enemy come. They'd stumbled upon the Tojo outpost almost by chance.

They'd built it on the top of a hill in a grove of particularly thick trees, secret tunnels running through the ground to emerge at the base of the hill. If the Marine unit hadn't been marching past one of the rat holes when a scout popped his head out, they would have gone past without a clue. As it stood, Captain Palmer had ordered the attack after their own scout reported that the garrison was only half their number.

But that was still more than enough to hurt the unit.

It was a three-pronged attack: one from either side of the hill, and one through the tunnels. Alcide and the rest of the machine gun crews were on the front side assault. And it didn't look like the Tojos had any idea that two hundred or so men were quietly waiting to ambush them in the middle of their own encampment. All Alcide and the rest had to do was keep them distracted until the proper moment.

Easier said than done.

"*You're good*!" Trick shouted.

Alcide closed the ammo port, cocking his weapon and pulling the trigger once again. A Japanese soldier screamed as the bullets chewed through him, wet tearing sounds echoing even over the sounds of battle. Alcide saw the man fall face first into the mud and destroyed foliage, his guts spilling out like fetid worms where the .30 caliber had torn into him.

Beside him, Martino was screaming profanities as he fired into the men running down the hill. Basher was doing less cursing but about the same amount of killing. Alcide stared, lost in the trance of battle, focused entirely on the faces of the enemy, searching for fear or something else to remind him that they were men like him. All he saw, though, was targets, and worried what that meant about his soul.

They fought up the hill, Alcide whispering words that he hoped would help, spells and words of power that would keep his squad unharmed from bullets. But his power had limits and the enemy's bullets didn't always miss their mark.

A private two men down from Martino screamed as his jaw disappeared, bloody teeth dangling from limp red strings. A whistling noise emanated from his throat as he struggled to breathe, toppling over to the desperate shouts of those around him crying, "*Corpsman*!"

But despite the death, despite the danger, they advanced up the hill.

"Boudin, Trick, right side!" Preach yelled, pointing toward three enemy soldiers, charging with bayonets fixed.

Alcide adjusted his aim and the bullets tore into them, revealing another Tojo crouched behind them with his hands up. Tears of dirt streamed down the man's face and he wore what barely amounted to a loincloth. His head lolled around on his neck, hands shaking as he raised them to the sky, not staring at the marines who had killed his friends but the bright sun. Alcide had, perhaps, rediscovered his pity.

From the top of the hill came shouts of terror and more

volleys of gunfire. The other two prongs of the attack seemed to be succeeding, and, for the moment at least, they had been granted a respite.

"How are we looking?" Preach called out.

"All clear left," Alcide called out, and the other men reported the same in their respective areas.

"All right. Hold here."

Preach fired off a flare to signal they had captured the position and, hopefully, avoid any friendly fire.

"Aw, come on, Preach," Martino said, "let's take the fucking hill ourselves. We could be waiting on top when the goddamned skipper arrives, like the rabbit in that fucking story."

"You might have missed the point of that fable, Martino," Alcide said, and the other men laughed.

"He's got you there, Martino. Orders are to wait here, watch for a counterattack, and don't kill anyone coming down off that hill wearing green. Anyone confused?" Their heads all shook. "All right. Smoke 'em if you've got 'em."

Preach put his back against a tree, sighing heavily as he slid down until he was sitting in the chewed up remains of a bamboo patch. He pulled out a small silver case, retrieving a makeshift cigarette. He looked over at Alcide and the rest.

"Any of you have a light?"

Alcide nodded, but knew better than to give another man a perfectly good pack of matches. He'd never get it back, even from a choirboy like Preach. He joined the corporal where he sat, pulling out a small matchbook as he did.

They might have defeated the enemy here, but barely more than a hundred yards up the incline, the sounds of death reached them. Alcide had long since gotten over the worry that it was wrong to slack off when others were working. Life in the Corps was a death of a thousand details, so Alcide took his breaks when he got them.

"Thanks, Boudin," Preach said, taking a long drag of his cigarette. "Basher? Why don't you get a tally of our wounded? The skipper will need to know and we'll be ferrying them back to Lunga Point tonight."

Basher grumbled but set about his never-ending task.

Once, after nearly being shortchanged during pay call, he had protested that despite being from Alabama, he knew how to count. Ever since, he'd been tasked with every inventory, ammo count, and casualty report in the platoon. In a way it was a running joke, but it was also just how these things were. Alcide knew a guy in second platoon who'd been a plumber before the war and now had to dig every latrine.

The Japanese soldier had begun to wail, screaming things in his language that neither Alcide nor Preach understood.

"Oh, I know what'll fucking shut him up," Martino said, brandishing his Springfield in the man's face.

The young corporal sighed and took another puff of his cigarette. "Don't even think about it, Martino. Shut him up without hurting him. We'll send him back to battalion and let the MI boys deal with him."

"Military intelligence," Basher said, looking up from his figuring, "ain't that an…oxen moron?"

It had probably been a hoary old joke during the last war, and Basher had still managed to butcher it.

"No," Martino spat, "you're a fucking oxen moron. The rest of you assholes want to give a guy a hand?"

A few of the others helped him secure the prisoner. Alcide slid into the bamboo next to Preach, staring at the crying Tojo and failing to understand the dark feeling that nestled itself in the pit of his stomach. It wasn't until two men attempted to pull the prisoner to his feet that Alcide realized what it meant. The Japanese soldier was holding what could have been a tiny green pineapple.

"*Grenade*!" Boudin shouted.

The cry echoed through the hillside as the two Marines who had tried to restrain him tried to throw themselves away. They were too slow.

There was a small flash and the Japanese man was thrown into the mud, his body pulped into a mass of unrecognizable meat by the Type 97. The screams began in barely the blink of an eye. Alcide saw a Marine clutching the bloody stump where his arm had been just seconds before, screaming as he stared at the severed limb at his feet. The other man made some sort of gurgling sound as others tried to fill the holes in his stomach with whatever they could find to stop the bleeding.

Preach dropped his cigarette and leapt to his feet to begin handling the disaster. As Alcide jumped up to help, he noticed Preach's eyes looked out of place, like they were already dead.

"God damn this war," the most religious man Alcide knew muttered under his breath.

16. AUGUST, 1942

Ezekiel staggered, trying to process the death and destruction that was happening around him. Jake Dempsey was aiming his .45 at the enemy, screaming at them to put their hands over their head. Not too long ago he'd been more worried about America's loss of face at Pearl and the Philippines, or the hundreds of places where Tojo had stretched out his hand to take what didn't belong to him.

Those worries faded away completely the first time the smell of burning palms and fresh blood had reached his nose.

The Japanese dead were left where they fell, rifles still clutched in their hands, dead eyes staring as the flies began to walk across the open orbs, suckling at the fluid or ragged tissue if a bullet had found its way there.

The lucky ones, if they could indeed be called lucky, were kneeling with their hands covering their heads. According to the War Department propaganda, Japanese preferred death to the dishonor of surrender. Here in the field, though, they were just men, and most men didn't want to die, regardless of what posters told them to think.

Ezekiel sat on a small hill of dirt, letting the sweat run and leaving faux trails of tears across his eyes. Blood ran too. He'd taken a small graze across his cheek and now the crimson drops fell into the dirt where water and trampled thatch formed the tableau of war.

He'd wanted the violence. When they'd charged up this hill the exhilaration had hit and Ezekiel had given in to the small voice whispering for blood and death to win the day. He'd led the charge and only that Arisaka rifle bullet that had knocked him on his ass had brought him back to his waking mind. But even now, as he stared at the smoldering corpse that the flame from the M-2 had found, he couldn't find any righteousness in the violence.

Nightmares would come. They'd already started to intrude on his dreams. The men he'd killed. The men he hadn't been able to save.

Jake sat down next to him, staring at the melted eyes of the dead Tojo. "You still with us, Zeke? You've got that two-thousand-yard stare."

Ezekiel nodded, pointing at a group of men who were busy overturning tables in the bunker, looking for cigarettes and those awful rice-and-barley tins the Japanese ate. "Take control of the Keystone Kops over there. They need to be looking for intel, not chocolate."

Jake looked at the men, then at his friend. "Yeah, sure. What're you going to be doing?"

Ezekiel stood up, not sparing a glance at the burning enemy, his face hardening as he picked up his M1, making sure the clip was reloaded."I'm going to find Cantor and his detail, do a sweep of my own, and then get us the hell back to Lunga Point. And Jake? Get the prisoners on burial detail. Our men go in the ground before theirs, you hear me?"

Jake nodded grimly and began calling the NCOs together. Ezekiel looked over the crouching prisoners, maybe some dozen in all. One struck him as serene, his eyes closed and hands clasped, a telltale string of beads in it.

Ezekiel felt a lump in his throat and leapt at the man, ripping the rosary out of his hand, sending beads flying.

"Where did you get this?" he shouted. "Who did you steal this from?"

The man looked aghast and said something in Japanese, but, seeing the rage and incomprehension in Ezekiel's face, made the sign of the cross.

A Japanese Christian. He hadn't realized there was such a thing. He let the ruined rosary drop to the ground. The man waited, as if expecting to be shot, then tentatively began gathering the scattered beads. He'd never be able to find them all in this undergrowth.

"Sorry," Ezekiel whispered.

Ezekiel was a lapsed Catholic, and for a moment he wondered why God had put this man here to oppose him when they believed the same thing.

Ezekiel hardened his heart and began to patrol the scattered remains of the camp, poking his head into holes and checking dead bodies to make sure they were really dead.

He found papers, written in the scrawling symbols of the enemy, of which he had no understanding, but it was the art that fascinated him. Images of dark figures in blue surf, lobster-like monstrosities that looked like a combination of a crustacean and a scorpion.

Ezekiel chuckled and threw the drawing in the dirt. This wasn't intel. This was the Japanese version of a Tijuana bible. Overactive imaginations were universal wherever you went.

17. AUGUST, 1942

The mood was grim at Lunga Point. More than a few divisions had fallen back to fortify the beach and airfield from Japanese attack and they'd brought their dead with them.

Like most of the officers, Captain Palmer was getting debriefed over his assault on the outpost, leaving the enlisted men to lounge in their foxholes just off the beach. Alcide's squad was down to two fire teams (him and Trick alongside Basher and Martino) and a corporal (Preach.) It wasn't great, but neither were they the most decimated unit in 1st Marines. The men had pooled their efforts and dug a foxhole large enough to sleep all five of them.

Searchlights peered through a darkness that was broken by the sound of waves crashing against the sand. No lights were allowed, and lighters only if they were under cover. Even cigarette cherries were supposed to be kept hidden. Any slip-up could result in a Japanese bombardment.

Alcide stared at a few smoke plumes that still rose from the water in the strait. Every once in a while the surf would carry some piece of metal up onto the dunes. Martino had even been brave enough to rush out to retrieve one after the others had noticed it reflecting in the light of a passing PT boat.

"You keep peeking your head out, Boudin, you're liable to lose it," Preach said beside him.

Alcide had been carving protective designs into the sand, small workings that would divert attention, maybe a bullet if things got hairy, but each one was a frail thing that would be washed away when high tide came during the dead of night.

"Don't worry any which way about me. Just doing the things

I believe to keep us from going home in a pine box."

Preach chuckled, coughing a bit and shaking his head to clear his throat. "You're a funny one, aren't you?"

Alcide sat back down after his circuit of the foxhole was complete, leaning his head back against the dirt and staring at the stars. "Not any more than the rest. Just trying to do my part, find my fate." He looked at the corporal's rosary hanging with his dog tags. "You believe in that, Preach? That the Big Mambo is sitting up in heaven directing our lives to the destruction of evil?"

Preach nodded his head, but it was with a reluctance that Alcide was quick to notice. "I think that He directs things to their proper places, but we make our own choices. Free will and all that."

Trick spoke up from behind, "Well He's certainly put us all in the right place. All the way across the ocean in a dirt hole, feeling like I'm about to shit my…"

Trick never managed to finish his sentence. A yelp escaped his lips. Alcide and Preach both jumped to their feet, rifles sweeping the darkness, the men in the nearest foxholes doing the same.

"Boudin! Boudin! Get it off!" Trick held up his hand and Alcide had to choke down a laugh. A crab had fallen in and latched onto his thumb, a thin line of blood running from where the claw had bit into his flesh.

Preach reached over, holding the crustacean still while Alcide took the tip of his knife and wormed it between the pincers, twisting it until the crab released its grip and fell to the dirt.

Trick sucked on his finger, trying to stop the flow of blood. Alcide reached down and extended his hand to the crab, whispering, "Come on now, gumbo stirrer, caused enough trouble in this hole."

The crab's twin eyestalks wavered for a second and Alcide was briefly reminded of the Clicker he had seen feasting on the dead men, the monster that had consumed his thoughts since he had seen it. As the crab scuttled into his palm, he mused on why the Clicker had been that far inland.

It had to be trolling the waterways, just like the ones back home in Texas, but there was plenty of game there to satisfy them in bayou. Besides the odd saltwater crocodile, there couldn't be anything here that could sustain one of that size. Unless it was the bodies, all the dead men that floated in the tide from the sunken ships, sinking to the bottom and tempting the monstrous crustaceans with blood.

Alcide stood and let the crab crawl out of his hand and back onto the sand. Staring at the surf, he noticed an unusual number of sea creatures making an exodus. Crabs of all sizes scuttled out of the waves. Sea fleas jumped and burrowed themselves into dry sand. Two sea snakes quickly entered the woods and even a massive sea turtle was making its way up the beach. The meaning of it all didn't escape him. When the river flooded back home, plenty of creatures went seeking higher ground to avoid the gators who could now make their way easier.

His grip on his Springfield tightened and his eyes never left the surf, even when Preach appeared next to him, staring at the crabs scuttling past the foxholes.

"What the fuck is that?" Martino asked. "Did the Navy start dumping goddamned draft notices overboard?"

"Those are some might fine meals scampering past," Basher said, licking his chops.

Alcide thought that he could feel Basher's hand twitch towards his knife. The temptation to kill a few of the choice cuts coming their way was strong. The rations had gone down with the ships off Savo and now they were subsisting on whatever the Tojos had left behind.

Alcide managed to find his voice. "I can catch us more than a passel if you think you can cook them up, Basher."

Alcide thought that he saw the private from Alabama give a hint of a smile before he spoke, staring off across the sea like he could actually see home on the other side. "Can't say I'm much of a cook. I've always let the missus handle that."

More sea life was beginning to pour up from the depths. Alcide thought that he could even spot sharks swimming as close as they could to the shore. He gave the "come hither" gesture to Basher and Trick, who low crawled out with him. Between them, they bashed in the brains of a few crabs and sea snakes and crawled back into the hole, arms full.

No bayou boy worth his salt needed hoodoo to catch a few crawdads, especially when they were running right at you. But now, back in his hole, he had a sudden panic about the strange migration. He found himself whispering more workings under his breath, drawing designs almost frantically into the sand, sweat that had nothing to do with the humidity dripping off his arms.

But Preach didn't notice, his mind on the comforts of home. "You have a sweetheart back home, Boudin?"

Alcide shook his head, wishing that the men who shared this small stretch of hell would leave him to his work. "Haven't happened for me just yet. My two brothers both call me the *couillon* of my mama's brood. Probably why I'm out here halfway round the world."

Preach patted him on the back before looking at Trick. "What about you, Trick?"

Trick shook his head. "Youngest of seven in a town of two hundred. Paul and Callum always got their pick of the girls and then I shipped out."

Alcide paused in his drawings, feeling the invisible pressure of the workings forming around him. He glanced back at Trick and Preach, wondering if they could feel it, the protections he had woven... and if he'd need more by the time the night was over. But for now he stilled the beating of his heart, taking a deep breath and trying to satisfy his curiosity.

When he was finally finished, he turned back to see Preach looking as white as a sheet.

"What's the matter, Preach?"

The corporal's finger rose, trembling in the air, pointing at Alcide's workings. Alcide raised his hands up in a conciliatory gesture.

"I told you before, Preach, they ain't devil markings."

The corporal eyed him, his hand going to the rosary at his neck and rubbing it between his thumb and index finger as if it were a talisman like the one around Alcide's neck that would protect him from the horrors that were waiting out there under the green palms.

"What's shadowing your thoughts?" Alcide asked.

Preach shook his head, seemingly unwilling to say more. Then Alcide knew.

"You've seen something like this before?"

"Christ, Preach," Trick said, "it's just superstition, like tossing salt over your shoulder or not walking under a ladder. Don't take it so serious."

But the corporal wasn't mollified. He and Alcide locked eyes, both searching for something in the other.

"It's more than that, Trick. Something happened to me. It was back in Oklahoma, covered in dust everywhere. I can't rightly describe it to you. Seems so unreal looking back on it now."

Preach told his tale and every man in the foxhole listened, never losing focus on what the corporal was saying. If the Tojos had chosen that moment to attack, they would have found easy targets. But Alcide knew that a tale had power, and it was just right, even back in the dark alcoves underneath the cypress trees and Spanish moss, to listen when a man told his story.

When it was finished, Preach retrieved another cigarette from his case, shrugging his shoulders. Basher had finished making some kind of gumbo out of their seafood combined with Japanese rations and began ladling it into mess bowls.

"At least, that's what happened. I sure don't expect any of you to believe me, but that's why your drawings are giving me a start, Boudin."

Trick, naturally, broke the spell of solemnity by laughing at the both of them. "Man, you two are cards. I mean, I saw Boudin on the ship weaving his little trinkets, but damn if you two can't wind up a tale!"

Preach smiled, but there was no joy in it. He popped the buttons on his blouse, exposing his skin underneath. No matter where they'd dug their holes, no matter how hot it got, no matter the state of undress that all the other men had reduced themselves to, Alcide had never seen Preach remove his uniform. Up until now he'd assumed it was a religious thing.

The amount of scars crisscrossing his skin proved everything to Alcide, who looked at the raking claw marks that only a large animal could have made.

Trick stared wide-eyed. "That's…" he nodded his head, licking his lips and swallowing a lump that had formed. "It's true, what you told us?"

Preach nodded, buttoning his uniform again. "Tojo can't scare me. I've seen what's really out there in the dark."

Trick seemed to digest the words the same way that the rest of the men had been digesting their stew. He went pale and lapsed into silence in his section of the foxhole.

Preach sighed. "How'd you get involved in…" He made half-hearted waves at the designs etched in the sand, "all of this anyway, Boudin?"

Alcide shook his head. "Family tree goes back quite a ways. Picked up things over the years." He shrugged, reaching out to toss another crab that was getting too close back into the surf. "Just know a few things extra about what's out there."

The men lapsed into silence after that, watching the moon make its way across the sky, ducking when patrol boats came by, and always on the lookout for movement.

It couldn't have been more than an hour but Alcide noticed the sea life was coming fast now, practically frantic. The men in nearby foxholes were grumbling loudly and occasionally crying out as crabs and stranger things dropped into their holes with them.

Alcide clutched his mojo bag tight and whispered to all the powers that he thought could hear him. But when he saw the dark shapes in the waves, and the wavering tails that jutted from the surf, he knew that it had been in vain. No amount of workings could save most of them from what was coming.

But he could save a few. He started shaking them awake, eliciting annoyed groans.

"Basher? You have a little one back home, right?"

Basher stirred from where he had been sleeping and stared at Alcide with tired eyes. "I was trying to sleep."

The first Clicker came, a large one, headed straight for a foxhole filled with four men from another company.

"I know you were," Alcide said quietly, staring at the monstrosity and trying to swallow his own fear, "but if you want to see your family again, you won't leave this hole."

Basher didn't have time to ask before the screaming began.

18. AUGUST, 1942

Ota watched from a nearby rise as the *Kurikka* hit the American positions. Back home he was the sort of man who felt a pang of conscience every time he had to wring a chicken's neck. Long years in His Imperial Majesty's service, though, had taught him to appreciate suffering in the service of a greater goal, and the suffering of enemies was always preferable to the suffering of his brothers in arms. The Americans would be fleeing into the jungle soon, unable to resist the multitude of creatures. That was where the second phase of this operation would begin.

The specimens the *Umibozu* queen had provided were turning out to be enough to keep the Americans on their back feet. He only needed to sow terror in their ranks in order to buy himself enough time to finish his real work. The work going on in his labs was going to secure his homeland and ensure the Emperor's power over the Pacific and Asia was ironclad.

Ota was suddenly aware of movement behind him and turned to see Atagi, a scrap of paper held in his hand. Since Shinsato's disappearance the rest of the Army regulars had fallen in line, and he'd been able to put his trusted men from Unit 731 in positions of power. Atagi was no longer his aide-de-camp, but officially his second-in-command.

Atagi bowed before Ota and immediately began speaking. "The Americans are moving up their tanks."

A distant scream came drifting above the cacophony of gunfire and he briefly wondered how many Americans would make it into the jungle and how many specimens he was sacrificing to make it happen.

"Then it's time to reveal our countermeasures. Come with me."

He took a deep breath, smelling the saltwater even over the heavy humidity, and turned to walk up the mountain, Atagi trailing in his wake. The Americans had to withdraw into the jungle; this was the lynchpin of his plan. The specimens attacking them were numerous, but they alone could not turn back the American invasion.

Ota pulled the thatch covering that led to the underground tunnels beneath the mountain, hollowed out and fortified by forced native laborers. The warren was a veritable fortress, with only one approach, covered by enough emplacements to thoroughly eviscerate any intruders.

Men hurried through the tunnels, blurred faces that Ota scarcely recognized, his thoughts consumed by what he was about to unleash. Now that he was in command, his experiments could be tested in the field. Dust occasionally fell from the ceiling, the heat was nearly unbearable, and even in the dim light, he saw that every man was coated with a sheen of sweat.

His creations were housed in the bunkers closest to the base of the mountain. A man stood shivering next to the opening, trembling hands wrapped around his rifle. Beyond him was a deep lagoon, green algae floating over the water and only occasionally disrupted when barest hint of a white shell broke the surface. Some of the algae had been stained crimson, a few human limbs still bobbing close to the shore. Two men had been lost after they had ignored his orders not to approach the water, their desperation to refill their canteens proving fatal.

Ota strode purposefully to the edge of the lagoon and lifted his sword high. Immediately, the water began to roil and churn, the *Kurikka* inside rising to the surface. Ota thought that they looked like massive white jewels.

These held a special place in his heart, his first successful original breed, and even if they weren't what the *Umibozu* desired, they had already proven to have military applications. These *Kurikka* did not belong to the magic or heathen science of those who dwelt beneath the waves. These belonged to the Emperor. It was fitting, if not a sign of divine providence, that their shells had bred one of the colors of his homeland's Rising Sun.

Ota felt a surge of pride as the blood red *Kurikka*'s eyestalks fixed firmly on the sword he held high. He'd hand-reared the first breeding pair of them himself months ago. When transporting the parents and the first brood of ten to this breeding pool he'd lost one, to his great shame. But if Shinsato's reports of monster sightings were to be believed, even that little lost *Kurikka* had survived in the wild.

He held the sword out to Atagi, who bowed and grasped the blade like it was celestial treasure. So that Ota's side would not have to be naked, he handed over his own modern *showato* blade with much less ceremony, then stepped back to salute.

"For the Emperor," Atagi whispered.

"For the Emperor," Ota agreed reverently.

The *Kurikka* swarmed, their claws echoing off of the palm trees and sending every living creature that could hear fleeing into the wind and the deep green of the jungle.

19. AUGUST, 2020

Cam sighed as the RV's engine sputtered to a halt and the air conditioning went out. Almost immediately his lungs filled with the hot, salty New Mexico air.

"Well, this is another fine mess you've gotten us into, Ollie," he said to the empty rear of the RV.

He checked his cell phone which, naturally, had no signal, and therefore no GPS, and without the engine to recharge it, would be dead soon enough anyway.

"Fuck," he roared, slamming his hand on the dash.

As if on cue, the glove compartment door fell open and a pile of random papers fell to the floor. He had noted the broken latch upon purchasing this decrepit vehicle, but had not expected it to result in such an annoying circumstance so soon. But then his eyes narrowed.

"All right," he said, again out loud but to no one, which made him worry whether he was starting to go mad, "at least we still have analog GPS."

His hand fluttered through the empty fast food wrappers and receipts for various car-related expenses, before finally lighting on a map of New Mexico. The air inside the van was starting to get so hot, he climbed outside, but the furnace of the Chihuahuan Desert was little better.

"Motherfucker," he muttered under his breath as he laid the map out on the overheating engine block.

The map sizzled and for a moment he worried it might burst into flames, but after seeming to threaten to, it remained simply paper. He ran his finger along the highways and byways of the southwest, trying to retrace his steps after departing the Santa

Fe airport. He nodded along with the route.

"Huh," he said, glancing up at the nearest mile marker to where he had broken down, "actually, I'm not in that bad shape."

It was four miles to his final destination. That, though, on foot and in the sweltering midday heat. Christ, why couldn't he have just broken down in the middle of the night? Or, hell, gotten four more miles out of this ridiculous RV?

"Okay, he said, rummaging through the RV for supplies.

Of course, there were none. He hadn't expected this to turn into a foot-borne expedition. All he had was half a large plastic cup full of ice, which, thankfully or not, had melted into water. He'd already devoured an armload of tacos from the local taqueria, a nice place in the airport with what he guessed was an authentic Mexican mission bell as the logo. But, anyway, those were all gone. So all he had was a few fluid ounces of water and all he wanted to do with it was splash it over his head.

With a sickening, sinking feeling he realized what he'd have to do instead. Because while he might have forgotten about the half gallon of authentic local beverage he'd just downed (a drink called "Baja Blast" if he was remembering it correctly), the liquid had not forgotten about him.

"All for your legacy, this is all for your legacy," he reminded his (thankfully) still invisible imaginary friend as he tugged off his sweat-soaked trouser legs one by one.

He urinated on his jeans and, fulminating in discomfort, wrapped them around his head, turban-like.

Plastic cup in hand he sauntered off, underpants his only protection as his legs slowly turned crispy and brown. As a longtime mariner, he wasn't as fair-skinned as perhaps he had been born, but that didn't mean he was enjoying the high desert sun. He was glad he'd left the Clicker under lock and key back in town. He'd been reluctant to leave it even for this brief jaunt, but now in hindsight he was glad he wouldn't have to run the risk of either leaving it on the side of the road with the RV or drag it four miles through the desert.

What felt like seven hours later, but, in retrospect, couldn't have been much more than two, he found himself tossing his now empty cup off into the juniper bushes and sage. The air around him was almost literally burning, and for the first time he understood what a mirage really was: not a literal oasis replete with palm trees as in the old Bugs Bunny cartoons, but simply the weirdness of the sizzling air making it constantly appear as though there was something in the distance that could be reached.

Now, though, something in the distance wasn't simply receding into a semi-hallucinatory background. Towers grew taller as he approached, rather than simply disappearing. Concrete bunkers and chicken wire fortifications slowly came into focus. There it was: the location of possibly the only corroboration for his story in the world.

At the guard outpost a lone soldier, somehow not looking completely miserable in uniform, helmet, about twenty additional pounds of armor, and an M-16 slung over his right shoulder, squinted in Cam's direction. As he approached, the soldier's lips started moving, silently mouthing his incredulity. Well, maybe this wouldn't be so hard after all.

"Do *you* believe in undersea worlds?" Cam asked as he reached speaking distance.

The guard's eyes were as wide as saucers. "It *is* you!"

"It's me," Cam agreed, "your friendly neighborhood marine biologist."

The guard did a double-take. "What are you doing in the middle of the desert, Dr. Custer?"

Cam took a deep breath. He had no fucking idea anymore.

"My car broke down," he said, jerking his thumb over his shoulder, "and I'm supposed to meet with General…Colonel… Christ, what was his name?"

"General Kiste?"

Cam snapped his fingers.

"General Kiste. How is that old piss-and-vinegar sourpuss? Boy, I haven't gone golfing with him in probably six months. We're due down on the…down on the range."

The guard paused for a moment. "Well, sir, I mean, General Kiste is a lady of the female persuasion, but…"

"Yes, of course. That was what I meant. We go to the same… gynecologist," he trailed off.

The guard stared at him for a moment. Cam jerked his thumb over his shoulder again.

"Could you help with my…?"

"Your car? Yes, sir, Dr. Custer!"

The guard immediately abandoned his post and went running down the road. Cam stopped to scratch his head, remembered he was wearing a piss-soaked turban, and tore it off. That had been easy after all, although very, very strange.

"All right," he said, "I'm not going to look a gift horse in the mouth."

He walked past the guard shack, stopping only to consider whether to take the guard's open bottle of Dasani, but decided against it before proceeding on. The good news about Los Alamos was that it really only consisted of one cluster of buildings. As Cam reached the first bastion of shade he'd seen all afternoon, he pulled his now dry and salt-crusted pants back over his legs. He walked into the nearest building.

The area was just a foyer, and the door leading further in was massive and wouldn't budge. A series of miniature lockers almost like post office boxes lined the wall, most with orange keys dangling from their locks, although a few were keyless.

Various signs indicated that cell phones and cameras were not allowed inside, and had to be placed in the lockers before entering. Other signs listed phone numbers of secretaries to call to gain entrance. Cam briefly pondered who sounded the easiest to bamboozle purely based on their name, when the massive door unexpectedly opened.

"…these motherfuckers are not completing their PRs in time," a voice growled.

"I hear you," a second person agreed.

Cam caught the open door and smiled as the two civilians, barely looking at him, made their egress from the building. Cam shrugged again, and then slipped inside, pulling the door closed so it wouldn't make a sound. He noted a clipboard hanging on the wall, with a stack of guest IDs underneath it. He gathered that this was where guests had to sign in to enter this building. No one was watching him, though. Even the security people who presumably were supposed to be were instead discussing lunch plans.

Cam grabbed an ID, then, in a moment of inspiration, took the clipboard, too, and dove into the building. He found as he continued along that there were few problems which could not be solved by nodding at a nearby person and then appearing to consult his clipboard. He caught every door as it opened from the inside, waiting not very long at most, and never subject to any scrutiny. He soon found himself, almost inexplicably, in the deepest heart of the government's most secret base.

When he finally found himself in a place that no one else seemed to occupy, and where he could move no further, he saw a short, impossibly busy janitor still scrubbing the floors. Her nametag identified her as Sylvia.

"Excuse me," he said, putting on his best *I'm a fuck-up* grin, "Is there any way you could…?"

Without even having to finish his sentence, the woman sighed heavily and put her identification card against the door he could not enter. It buzzed, and he grabbed the handle.

"Thanks so much," he said with the widest smile anyone had ever worn.

He stuck his shoe in the doorjamb, desperately not wanting to get stuck down there.

"Who are you?" a voice, impossibly ancient, yet unbelievably modern, croaked in perfect English.

Cam's eyes widened. The creature within was human-shaped, albeit covered with scales and possessing webbed hands and feet. Were he not a man of science, he would have called her a monstrosity, a being beyond space and time, something which shouldn't have existed period, let alone a marine creature secreted away far in the depths of the New Mexican desert. Had she held a trident, she would have been a perfect, exemplar of the creature which some eighty-year-old Japanese drawings had identified as an *Umibozu*, yet here, now, and in living color. He, though, had heard another name for them.

"Dark One," he whispered.

The Dark One's scaled non-eyebrows rose.

"My name is Jade," she replied, "Who are you?"

20. AUGUST, 1942

The men in the foxhole closest to the beach didn't even have time to call for help. Alcide heard a startled yelp followed by the wet tearing of flesh. He ran to the lip of the foxhole just in time to see the Clicker yank the man it had impaled with its stinger onto the beach, his skin already beginning to slough from where the venom did its work. The creature's mandibles shredded eagerly, spattering its black eyestalks with blood.

Trick and the others stood wide-eyed with shock, no longer grumbling about Alcide waking them.

A private that Alcide had never spoken to, Bailey from Iowa, stuck his rifle directly under the crustacean's hellish face and fired. Hot, thick, orange blood gushed out of the wound thick enough that it reminded Alcide of syrup. The effluvia splattered into the private's open mouth even as a high-pitched squealing escaped the creature as it died.

Bailey locked eyes with Alcide. It was enough to get a measure of the man, a scared kid, miles from comfort who suddenly realized that he wasn't going home. He'd killed one Clicker, but swarms more were lunging out of the water and onto the shore.

Trick tried to call a warning, but a massive claw wrapped around Bailey's head. His scream cut off with a sound like a squashed apple, blood dribbling from the twitching corpse held in the monster's claw, while three other creatures swarmed into the foxhole.

Alcide didn't think he would ever forget those screams.

Each creature was already beginning to rush past the first line of foxholes and the screams were growing louder than the smattering of gunfire answering them. Alcide held his breath and braced for impact, but the wall of Clickers emerging from the ocean parted and passed around his foxhole, like a river around a rock. So, the spell was working. It might have been taxing him something fierce, but directing the will of simple predators was easier than bending men.

Still, the Clickers were churning up a lot of sand and dirt. Alcide focused, hastily redrawing the designs every time one of the Clicker's segmented legs disrupted his workings.

It couldn't have been more than a few seconds, but the blood already ran deep on the sand, mingling with the tide and the never-ending horde of nightmares pouring from the water. Preach, Trick, Basher, and Martino, shaking off their collective trance, finally grabbed their weapons and started taking up positions. "Hey, Basher," Trick said, "I'll bet this is the second worst case of crabs you've ever had."

"Ah, shut up," Basher replied.

Chuckling, Trick slammed his Browning down in its customary position, ready to start chewing up the monsters, but in doing so he had mashed in one of the keystone sigils of Alcide's working.

Alcide could barely open his mouth before the sound of whizzing bullets swallowed up his warning. A Clicker the size of a large dog leapt directly over the Browning barrel and landed squarely on Trick's chest.

Preach was knocked to the side as Trick flailed, but without even trying to regain his feet immediately aimed at the monster on the kid's head, firing twice. The Clicker wheezed and its mandibles ceased their movement.

Despite the onrush, Alcide still thought that they would make it, that he and his squadmates would climb out of this hole, fall back, and live to talk about the night the Clickers came ashore. But as Trick jumped upright sharply and the monster slid off his chest, they could both see the stinger embedded in his upper thigh. Alcide's heart stopped cold. Three more of the monsters leapt through the broken ward into their hole, eager mandibles clicking. Preach, Basher, and Martino all struggled wildly with them, but Alcide couldn't take his eyes off his partner.

"Boudin, *Boudin*!" Trick took a step, dragging his injured leg, which was leaking bright blood and swelling bigger than a balloon at the fair.

Alcide had seen it plenty back in the bayou. More than one boy had gone looking for mussels and come back, limb swollen with venom from what they had thought had been a big crawdad.

Trick's leg wasn't any different. His flesh dissolved as the skin melted off and ran in a slurry, pooling at the bottom of the foxhole. Trick fell into the mixture of sand, venom, and his own juices, howling in agony as he stared wide-eyed at his leg bone, barely clinging to his thigh and dripping wet with gore.

A desperate pleading passed through Trick's eyes, and Alcide raised his Springfield and put a bullet between his best friend's eyes. It took Preach and Basher both, one to a shoulder, to haul him out of the hole before it was overrun.

He didn't recall running. Perhaps the others had dragged him. All he remembered was whispering workings under this breath and trying desperately to turn the Clickers' gaze away from him and his remaining squadmates.

Basher's heavy hand on his shoulder pulled him out of it. "Had to be done, Boudin. It was an act of mercy."

Alcide didn't believe that at heart. The core of him couldn't accept that not everyone could be saved. He struggled against the Alabaman's grip, costing them precious seconds, enough time that the next wave had reached them.

Alcide sighed heavily and muttered prayers under his breath. There were monsters behind and more coming by the second. All he had was his Springfield and it wasn't going to make much of a dent in those numbers. A quick glance showed that there was no escape. The foxholes closest to the sea were blood-splattered open graves, Clickers clustering tight and shoveling still-steaming viscera into their mouths.

A few dozen of the red and black monstrosities were behind them, rushing battalion's machine gun emplacements. The Brownings thudding away, turning each charging crustacean into a pulp of orange and red meat, but it didn't stop the creatures. More and more of the repulsive crustaceans scrabbled after the retreating men, running them down. Alcide saw a Clicker rip the Achilles tendon from a fleeing buck sergeant, holding its bloody prize high as the man went toppling into the sand. The stinger did its work and the man swelled, agonized wailing growing higher and higher as his throat began to shut. Then the claws slammed into his skin and the man dissolved in a mess of steaming, bubbling sludge.

Alcide realized that his squad was an island in a sea of monsters, only held back by the remaining power in the minor workings he wore on his person. And even that power was ebbing like the tide.

From a nearby emplacement, a suffering man screamed for help. But before they could even respond, his voice trailed off into pained gurgles as three Clickers scrabbled up onto the sandbag wall, their segmented tails striking over and over again.

Preach swept his rifle from side to side, but even he seemed to know that it was pointless. The Clickers inched ever closer to the invisible circle of protection around them. Alcide closed his eyes and whispered out whatever power he could muster, trying to keep them back. But he might as well have been trying to stop a train by holding out his hand.

Despite normally being profoundly profane, it was Martino who said, "Maybe time for a few words for our souls, Preach?" Basher, too, looked to the corporal with uncomprehending eyes. "I…I have a little girl, she needs me. She…"

Alcide listened to him, but it was drowned out by the sound of claws. *Click-click, click-click.* But even above that, he heard another sound, a whistling that seemed to be getting louder. That was definitely the whine of a "friendly" mortar, not a Japanese 81mm. Preach turned to Alcide in wordless panic, then all sound faded and the world went white.

The last thing Alcide remembered was flying through the air.

21. AUGUST, 1942

Doodles was the happiest he ever remembered being. Nothing could compare to this. Not Christmases with his family, not graduating boot camp, not even losing his virginity to Mary Ann Higgenbottom at the old Albatwitch Festival in Columbia the year he turned sixteen.

No, somehow, out of the blue, he'd found his paradise on a tropical Pacific island. Well, on the surface of it that didn't sound so strange after all. It was more the circumstances of it. He was hardly surrounded by Polynesian beauties and endless mounds of roast whole pork with pineapple slices. Instead, he was barely subsisting on breadfruit and oceanic crabs. And speaking of crabs, he was being accompanied by the weirdest, wackiest one he'd ever heard of in his whole dad-blamed life.

After the whole "trying to kill each other" thing, Pinchy and Doodles had fallen into a fine rhythm. That was just always the way, he supposed. He and Rob Swartwood had nearly beat the shit out of each other in sixth grade over some nonsense he couldn't even remember now. In any case, the insult had been dire, and they'd fallen to tumbling through the dirt like a couple of Katzenjammer kids, pummeling each other with their fists. After that they'd played aggies together practically every day. Sometimes you just had to clear the air.

And that was how things had ended up with Pinchy. After trying to bash his shell in, and Pinchy trying to dissolve and devour him, they'd realized they had more in common than a man and his crustacean monstrosity friend should have.

In the last few weeks, for some reason, the Japanese patrols had gotten much, much heavier, and they'd stopped sleeping in the open. It seemed like they were building up to something, and while Doodles probably could have snuck around a bit to figure out what, these days he just didn't feel like it anymore. All he wanted to do was play with Pinchy and get about the business of being a castaway.

So he'd started hiding out in a cave, and had found that it kept him much more secure. One night he'd seen Private Yotashi and Sergeant Ohno pantomiming Pinchy, essentially. So they knew that there was a giant crab monster on this side of the island, though they evidently did not know that Doodles had effectively neutered him. From what he knew of the Tojos, they were a deeply superstitious lot and he'd gathered that Pinchy was becoming a bit of a bigfoot legend among them.

It was a chilly night, despite being a seasonable summer, and Doodles woke up in the middle of the night to something hard and unyielding under his head. It sure as shit wasn't the burlap-wrapped coconut he normally used as a pillow. Nope, the fire had gone out and Pinchy had crawled up under him, seeking warmth and Doodles learned exactly how flipping cold the carapace of a massive, ocean-dwelling monstrosity was. Doodles was shivering, and though he knew in a few hours the sun would be high and he'd be back to being baked like a loaf of pumpernickel, right now he was freezing to death and hating every second of it. Glancing down at his feet, he worried that he might actually be about to get frostbite. Being on the equator that sounded ridiculous, but nonetheless that was how he felt.

The fire had been reduced to embers, so he lumbered to his feet.

Click-click? Pinchy semaphored plaintively.

"You're killing me, crab salad."

Click-click. Pinchy replied, forlorn.

"I'm not leaving you. I just need to stoke up the fire."

He always hated keeping a fire at night, though it was necessary evil. He knew the island better than the Japanese, or at least the clowns they sent on patrol, so he knew where was safe and where wasn't, but really nowhere was 100% safe from their prying eyes. He'd recently been getting the feeling, too, that there were other, darker eyes prying in on him and his one-man resistance operation, though he usually chalked that up to loneliness and island madness. Still, he couldn't help feeling at times that there were evil, alien eyes staring up at him from the seas.

Click-click? Pinchy asked, perhaps reading his mind.

"No, not you. I mean, I don't think you. They're different eyes. Like a crocodile's eyes. Or a reptile's. I've never seen them, I mean, so I guess maybe that doesn't make sense. But it feels sometimes like they're looking in at me."

Click-click-click.

"Well, you can go straight to H-E-double hockey sticks with that attitude!"

Doodles harrumphed off, his initial completely logical concerns about the Japanese spotting his fire completely forgotten. They came rushing back, but so, too, did the cold in his veins.

Doodles kept the fire pit just outside of the cave mouth, so that it would warm the interior but the smoke could escape and not asphyxiate him. He yanked some piles of driftwood and dried palm branches from his camouflaged wood pile and began to pile it onto the dying embers of the fire. He knew from hard-won experience that too much fuel could smother the flame and too little wouldn't catch. He crinkled up some palm leaves and let them sizzle, added a frond, then some smaller chunks of wood, and after five minutes, decided to heck with it, and pulled his entire fuel pile onto the fire.

Soon, he and Pinchy were dancing around a raging bonfire. Every time he whooped he stopped and looked back at Pinchy, who responded with a click. After the third loop around the fire he didn't even have to look back anymore. Pinchy had just picked up the rhythm. They were island animals now.

"Whoop!"

Click!

"Whoop!"

Click!

"Whoop!"

Click!

"Whoop!"

BLAM!

Everything was blackness for, well, it might have only been a few seconds, but it felt like an eternity. Doodles opened his eyes, having no idea how long he'd been unconscious. He blinked, and pulled himself up out of the sand. He wanted to wipe it out of his eyes but knew better, after long months on the island, than to do so.

He looked back to see the bonfire still flaming high into the night. But not far from it a crater distended the pristine surface of the beach. A shell had obviously struck and sent him flying. Glancing skyward he saw tiny streaks of light, indicating more ordnance incoming. He'd seen such volleys before, but in relative safety aboard the *Lexington* they had always reminded him of fireworks during the Fourth of July celebrations back home. Now, though, the destructive force and danger of the little light show was terrifyingly real and close to home.

He scrambled away from the onslaught, hiding behind the rock outcropping he'd planned as the Alamo of his little camp. But judging by their trajectories, he soon realized that the shell which had struck his campsite had been the fluke. The others were targeted elsewhere.

Then he felt his heart sink into his stomach. He rushed toward the crater, heedless of all danger, accidental though it may have been. Were the black flecks in the shell crater merely chunks of firewood or were they the smashed-up parts of a giant crab-lobster monster? It was impossible to tell.

"Pinchy!" he screamed to the high heavens. *"Piiiiiinchy!"*

22. AUGUST, 1942

Ezekiel Palmer looked over the lip of his foxhole when the screaming began, his face still dripping with shaving cream. His men were running everywhere, occasionally turning to fire down towards the beach.

"What the hell is happening!?" he shouted. "You men need to take cover!"

But the whole area was a howling scrum. Only Gunnery Sergeant Webb even seemed to be trying to restore some discipline. The non-com was trying to restore some semblance of sensible battle lines, though it seemed hopeless. Failing that, he began tossing men to the ground to lower their profiles, ironically raising his own.

"Low crawl, you idiots! You want to get shot? Where are Williams and Gonzalez!" Webb shouted.

"They were the first ones to get stuck in with this bullshit!" someone shouted back.

Webb grabbed a marine running in the wrong direction. "Keene! Get in there and replace Williams!"

The Irish kid from West Virginia looked petrified. "I…I…I can't replace Williams," he stuttered.

"No one said you could. Now get up there. I'll send two more jackasses to replace you and Gonzalez in a few minutes."

Ezekiel crawled to Webb's position, and practically tackled him to the ground so he would take his own advice about not being a target.

"What's going on, Gunny?" Ezekiel was shouting, but oddly, there weren't that many gunshots. It sounded like no pitched battle he'd been through.

"We're under attack! Tojo's coming straight out of the water!" Gunny shouted back.

"Will it hold?"

"There's nothing left to hold, sir." Webb wasn't one given to exaggeration.

"I'll try to get battalion to ready a counterattack. Any man who isn't already lost in the jungle is probably headed back to Henderson Airfield."

"I'll get as many men as I can there."

Webb put his weapon in the crooks of his elbows and crawled toward a tangle of men heading towards the line of foxholes Ezekiel had ordered dug in at the beach.

Everything was chaos. Ezekiel strained to see where the Tojos had decided to push. There were flashes of light and screams down at the beach. A grenade went off, an orange fireball that superimposed the images of screaming men and something else that he didn't understand.

Jake appeared next to him, his jacket hanging loosely over his bare chest, dog tags clinking as he slowed. One of the platoon radiomen, whose name was Holt, but everyone just called Microphone, was dutifully following the XO, the massive SCR-300 strapped to his back. "Zeke! Radio is going crazy. There must be attacks all up and down the line. I can't even get battalion."

"We've got incoming from the fucking water!" Ezekiel shouted. "We'll just have to signal them the old-fashioned way."

Grabbing his pistol, he made his way toward a brave or foolhardy mortar crew which had not yet abandoned their position."Get some flares up!" he told Jake.

He, Jake, and the radioman slid into the foxhole, watching as the crew dropped another shell into the pipe, the heavy *thunk* echoing off the surrounding sand and sending the screaming explosive downrange.

"What are you targeting?" Ezekiel shouted as Jake dug around in the crates of munitions for the flares.

The mortar chief, a corporal named Sandow looked at him like he was crazy."Begging your pardon, sir, but there's no lack of targets. And no friendlies to avoid." He tapped his gunner on the shoulder and the mortar fired. Jake handed the ammunition bearer the emergency flare.

"But, Skip, what about the Tojo ships?" one of the mortarmen asked.

Ezekiel ground his teeth, staring down towards the beach and listening to the screams of his men. If the Tojo fleet was out there watching, it would be like waving a red cape in front of a bull. But if he couldn't signal for reinforcements, they'd be wiped out.

He crouched next to the radioman. "You can't get battalion, Microphone? Brigade?"

The kid looked like he wasn't out of diapers yet, but he wore an expression as grim as a two-war veteran. He pushed his glasses back up on his face. "I can't get anyone, sir."

He held up the handset and clicked it. Nothing but unholy screaming came through as he scrolled through a few channels. Ezekiel wished he hadn't.

"All right, Sandow. Flare."

A streak of light shot into the sky and blazed, illuminating everything from the ocean to the mortar emplacement. Ezekiel felt his mind leave him as he stared at the scene, trying to comprehend what was happening.

Men were climbing out of foxholes like boiling ants. Only a few within immediate earshot of Webb were even bothering to hold their positions long enough to fire back at their pursuers. It was here that Ezekiel thought that he had gone mad.

Where are the Japanese?

It was a thought that continued to repeat as he looked over the scene. The scuttling monsters overtook another foxhole. One of his men screamed out a high-pitched wail as five different claws seized his limbs and pulled him apart, red blood splattering on the sand.

A Browning chattered away. It was one of the last, about halfway between Ezekiel and the beach. The gunner swiveled the weapon back and forth, catching a crab monster under its merciless torrent and reducing it to a gooey mess of orange pulp.

More scuttled into the fine mist to feed on their dead brother, happily lapping up the orange blood. The Browning gunner screaming as he focused fire, bullets chewing into the monsters' shells.

The situation was teetering on a knife's edge. The first two rows of foxholes were overrun, replaced by the monsters. Ezekiel could see their scorpion tails waving as they feasted. Two machine gun crews were desperately holding off the seemingly never-ending tide from moving towards the last row of foxholes, but they were surrounded on three sides and couldn't withdraw. Survivors ran between the alley of safety created by the two crews, carrying friends and weapons, never looking back, their eyes full of panic.

But where are the Tojos?

"Skip? Captain Palmer? *Zeke*!" Jake Dempsey's voice snapped him out of his delirium. Sandow's crew and Microphone the radioman were already gone, most of their gear left behind. He looked into his friend's eyes as Jake yelled, "It's over. We need to get everyone to the airfield!"

"Yes… yes!" Ezekiel agreed. "I'm going to get those men. They've saved half the company."

He jumped to his feet just in time for one of the machine gun nests to fall silent with a steaming hiss.

"Son of a bitch," Ezekiel muttered mournfully.

Men screamed and the scuttling monstrosities hissed in response. Jake hefted his gun. "The men are still alive. *Come on*!"

He charged out of the foxhole, firing as the next wave advanced, claws clicking in steady rhythm. Ezekiel watched one the size of his grandfather's farm truck scurry over the lip of the foxhole and knock the frantically reloading machine gunner to the ground.

Ezekiel aimed with his .45, fired, and reduced one of the thing's waving black eyes to paste. The monster squealed and reared back, blood spraying out of its eyestalk and coating the screaming rifleman as he struggled to keep the thing's claw from bisecting him.

Ezekiel took a knee and fired again. The bullet found the space between the monster's eyestalks and a section of orange gore splattered against the machine gun, immediately steaming from the overheated barrel.

The smell hit him, reminding him of his mother's crab boils, overlaid with vomit. Then he heard the scream as the assistant gunner lost his battle and found a stinger impaled directly through his sternum.

The man's eyes bulged and he tried to cough something. "Ski…Skip…"

Thin red lines of blood ran out of his mouth and then the crustaceous monstrosity finished him, claws digging into the man's guts.

The man's pleading gaze was still locked on Ezekiel as he melted. The clicking things began to lap up the soupy remains, and Ezekiel began screaming as he fired, his .45 blowing chunks out of the dog-sized monster.

The thing's segmented tail and legs twitched for a moment before curling in on itself. He breathed deep, panting hard as he realized that he had killed it. He wondered what his father would say when he learned that his son had slain two genuine monsters. It didn't fill him with pleasure or pride, and he would've traded any future accolades for the man whose remains were busy feeding the things that had killed him.

The machine gun nest was lost. Ezekiel and Jake helped the remaining men out of the foxhole. He turned and saw the other machine gun crew finish reloading.

"Lay down some fire over here!" He hollered, waving his hands at the onrushing crustaceans. The gunner nodded and pulled the trigger. Ezekiel scrambled back, pulling a private after him, struggling to gain his feet.

For a breath, Ezekiel thought he might have been able to save the other crew, until he saw the newest horror marching up the beach. The numerous clicking monsters parted before it, and if it hadn't been for the flare's light, Ezekiel wasn't sure that he would have seen it coming.

Its shell was as dark as night. *Obsidian,* that was the word Ezekiel was looking for to describe the color of the thing scuttling up the beach. Its tail dripped the same caustic goop that the rest of its kind did, but unlike the others which varied in size, this one was gigantic, easily the size of two tanks stacked on top of each other.

It hissed and its claws clicked, each snap sending a vibration that echoed inside of his chest and nearly made him tumble back onto his ass. He'd seen an elephant once at a circus when he'd been a boy and it was the same feeling then as now: a sense of awe at the thing's power and size.

He tried to call out a warning only to find that his breath had seized in his throat and the only thing that came out was some sort of hacked coughing. The corporal in the hole cried out a warning and the gunner immediately swiveled the weapon to destroy the creature. Hope swelled in Ezekiel's chest. The creature was still too far away, its killing claws and venomous stinger out of range. The Browning would chew through it in seconds.

His hope drowned at the same time as a jet of clear liquid jumped from the thing's tail and splattered across every man in the foxhole. The results reminded Ezekiel of the flamethrower victim up on the hill, though there was no flame. Wherever the liquid dripped, the men's skin began to bubble, sores opening up and blood splattering against the sand as their features fused together like melting candle wax and their uniforms dissolved into their skin.

They wailed incoherently, perhaps crying for their mothers before their lungs also melted and their blind, eyeless faces revealed bone before that sizzled and sloughed off, too.

And then the creature turned, letting the smaller red ones feast on the mess it had created. Its eyestalks centered on Ezekiel, tail raised to disgorge another volley of death.

The Marine captain didn't hesitate any longer, or focus on any other last minute heroics. He just screamed at everyone to run and regroup at the airfield. But even as he ran, he felt the weight of every single man who had fallen beneath the twin tides of claw and venom.

And over it all, there was no escaping the clicking.

23. AUGUST, 1942

Alcide stumbled through the jungle, supporting Preach's weight as the corporal hacked and coughed bloody spittle into the bushes. He was going to have words with Corporal Sandow if he lived long enough to see him again. The mortar's concussion had flung them into the jungle scrub that bordered the beach, knocking him senseless when he hit the ground. It couldn't have been more than a few seconds, but that was more than enough time for a Clicker to find the pair of them.

Alcide had come to in time to find the creature's venomous tail striking, and only his panicked jerk kept him from becoming the thing's next meal. The tail had torn through the fabric on his shoulder and embedded itself into the sand. The Clicker's beady black eyes had swiveled and a hiss had escaped from between its mandibles. Alcide hadn't hesitated as he'd rolled away, scrambling across the sand to where Preach lay groaning.

Alcide had grabbed the man's rifle, acutely aware of the clicking growing louder behind him, and rolled over to shoot at the vague scuttling shape barely a hair's breadth from his leg. He had shot until the gun was empty, each bullet shattering another section of the monster's carapace and spreading orange gore across the bushes. The Clicker's hissing had become a violent squeal and its pincers had clacked furiously as it tried to retreat.

Alcide had still been pulling the trigger when the thing had collapsed, segmented legs twitching weakly in the sand. He'd turned to see Preach, grasping his rosary and whispering, "... and deliver us from evil. For thine is the kingdom, the power..."

"Not yet, Preach," Alcide had muttered, hoisting him up

and plunging into the jungle towards what he hoped was Henderson Field.

Briefly he'd considered turning back. He hated being separated from Basher and Martino, but didn't see any sign of where they'd gone in the chaos. He also hoped that given some time and the right ingredients, he might have been able to push the monsters back out into the sea.

Another round of explosions and distant screams reassured him that he wasn't forsaking men or duty. Couldn't help anyone if they were dead, and even what spell work he knew wasn't going to matter a lick without the preparation. For right now the only reasonable option was to regroup and try to find the rest of the company.

He heard his Pa, Jean Renard, whispering in his ear. The old hoodoo man had made sure that all of his children had been trained in the Art same as him; there was no working that Alcide or his brothers weren't proficient in.

But this working was going to test his knowledge and his limits. Finding the ingredients alone was going to be hell. Alcide steeled himself and tried to forget the odds against him. The Clickers were swarming, and if he couldn't turn them back, they'd overrun everything.

He said a quick prayer under his breath, entreating the divine that the Clickers were all that would come from the depths.

24. AUGUST, 1942

Ezekiel felt like he was in one of the action pictures that played for thirty cents at the cinema in his hometown. His men, only a few dozen left, scrambled through the palms, occasionally firing desperately back into the darkness.

The flare had gone out and now there was nothing but the all-consuming darkness and the occasional muzzle flash from a rifle. In those quick flashes, Ezekiel saw nothing but a writhing mass of red and black chitin, coated in macabre offal and eager for more.

"Come on, come on! Move with purpose!" Webb was shouting so loudly Ezekiel was sure his throat would be sore come the morning. If any of them made it to the morning.

They'd been forced to abandon their heavy equipment, leaving behind Brownings and mortars covered in various bodily fluids. Normally they would have spiked equipment left behind so the Japanese couldn't turn their own guns back on them, but he doubted the clicking monsters were going to start growing trigger fingers. Then again, the way this day was going...

Their only hope was to make it to the defensive line that the 1st and 2nd divisions had erected around the captured airfield. He'd always politely avoided "Preach" Cantor's impromptu religious services, but in that moment, Ezekiel wished he were here to lend him some faith. He barely remembered how to pray anymore.

"Get the lead out of your asses!"

Though he didn't let it show in his voice, Webb's exhortations were growing more urgent. The ammo situation was growing desperate. A quick burst from a Thompson Ezekiel had inherited turned a poodle-sized Clicker into just another stain in the sand. His hand drifted to the last two drums nestled in his jacket. It would have to last.

Cursing, he tripped on some log or divot in the dirt. Shit. Why had he been checking his ammo instead of watching where he was running?

He struggled onto his back just in time to fire at a blue-shelled clicking monster nipping at his boots. Its eyestalks seemed to ask, "What did I ever do to you?" just before it collapsed. He rocked back and forth, but it was too damned hard to right himself with his rucksack and gear. The best he could do was kick forward like a dog with worms across a rug. A swarm of wildly chittering monsters poured toward him.

Jake dropped to his knees by Ezekiel's side, firing his rifle with wild abandon, not pausing to see if any of his shots had scored a kill. He grabbed Ezekiel's shoulder and dragged him, but even with the two of them, they were not moving fast enough. The wave of monsters was about to crest over them.

"Get the fuck out of here!" Ezekiel shouted.

"Oh, all right then," Jake grunted as he strained to continue pulling Ezekiel, "I guess since you say so, we'll just start leaving men behind. Fuck it."

"God damn it, Jake!"

But suddenly Ezekiel was lifted practically straight up to his feet. The enormous farmboy Basher had emerged from the darkness, firing, and pulling at Ezekiel's other shoulder.

"Let's go, Skipper!"

All three of them headed further into the darkness.

He heard a scream and saw two desperate shots, illuminating a skewered shadow as one of his men attempted to fight for his life and lost. Everywhere around him, men were fighting or running, but the horde of primeval crustaceans did not grow weary of killing. They weren't men. They didn't grow tired. They couldn't be sated. And they wouldn't stop.

It was only a few seconds later that Ezekiel heard another sound over the disgusting din of clicks behind him: shouts of encouragement, the sounds of frantic yelling…

Flares launched into the night and tears of joy jumped into Ezekiel's eyes as he saw the flat open ground of Henderson Field.

And the defensive line surrounding it.

Most of the defenders stared dumbfounded at the creatures. A few that had managed to keep their wits about them were shouting for Ezekiel and his retreating men to hurry. They were withholding their fire in order to avoid killing the survivors, though they couldn't refrain forever. It was now that he felt most afraid. His academy training echoed in his head.

You're in the most danger the moment you feel safe.

He supposed it luck that he was more scared than he had ever been his entire life, but the initial relief that flooded through him, stalled him a half step.

It was all the monsters needed.

He felt a sharp tug on his boot and the ground disappeared before it found him again and knocked the wind from his lungs. Ezekiel stared up, dazed, watching the flares cast dark shadows across the dirt and palm fronds, before he felt the sharp pain in his leg.

A clicking monster hung to him, pincers digging deep into the meat of his calf. Ezekiel shook his leg, trying to dislodge the thing, which just dug in deeper. He'd never felt such pain or pressure. Through the rips in his pants he could see his skin begin to turn a dark shade of purple. It felt like his leg would burst. The thing raised its tail and Ezekiel squirmed in panic, pathetic noises escaping him, smashing his ravaged leg into the ground to dislodge the creature.

To the Marine captain, it felt like an eternity. Everything seemed to move in slow motion: the striking tail, the hand catching the appendage midair and yanking the beast off of him…

Basher hurled the creature, pincers clicking futilely as it landed back into the horde of its other brethren. God, the man had to be stronger than King Kong. He shoved his arms under Ezekiel's armpits and yanked him toward the wire as Jake laid down suppressing fire with the Thompson which had briefly been Ezekiel's.

He could make out urgent shouts, the staccato beat of rifle fire, and the clicking. Then he felt an incline and the cool touch of freshly dug earth.

Jake was frantically discussing casualties with Basher.

"Cantor? Robichaude? Anyone else?"

"I don't know, sir. We got separated."

Jake looked to Ezekiel. The agony in his leg was almost overwhelming, but he could see Jake was torn up emotionally. It wasn't a college degree or seventeen weeks of OCS that made an officer. It was moments like this, when decisions of life and death had to be made, that made an officer. And though Jake was trying, the tough call really belonged to Ezekiel. He glanced around at his surviving men. No more were outside the wire.

"Any man who isn't here yet will have to survive until we can get rescue parties out. Button it up."

Jake stood back up and motioned to the guard towers. "Light up the bastards!"

Ezekiel smiled to himself as he heard the chattering Brownings and the fresh squeals of the dying monsters. His lips felt dry and everything seemed to twist in his vision.

He lapsed into the comforting darkness without knowing the outcome of the ongoing battle.

25. AUGUST, 1942

The immediate threat dealt with, Jake Dempsey turned his attention back to where Ezekiel Palmer lay on his back, mangled leg sticky with the blood. There was already too much of it pooling on the ground. Ezekiel was as pale as a bed sheet and even a hard slap didn't wake him.

"Corpsman! I need a Corpsman!" Jake shouted it over and over, tearing at his uniform and wrapping the makeshift bandages around his friend's leg.

"Come on, Zeke, you're not leaving me yet. Drinks in Sydney when we're off this shithole, yeah?" It was a promise they'd made to each other and now Jake repeated it like a magic spell that would keep his friend amongst the living. "A couple of nice Aussie girls, a few pints, maybe even ride a kangaroo buck ass naked. That's going to be a sight."

"Sir..."

Jake looked up sharply at Basher. The man was holding one of the machete knives that they used to clear brush. Jake's immediate instinct was to fly off the handle at the suggestion, but this was war, he was an officer, and Basher had proven himself nothing but loyal and competent.

"You're going to take it?"

"I need to cut away the bad flesh at least, sir."

"Are you sure?"

"Trick didn't even make it this long, sir."

The venom was surely spreading up the leg. The stinger had struck at Ezekiel's ankle and now his thigh was turning distended and black. Jake nodded and stepped back.

Basher had been the right man to do it, too. For him, shearing off huge chunks of diseased flesh was no harder than a morning shave. Blood and pus were beginning to spew from the wrecked leg, and he sighed in relief when a pair of overworked Navy corpsmen arrived with a litter and took over, tourniqueting and everything with utter competence.

Jake breathed out a sigh of relief when he saw Ezekiel's eyes flutter, mumbling something about the men.

"Don't worry about that now. We're going to get you patched up."

"We've got him, sir," said one of the corpsmen, and they began double timing it to the aid station. He could tell from their sense of urgency that this wasn't their first or even hundredth trip that night.

A cry went up from the gun towers, echoed a moment later by the men on the ground. The laugh practically undulated out of Jake as the shower of orange meat filled the air. The big obsidian bastard with the spraying tail was nothing but a vaguely lobster-shaped pile of goo. Its size had been an advantage when slaughtering men in the open, but up against fixed defenses it simply became the easiest target.

He'd barely had time to pull Ezekiel into the airfield before the clicking bastards were at their lines. Bullets had met shell and the chitinous abominations had been found wanting.

They'd killed enough of them from here to the beach that the humid tropical air hung heavy with the scent of their deaths. It smelled like ammonia, and each new crustacean that died just added to the odor.

But they just kept coming.

It wasn't natural. Any other animal that hunted in packs would've been sent running, but this wasn't a pack of coyotes or wolves nipping at the cattle. This was an army.

They were outnumbered, even with the big obsidian one dead. There were at least twenty of these things for every man in fighting shape. The only reason they hadn't been overrun was that the living stopped to feast on the oozing remnants of the dead. Jake momentarily wondered if the monsters knew they were eating their own.

Then Jake realized that the clustered feeders made prime targets.

Webb was counting heads and getting after actions reports from the survivors of the company. The information would be valuable, but Jake knew he was probably doing it mostly to distract the men from the trauma they had just experienced. Microphone the radioman was one of the few trying to do something other than look dazed, as he continued trying to get in contact with higher.

"Gunnery Sergeant Webb," Jake said, "I'm taking Microphone."

Webb glanced over. He ticked something down in a very grubby notepad.

"Holt's with you, got it, sir."

"Come on," he said, gesturing to the radioman.

He scrambled up a sentry tower with Microphone climbing behind him.

"Who the hell are you," the Marine on the tower said, belatedly adding "sir" as he noticed Jake's bar.

"Don't stop firing," Jake said, "I just came in from fighting these clicking…these fucking Clickers. You ever see a Tojo sniper shoot a man, then wait until he calls for a corpsman, then shoots the corpsman?"

Despite Jake's admonition not to, the machine gunner did stop shooting for a moment. Then it was like a light went on. He turned his attention to the Clickers who had been drawn in to feast upon the obsidian giant. He began chopping those up, making the circle of feeding Clickers expand outward, like the concentric circles of a rock tossed into a lake. The area around the obsidian Clicker became like a drain, drawing in all of the monsters around it and greatly weakening their attack.

Jake shook Microphone by the shoulder. "That's the ticket. Direct those M2 tanks toward the clusters. Pass the word along to anyone you can get ahold of. I'll see if any of our boys feel well enough to act as runners."

The radioman nodded and began shouting into his set. Communications didn't sound much less chaotic than earlier, but at least a few channels had men answering and not just screaming. Microphone's voice sounded like some washed-up lounge singer, breaking at every other syllable after a lifetime of too many drinks, even if the kid was barely pushing twenty. Jake practically slid down the ladder without touching any of the rungs, a smug smile on his face, which Gunny Webb was all too happy to wipe off with a stark declaration.

"They're coming from the fucking jungle, sir!"

Jake's heart practically stopped as he saw a swarm of Clickers streaming from the trees on the opposite side of the field. To Jake's surprise, they were all a uniform bright white color, and he had never seen a white one before.

Jake had to squint to see in the light of the spotty flares, but as soon as he saw one closely enough, he was sure. Painted on the backs of these Clickers was the Rising Sun of the Japanese Empire.

The pieces fell into place at the same time one of the white ones reached an M2, claws digging into the treads as it threw itself under the light tank. The explosion that followed threw the tank's tread, leaving it all but useless.

Jake turned to look at Webb, unsure what he was seeing, but luckily the no-nonsense NCO made it clear as only he could.

"That motherfucking crab just blew itself up!"

26. AUGUST, 1942

Doodles frantically dug through the shell crater, nails caked with wet clay and sand, looking for his friend. His heart jumped every time he uncovered another rock or piece of driftwood, thinking it was a splinter of Pinchy's shell.

"You can't be dead, Pinchy! You just can't!"

He knew that he shouldn't cry, not over an enormous crab, but the tears came unbidden. They'd built a life together. As a boy he'd had dogs, but in his soul, he knew his relationship with Pinchy was a once in a lifetime friendship.

You can't be dead.

It sounded like the war had finally come to his isolated beach. He heard distant explosions and the occasional faint scream, but never thought to run toward it, not even if it meant finding his countrymen and being saved. All his thoughts were bent on Pinchy.

A string of pseudo-profanity began tumbling out of his mouth. If only he hadn't lit that consarned campfire. If he'd just let himself freeze, everything would be different, and he and his best friend would still be together right now.

His hands trembled as he dug, dry skin splitting from his efforts and bleeding into the sand and surf, but he refused to give up. Doodles wasn't sure what he would do if he couldn't find his friend.

At last the thought came: if he'd been thrown by the explosion, maybe Pinchy had too. Doodles stood and leapt from the hole like someone had put hot coals to the bottom of his feet, scampering to the forest and rooting through the scrub brush and fallen palms for his friend.

27. AUGUST, 1942

Ota removed the spyglasses from his face. A single tear flowed down his cheek, tracing a line like the mighty Abashiri River back home. He'd lost no more than a dozen men. The Battle for Guadalcanal would be the last of the Pacific War, the long-awaited *Kantai Kessen*. With his simplest creation, the *Kamikaze Kurikka,* Ota had redefined the battlespace entirely. He had, after all the work he and his men had put in, finally and decisively saved the Empire. More importantly, the lives of countless of his countrymen, though willing, would no longer need to be laid down to secure East Asian Co-Prosperity Sphere.

He looked around. Atagi was leading the battle, or he would have been near to hand. He spotted one of the infantrymen he had inherited from General Katou at the base of the lookout tower.

"Sergeant Ohno!" he called out.

Ohno came hurrying over, looking terrified to be called upon.

"Yes, Colonel?"

Ota held out the key to his office.

"In my office are the only green-colored flares on the island. I want you to set one off westward toward the ocean."

"*Hai,* Colonel. Right away."

Ohno hurried off to see to his task. No doubt he would think Ota was signaling the Navy. He had no intention of disabusing the man of this notion.

As he waited for the *Umibozu* chieftainess to arrive, his thoughts turned to the future.

He had no doubt there was a general's tan collar patch

waiting for him when he got home, and likely a position on the General Staff. If he could be stationed on Hokkaido, that would be best, but even if they kept him in Tokyo he would be able to see Haruki and his child much more often. He might take Atagi along with him, a pet subordinate as they sometimes said back home. The young man had proven his mettle many times over.

Something struck his foot and a wet splash stung his face. He reached up to touch his chin and his fingers came away red. He did not wish to look down at the soccer ball shaped object which had just struck him, but he forced himself to.

"Regrets, Ohno-*san*," he whispered wistfully.

He slowly reached down and lifted the unfortunate sergeant's severed head off the ground. Why, when the war was so close to over, did good Japanese boys have to continue dying? A twelve-foot-tall figure loomed in the shadows. Slowly, fighting his real emotions, Ota bowed deeply, nearly putting his forehead to the sand.

"I regret that my subordinate insulted you so direly," he said as best he could in their language, not raising his eyes in awaiting a reply.

"It is you who insults me, human, with your scraping and bowing and obsequious manner."

Ota nodded and slowly raised his head. A shell flashed in the air, lighting up the complex behind the *Umibozu* chieftainess.

"I wanted to thank you from the bottom of my heart. In churning up your monsters from the bottom of the ocean, you have saved my people. You personally, and your people, will always carry a place of great honor in the halls of power of my empire. I look forward to establishing a relationship between the dwellers of the land and you, the true lords of the deep."

"I was not finished," the creature replied, holding up one of her massive claws. "You will stop speaking."

Ota nodded his acquiescence.

"You insult me not just with your manner, but with your very existence. Your pink skin. Your hairy scalp. Your soft, brittle bones, and your complete lack of any meaningful way to defend yourself."

Ota nodded again. This was odd behavior from his patron,

but he had long since learned the value of patience when dealing with the *Umibozu*. They had never exactly restrained themselves from showing disdain for humanity, but had perhaps never been quite so overt about it.

The chieftainess stepped forward, her grotesque face illuminated briefly by a flying flare.

"You would welcome us as allies of your empire. What a joke. What do you know of the ancient Empire of the Dark Ones?"

"Very little," Ota admitted.

The chieftainess walked past him, putting her claws on the railing of the high tower they were sharing together. Ota decided to place Ohno's head somewhere a bit more respectful than carrying it around like an overripe durian, and placed it down. The thing cast a wide arc with her claws.

"All that you see before you, weakling, was once our empire."

"Yes, I can appreciate that," Ota said.

"No. You couldn't possibly. Every inch of the ocean you see before you was crawling with our kind. Our merest farmsteads would have put your mighty capital Tokyo to shame. And our cities, our true cities, were glittering jewels, extending thousands of miles in every direction."

Ota wasn't sure how to respond. All of their previous encounters had been mostly transactional, and she almost never told him anything more than was absolutely necessary. And though the chieftainess was given to fits of exaggeration, if even a tenth of what she was saying was true, then the ancient *Umibozu* empire had been mighty indeed.

"What happened, if I may be so bold?"

"Your kind. When you began to breed and dominate the dry land above, we were riven apart discussing what to do about it. We had been united in glory once, the most potent force of all time on the planet. We used our magic and technologies to keep you weak, keep you primitive, little more than our Clickers. Every time your kind reached higher than your purpose, we turned you back to your place."

The chieftainess hissed, "Then came the great cataclysm.

Your primitive ancestors worshipped something, and it woke with great fury, destroying our great works within a tide. It secured this world for your kind. You've heard the legend of Atlantis?"

"Yes."

"Mu?"

"Yes."

"Mahabalipuram? Lyonesse? Cantre'r Gwaelod? Aztlan? Heracleion?"

Ota shrugged. Some yes, some no, but all were generally the same. Underwater kingdoms which had offered succor to the mythological heroes of various cultures.

"Those were all us at different times, around the world, in different states of disarray. Every time one of our factions reached out to humanity, we were rocked by destruction."

"Well," Ota said, wracking his brain, "I can assure you this time it will be different. I have already pledged you our undying loyalty."

"It will be different this time, I agree," the chieftainess said, nodding.

As a shell flared behind him, Ota felt a knot in his stomach. Shadows danced around him. Though he was terrified to turn away from the *Umibozu* chieftain, or even to risk breaking his eye contact, he could sense a flurry of activity around his base.

"We are reduced now to a few scattered tribes of which mine is not even the largest. But do you know what our one saving grace is?"

Ota shook his head. The chieftainess nodded and closed her eyes, seeming to concentrate, perhaps meditating or casting a spell. A *Kurikka* about the size of a large tiger Ota had once spotted in Manchukuo approached, as if called. It scrambled up the stairs of the lookout tower, creating a cacophony of chitin on steel.

Ota's heart fluttered, but he wagered that his value to the *Umibozu* was not yet spent. Besides, if she wanted to kill him, she could easily dispatch him with her massive jaws or thickly muscled arms.

"Our friends, our kindred, the Clickers," the *Umibozu* said.

"They were once everything to us: pets, livestock, in some ways, trusted counselors. They were everywhere throughout our empire. I had a small one I kept in my lap, and ten larger ones I kept outside in a barn to milk for venom. Before my time they were even more populous, and we bred them extensively."

"You can control them?" Ota asked. The exact nature of the relationship between the *Umibozu* and the *Kurikka* had long been a matter of some discussion among he and his more senior scientists.

"No," the thing replied, "not entirely, though they respond to our wishes and desires to some extent. Which was why I came to you."

She took a step forward, and her *Kurikka* did not shrink either. If the crow's nest were any smaller, she would practically have been breathing in Ota's face.

"I have far superior technology to yours down on the ocean bed. Devices that make yours look primitive. Even devices that can turn your people into primitives. All of it from our golden age, and all of it lost. I would have needed an army of scientists without even a shred of a conscience, experimenting around the clock to learn how to use it all. So perhaps I should thank you."

The thing produced from within her cloak of nets a massive tome, which Ota recognized as his own personal notebook, full of extensive notes on all of the experiments Unit 731 had conducted on Guadalcanal. His breath caught in his throat. He didn't know that the *Umibozu* had known about that journal.

"I'll be happy to translate it for you," he said, subtly trying to remind the thing that she still needed him.

She barked in what passed for a laugh among her kind.

"That won't be necessary, of course, you buffoon. I've known your language, and the language of all your many nations since before you were born."

Ota jumped with a start, realizing that the thing had switched from its own opaque language into flawless Japanese, even mimicking his light Hama-Kotoba accent.

"You've helped us master the science of biological weapons. And for that, I will be in your debt. But for everything else, your verminous race must be swept from the face of the surface world."

A fire exploded below. The screams were now impossible to ignore. Ota looked over the side railing. All around, under cover of darkness, neither Americans nor British nor Dutch, but their supposed allies, the hulking reptilian monstrosities, were attacking his people. Many carried tridents, littered with the heads of their victims, his friends and subordinates.

Ota jumped as he felt a massive, barnacle encrusted claw fall on his shoulder.

"Very well, then," he said, dropping to his knees, "at least I will die an honorable death."

The thing's mocking laughter filled the air again.

"Oh, no. Nothing like that. Nothing like that at all waits in store for you."

28. AUGUST, 2020

Cam's breath caught in his throat. Too many years as a biologist overrode his basic manners and even sense of safety. Fueled by nothing more than curiosity and instinct (if "instinct" was what drove a scientist to explore the unknown) he reached out and grabbed the green-skinned girl's wrist, turning it upward for examination. And then he realized his mistake.

He was an inch from her face and her eyes were black and bottomless, in a way wholly alien and yet possessed of a primeval fury Cam was all too familiar with. He had been surrounded by marine animals all his life, from harmless jellyfish to merciless great whites. And all of them, when backed into a corner, looked like this.

Her muscles tensed. Her lips rolled back revealing teeth as long as toothpicks and sharper than any flaying knife. If she wanted to—and he could tell that she deeply, deeply wanted to—she could have lunged forward and ripped his throat out of his neck with one meaty bite.

But there was something...different somehow, too. As though the Dark One, who had identified herself as Jade, was at war with her own nature. He had never encountered a sentient non-human before, the closest being certain primates, who thought they could communicate did not alter their behavior very much for man's benefit. He had always wondered about this part. Could intellect overcome instinct? He had already intuited from the fact that she had addressed him in English that she had been raised by—or lived for many years with—man. That meant she was more than simply intelligent. She was acculturated.

"I am sorry and deeply ashamed. I know it's not an excuse but I'm very used to examining animals and for a moment my excitement got the best of me. I won't touch you again without your permission. I hope you'll forgive me."

He kept his eyes locked on hers. To look away from a predator was to identify oneself as prey. Instead he gradually, but as obviously as possible, released his grip on her arm and took a step back. Having successfully kept her most murderous impulses in check, she now seemed to relax. The rage in her eyes slowly transformed into curiosity.

"My name is Cameron Custer. I am a scientist…"

"I know you! 'Do *you* believe in undersea worlds?'"

Well, that was a surprise. But he supposed even convicts had cable. "That's me."

Jade slunk back into her cell and sat on the lonely cot that served her as a bed. Looking around, Cam was surprised to find himself thinking it could have been the bedroom of any teenage girl, albeit if her parents really loved naked steel. She had a stack of books on one nightstand, magazines at the foot of her bed, pictures of celebrities tacked up on the wall. She really was just a girl, separated from her people, and held captive here.

"I suppose my father's hired you to examine me or something."

So she had a father. Or, probably more accurately, someone who insisted she call him father. He suspected this facility would make for a fascinating case study on abusive scientific practices, but he had no time to worry about that now. In fact, he really had no time to be standing here discussing much of anything with her. They had to escape, and sooner rather than later.

"In fact, Jade," he said, testing out the name and, as with the mundanity of her possessions, found that simply using it humanized her in his eyes, "I am nothing of the sort. I broke in here to see you."

"To see me?" She sounded surprised. "I thought nobody knew about me. That's what my father…sorry, that's what the scientist in charge of my project always says."

"Well, nobody does know about you. Not really. I was

fortunate some years ago that someone rather high in the corridors of power was trying to impress me with the secret of your existence. Believe it or not there was a time when people used to try to impress me. And I don't mean to rush you, but I was hoping you'd want to escape from here."

Her eyes grew as wide as saucers. He realized that he had been using that metaphor improperly all his life to describe someone whose eyes had simply bugged out. In the case of this marine girl, her eyes genuinely were as large as saucers.

"I…of course I'd like to, but we'll be killed."

"Not if you come quickly and we're not caught. I know this is a life-altering decision, and one that probably requires some time to…"

She leapt off of her cot, clapping her hands together in such a girlish motion that Cam chastised himself for thinking of her as some alien thing.

"Yes, of course I'll run away. I've dreamt about this all my life. Let's go now, before the next bed check."

"Uh…you're sure? I was hoping you'd say yes, but you understand you'll never see anyone here again. You'll be a fugitive. You'll never see your friends or your father…"

And now, after her manner had nearly convinced him she was a teenager just like any other, that, deep, primal, rage returned to her face, reminding him that she was an abomination from the antediluvian depths of the ocean and of time. In fact, he was frightened by how quickly she could alternate between the two ways of being.

"Fuck them," she hissed. "No one here has ever done anything but torture me. No one here has offered me so much as a scrap of human kindness. If you want, I'll kill every one of these bastards on our way out. Oh, except Sylvia. She's cool."

His heart nearly leapt out of his stomach. Now this was a truly frightening thing to behold: the assuredness and certitude of an adolescent combined with the raw killing power of a marine apex predator. "Well, *that* level of murder won't be necessary…I hope. But there is something rather large I have to ask for your help with."

"All right," she replied inquisitively.

"The most important thing is getting you out of here safe and whole. But there's something else here that might help with my cause."

"Is this like a guessing game?"

And once again she was a sarcastic teenager. He'd really have to keep an eye on her. "No, it's not. What I'm looking for is…"

"What the hell is going on here?"

Cam nearly jumped out of his skin. In a flurry of motion, Jade flung herself against the far wall. He whirled around, slapping at his pockets, wishing he had brought a gun or something equally threatening.

Actually, looking at the intruder, Cam felt a bit less threatened. His lab coat was embroidered with the name Davis and though he looked a bit athletic, he was carrying a manila folder, not a gun. Nor did he seem to have pepper spray, a taser, or any other kind of weapon.

"Oh, hello, Dr. Davis," Cam said, hoping he wasn't giving himself away with his halting cadence, "I'm the new, erm…"

"You're that hack Jacques Cousteau wannabe from TV."

Well, that jig had lasted shorter than usual. Davis pointed at one of the cameras in Jade's room, indicating that his appearance had not been a mere coincidence. They must have monitored her non-stop. "Oh, yeah, I am that. I'm actually pretty well respected in my field, and your boss…"

"I don't have a boss. I'm the boss here."

Cam scoffed. "I believe General Kiste would beg to differ."

"Kiste is in charge of facilities. She just has to make sure tenant commanders like myself have electricity and parking. Jade! Come out of that corner."

The Dark One, her head hanging like a whipped dog, slowly stepped out of the shadows. "Father," she whimpered.

Ah. So this was her proverbial father. And, like a stereotypical sitcom father, Davis put his hands on his hips.

"What were you talking about with this man? You'd better answer me, young lady, or it'll go poorly for you."

Cam cleared his throat. They both turned to look at him as though he were an unwelcome interloper in a family quarrel, which, of course, he was.

"Actually," Cam said, "We were just discussing whether Jade here would turn on the people who had raised her. And she seemed to indicate that murderous rage was in the cards for everyone who had ever wronged her. Or did I misinterpret that, Jade? Because now would be the time to unholster that aforementioned rage."

And just like that the cheerleader was gone and the Dark One was back. Frills rose along her back, a sign he recognized from many species as predatorial. Killers had to appear larger to intimidate their prey. Davis turned, mouth agape, to look at the creature he had raised.

"Now, you listen here, young lady. I don't know what you think…"

Jade lunged at him, her long, lanky fingers outstretched toward his throat. Davis seemed shocked in the way that only a master who has beaten his attack dog all its life can when bitten. He clutched at a whistle around his neck, but didn't manage to grab it before Jade brought her jaws down with a *crunch-crunch-crunch* on the knuckles of three of his fingers. His hand exploded into a firework of hot, spurting blood that spattered Cam's forehead. He reached up to wipe some out of his eye.

Jade's fingers were so long that her nails met at the back of Davis's neck as she throttled him. The man stumbled backwards, arms windmilling like a comedian from the thirties tripping on a banana peel. Loud crunches and pops filled the steel chamber as Jade lazily munched her father's fingers while crushing his windpipe.

His face was purple and his mouth was open, as he wildly tried to scream for help, but no noise escaped. Jade put a further damper on the notion of calling for assistance by seeming to give him a long, deep French kiss. When her head snapped back, it was with a long, wriggling tongue clenched between her teeth, seemingly ripped from the very back of her father's mouth. She let it slide down her throat and Cam was reminded of nothing so much as the thousands of times he'd seen dolphins be fed a fish.

With another abortive snap of her jaws, Davis's face turned from a healthy, albeit strangling and tongueless human's into a half caved-in skull. She'd sheared away his entire nose and most of his cheeks with a single bite, revealing the skeletal sinus passages and facial muscles on his still-living face. And either from shock, blood loss, asphyxiation, or a combination of the three, that was the end for the government scientist. He collapsed like a rag doll under Jade's ministrations, and, with a surprising tenderness for someone she had just brutally butchered, she lowered his body to the ground. She wiped the blood from her face with the back of her arm and with that the Dark One was gone and the cheerleader was back again. "I've waited a long time to do that."

"I can see that," Cam agreed.

"Now, what was this other thing you needed before we left?"

He paused, genuinely not remembering for a second in all the commotion. He snapped his fingers after a second. "Oh, right. Some files and blueprints from the 1940s."

"I know this base well. Lived here all my life. I can take you right to the record archives."

"Great!" Cam said, finally excited.

Everything was coming back. He was going to get his fortune and his standing back, all in one fell swoop. Everyone on the planet was going to believe in undersea worlds once he was through. Damn it. Now he was using his own stupid catchphrase in his mind.

"I hope there are some guards along the way," Jade said, as she led him out into the corridor, "I'm still a bit peckish."

29. AUGUST, 1942

Alcide could see the ocean flickering through the trees, moonlight reflecting off of the waves. Preach was breathing hard, an occasional cough producing more blood. Neither man spoke of it, but it was obvious that he wasn't a long way off from shuffling off the mortal coil.

"Put me down… I can't go on…" Preach wheezed out, blood dribbling from the corner of his mouth.

"Don't be talking like that, Preach," Alcide grunted, positioning the man against the trunk of a palm tree. "Plenty of road still to come, yeah?"

Preach laughed. To Alcide's ears, it sounded like the squeaking fan belt on his family's old ruster. The corporal looked up into Alcide's eyes and reached a hand into his jacket, rosary and dog tags clinking as his hand shoved past them.

A pair of stained and misshapen letters came back in his trembling grip.

"Boudin? Will you give…give these…to my sweetheart? We were going to get married…when I got back."

Alcide slowly pushed Preach's hand back into his lap. "Can't do it, Preach. Pshaw, this ain't nothing. And I've got the power, me."

Preach looked puzzled, but Alcide paid it no mind as he sighed and slipped a pouch wrapped in red cloth from the inside of his jacket. His footlocker containing most of his other workings was still back at Henderson Field, but a good practicing man never traveled anywhere without some mojo, and this was powerful medicine.

Unscrewing the top of Preach's canteen, he poured the

powdery contents of the red pouch inside. Alcide closed his eyes and began to whisper words. "I call upon the east gate and the west wind. Burn his pain and ailments from him, with fire cleanse and water cure, with this power I entreat you."

Then he pressed the canteen to Preach's mouth as he struggled and tried to resist drinking it, but Alcide held his nose closed until he was forced to swallow the worked water. Preach choked, small dribbles running down his chin as he stared up into Alcide's pitying eyes.

"Hold fast, Preach," Alcide said. "It's going to hurt."

Preach shuddered, his eyes bulging. Alcide saw him take a breath as if to scream and quickly placed a hand over the corporal's mouth, muffling the sound. He looked around the dark jungle, worrying about the noise. He could only quiet the man for so long before something noticed them. He wasn't sure where they were, but they'd heard of Tojo patrols combing close, and from his experience, Clickers would follow blood for miles if they got the smell of it.

Preach reached up and pulled Alcide's hand away from his mouth, panting hard as he wrestled himself into a sitting position. "What the heck did you just give me?"

"Little ground up rattlesnake skin and some water. Potent working for putting the healing touch on someone."

Preach stood, his hands balled into tight fists. Alcide watched warily. The mojo bag he wore around his neck was powerful enough to turn away any lasting harm, but it wasn't hoodoo he was willing to put to the test against a comrade-in-arms.

"What kind of curse did you put on me?" Preach hollered, the normally long fuse of his temper finally spent.

Alcide dodged the man's fist as he swung, overextending and stumbling past him.

Alcide had spent his childhood wrestling with his brothers on muddy bayou banks. He was heavier than Preach by a quarter and some change, and he was also still recovering from the concussion blast and the side effects of Alcide's spell.

Alcide kicked his leg out and caught Preach in the shin, sending him sprawling in the sand. He sat on the man's lower back, easily pinning him in place. Preach struggled, attempting to fight, spitting sand and turning his head to glare at the Cajun.

"Hush now, you're going to give away our position going on like that."

"This is the Devil's work, Robichaude. This shit comes straight from Hell!"

Alcide blinked. He didn't think he'd ever heard the religious corporal swear before. He shook his head, wondering what had brought this kind of reaction to him saving his life, not to mention the intense paranoia when Preach had seen his drawings.

"Powerful wound on the soul that would make you jump angry at me, yeah? Something work black magic on you? Hard to forget things like that, or the monsters that do them." Alcide spoke plainly, calmly.

He had recognized the holes in Preach's story earlier. They were the kind of holes he himself left, when hoping to conceal his workings. He rose off the corporal's back, letting him clamber to his feet. "I'm not a monster, and I'm not out to put a spell on anyone. I'm just a man who knows a little more than most."

Alcide couldn't be sure how long they stood there eyeing each other. He didn't want to kill the corporal, but he would if he didn't see reason. Another hard lesson growing up: at the end of the day everything came down to kill or be killed.

"I…" Preach began, cut off by the sound of faint movement coming out of the trees. An understanding of truce passed between the two of them and Alcide pointed to a thick tangle of undergrowth. Preach nodded and picked up his rifle, jogging and pushing aside the foliage.

Alcide crouched in the sand, keeping one ear to the wind for the sound of the incoming creature. If he had to hazard a guess, the creature had cottoned to Preach's blood, following the trail to what it thought was going to be an easy meal.

He found a small pool of blood that was still fresh. He had to be careful with what he had in mind, unless he wanted to turn Preach into a piece of bait. He drew three symbols in the sand around the pool of blood, equidistant from each other, each design precise. Ripping the red mojo bag from around his throat, Alcide felt a pain as it unraveled in his hands, the careful working bleeding away into the night, magic sacrificed for something new.

He stuffed the roots, loose coins, powder, and the fabric of the bag back into his pockets. No use in wasting ingredients, especially in the middle of a war. He grasped the three coffin nails he had brought with him and embedded them in the sand, whispering the working. "Thrice I work thee, and thrice I bind thee, thrice it is done."

As soon as he had driven the last nail into the sand, he saw the stirring of the scrub brush close to the beach. The Clicker emerged, eyes focusing on Alcide. It was bright white and about the size of a small dog. He contemplated shooting it, but the shot would give away their position.

The creature paused at the end of the clearing and Alcide wondered why the blasted thing wasn't clicking its claws like the rest of his kind before deciding he didn't care.

A breeze kicked up and blew the scent of blood towards the creature. Its eyestalks wavered and focused in on the patch of blood. A warbling hiss escaped the creature's throat and it charged headlong across the sand. Alcide smiled and whispered to himself, "That's right. Come on, beastie."

The small Clicker never let up as it plowed into the trap. Preach appeared from the brush and both men watched as the thing futilely attempted to swipe its claws at Alcide's knees, only to stop at the barrier line created by the three nails.

"Does it have…rubber bands on its claws?" Preach asked, dumbfounded. "And one of those cartoon faces drawn on its back?"

"Missing its tail, too," Alcide replied, squatting down to look at the animal, which had given up trying to kill the two of them and was now eagerly shoveling the blood drenched sand into its craw.

Preach squatted next to it, examining every facet of the thing. "Didn't get a good look on the beach. Ugly suckers, aren't they?"

Alcide nodded, thinking of the times he'd gone to check his trotlines on the river back home only to find a pissed off Clicker waiting for them. "Vicious bastards, but easy enough to bind if you know the right ways."

Preach didn't smile. "What you do doesn't sit right with me."

Alcide put a hand on his shoulder. "We'll shake it out when we're eating something proper in Sydney. Just trust me for now, yeah?"

A moment passed between the two men before Preach offered his hand and Alcide gratefully took it. "Alright, Boudin. What do we do now?"

"Suppose we need to link back up with Basher and Martino and the rest of the company, assuming they made it off the beach. I've got the ingredients in my pack to do a massive working, turn these fuckers back into the sea…" His eyes glanced back down to the Clicker, finished with its meal and once again attempting to escape its captivity."…but first, hand me your knife."

Preach passed his KA-BAR to Boudin who grabbed it tight and positioned his hand just out of reach above the animal's body.

Alcide smiled grimly. "Going to stew you and your big brothers, you little son of a…"

"Wait!"

The piercing cry echoed through the jungle and Preach snapped his Springfield into position as a man stumbled out of the trees, hands waving frantically. His sun-kissed skin and unkempt face emphasized the wild eyes that shone with a panicked madness.

"No! He's my best friend!"

30. AUGUST, 1942

Doodles put his body between Pinchy and the two strange men. After the adrenaline rush of running across a beach as shells lit up the night sky and bullets cracked in the not-very-distance, he suddenly felt very stupid.

He had just been a cook aboard a carrier. Sure, there'd been booming and attacks and such, but he'd always been able to hide out from those below in his galley for the most part. As long as everybody got fed he didn't have to worry about dying. This was a very different animal. And now with the adrenaline seeping out of his body, it occurred to him exactly what was going on here.

This wasn't Sergeant Ohno. And it certainly wasn't Private Yotashi. These were Americans. And they could understand him.

"Hands up, son," the one on the left, a Corporal Cantor if his nametag was in order, said, slowly lowering his rifle to be perfectly level with the mad cook.

Doodles just stared for a moment, dumbfounded. He hadn't heard another human voice speak English in months. And he always avoided the ones speaking Japanese. He took a step forward, causing both of the men to jump back and cock their weapons.

"I'm American," he said, pounding his chest, "American. You can understand me, right?"

"Yeah, all right, screwball," the other one, Robichaude, said in the thickest swamp accent Doodles had ever heard, "we can understand you. What the heck is wrong with you? And why are you protecting that thing?"

Doodles put his hand over his mouth. He thought he was

about to start crying, but it was too late. He already was. And he wasn't sure if it was due to joy at being found or misery at his life on the island coming to an end.

"I'm, ah, SD1 Enterline. Christopher Enterline. I don't remember my number thingy. It might be on my dog tags if I can find them."

"What's that mean, SD1?" Robichaude asked. "That ain't no American rank I ever heard of."

"He was a cook, Boudin," Cantor said, "in the Navy. Didn't you ever pay attention to that weird rate system they have?"

"Aw, Navy," Robichaude replied, spitting on the ground, "that's even worse than being a Tojo."

"Actually," Doodles said, "the Marine Corps is a part of the Department of…"

Both of the Marines fixed him with such deadly stares that he just shut up without being told.

"All right, well, what's your deal, sailor? You look like you've been stuck on this island for more than a minute," Cantor said.

"Yeah," Doodles replied, running his hand down his face, "I have. A long time now. I'm not even sure how long. I was on the *Lexington* when it sank in May."

The Marines exchanged a shocked look, but their attitude toward him softened.

"What? What is it?" Robichaude shrugged. "You tell him, Preach. I haven't the heart."

Preach. Cantor was wearing a rosary, so that made sense. Must've been a Bible thumper. And a *boudin* was a Cajun sausage, so maybe that was why the corporal called Robichaude that.

"It's August, Enterline,"

Doodles paused and nodded. Yeah. Yeah, that sounded about right. A few weeks alone, then a few with Pinchy.

"You're a regular Robinson Crusoe," Preach said. "I guess this wasn't how you imagined your rescue to be, but come on, we'll do what we can for you. We have some C-rations back at Henderson. If it's still standing."

Hearing him say it like that crystallized the decision in Doodles's mind.

"No, no. I'm good. I just needed to find my friend here. I know the island inside and out. I can make my way over to the airfield."

The two Marines exchanged a sidelong glance.

"They ain't going to let you take that thing in with you," Boudin said, "and they sure as shootin' ain't going to let you take it home with you."

"Yeah," Preach agreed, "I don't think you know how dangerous those things are. Best for all of us if you let us put it down. I know you like it for some reason, but you've put down your dogs and horses back home, haven't you?"

Doodles dropped to his knees and wrapped his arms around Pinchy. Pinchy seemed to be rooted to the spot for some reason.

"He's tame. He wouldn't hurt a fly. And besides, he can't hurt anybody even if he wanted to. I binded up his hands and his tail already broke off. He's totally fine."

Click-click, Pinchy agreed.

"Listen, Enterline," Preach said, "I know you think that because you've been stuck on an island with only the voices in your head to keep you company for a couple of months, but that thing will kill you as soon as look at you."

"I'm not leaving him," Doodles said. "He's my only friend in the world."

"Well, hang on, now, Preach," Boudin drawled. "Now that you've got me thinking about it…maybe it's not a bad idea to have a living one. For…what we was discussing earlier."

"Oh, no," Doodles said, "you mean cut him open and see what makes him click. They aren't even going to treat him like a POW. They'll treat him like an animal."

"That ain't what I had in mind. Listen, Christopher…"

"Doodles," Doodles said, the word sounding strange in his mouth. Nobody ever called him Christopher except his mother. Most of the boys on the boat hadn't even called him Cookie, which was strange. It had always just been Doodles.

"Doodles," Preach repeated in a tone you might use with a schoolboy, "we've got to get off this beach, before your buddy's buddies come and eat us."

A long, loud whine pierced the night sky. All three of their eyes turned upward as a wing of B-29s flew toward the island.

"Oh, that's bad," Preach said.

"Why's that bad?" Doodles asked. "Those are our planes?"

"Yeah, but they don't look like they're on a support run to me. They're about to bomb this island to kingdom come. And we're about ten miles from where we're supposed to be."

31. AUGUST, 1942

Microphone was desperately trying to raise the last M2 on the radio, shouting and waving his free hand as if they could see him. Jake was proud of how what was left of Ezekiel's company had rallied, even after the slaughter down by the beach. Two of his men had taken over one of the guard towers when the sentries had fled, and Jake was up there with them now. But the crew manning the Browning were on the edge of panic, like their predecessors. Ammunition was beginning to run low.

The smell of death was everywhere, the coppery tang of blood and the rich ammonia of dead Clickers filled the air. The airfield was overrun. The white Kamikaze Clickers were all gone now, having sacrificed themselves to blow up tanks, guard towers, gun emplacements, and most of Henderson's defenses. The remaining wild crustaceans were everywhere and where they could, men fled.

But not his company, not while Jake could still draw breath. The wild ones that seemed to be the most numerous had scurried over the light tank, tales striking and trying to gnaw their way through the metal to no avail. Even one of the bigger obsidian ones had tried to spray it down, but the M2 had fired and the black monstrosity had sprinkled into a fine mist over the crater-pocked airfield. It had become a matter of great personal pride to Jake and his men to do everything in their power to save the one remaining tank crew.

Then, in a night full of horrors, a new one emerged. An albino Clicker, almost translucent, and about the size of a pickup truck skittered onto the scene. It reminded Jake of a ghost the way it scurried quickly over the battlefield, the smaller ones moving out of its way as it came straight for the tank. And once it was in view, he saw that someone had painted a Red Rising Sun on its back.

While he had a weird suspicion that the obsidian Clickers were "natural"—if that was the right word for it—he knew that the white Clickers had somehow been bred or engineered by the Japanese. The damn Tojos; they'd gone and done something monstrous, unholy. He'd eaten crab, stomped on scorpions, but neither one of them had been the size of a fucking Ford. There'd been scuttlebutt after Pearl Harbor, about the Huns across the pond, about the Tojos here, what they did in the dark shadows wherever the Axis touched.

They were mad, and they'd perverted creation. And he didn't want to find out what this latest monstrosity would do.

Jake tapped Microphone's shoulder, pointing frantically at the ghostly white Clicker. "Tell that tank to take it out!"

The man's eyes widened as he listened to the handset, shaking his head at Jake. "I think it's all over, sir. Command's authorized a bombing run!"

Jake felt the blood drain from his face as he glanced up at the sky, dark but for the stars and light reflections of burning tank hulks. He could already see it, the wing of bombers, their doors opening wide and the deadly whistling that would signal death. They had to get off the airfield.

The white Clicker's tail struck left and right, as it gleefully attacked its own kind. Its stinger, Jake saw, was impossibly sharp and strong enough to strike through even the shells of its wild brethren. And as it did, the brown ones would inflate like a balloon and pop, almost instantaneously. He was no egghead, but after seeing what Clicker venom had done to Ezekiel's leg, and what Basher had reported about Trick, he guessed that albino Clicker venom was ten, maybe a hundred times more potent.

A blast from a Browning caught the massive beast's attention. It turned and scuttled quickly toward a pillbox still occupied by men from Division, safely encased in concrete. The thing's stinger came down and punched through the top of the pillbox like it was nothing.

Jake heard a wet *pop*, and the pillbox began to disintegrate from the inside. Bile rose in his throat and he had to look away as the men came tumbling out of the melting concrete, their howls silencing as their tongues melted with the rest of their flesh into a slush on the ground.

He watched helpless as the white Clicker turned toward the tank. Having seen dozens blown up by Kamikaze Clickers, Jake knew the procedure. He saw the M2 try to reverse, treads chewing into the mud and dirt as they tried to escape. The enormous and gleefully ghoulish albino seized the treads in its claws and squeezed tight.

The treads snapped in half and the tank didn't move. The monster chittered, and if Jake didn't know better, he could have sworn that it was a laugh. The top of the tank popped open as the creature began to climb, legs piercing into the metal.

The tank captain fired his sidearm and one of the thing's eyestalks blew off. The man fired until he ran empty and then screamed as the Clicker's body began to undulate. Apparently the tank commander had killed it with one of its shots, and now there was nothing to control its venom sacks or glands or whatever. The shell wiggled like an overfilled water balloon and then popped, Clicker innards about the consistency of buckwheat pancake batter splattering all over the M2. The brave commander dissolved instantaneously, the tank following soon after.

Jake heard the sound of tapping on the metal ladder of the guard tower and turned, Thompson raised, expecting to see a Clicker scuttling up toward them, but to his relief, three men were climbing instead.

"Situation's fucked, First Lieutenant Dempsey!" Basher hollered, patting Martino on the shoulder to let him know it was safe to give Jake a sitrep.

"I fucking saw Goblirsch and Chizmar bite it myself. Everyone else is gone, scattered. They're all probably fucking dead too!" Martino was on the edge of losing it. Jake could hear it in his voice.

"We're going to be scattered to Hell and gone if we don't get off this airfield," Jake said."Bombers are coming. This place is going to be a giant fucking hole in three minutes!"

The corporal who'd commandeered the Browning turned. "We're out of ammo for the machine gun, sir. And we're surrounded."

Jake gestured for them to leave. It was getting crowded up there anyway with Microphone, himself, Martino, Basher, and… he didn't recognize the third guy they'd brought with them.

There was a finality to it, the realization that there was nothing holding the monsters back anymore, that they'd scuttle up into their tower or knock it over and then devour them. Jake felt a sigh escape him and he sat back down, looking down at Ezekiel who was still lying unconscious. The doctors at the aid station had patched up his leg and returned him to his unit, for all the good it would do him now.

He knew that his friend couldn't hear, but regardless he spoke, "I was just supposed to pass along what you wanted, back you up. I was never supposed to be the one leading. These things don't have a command structure, they're just fucking animals."

"Wouldn't be so sure about that, sir," the third man who had accompanied with Basher and Martino said.

Jake noticed a couple of things immediately: the three stripes indicating he was a buck sergeant, and the M1903 rifle with scope attached. A sniper. The man carefully aimed his rifle across the battlefield. He licked his thumb and put it to the wind, either an affectation or a real sniper's trick. Jake couldn't tell which.

"What's your name, Sergeant?"

"John Pike, sir. I've got an overly eager Tojo in the trees next to the river. Got a fancy sword with him."

Jake picked up the binoculars the machine gun chief had left behind, followed Pike's trajectory, and saw the barest hint of a human figure gesturing at the edge of the airfield. The sniper was right, it seemed.

"When did you spot him?"

"The moment I climbed up here."

"Why haven't you killed him?"

Pike licked his thumb and put it up to test the wind.

"My targets are supposed to be approved by division command or higher, sir. You see…well, but perhaps that's not important right now. What's important is I'm supposed to have orders."

"Sergeant, I order you to kill that son of a bitch," Jake replied.

"Gladly," Pike replied, taking aim.

32. AUGUST, 1942

Atagi watched the killing field with a well-trained eye. This was Colonel Hanshiro's vision accomplished on a small scale, and ready to expand from this island. He'd been privy to Hanshiro's plans; the oceans flooded with *Kurikka,* battleships and submarines plunging into the dark depths as the creatures swarmed, all under the banner of the Rising Sun.

The IJA brass would celebrate the unit as heroes when they returned to the home islands, flanked by the results of their research. These were the things that he had dared to dream. But the *Umibozu* made him worry he would never get back to Gifu. He didn't trust the sea lords.

The sword in his hand almost thrummed. He could practically feel the excitement of the *Kurikka,* like a wave in the ocean rushing towards the shore, inexorable and unstoppable. The creatures destroyed everything they came in contact with. They had no fear, they were efficient and obedient to whoever commanded their will. They were the ultimate tenets of *bushido* distilled into an animal, the perfect weapons.

Atagi could not say whether the beasts had been trained to follow the sword or if it was magic. The way he could feel the creature's instincts like a sixth sense made him inclined to think the latter, but he had decided he did not care. Magic or simple science, they would be the Emperor's divine right hand.

The roar of a diesel engine cut through the night, and an American tank pulled into view. Atagi gestured with the sword.

"*Banzai*!" he shouted.

He watched as one of the white *Kurikka* charged towards the

American tank, ending its life in a glorious *Kamikaze* attack as the bomb strapped to its back exploded.

The five machine gun nests had been reduced to one, but the tenacity of its defenders was breathtaking. The machine gun swept in a wide circle, bullets killing any of the *Kurikka* that massed, with the other men emerging to fire a volley before ducking back into cover. They fought bravely and Atagi raised his sword to his face, saluting their tenacity in the time before their deaths. He focused intently, feeling the instincts of the *Kurikka* and urging them to rush forward and end this resistance.

Atagi saw a flash from a foxhole, some three hundred or so yards distant from the copse of palms he stood in, before he felt an impact and something wet splatter across his uniform.

Hanshiro's sword was still in his hands, but the bullet had snapped it in two. With one last, fading thought, Atagi felt shame that he had allowed the weapon to come to harm. Then he toppled forward into the mud, the blood from the hole in his head staining the churned-up clumps of grass red.

33. AUGUST, 1942

"One dead Tojo," Pike said simply, lowering his rifle.

"The fucking things have gone wild!" Martino called, Basher confirming the same in less profane terms. The machine gun crew whooped, and Jake even saw the radioman smile uncertainly.

The Clickers were swarming on each other, claws tearing and reaving everything in reach, singular will giving way to instinct in the hundreds. They were no longer united as an army; they were now just animals fighting for food.

Jake heard the faint drone of propellers.

"Oh shit! Basher, Martino!" He pointed down at Ezekiel. "Grab the skipper. Everyone else grab a weapon, and make for the trees. We've got to get the hell out of here!"

They scurried like madmen, all of them able to hear the approaching bombers, and then they were running in a desperate scramble.

A few of the Clickers snapped or tried to sting them as they passed, each man quickly forgotten as they made it past the slaughter. Jake looked up, and in the night sky, he saw the vague shapes of the bombers, then he heard the whistling.

"Move! Move! Mo..."

They were at the edge of the trees when the night exploded.

34. AUGUST, 1942

The acrid smell of burning flesh and buildings was distinct from cordite. One smelled of vigorous combat, the other of massacre. Right now Ota Hanshiro could only think of massacre. The *Umibozu* chieftainess shoved him forward, withholding her strength as Ota might have when catching a butterfly in his hands, but nevertheless hurling him violently.

The *Umibozu* apparently thought so little of humans in general, or Ota in particular, that she had not bound his hands. Or perhaps, such things were not common practice among their kind. Out in the darkness, the *Umibozu* prowled. Some of them walked upright, others on all fours, and still others with their knuckles on the ground like apes. All watched Ota hungrily, held back from slaughtering him only by their primal fear of their mistress's wrath.

The *Umibozu* chieftainess was massive, towering at nearly twelve feet tall, and judging by the look of the others, the creatures continued to grow throughout their prolonged lives. That meant the chieftainess was a particularly ancient specimen. A lithe, lanky *Umibozu* not much taller than Ota strode through the chaos which had become of Ota's base, pulling what Ota thought might have previously been Superior Private Yotashi along behind him. The stringy *Umibozu* had devoured Yotashi's face, chewing down to the bone and leaving him with the unsettling look of a skull with eyes still in its sockets.

The lanky one stopped to stare greedily at Ota. The chieftainess growled murderously, a sound which must have carried for miles underwater.

"Not for you," she uttered in her guttural language.

"Yes, of course, mistress," the lanky one hissed.

He turned his attentions back to Yotashi, clamping onto his socket and sucking out the eye with a loud, squishing pop. Ota watched in disgust, but unable to tear his eyes away, as the lanky *Umibozu* sucked down Yotashi's optic nerve like a long string of soba noodle. Then it dug into the now empty socket, pulling out chunks of the still screaming Yotashi's brain and popping them into his mouth like rice balls. Yotashi's rag doll twitching became increasingly agitated.

Ota hissed in pain as a sharp spike dove deep into his back. The chieftainess was urging him on with her trident, but either didn't know or didn't care about the difference between a harmless poke in the butt and a potentially life-endangering poke in the kidneys.

"Move, pink meat-slave," the chieftainess hissed, and though she had now demonstrated her fluency in Japanese, did not deign to continue to speak it.

Ota nodded, clasping his wound with the blouse of his uniform. He could not die like this. To be taken prisoner lacked honor. There was no time for the ritual of *seppuku*, but perhaps he could provoke the *Umibozu* into granting him a clean death in battle.

Rows of crude driftwood torches formed a path before them, trailing off into the ocean. The *Umibozu* had no doubt marked this path for their fellows coming out of the sea. Up ahead something was flying through the air in repeating figure eights. For a moment, Ota could not identify it. No insect or bird flew like that.

As he drew nearer he understood. Two *Umibozu* stood on opposite sides of the path. Ota had observed that the amphibious creatures delighted in the change of physics from being out of the water, the same way a human child in a bath might repeatedly submerge a toy. These two were juggling, the one on the right tossing overhand and the one on the left tossing back underhand, resulting in the whirring blur of figure eights which seemed to stick in the air.

Instead of balls or blades or bowling pins, though, they were tossing thick brown livers to each other, grabbing a replacement every time one fell in the dirt. Ota glanced to either side of the torchlit path and saw a half dozen of his men, their bodies piled up like cordwood, each of their chest cavities ripped open and steaming in the cool Pacific night.

The *Umibozu* chieftainess seemed displeased by the grotesque carnival display. She stamped her foot, once, loudly.

"What is this?" she shouted in his undersea language, "I have no time for your foolishness. There is slaughter afoot, and much to be done, and you toy with the prey. Return to your work!"

The chieftainess made the mistake of stepping forward a few feet to yell at her people. That put her back to Ota.

The Emperor had favored him, at least inasmuch that the chieftainess had thought him so weak she had not taken his weapons. Ota drew his pistol and leveled it at the monster's head. He fired, and though as a scientist Ota was not famous for his marksmanship, from this distance he could scarcely do worse than strike the beast square in the back of the neck.

The bullet pinged off the thing's scales, harmlessly zipping away into the night. Ota's eyes widened in horror. He'd seen the corpses of a few *Umibozu* felled by his men with rifles, so he knew they were not immune. But then again, the thing was ancient beyond all reason, having spoken earlier in no uncertain terms about watching the rise and fall of her grandiose empire. Her scales must have hardened over the centuries, and filled in with barnacles and other hard sea parasites, like the ones which had consumed her eye.

The chieftainess growled in anger, her frill rising in a grotesque display. She whirled on Ota, who defiantly fired two more shots, hoping to strike her in the eyes. The chieftainess flung her arm through the air, attempting to cast the bullets away like annoying flies. It was unsuccessful, of course (that would have been an astonishing feat, to be able to strike bullets out of the air) but Ota nonetheless missed his target and failed to blind her.

The prowling *Umibozu* and the jugglers alike all froze in place, either shocked or bracing for a fight. Well, Ota would give them one. He raised his pistol again, but the monster, with her incredible reach, struck the weapon out of his hand without even taking a step. Ota's wrist shattered and his right arm, dislocated, flopped behind his back like a rag doll's.

Ota spat defiantly, and, ignoring the pain as adrenaline dosed his system, reached for his scabbard with his left. He would rather have died with his ancestral heirloom in his hand than Atagi's *showato,* but even a modern sword was better than none at all. With a long snick, the blade burst into life, the torchlight glinting off it in the darkness.

"Your empire, such as it was, was a joke. It deserved to fall and no one will mourn you, you half-addled dead ends of evolution." He spoke in defiant Japanese, knowing the creature would understand his insults, and its lackeys likely would not. "No one will remember you, nor even ever know you existed. My kind will continue to dump our excrement over the ruins of your once fabled cities. And we'll laugh about ripping you out, root and branch, simply by polluting your environment."

The chieftainess's lips peeled back. Now she was angry. Now she would strike the killing blow. Good. With an ear piercing *"Banzai!"* Ota rushed headlong, sword brandished one- handed, and made it no more than three steps before the chieftain snatched him up like a baby, palming his entire head like a pear.

Ota's sword clattered to the ground. His legs continued pumping, his good arm continued swinging (his bad one did, too, but that was of its own accord) but he was held aloft, five feet off the ground.

"I know what you want, you petty bureaucrat," the thing growled. "I know all about your crabshit *bushido* code. And these young broodlings might just be undisciplined enough to give it to you. But I am ancient beyond reason. I have the patience of the ocean's rolling tides. I am a royal-blooded Dark One, last of the great stock, and I will grant you nothing you desire, least of all the icy grip of death."

Ota could barely see between the thing's fingers, and blood from his compressing scalp dripped down into one of his eyes. The chieftainess turned and shouted at one of the jugglers.

"Bio-vizier! Bring me a Clicker of the fourth sigil."

"Yes, mistress," the juggler replied, scraping and bowing as it disappeared under the water's surface.

Not releasing his grip, the chieftainess strode down to the beach in just a few of its long strides. She squeezed Ota's head like a housewife testing a melon, just to remind him that she was so physically potent she could take his life at any time and refused.

"You don't have the balls to kill me," Ota spat, his mouth sputtering blood along with the words from a bitten through lip and tongue. "Unsurprising," the thing responded, "as I am a female. Nevertheless, I have something far better in mind for you than simple death."

The juggler *Umibozu* emerged from the sealine, feet stomping loudly as though it were a man in a rubber suit emerging onto the Japanese coastline rather than a real-world monster. In its hand it held a new juggling ball… a *Kurikka*, about the size of a child's plaything. The mini-*Kurikka*, unlike the rest of its kind, had a near translucent shell, perhaps just a thin layer of membrane, and in the fluttering torchlight its crab-like meat pulsed like an exposed human brain.

"A fourth sigil Clicker, as you requested, mistress."

"Thank you, bio-vizier. You may apply your craft."

The juggler stood nearby, smiling, and Ota noticed that it, unlike the other, mostly naked *Umibozu*, wore parti-colored sheaves of algae.

Noticing his interest, the chieftainess lifted its fingers to free Ota's eyes. "Yes, look at her, meat-slave. In her you have a kindred spirit. My very own Ota Hanshiro. You spent five years trying to make a Clicker that would blow up. Congratulations. Three hundred years ago, she perfected this!"

The juggler…bio-vizier, rather…stepped forward and placed the brain Clicker on the back of his neck. Ota nodded, accepting that he might not die in glorious battle, but welcoming death if it would spare him the agony of his ruined arm and half-crushed skull. He waited for the creature's pincer to strike, and fill his nervous system with melting acidic venom.

Instead, he flinched as it wrapped its long, spindly legs

around his neck. As a youth he had rarely fought with his brother, but one time Yoshi had throttled him, and he was instantly a child again being choked. The *Kurikka*'s claws waved through the air, Ota sensed, though he could not see them, and worried where they would find purchase. An instant later the brain Clicker seemed to decide, and snapped deep into his clavicles, biting through skin, meat, and bone, apparently seeking nothing more than purchase.

He found himself hyperventilating. This was some kind of torture, he knew. But perhaps he would find peace with his ancestors after all for suffering it. Perhaps he was being tested. Denied his ancestral sword and everything else, including the clean blow of a sword strike from his second after evisceration began , surely this was just as torturous and would satisfy his ancestors? So let the killing blow fall.

The creature drove its pincer deep into his neck and he felt the spike come to rest sickeningly between two of his vertebrae. Then the chieftainess let him fall to the beach. He coughed, sputtered, and tried to sit up, but found that he could not. Nor could he kick. He was, in fact, paralyzed, and began hyperventilating as he realized his body had become nothing but a block of ice beneath his neck.

So that was it, then? They would paralyze him and leave him to die of exposure? Perhaps it would not take so long. Perhaps an American would find him and put him out of his misery. Or a roving island animal. Or a *Kurikka*.

But then his useless, ice-cold body sat up in a herky-jerky motion, like a child's marionette with strings being tugged by an inelegant puppeteer. Only…he hadn't told it to. Then he was standing, bobbing back and forth as though he had never stood on two legs before.

The bio-vizier approached him, and checked each of his eyes.

"What are you doing to me?" Ota whispered.

The bio-vizier fingered the *Kurikka* on his neck.

"Can you hear me, Brother Clicker? Can you understand?"

"Yes," Ota croaked in Darkese, stretching out the syllable as though trying to speak for the first time. But it wasn't Ota speaking. It was the thing on his neck, making him dance, controlling him.

"Good," the chieftainess purred, her tone considerably less furious than previously. "Do not let this blob of meat speak again. Congratulations, bio-vizier. I think you finally have a new assistant who will be of more use to you than hauling rock or catching specimens."

"I thank you, mistress," the bio-vizier said, bobbing her head in a chilling approximation of a terrestrial nod.

Ota screamed, long and loud, but no noise came out. It stayed locked away with the rest of him, trapped in his own mind. Against his wishes, he began to walk to the shoreline, and followed the bio-vizier into the deep. His mouth and lungs filled with saltwater, and despite the *Kurikka*'s overwhelming control, his body began spasming as he drowned. The pain was excruciating, and the monster attached to his spine didn't even acknowledge it, simply walking along the ocean's surface, foot after foot. The bio-vizier fluttered along beside him, swimming with the practiced ease of a seal.

By the time they reached the wondrous gates of her undersea laboratory, in a cyclopean and ancient city exactly as mesmerizing, terrifying, and awe-inspiring as the chieftainess had described, perhaps moreso for its emptiness, Ota was already dead. But his brain continued to serve the *Kurikka* as he busied his hands with the experiments of the *Umibozu*.

35. AUGUST, 1942

"So this thing is what? Your pet? You paint that face on its back?"

They were picking their way through the jungle, all three men panting hard. Doodles reached over and lovingly stroked Pinchy across the shell.

"You don't understand. He's not violent. He's been living with me while I've been stealing from Sergeant Ohno," Doodles said.

Corporal Cantor, who his friend called Preach, mouthed "Sergeant Oh, No?" to Boudin who shrugged in response. Doodles didn't let the confusion of the jarheads dim his joy. He'd found his friend. Pinchy wasn't just splattered hunks of meat on a remote beach. He'd mark that in the "win" column.

Boudin pushed aside a large fern and the three men stopped in their tracks when they heard the sudden roar of exploding ordnance."Jesus, sounds like they dropped the entire AAF's payload on Henderson!"

The jungle glowed with distant fire. They were still a mile off from the airfield, but Doodles didn't have any intention of going further.

He decided to plead his case instead. "Can't get there now. Why don't you two come with me? I know all the best hidey-holes that the Tojos have abandoned. We can stay there, wait until Admiral Fletcher shows back up with the Navy."

Doodles was hoping to appeal to Preach's faith. He'd be able to teach Pinchy the ways of the Lord, tame his innate savagery enough that he could take off the rubber bands keeping his claws bound. His dreams of living out his days surrounded by people who understood the magnificence of Pinchy were interrupted by the sounds of footsteps and hushed voices.

Preach raised his Springfield, but Doodles saw Boudin raise his hand and call into the trees, "Lightning!"

There was silence before a gruff voice responded, "Rolling!"

Boudin and Preach both lowered their weapons as a large, bald Marine Gunnery Sergeant in a tattered uniform proclaiming his name to be Webb emerged from the brush, followed by six other men.

"Glad you made it, Gunny," Preach said, stepping forward and sticking out his hand for Webb to shake.

Webb did not take it, but stared at it like it was a dead fish until Preach lowered it in embarrassment.

Webb hooked a thumb back at the men following him. "Got guys from the 2nd and 3rd. That's all I've been able to find from Henderson. Those damn crawdads didn't stop. What's the situation down at the beach?"

Boudin gestured with his rifle at Doodles. "Just this fruit basket. Our positions are scattered to hell and gone. Plenty of the guys are dead."

Webb grunted and cast his eye at Doodles, who instinctively held Pinchy a little tighter as Webb asked, "Who's the squid?"

Doodles introduced himself and briefly outlined where he came from, trying to keep the timeline of things straight in his head. His experiences on the *Lexington* felt like a lifetime ago. Boudin and Preach occasionally would chime in with their own observations.

Webb grunted when he was done. "So you caught one of the damn things? And you know where Tojo is dug in?"

Doodles nodded emphatically, gesturing towards the east. "They have lots of little hidey-holes, but the biggest is on that big hill south of the airfield. That's where Pinchy and I go to forage for the good stuff."

The good stuff was just a higher quality of rice and barley ration canisters, but that didn't matter to a man that was on the verge of starvation. Webb nodded and looked over at Boudin and Preach.

"We'll take him with us, link up with Lieutenant Colonel

Puller and the 7th, and see if we can't find a way to get past those damn pillboxes and these fucking clicking monsters." He then pointed at Doodles. "Someone get that damn thing out of his hands and kill it so we can hand it over to the boys in Intelligence."

36. AUGUST, 1942

Alcide stepped between Gunny Webb and the screaming cook, glancing back to see that Doodles had curled around the maimed Clicker and was ranting about how they couldn't take his friend from him. He didn't care much about keeping the man's pet monstrosity alive, but if he was to conjure a working that was going to affect the minds of an army of Clickers, he'd need a live one. An already captured and seemingly harmless one went a long way towards solving that problem.

"Move it or lose it, Robichaude," Webb said, his eyes brooking no defiance.

Alcide shook his head, trying to think of how he was going to explain to a rigid rail of a man like Gunny why he needed Pinchy alive. His father Jean Renard had always been the one with the sweet tongue, telling lies to folks who pried too close to the family homestead. He had just been the muscle when things required a more permanent solution. But no lie was going to satisfy the non-com, especially when he'd already made up his mind about killing Doodles' pet.

"Gunny, I'm familiar with these things. Back home in the bayou we call them Clickers. They're as aggressive as cupid's itch, but they're plenty easy to train. We can fight back, but I need a live one."

It wasn't exactly a lie. Alcide was sure that Webb wouldn't tolerate any gaff or reasoning about magic, but what he'd said was close enough to the truth. The rest of the gravel stompers in his unit had a tendency to think he'd spent his free time wrestling gators and cooking up jambalaya. Playing on that reputation seemed like the smoothest course.

His suggestion seemed to go over well with the rest of the men. They were ready to dole out some payback.

But Gunny shook his head. "We're not training them, Robichaude. This is the Marine Corps, not the goddamned humane society. The air forces just blew the hell out of the ones in the field and the rest are in disarray. We rendezvous with the 7th and take the fight to Tojo."

Alcide glanced back at Doodles rocking back and forth. He took a step forward and leaned in to speak a bit lower, while keeping a respectful distance from Webb.

"You're right, Gunny. Lieutenant Colonel Puller's going to want to know what that *folle* found out about Tojo's positions, though. He probably not going to be disposed to tell you if you kill his little crawdad."

Webb's eyes bounced back and forth from Alcide to Doodles, considering. It had been docile enough to let the man put rubber bands on its claws and paint its back, after all. But Webb's face hardened.

"Too dangerous, Robichaude. It needs to be put down. I'll take care of it. You won't be responsible. Step aside."

Alcide clenched his fists. Even if Webb couldn't see it, he was trying to save everyone who was still alive, even the Japanese. Where there were Clickers, there were Dark Ones, and while he'd had experience dealing with them, he wasn't willing to fight them mojo to mojo. Hoodoo only stretched so far when it came to primitive strength, and by the time he'd finished a working, they'd have ripped his head clean from his shoulders.

He turned to Preach, hoping the man who'd seen what he could do would back him up. But Preach didn't step forward.

Alcide took a deep breath. "I can't do that, Gunnery Sergeant."

The men, Preach included, stared with wide eyes.

Webb's face hardened. He didn't raise his rifle, but the threat was implicit. "I'm not asking again, Robichaude."

Alcide took a deep breath and prepared to enthrall Webb's mind with a spell. It was black magic, but the stakes were high enough he was willing to risk it.

"Lightning!"

The voice rang through the trees and everyone seemed to sigh in relief. Webb forcefully ripped his gaze from Alcide and called, "Rolling!"

First Lieutenant Dempsey appeared. Basher and Martino followed directly behind him supporting Captain Palmer on a litter between them. Gunny immediately snapped to attention, knowing better than to salute in a combat zone. Alcide had never seen a man look so relieved while simultaneously so stiffly military.

"Good to see you, sir."

"You, too, Gunny. Let's have a pow-wow. The rest of you, form a perimeter and set the skipper down."

The men jumped to follow Dempsey's orders as Webb filled him in. The XO looked tired, haunted, his uniform reduced to tatters. Throughout his discussion with Webb, his eyes kept darting to Captain Palmer.

Palmer looked like he and Death were sharing a cup of joe. His head rolled around like he was swacked and he was sweating profusely. Basher and Martino set him down as easily as they could next to Doodles, the only other invalid in the area, who took one look before going back to muttering and stroking his pet Clicker.

The old squadmates took up their positions on the perimeter. Martino clapped Alcide on the shoulder, looking at Preach. "Thought you boys had fucking bought it."

Alcide returned a grin, the thought of their disagreements earlier in the day long forgotten. "Couldn't let you two hog all the fun." His smile disappeared when his thoughts returned to Trick. He pointed at Palmer with his chin. "How's the skipper?"

Basher shook his head. "One of those oversized crabs nicked him good and we had to take his leg. Don't have a corpsman to look after him anymore. Janz bought it in the retreat back to the airfield."

"What's with the fucking squid?" Martino asked.

Preach shook his head. "He's been stuck on this island for months. Sun's baked all his brains away. He thinks that Clicker thing is his friend. Marked it as his own and everything. That's what Boudin was fighting with the gunnery sergeant about when you fellows interrupted."

Martino whistled in appreciation. "You went chest to chest with fucking Webb? What were you thinking, you crazy fucking Cajun?"

Alcide's eyes went dark. "I was thinking about Trick."

Preach shook his head. Martino and Basher's faces both fell. "Good kid. Shouldn't have died like that," Preach said quietly.

"Don't worry, boys," Alcide said. "If I have my way, no one else is going to die to these things."

Webb was apparently simultaneously finishing telling Dempsey about their altercation.

"Private First Class Robichaude," the XO snapped sharply.

Alcide jumped up from his prone position and double-timed it over to the leadership. Dempsey was wearing a serious face, one that was rare to see on the playboy XO.

"The gunnery sergeant here tells me you've been disobeying orders. That true?"

Alcide shook his head vigorously. "No, sir. I wasn't trying to mutiny or nothing and my apologies to you, Gunnery Sergeant, if it seemed that way, and I'll take my lumps if need be. I'm just hoping I can convince y'all of a different course."

Dempsey looked to Webb, who seemed less angry but no less stiff. "I appreciate your conviction, Robichaude, so I'm not going to bust your ass or beat the shit out of you, but this still isn't a democracy. That being said, sir, the decision is really yours."

Dempsey nodded and sighed. "I've seen about a hundred of those white Clickers tonight. They blew up half the defenses of Henderson tonight. Is it aggressive?"

"Seems safe for now but if the Tojos are controlling them somehow, it's a danger just to have it around." Webb said.

Dempsey nodded. "Sorry, Boudin. I agree with Gunny. The best course of action is to make crab puffs out of that bastard."

"Well, begging your pardon, gentlemen, but if this isn't a democracy, isn't it really up to Captain Palmer?"

Dempsey's words were slow and pained. "The skipper isn't in any condition to be doing anything."

Alcide nodded. "I know that, sir. But one minute of me

working on him and he'll be right as rain."

He dug into his pockets for what he'd need.

"He needs a boat to Sidney, Robichaude, not whatever half-assed cornfed remedy your mama taught you," Webb growled.

Alcide looked to the XO, who was visibly torn. He and the skipper were friends. "I can save him."

Silence reigned as men twitched, every eye in the makeshift perimeter that was supposed to be watching for snipers instead watching the drama unfolding.

Then Preach's calm voice broke the silence. "Let him try, sir. What he's packing, it's potent stuff."

Dempsey sighed deeply and rubbed his head like he was trying to expunge a headache by sheer force of will. "What the Hell. Go ahead, Robichaude."

Webb looked like he was chewing on a whole raw onion, but didn't say anything.

Alcide crouched next to the captain, and pulled out the teeth of the dead marines. Out of the corner of his eye, he saw Basher and Martino glance at each other.

"Pried them out of a dead Tojo when you boys weren't looking," Alcide said, etching the widest grin he could muster on his face, hoping they bought it, but not too concerned if they didn't. Bigger stakes at hand than worrying about what a few men thought, especially if they would most likely be dead before night's end anyways.

He wrapped the teeth in the red velvet cloth he'd taken from his mojo bag. Taking his canteen, he poured water inside, and then pulled the drawstring tight.

The water was leaking through the pouch, but Alcide didn't worry. Healing was simple magic when it came down to it.

He held the object over the captain and whispered the words: "Thrice I call and purify you from the table of death, with former life, I give to you strength."

Upending the pouch, he released the draw string, letting the water pour onto Palmer's wound. The captain winced, a small moan leaving his lips. Alcide watched the water soak in, flesh knitting back together as the color slowly settled back into his face.

Half the men fell on their asses in shock when Palmer sat up, gasping for breath, eyes wide and focused entirely on Alcide, who smiled. "Welcome back to the Canal, Skipper."

Palmer looked around the clearing and then grabbed at his leg. Alcide stepped back and glanced at Webb, who was staring widemouthed. He grinned at the non-com, saying, "Might've left off a few applicable skills when I signed up."

Dempsey jumped to his feet. "I'll fucking say. You all right, Skipper?"

Palmer gratefully accepted the help and stood, tenderly putting weight on his leg before resting easily. "What the hell happened? I thought I was done for?"

Dempsey shrugged. "Boudin…did something to you, Zeke."

Palmer eyed Alcide, more than a bit skeptical. "You ever thought about a career in medicine, Robichaude? I could put you in for a transfer to the Navy Medical Corps."

Alcide shook his head. "Hell no, sir. I'm a Marine." That elicited an unwise but nonetheless hearty cheer from the men. "Just know a little bit extra."

Palmer glanced at Doodles holding Pinchy tight. "Would knowing a little extra happen to include those oversized lobsters?"

Alcide crouched on his haunches next to Doodles. "Skipper, you might want to have a seat. It's a deep ocean, and there are fouler things in it than just Clickers."

37. AUGUST, 2020

"Come on, Dr. Custer."

"I said, 'no.' No it remains."

"Come on," the Dark One girl repeated, with a weird come-hither tone in her voice.

"Do you think if you just keep saying 'come on' it will convince me?"

Sighing, she flopped backwards onto the motel bed. God, there were times with her body language when she could absolutely pass for a teenager, were she not almost seven feet tall with green, scaly skin.

"It's 3:00 am," she moaned.

"I know that."

"We're in Socorro, New Mexico."

"I know where we are."

"There is no one that is going to see me."

"I already let you take a shower and three baths today."

She slammed her head back against the headboard, a move so severe that it would have snapped any human's neck, and he worried it might have permanently damaged the bed frame. The shaking must not have stopped for a solid five seconds.

"It's not the same," she said, exasperatedly dragging out the last word for far too long.

Cam raised his eyes to the ceiling. They'd been having this conversation all day. While the sun had been up, he'd at least been able to make her see reason. But now that night had fallen, the dimly lighted motel pool was calling to her like a siren, and she'd been babbling about it like a Valley Girl.

"I don't even think it's going to be good for you. It's all full of chlorine."

"Yes, thank you, Florence Nightingale, I know what chlorine is and I know I'll have to shower it off when I get back inside. But Doctor C., you've got to listen to me. I've never been allowed… my father, I mean Dr. Davis, never would let me submerge myself in water. He thought it would bring out my Dark One heritage. He called it my feral side. Like I was Dr. Jekyll and Mr. Hyde or something."

"He never let you bathe?"

She shook her head. "I had to scrub my scales with a sponge and a bottle of water. It was all he ever allowed me at once. Sometimes I would put my head in the toilet just to feel it on my skin."

She was itching all over now, either a psychosomatic reaction to all this talk, or the genuine result of forcing a Dark One to live on dry land for seventeen years. Cam's mouth opened to protest, but, really, how could he?

"You promise to keep your clothes on the whole time?"

She sat up and bounced up and down on the bed in excitement. "Yes, yes!"

"And you promise if anyone comes, and I mean anyone, you and I are out of there like a bolt?"

"Of course. Scout's honor." She held up three fingers on her right hand.

"Where did you learn that?"

She shrugged her shoulders. "Where does anybody learn anything? TV and the internet."

He shook his head. This was a really, really bad idea. But he wasn't a damn war criminal like it sounded the man who had been raising her for seventeen years was. He scooped up the files they had gotten from Los Alamos and a flashlight.

"I'll be okay. You don't have to come."

"Uh, I am damn sure coming," he said. "Now get in your clothes."

Jade clapped her hands together with glee and hurried into the bathroom to change, which, Cam reflected, was a bit like Donald Duck covering up his private parts even though he never wore pants. She'd been naked all her life, and was naked now, in the room, though, of course, he found it impossible to think of her in a sexual way.

Or could he? No, no, that would be far too strange. Besides, she was only seventeen or so. But, then, what did seventeen equate to in Dark One years? Did underwater devils have jailbait?

"Ready!" she said, exploding out of the bathroom before his decidedly unsettling train of thought reached its destination.

He hadn't known what to do, exactly, about the obvious logistical hurdles of being on the road with a Dark One as a traveling companion. On TV shows and movies aliens always seemed to be able to just dress up and blend in. But ET or Paul or Roger Smith were all deliberately small. Jade was enormous, if not for her kind, then for the average person. And unlike a grey-skinned creature whose flesh might be mistaken for human by someone not paying attention, there was no way to hide Jade's obvious green scales.

So he'd done his best. Galoshes fit over the largest pair of jeans he could find. A flannel lumberjack's shirt was big enough to cover most of her body. She wore yellow dishwashing gloves, a huge fabric face mask (which thankfully was not so weird anymore after the 2018 pandemic), sunglasses that covered pretty much the rest of her face, and a hat with a back flap that came down to cover her neck. Between all of that she was pretty much completely covered.

"Jesus, you must be hot."

"That's what all the boys say," Jade agreed, striking a pose and smacking her own butt.

Cam shook his head, trying to clear himself of what he hoped wasn't a weird, perverse attraction. No. It wasn't sexual. She was just a fascinating, truly unique specimen. He opened the motel door and she was already out, skipping and wringing her hands in delight, rushing headlong toward the pool before he could even say "Follow me."

He glanced back at the white Clicker, near comatose in its tank. After picking it back up safely before departing Los Alamos, he had been loath to leave it unattended, but he supposed they weren't going far and could keep their eyes on the door to their room. He'd assumed he would have to at least fend off cleaning personnel, but, perhaps not surprisingly, that had not turned out to be much of an issue at this particular motel.

The pool was closed, and consequently poorly lit, although he doubted anybody attended to it even in the best of times. And judging by the beer cans and cigarette butts strewn around, the clientele was more likely to be nightswimming high schoolers than actual motel guests.

With a loud splash, Jade and all of her bulky clothes disappeared into the water. He pulled one of the non-lounging chairs over to the side and began poring over the files they'd liberated from Los Alamos. He could almost see by the lights of the pool, but pulled out a flashlight just in case.

When a solid minute had passed, he looked up in alarm, suddenly realizing Jade had been under the whole time. But he saw that she was down there doing figure eights, as elegant as a naked fish even in eight layers of clothes. Of course. She was unlikely to drown. He continued to have trouble seeing her as both a cheerleader and a horrible monster from beneath the ocean waves. He could only ever really keep one image of her in mind at a time.

After ten minutes or so, once Cam was fully absorbed in his work, Jade's no longer masked, sunglassed, or behatted face broke through the surface of the water. In doing so she recreated any number of Cam's fantasies of a bikini model breaking the surface of the ocean and throwing her hair back in the glistening sun, despite being a reptilian horror with an outstretched crest and it being the middle of the night. She put the items she had stripped off her head on the side of the pool.

"What are you doing?" he asked, clicking his tongue in irritation.

"Just the head stuff," she said, "It's dangerous. I'll bash my head into one of these concrete walls and crack my skull."

"Based on what I've seen of your biology, Jade, you'd be more likely to break the concrete."

She shrugged, not trying to deny it. He leafed back to a

different page in the portfolio. This really was fascinating stuff.

"What are you reading?" she asked, seeming to discover the doggy paddle with the delight of someone learning something new about their body for the first time.

"Well," he said, "It seems that twenty years ago your people and this, uh, symbiotic species I've been telling you about..."

"The Clickers?"

"Clickers, yes. I mean, they have a bunch of names. In Australia they're called Chazzwozzers. Anyway, about twenty years ago there was this minor, short-lived incursion in a place called Phillipsport, Maine."

"Never heard of it," she admitted.

He shook his head. "No reason you should've. I've never heard of it, either. Tiny town. And it was wiped out, root and branch."

"I thought you said nobody knew about my kind."

"They don't."

"So how do you wipe out a whole town and get away with it?"

He quirked his head. "That's a very good question."

She nodded and plunged back under water. He continued to devour the information furiously, so furiously, in fact, that the sound of the rest of Jade's wet clothes plopping on the pavement practically pulled him out of a fugue state.

"Jade," he said sharply, although he found some of the edge bleeding out of his voice as he saw her naked body. He'd seen her naked for days but now, flickering under the water, there was something perversely erotic about her.

"It's not comfortable like that," she said. She scratched the back of her head. Maybe the chlorine was getting to her.

He sighed. Realistically, he'd known this was going to happen.

"Has your feral side been coming out since you've been getting wet?"

Her eyes lit up. "The exact opposite, actually. I've never felt so alive, Dr. Custer. I think what made me angry and violent was being on land. In here I feel like I could just swim and luxuriate for the rest of my life."

"Well, don't luxuriate too long or that chlorine's going to give you ich or fin rot or something."

"Hey! That's racist!"

He looked down at her, raising his eyebrow. Her face, alien as it was, was hard to read. "Is it?"

A toothy smile bifurcated her face. "I don't know. Maybe. Do young people get upset about that kind of thing these days?"

"I assure you I have no idea what young people get upset about these days. Oh!"

She stopped treading water and moved over to the side, placing her elbows on the concrete and cradling her chin with her hands. "Something interesting?" He could tell by her reaction that he was not hiding his perturbation well. "Something bad?"

He nodded. "Something a little close to home, in fact."

He held up the file, and fumbled with the flashlight to illuminate it for her. She held up her hand to wave him off. It made sense that as a deep ocean dweller she would have phenomenal dark vision.

"One of those is me, huh," she said grimly.

He nodded. He'd discovered a picture of a clutch of Dark One eggs which the government had recovered from the Phillipsport massacre.

"That would make you about twenty," he said.

She nodded. "Sounds right."

"Good," he said quietly.

"Why is that good?"

Damn, he hoped the blood wasn't rushing to his cheeks. Internally, he mentally chastised himself. He wasn't going to be one of those dirty old men who thought it was okay to date someone a third of his age because she was technically of legal age. Hell, that was probably the least of the issues between them.

"I suppose it doesn't matter. I don't have any specimens of different ages to compare you to."

"So charming. Every girl loves to be referred to as a 'specimen.'"

"I apologize."

"Just fucking with you, Doctor C.," she said, smiling devilishly and backstroking away.

She continued to swim and he continued to read. Finally, despondent, he put the file down. Perhaps noticing his mood, she climbed out of the pool and sat by his feet, hugging her knees.

"You done?" he asked.

"I guess," she said, scratching her neck and the backs of her legs. "You were right about the chlorine."

"We can head up and shower."

"Well, tell me what's bothering you first."

He sighed, not knowing how to put it. "After they recovered you…"

"'Kidnapped' might be a better word."

"Agreed. After they kidnapped you and your siblings the Navy dropped a nuclear device into the ocean off Phillipsport."

"What?"

"They seemed to feel it was the only way to stop any further Dark One or Clicker activity. I suppose genocide is a rather… final solution, as someone once said."

Jade looked somber.

"Listen, Dr. Custer, I don't know how I'm supposed to feel about this. I know what I am, but I was also raised by humans. I have instincts I don't know what to do with, but all of my personal, intellectual, internal life has been spent rooting for humans. I grew up playing with Bratz and watching Kim Possible, you know."

"Stockholm Syndrome," he said, shaking his head.

"Maybe. Maybe I'm Stockholmed and to get my head right I need to get back to my people someday. But right now I feel like one of yours. And I have to say you could imagine how things would have gone the other way. You can imagine a world where they didn't drop the bomb. There might have been other invasions by the Clickers and my people in the aughts and the teens. It could have been tragic for lots of people."

"Yes," Cam agreed, "in some alternate world the Clickers invaded, maybe multiple times, and it was apocalyptic. In ours, every time the government spots one they drop a nuke."

"What do you mean, 'every time?'"

He flipped open the file again.

"Oh, yes. Phillipsport was not the first time. Twenty-three times they tried to invade the Bikini Atoll, and the government claimed it was just testing nukes. I didn't know about this, the Feyzin Disaster in 1966 was actually a European Clicker incursion. Apparently a Clicker stowed away on the *Challenger*. Not sure how that happened unless it had wings, but I know the result. Even the first nuclear test ever was to beat back the Clickers."

"Oh, I know that one. Trinity. Los Alamos."

Cam pulled his legs into a hug, perhaps in imitation of his young charge.

"That's just it, Jade. Trinity wasn't the first nuclear test ever. According to this, the first ever nuclear weapon was actually dropped three years before Hiroshima, at the Battle of Guadalcanal."

38. AUGUST, 1942

Ezekiel wasn't sure whether he wanted to deny everything or run screaming into the jungle. But it was true, he knew in his bones that it was true, and one glance at his leg was all he needed to reaffirm that his reality was still intact.

The monster, the *Clicker* as Boudin called it, had taken more than a chunk out of his leg, pincer squeezing so tight that the bone had been shattered and Basher had hacked away half of the diseased flesh. Now he was walking not an hour later and none the worse for wear. And this man was telling him that they were just the beginning.

"So, the Clickers are pets of these Dark Ones?" Ezekiel asked glancing at Jake who looked equally as mystified.

Alcide nodded. "And weapons. They aren't afraid, just hungry. Even with what I do, the workings have to be specific. One mistake and they're just as likely to devour you as the person you're trying to sic them on."

He, Jake, and Boudin sat in a circle while Gunny Webb directed the rest of the men to form a perimeter. John Pike, a late addition, apparently, to his command, had noticed an empty Tojo sniper nest in a palm tree and had scaled it to keep watch.

Alcide had directed the men to carve a specific symbol into the sand. Webb had given an imploring look to both Jake and Ezekiel not to abide this superstitious nonsense, but the captain had merely pointed to his leg in response.

Whatever Boudin said went. The whole operation was sideways, and if he claimed that these drawings were diverting Clickers from their location, Ezekiel was inclined to believe him.

The Navy cook Doodles was supervising the application

of the designs, occasionally reaching down with his hand to make the drawing longer in places, his finger tracing flourishes, erasing the errors in the other men's work. He had come back to himself, sort of, at the promise of artistic work to do.

"What do the Dark Ones want?" Ezekiel asked, trying his best to picture what Alcide described: seven feet of muscle and scale, with magic even more potent than the hoodoo man sitting before him.

"Wouldn't know it. A tribe of them exists back home and my Pa has dealings with them occasionally. By their reckoning they used to rule the world, before some cataclysm broke their civilization apart," Alcide said shrugging. "Of course, that's all in their own tongue, what they believe. They're not ones for engaging with us humans."

"How do you know, Boudin? How do you know these things are behind the Clickers? It could be the Tojos for all we know," Jake said, casting a wary eye around the trees. "Those albinos wore the Rising Sun."

Alcide chuckled wearily, his finger tracing his own designs, not bothering to look at the XO. "If it walks like a dog and talks like a dog. Trust me, unless the Tojos have gone and learned some magic, this is Dark One work. I have no doubt the Dark Ones are letting the Emperor believe he's in charge, but they're the ones really calling the shots."

Ezekiel hoped he appeared more confident than he felt. Annapolis hadn't prepared him for fish-men or lobsters the size of small cars any better than it had covered the proper protocol for dealing with an enlisted witch doctor.

"Any weaknesses to these things, Boudin? The Clickers and Dark Ones? They seem to come in all varieties. A big obsidian one sprayed acid out of its tail. Killed our contractors, Golden, Maberry, and Moore. Those bearded bastards never saw it coming."

It didn't breed confidence for Ezekiel when he saw the Cajun private's face furrow in confusion. "Never seen a black one before. All the ones back home are the brown kind that are crawling all over the place. Heard tell of different breeds, but none ever trolled the bayou."

Jake snorted. "Good to know, Boudin, but guess what? Now there are white ones running around with Tojo flags on their shells fucking exploding."

Boudin crossed his arms, staring down at his designs. Ezekiel bit his tongue, trying not to be frustrated at the fact that their only source of intel was only working with a half picture.

He addressed Jake. "You might be right, sir. Suicidal, attacking Clickers doesn't sound like anything natural, magic or science. They've got *Kamikaze* Clickers now."

Alcide looked back over at Ezekiel. "Red, black, white... I'm assuming it's all the same. A good shot with the rifle might be able to take them down if you hit them right. Have to be precision fire though. The shells are thick. As for those stingers? One sting is fatal unless you can amputate. Better to avoid it entirely."

Ezekiel had seen the effects firsthand and he wasn't eager to see it repeated.

"Well, unless'n I can get to it in time. The Dark Ones are similar. Rifles should penetrate just fine anywhere you shoot, but they're faster than their pets, tougher when all is said and done. If you don't have a good shot, they'll have your guts in their hands faster than you can blink. And if they get their magic into your minds, they can subvert you." Alcide's face darkened. "I've seen that firsthand."

The tropic night was humid, bits of moisture dropping off the palms, but a cold chill ran up Ezekiel's spine. He tried to think of a plan. The logical thing to do would have been to follow Webb's suggestion and link up with Lieutenant Colonel Puller and the rest of the 7th, but if any of the creatures followed them, they'd be bringing Clickers into the heart of the American presence on Guadalcanal.

"I can send them back into the sea, sir. Just need something for them to follow." Ezekiel watched as the Cajun man's eyes drifted to the castaway still cuddling his pet Clicker tight, before he continued. "It's a powerful spell, but I've got the ingredients on the island. Just need to go get them."

Ezekiel had been on the other side of enough briefings to hear the unspoken bad news that Alcide was leading up to. He didn't even have to bother asking before Alcide finished.

"But my ingredients are in my pack, back at the airfield."

Ezekiel looked at Jake. "You said the Air Forces bombed it?"

Jake nodded. "Real firestorm. Nothing should be crawling or creeping over that blast crater."

Ezekiel had heard promises like that as well and had learned that what *should* have been was often different from what *was*.

He sighed and looked over at the private. "Boudin, you promise you can do this?" The man nodded and Ezekiel steeled himself, realizing that the night's horrors weren't over yet. "Jake, round up everyone. We're going back to Henderson."

39. AUGUST, 1942

"Sir?"

Vice Admiral Frank Fletcher looked up from the stack of papers on his desk. The steward was holding a silver tray with what looked to be a pork chop dinner. He gestured with his hand at the side of his desk.

"Yes, you can put it right there, Enterline."

Fletcher's hand shook, pen poised, but unable to write his own signature. A pall had fallen over the room. The steward, who he remembered now was actually named Triana, paused just a moment too long before placing the tray down. Why in God's name had he called him that? Triana had been serving him for months.

Of course, Enterline was probably on his mind because he had recently seen a dispatch declaring the kid officially lost at sea. Leave it to the Navy to wait more than three months after the Battle of the Coral Sea to make a decision. He never should've allowed that boy's transfer to the *Lexington*.

"They taught me at Annapolis that an officer never apologizes," Fletcher said, "so I…regret calling you by the wrong name, Triana."

"It's all right, sir. It happens to all of us. If you'll pardon my language, sir, it's this damnable war."

Fletcher chuckled wryly. Being a flag officer was a damnable business. It was like he wasn't even a man anymore. He was a little porcelain doll who other sailors thought couldn't bear to hear them swear. Or perhaps Triana had caught that particular character trait from Enterline during their training together. The man had never met a cuss word he wouldn't avoid.

Dammit, his old steward really was haunting his thoughts.

"Have you eaten yet tonight, Triana?"

"Yes, sir."

"Do you know lying to a superior officer is a court martial offense?"

"Well, no, it ain't sir, not by its lonesome. But all I meant was, I was just headed back to the galley now to fix myself something."

"The hell with that. Secure that hatch and have one of these pork chops with me."

Triana shook his head. "That wouldn't be appropriate, sir."

"Bombing Pearl wouldn't be appropriate. Goose-stepping into Poland wouldn't be appropriate. Stabbing a bunch of folks at Nanking wouldn't be appropriate. I'd say the gloves are off when it comes to this damnable war, as you so appropriately put it."

Triana was rubbing his chin. "Well…"

Fletcher reached into his cabinet and pulled out a decanter of Old Crow and a couple of glasses. Without a word exchanged, the deal was sealed. Triana quickly closed the hatch and, with all the confidence of a kid stealing from the cookie jar, pulled up a chair by Fletcher's desk.

Fletcher dumped the salad onto the main plate and started pulling a pork chop and a generous portion of potatoes onto the salad plate for the steward. Triana would have to figure out how to eat his chow with the salad fork and butter knife, but he was confident in the boy's abilities. Wordlessly, they ravaged their food, though he noticed Triana didn't touch his tumbler until Fletcher signaled it was okay by taking a long swallow of his own.

"I've got to tell you, sir, this is awful kind of you. But I don't entirely understand why you would want to eat with me when you've got the captain and all them educated officers to eat with instead. I don't know much about anything except the price of eggs, and in my case that ain't just a sayin'."

"I'll tell you why, Triana," Fletcher said, talking with his mouth full and not even caring, "it's gotten away from me."

"Sir?"

"The Navy. The sea. Look at this. You think I joined up to fill out forms and sign ration requests?

I was a young ensign once. I used to chop it up, get into trouble, girl in every port, rubber in every pocket. You get up to some hijinks down in the galley?"

Triana shook his head vigorously. "Oh, no sir. Chief Malerman runs a tight ship. We don't get up to no mischief."

"You'll make a very good politician one day, Triana. I suggest you run for school board when you get home."

"Thank you, sir."

"Where is home, by the way?"

"Mooresville, North Carolina."

"Is it nice?"

"No, not really, sir."

"Hmm. I'll make a note not to visit there."

Fletcher chewed mournfully. He wasn't lying, but he wasn't exactly telling the truth, either. He didn't miss being a young officer because he wanted to sow his wild oats and raise Cain. He missed those days because the weight of darker responsibilities hadn't been on him. Someone like Triana didn't have to worry about that thing in the hold. Or the men it had killed.

The intercom buzzed. Sensing his brief breach of protocol with the admiral was up, Triana rose from his seat, but Fletcher gestured for him to sit. "I'm sure it's nothing." He pressed the intercom button. "Vice Admiral Fletcher."

"Relay for you, sir," Captain Dewitt Ramsey's unmistakable voice said, "from Pearl."

"Damn," Fletcher muttered. "Thanks, Dewitt. Put it through. Vice Admiral Fletcher."

"Good to hear from you, Admiral Fletcher," a scratchy voice sounded, "This is Admiral Nimitz."

Fletcher frowned. He'd been friends with Nimitz for years. He always called him Frank and usually, unless there were men around, he called him Chester back. Someone else was on the line.

He glanced at Triana, who was petrified. "Relax," he mouthed.

"And a pleasant evening to you, Admiral Nimitz," Fletcher

replied, though it sounded clunky in his ears.

"Listen, I'll be brief, Admiral Fletcher. Well…in fact…I'm just going to hand you over to Washington."

Washington. So that was it. King or somebody wanted to yell at him. What could he possibly have done now? The battle on the land wasn't exactly going swimmingly, but he could hardly be held responsible for what the ground pounders were up to. He was keeping his end up.

"Ah, good evening, Admiral Fletcher," a pleasant, unmistakable patrician voice said, "or whatever time it is there at the, ah, landing at Guadalcanal."

The intercom dropped out of Fletcher's hand. It was a good thing he had told Triana to stay, because if there had been no one else there to witness this he might have believed he was dreaming. They exchanged a look, but neither of them were really unsure about the caller's identity, just confused.

Triana anxiously grabbed the intercom and pressed the button, holding it in front of Fletcher's face.

"Thank…" he swallowed, then tried again, "thank you, Mr. President."

"Well, ah," Roosevelt continued, "I've got Admiral King here with me and General Marshall and we've been discussing this, ah, situation for several days now."

"Frank, this is King," the head of the Navy said over the crackly line. "We've gotten all of your reports. I need to ask you one question. Have you seen these things with your own eyes?"

"I've got one in a cage, sir. Six of my boys got killed subduing it."

That had been an unpleasant time. Like everyone else, Fletcher had marveled at the near miracle of science when all the squids and fish had begun spontaneously beaching themselves. But then those damned monstrosities had scuttled up onto the island. The Japanese prisoners identified them as *Kurikka* and the Aussies had taken to calling them Chazzwozzers for God only knew what reason, but most of the men called them Clickers after the mind-melting noise they made. Even now the ship's guns were trained not out at the threat from the Japanese military, but down at the waterline.

"Normally, ah," the president spoke again, "my primary focus is on the Japanese threat. And the threat of Hitler in Europe, naturally. But the appearance of these, ah, monstrosities, must be dealt with. And swiftly. Admiral Fletcher I am about to ask of you, a great burden. But it is in the service of your country and I hope you will accept my, ah, unconscionable order."

Fletcher looked to Triana, his unwitting confidant, though Triana looked as confused as Fletcher felt.

"I'll obey any lawful order from my chain of command, Mr. President," Fletcher said, feeling limp as soon as the words were out of his mouth.

"Do you want me, sir…?" Fletcher guessed that was Marshall starting to speak.

"No, General. I will not shirk my responsibility as a leader, no matter how bleak the task before me. Admiral Fletcher, this is the President of the United States. I am sending you a weapon. A weapon of, ah, unimaginable destructive force. This is a single bomb which we believe will devastate much of the island of Guadalcanal."

"No single bomb can do that," Triana said, immediately clapping his hand over his mouth. But it was all right, Fletcher's finger wasn't depressing the radio button.

"You took the words right out of my mouth."

"It is apparent that these creatures will not surrender," Roosevelt continued, "They must, therefore, be destroyed. I am ordering you to set this bomb off on the island. Do you understand and concur with the orders I have given, Admiral King?"

"I do so concur," King's tinny voice spoke. "Do you concur, Admiral Nimitz?"

"Yes, sir," Nimitz, sounding somewhat clearer in Pearl Harbor said. "Do you concur, Admiral Fletcher?"

Fletcher swallowed a lump in his throat. If their estimates were accurate, that a significant portion of the island would be devastated by this magical bomb, then a whole lot of American boys were about to buy it. It was a terrible decision to be asked to make. But the president's staff, the staff at Pearl, all the greatest minds in the Navy agreed. Who was he, a lowly fighting admiral to dissent?

Still, he reflected, he knew why he was receiving this weighty call, and not merely an order telegraphed in from Pearl. Everyone in the chain had to be cognizant of what they were doing, open eyes and open ears. Well, Fletcher's eyes were wider open than anyone else's on the line right now.

He'd lied before. Not lied exactly, but misrepresented the truth by underexaggerating. He didn't just have a Clicker in a cage down in the hold. Two nights ago, sleepless, he had come up to observe the night's watch. The *Saratoga*'s deck had been surprisingly quiet, with a wing of bombers out on runs. A few swabbies were mopping down the deck, and he'd walked over to the leeward side to get a good look at the island.

A scratching noise hadn't quite burrowed into his subconscious, but he had noticed it. Looking over the side of the *Saratoga* he had seen not just one, not just a dozen, but hundreds of the crab-like creatures. And they hadn't just been floating uselessly in the waves. Pincer after pincer, they'd stabbed into the aircraft carrier's hull, leaving notches in solid steel as they'd awkwardly scuttled up a reverse incline. Still, they'd come.

Fletcher had drawn his pistol.

"Officer of the watch!" he'd called out.

An earnest looking young ensign, wearing a helmet and carrying a lantern, had hurried over. "Sir?"

"Rouse the crew. Have the master of arms dispense weapons from the lockers. And tell the gun crews to point their weapons down." The man had stared at him dumbfounded. "Move your ass, sailor!"

In the harrowing battle that had followed, several Clickers had managed to haul themselves, legs missing here and there but mostly unharmed, onto the *Saratoga*'s deck. Fletcher had watched with horror as one of the creatures, a fat one covered in disgusting green algae, had stabbed a marine in the heart. Even worse than being stabbed with a pincer, though, the marine had almost instantly disintegrated.

Fletcher had never seen anything like it before. One moment the marine had been standing his ground, firing his weapon. Then his tongue had lolled out of his head and his body had started to sink into his shoes like the Wicked Witch of the

West's. Fletcher had shot the stinger off the thing and kicked its shell in himself.

He tickled the intercom. "This is Admiral Fletcher. I understand your orders, Mr. President, and I concur. I will destroy the island as soon as possible."

40. AUGUST, 1942

"Damn Tojos picked us clean!"

Ezekiel tried to absorb the news as the scouting party returned. Henderson Field wasn't much more than a pockmarked hole in the ground. The airstrip was still intact, but it wasn't going to be servicing any planes in the near future. The ground was littered with monstrous remains, an occasional segmented leg twitching, piles of orange offal steaming in the night.

He'd sent Webb, Preach, the new man Pike, and a few others, ten men in all, with strict orders to find Boudin's pack and fall back to the jungle. They'd returned with two extra men in tow, survivors from the 2nd.They'd taken shelter closer to the edge of the airfield that met the forest and had been planning to pull back when they'd seen two dozen Japanese soldiers come creeping from the trees, picking over the American supplies, Boudin's pack among them. The Tojos had raided them and vanished back into the trees, barely more than ghosts.

"There was nothing we could have done, sir," Webb said, and if Webb said it, that was all there was to the matter. He was neither a hothead nor a coward.

"All right. Make sure you and your men get some water, Gunny," Ezekiel said.

"Yes, sir."

Ezekiel's eyes turned to Boudin, who was leaning against a palm, staring out at the dark. Motioning with one shake of his head, he and Jake headed to join the hoodoo man.

"Heavy thoughts, Robichaude?" Jake asked, finding a comfortable spot on another palm while Ezekiel stood between them.

Alcide glanced at the two before turning back to look out at the darkness. "Just trying to determine if there's anything natural I can use to work a spell, sir. I learned on all the things that grew and creeped through the muddy water…" He drifted off, no doubt thinking of home. When Boudin spoke again it was with a forlorn weariness. "…don't think a coconut is going to pass for a handful of cranberries, though."

Thinking that if he had a handful of cranberries, it would be a great change from the SPAM and rice diet they'd been subjected to over the past days, Ezekiel pressed him. "Can you work anything else with what you have? Make a Clicker crab boil?"

Boudin shook his head and booted a coconut. "Not without my pack. All that I could manage now is a few healings and maybe something that will get you some extra scrip when we get home. Nothing that is going to help us out here."

It wasn't an unexpected answer. Ezekiel had been planning for the possibility that Alcide's pack wasn't recoverable, but knowing that the Tojos had taken it at least gave a definite location and an objective to accomplish.

He glanced to the south and the massive hill towering over the jungle like a dark sentinel. Even now, the Tojos would have been watching the remaining fires, trying to mark any remaining American positions.

The Cajun's pack was there, and if they went for it, they'd die, simple as that. Recon had confirmed the place was a kill zone, hidden bunkers and pillboxes aimed down the hill, eager to churn the flesh of any attacker until they were nothing but bloody meat.

Ezekiel's eyes drifted to Doodles, sitting alone and throwing small bits of his ration to the dog-sized Clicker he called a friend, clapping as the animal scurried and eagerly chewed at the bits of canned pork.

"Maybe that cook knows a way in."

"Maybe, Skipper, but he's got all the sense of axle grease. We'd have better luck capturing a Tojo," Jake said, fishing a hand-rolled cigarette from his uniform pocket, eyeing Ezekiel expectantly.

Ezekiel fished his lighter out of his pocket and tossed it to his friend. Boudin turned his eyes to Doodles. "Don't have a Tojo on hand, sir, but we do have him. The sun might have stir-fried his head, but if you promise he can keep his pet, he'll lead us there."

Ezekiel shook his head. "My promise won't stand up to the first man we see with a leaf on his collar. Everyone in Washington is going to want that thing. OSS, MI, whoever. If the Tojos could weaponize these things, you know the brass is going to want to do the same."

Boudin nodded. "We all know that, but he doesn't."

Jake exhaled, sending a small plume of smoke out of his nose. "Mighty cold-blooded there, Boudin. I might put you in for a field commission."

Boudin shrugged. "Doesn't matter what we tell him, sir. In the end, that Clicker is going back in the water. The spell I have in mind will have any Clickers on this island following Pinchy down to the bottom of the ocean."

"Can't believe he named the damn thing," Jake said, taking one last drag before flicking the cigarette into the darkness.

Ezekiel thought that it wasn't too insane. He'd read stories of men adrift at sea forming connections with the schools of fish that followed them across the ocean. But at the end of the day Doodles's happiness was secondary to the success of their efforts here.

Despite what the propaganda said, the Tojos were just men. They could be made to feel fear, but these Clicker things kept coming even when five bullets penetrated their shells. No matter how many men they killed and ate they always lusted for more death.

Then there were their unseen masters, the ones Boudin had described as even more terrifying than what they had seen already. One man's scrap of lingering sanity wasn't worth the lives of his men or the rest of the leathernecks pounding all over this godforsaken island.

"Enterline," Ezekiel said.

Doodles' head shot up and he clutched Pinchy tighter. Ezekiel gestured for him to join them, which he slowly, reluctantly did.

"Can you get us into that hill?" He pointed.

Doodles's face screwed up. He looked back and forth between Ezekiel and the hill.

"I know it very well, actually."

He was smart enough not to say it to a superior (not to mention a score of angry men with guns) but everything about his posture read, "What are you going to give me if I do?"

"What if I said you could keep your friend there? All of us will make sure that you and…Pinchy both make it home."

The cook didn't answer. Ezekiel saw the conflict, wondering if Ezekiel was lying but then tasting the hope that he wasn't, that there was a happy ending waiting for him. "You promise?"

"You have our words," Jake said, in a voice that could have belonged to a tire salesman, "as officers and gentlemen."

Doodles's eyes narrowed. He pointed at Boudin. "I want your word. Your blood oath or whatever, magician man."

Boudin's lips quivered. "If they're lying to you, may I be struck dead before I make it home."

Doodles shrugged. "Good enough for me."

Ezekiel hoped that Boudin hadn't just laid a curse on himself. But he had no time to worry about such things. Most of them wouldn't need a curse to be struck dead before they got off the Canal. "Jake, get everyone together. Time to dole out marching orders."

"Yes, sir."

It didn't take long for the men to be gathered, staring at Ezekiel expectantly. He tried to steel himself, reminding himself that he was in command, that all of them were looking to him for answers. He wanted more than anything to point at Boudin and tell them to direct their questions towards the Cajun man, that he was the only one who knew what was going on and therefore should be the one calling the shots. But he wasn't about to start shirking his duty now.

Martino, unsurprisingly, sounded off. "What's the fucking plan, Skip? We lighting out back to the goddamn boats? Getting the fuck back to Pearl?"

"Your popsie is going to have to wait for your sugar reports a bit longer, Martino. Half of us are heading straight up Tojo

Hill."He gestured to the dark shadow dominating the south, watching the men squirm and wishing there was another way.

"They've got Boudin's bag, the one with all his mojo and tricks that are going to send these lobsters back into the pot where they belong." He looked at each man, trying to decide who he was going to take up the hill. They had barely eighteen between the guys that Jake had taken off Henderson and the ones Gunny had pulled out with him.

"So here's the plan. The XO and I are taking half of us up the hill. The other half of you are going to go with Gunny and link up with Lieutenant Colonel Puller. If we aren't back by 0600, have the Air Forces pound that hill until it's dirt."

Ezekiel wiped the sweat from his eyes, even as Basher raised a hand. "Yeah, what's the plan for getting up that hill, Skipper? Tojos ain't known for being great hosts."

Ezekiel smiled. "That's where our good friend the cook comes in. He knows the way through the tunnels."

The men groaned.

"Hey, you jarheads are lucky to have someone like me. And if you don't complain, I'll even cook you up a real meal."

Strangely that was what shut up the complaining. Doodles's reputation for foraging had gotten around.

Ezekiel smiled. "All right, then." He turned and picked out the men he was going to take with him. "Boudin, Preach, Basher, Martino, Pike, and Microphone."

Ezekiel approached Webb, who was already barking orders at the rest of the men. The big NCO glanced back at him. "I think this is a fool's errand, sir."

"So do I, actually. But if there's a chance Boudin can do what he says he can, it'll save a lot of good Marines. Just get in touch with Lieutenant Colonel Puller and find a radio. We'll try to send out a call every thirty minutes."

Webb, who he'd never seen break military protocol for even a second, held out his hand, as if unsure how this whole casual business worked anymore. Smiling, Ezekiel took it.

"Good hunting, sir."

"See you on the other side, Arthur."

There'd been no speaking once they had reached the base of the mountain. Doodles had held up the group more than once when they'd heard something moving through the underbrush. Not one of the men had questioned the man's bushwhacking experience, a fact that Ezekiel was extremely grateful for.

They'd passed more than a few rat tunnels, thatch coverings thrown aside to reveal an empty hollow. Even with no apparent sign of occupants, Ezekiel had still felt it safer to make sure they weren't going to suddenly find a Tojo grenade up their ass. He signaled to Basher who clambered up to join the captain, the M1 flamethrower they had scrounged strapped to his back.

"Burn it out," Ezekiel said flatly.

"Aye, Skip," Basher responded, the small wick of flame on the end of the hose igniting. The night blazed with light as Basher doused the hole in flame. The crackling pops of dry leaves going up masked their movements as they continued up the hill. Any Tojo watcher would be drawn to the light, their patrols converging on the area.

"We're close to the first bunker," Doodles whispered to Ezekiel.

He passed the message down the line as they proceeded, each man making sure that his weapon was at the ready. They might have proceeded another quarter mile up the hill when Doodles pulled a large fern back to reveal that the foliage had been cleared. Small, pulped remains of trees and pulverized slabs of concrete looked like they had once formed a bunker of some sort. Admiral Fletcher had done his job too well. It was hard to discern an entrance amongst the rubble.

"We'll have to move some rock, find a way in," Ezekiel mused, thinking that they were far too exposed to do the task safely.

Doodles shook his head. "Nope, nope, they know better than to just sit out in the big obvious bunkers." He pointed past a large triangular sheet of debris. "See the opening in the ground, the one by the tree?"

Ezekiel followed his finger and saw a square of darkness blacker than the rest of the night around it, wedged between a tree with scraggly branches and a slab of shattered concrete that a battleship shell had reduced to near rubble. It was a machine gun nest disguised as part of the hillside, and more than likely had two or three Tojos inside ready to pull the trigger and leave him and the rest bleeding in the grass.

Luckily, he had someone who could do the same, just in reverse.

"Jake, get Pike up here," Ezekiel whispered, watching the command be passed down the line. The ranks parted as the sergeant moved up as quietly as he could.

"What have you got, sir?" Pike whispered, eyes surveying the darkness, no doubt trying to pick out the telltale glint of a gun barrel.

"Machine gun nest, between that bunker and the tree. Mind seeing if anyone is home?"

Pike licked his thumb and held it to the wind. He glanced at Ezekiel and then squinted into the darkness. "Any way you can give me a flare, First Lieutenant Dempsey?"

Pike shouldered his rifle and aimed, nodding at Jake who pulled the trigger on the flare gun. The night suddenly blazed with light and Ezekiel heard Pike's breath catch in his throat. He fired twice in rapid succession, then exhaled, shouldering the rifle. "Two dead Tojos. Looked surprised to see us. Didn't invite us in for cake, though."

Ezekiel nodded, turning to look at the cluster of men. "Thank you, Sergeant Pike. Men, follow me."

Time always seemed to slow for Ezekiel in these moments. His senses seemed to heighten as he became aware of the sounds of insects buzzing, or the sputtering crackle of the flare overhead, the anxious breathing of the men as they prepared to run. It was possible they'd missed a rat's nest, that Doodles hadn't been as thorough on his scouting, or maybe he'd just gotten lucky. He felt his chest tighten as he held up his hand, raising his fingers. Then he was sprinting from cover.

The flare cast a baleful white light over the hill, long shadows stretching out from the bunker rubble. Ezekiel imagined the eyes of Tojos lurking there, hands on their rifles and ready to rush them, hollering as they stabbed their bayonets into his guts.

Then the shadowed figures of his mind changed. Human figures warped into segmented chitin, pincers, and waving stingers. The sounds of his own footfalls sounded like clicking.

He practically dove through the nest opening, wincing as he scraped his knee against the machine gun propped in the gap, falling and feeling the soft give of a body break his fall.

Ezekiel scrambled to his feet and aimed his weapon at a dead man. The rest of his men followed suit, sliding through the opening and landing on the corpses of the Tojos resting on the bunker floor. The flies that had been feasting on the splattered blood strewn everywhere buzzed in angry circles at the intrusion.

There were four corpses in the bunker and Ezekiel felt bile rise in the back of his throat as he realized that the man he had landed on was missing most of his throat and his chest had been hollowed out, pulped bits of internal organs laid across the dirt floor. The rifles had been snapped in half, the machine gun metal marred with long marks that Ezekiel could have sworn were made by claw.

"These two must have already been dead when I put two in them," Pike said, his granite voice softening as he pointed at two of the dead Tojos. Their mouths were slack, hollow eyes staring into a void, a small flap of skin and bone the only thing attaching their heads to their bodies.

There wasn't much to the bunker, just a rectangular space of dirt and mud, a flag emblazoned with the Rising Sun, a few crates of ammunition that wouldn't fit the American weapons, and a yawning black tunnel.

Jake nudged one of the corpses with his feet. "Shit, they bought it bad. Don't look like those oversized lobsters got them, though, or the bodies would be all melted." He looked to Boudin. "Is this the handiwork of your Dark Ones, Boudin?"

Boudin was crouching, fingers dabbing into the exposed flesh of a dead Tojo. "No doubt in my mind. They must've had some kind of truce with Tojo. But Dark Ones can't keep their aggression in check forever." He stood and nudged the corpse with the end of his boot. "And they love the taste of warm blood."

Ezekiel grimaced and forced himself to turn away. "Microphone, get on the horn and report our position."

The wiry man nodded and immediately went to operating the short wave equipment, poking the antenna out of the emplacement opening and whispering the code words for contact over the airwaves.

Ezekiel motioned for Boudin to join him at the entrance to the tunnel. He could feel the cool air radiating out of the darkness along with the copper scent of blood.

"What do you think is down there, Boudin?" he asked.

"More of the same, and a fucking filet of fish-men, I expect." Boudin said with a grim smile.

The light from the flare sputtered out and the darkness of the tunnel seemed to stretch out and overtake them, the men's low voices falling away into furtive whispers.

"What now, Skipper?" Preach whispered through the gloom.

Ezekiel left Boudin at the entrance of the tunnel. The men stood in a semi-circle inside the emplacement and Ezekiel braced himself, trying to seem as if he wasn't sending all of them to their deaths.

"How about a prayer, Corporal Cantor? Something…brief."

Preach looked surprised but nodded.

"Steady our feet, Lord. Turn our plowshares into swords and steady our hands for war."

"Good enough. The plan is simple, Preach, you're on point. Basher, you're covering him with the flamethrower. Everyone else is in a staggered line. First Lieutenant Dempsey is taking up the rear."

He could barely see the outline of the men's faces, but could tell that each one was uneasy. There was a certain comfort in facing men, but when you were crouching in the remains of a monster's work, it forced a shift in perspective.

Ezekiel sighed heavily, removing his helmet and running a hand through his own hair. "Listen, I can't promise we are all going to make it through this. You've all heard Boudin's stories, and I can't say I don't believe him, especially with what we've seen." He hoisted his carbine and stood. "But I can promise that we aren't going down without taking a bunch of the ugly fuckers with us." There was a round of chuckles as Ezekiel stood and motioned for Doodles. "You're with me."

All of them sat in silence for a moment as Ezekiel made sure that Doodles was secure between him and Martino. The man was jumpy and looked like he would rather be anywhere else. Ezekiel passed him his Colt sidearm, the sun-addled cook looking bewildered as he gently took the pistol, cradling Pinchy the Clicker in the crook of his left arm.

"That thing isn't going to do you any good if we run into trouble," Ezekiel murmured to him, patting him on the shoulder. "After you, Preach."

One by one, they each vanished into the dark.

41. AUGUST, 1942

As a child, Doodles used to whistle past a graveyard he passed every day on his way to school. Part of the reason was that the place was always so damned unkempt. Kudzu climbed the steel gates and it seemed like a puff of strong wind would push the concrete barriers over. If any Draculas ever tried to come after him, he didn't think the fence would do much to stop them, let alone slow them down. But the other reason was that he knew he'd end up there one day. Half the stones in there read Enterline, from his massive extended family in the area. He didn't even like to turn his head to look at them all.

He tried to whistle now, as he plunged into the darkness, but his lips were too damn dry. He licked them and tried to call up a jaunty tune that had gotten him through many walks to school.

A hard slap struck the back of his head.

"What the fuck are you doing?" Martino's voice stage whispered. "Keep it quiet."

Doodles nodded. The light was beginning to fade from the mouth of the cave. And he felt the ceiling beginning to rush up to his head until finally he had to crouch to move.

Click-click?

Doodles reached down and petted Pinchy reassuringly.

"Don't worry, old buddy," he whispered, an actual whisper unlike Martino's overloud attempt, ironically, to quiet him, "We'll be fine."

Soon he was down to crawling on his knees and holding his hand up in front of his face to make sure he could still see it when he could no longer spot Captain Palmer in front of him.

Then, minute by minute the darkness grew stronger and the hole grew narrower. Finally, he was crawling on his hands and knees, and could no longer move with Pinchy abreast of him. The friendly little Clicker skittered ahead of him, but didn't stop darting back to try to tangle up his arms as he moved.

Doodles's heart began to race as he realized he could see nothing and had no idea what was in front of him aside from Pinchy, and even that was based only on the abortive clicking of his banded claws and the skittering of his legs.

Suddenly his arms gave out in front of him, and he felt himself lurching forward into what had to be a bottomless pit.

"Great googly moogly!" he shouted, his words disappearing into the distance.

He pitched face forward and knew this was it. He was going to snap his neck at the bottom of some cave in some godforsaken island eight thousand miles from home. Heavy hands grabbed the collar of his blouse and he felt his feet flip out underneath him. For a moment he dangled, and while he could see that they had stepped into what looked like an underground grotto, he could not see the bottom of the gaping hole beneath.

He turned to his savior. Captain Palmer had caught him and the lighter in his hand explained why Doodles could see a little bit ahead. He was standing on a ledge that seemed to run the circumference of the grotto. Slowly, wordlessly, Palmer helped him until his stumblebum feet found their footing again.

"Tell the man behind you," he whispered.

Doodles nodded. In the sudden light he noticed Boudin, up ahead, was surreptitiously pocketing some weird supplies. He didn't believe the man was really a witch doctor or whatever. For one thing, witch doctors were supposed to be crazy and arrogant, and Boudin seemed to do everything he could to hide his talents. But maybe he'd just cast some kind of voodoo to save Doodles's life. Between being stranded on an island, sliced bread, and becoming best friends with a prehistoric crab monster, Doodles had definitely seen stranger things.

He crouched down.

"Look out for the lip," he said in a fairly normal voice, "pass it on."

Martino grunted by way of reply. With a moment to catch his breath, Doodles thought he would relax after his near-death experience, but sudden panic caught up with him. Where the hell was Pinchy? He looked all around, his sight limited by the wavering matches, lighters, and flashlights the men ahead of him were holding, but Pinchy was definitely not on the ledge. The men in front of him were starting to sidle along the ledge, moving forward.

He'd screwed up twice already, first by trying to whistle and second by almost falling, but he really wanted to call out for Pinchy. Instead, he patted his thigh rhythmically, as he did whenever trying to call his friend, and hoped the others wouldn't notice the low drumbeat.

Much to his relief, Pinchy came sidling up the side of the grotto, as though walking sideways up a sheer cliff face were no harder than falling off a log. He supposed if he had prehensile legs like that, it would be.

"You scared me," he muttered, patting his friend on the head as he fell into line with the other edging Marines.

Click-click.

"It's okay. I forgive you."

In front of him, fists rose and he raised his own to signal the halt. Preach, out front, pointed to the right. Doodles dutifully passed that signal back as well. When it came his turn he saw that somehow Preach had identified an even tinier tunnel than the one they had passed through to get to the grotto at about chest height. The men ahead were either crazy or fearless, because they just folded their arms back and began crawling in.

"Hey, Enterline, you fuck," Martino muttered.

"Huh?"

"You know why they fucking call it spelunking?" Martino tossed a rock into the grotto. It landed ten seconds later with a loud splash. *"Spelunk,"* he said.

Doodles rolled his eyes.

Click-click.

Doodles looked to Pinchy, but knew from long experience that those were not the dulled sound of his friend's language. No, those clicks had been sharper.

Click. Click-click. Clickety-clickety…

His gorge rising, Doodles looked over the side of the grotto. The telltale clicking sounds were echoing over every surface. Though it was deep and dark and a long way to the black water surface below, there was definite movement coming out of the water.

"Nice joke with the rock, you Garbanzo bean!" he said to Martino.

To his surprise, Martino grabbed him and shoved him out of the way, pushing his way forward to the spider hole Preach had managed to douse out. Doodles didn't quite fall this time, aware of the ledge and its limits, but Martino had not been kind in shoving him aside, and his feet scrabbled for purchase, only his toes grabbing onto the ledge. Then they weren't even his toes, and he felt himself sliding nauseatingly down toward the briny depths below. He managed to just cling to the edge of the cliff with the tips of his fingertips as the other ground pounders rushed by, either not noticing his precarious position or not caring.

All around him, but maybe fifty feet below, a scrum of angry, chittering Clickers boiled up toward him like the New England clambake from Hell. He wasn't a praying man, but he guessed this was it.

"Well, God…" he said, but got no further before two enormous claws wrapped around his waist, gently cradling him instead of slicing him in two as he knew they easily could have. Pinchy lifted him back up onto the lip. Two ruptured rubber bands lay on the cliff face.

"You broke your bands?"

Click. Click-click-click.

"You could have any time and just chose not to?"

Pinchy shrugged, such as it could. It wasn't really saying any of this, and even in his addle-brained state, Doodles knew it was still just a lobster monster, not a human or even a smart chimp. But he guessed that was the gist of it when Pinchy didn't immediately decapitate him with his newly liberated claws.

A bit unnecessarily, considering how easily he could move horizontally, Doodles grabbed Pinchy and lifted him up to the chest-height hole. Pinchy skittered down.

Doodles looked back up to Heaven. "Not today, motherfucker!"

Then he plunged into the tiny tunnel, just as a million claws began to appear over the lip of the grotto.

42. AUGUST, 1942

Alcide found himself pulling at the roots of exposed plants as the group crawled through the tunnel. He wasn't sure if any of it was going to be helpful in the short run. Most magic was built on knowledge passed down and experimentation was dangerous. So dangerous, in fact, that it usually ended with the wet mass of something that had once been human quivering on the floor. Only madmen risked it normally. Needs must when the devil came knocking, but this time he had come clicking.

Pike turned around to him. "Cantor says it opens up. Looks like we've reached the main corridor."

Alcide nodded and passed it to Microphone. The man nodded so hard his glasses flew off into the dirt. His hands immediately scrambled to find them, a hard task in the pitch-blackness of the tunnels.

Poor bastard.

The thought came unbidden, but Alcide couldn't help but think it was true. If things got hairy, if an already fucked up situation became even more hopeless, he didn't expect Microphone to make it far. He was just a kid. Same as Trick. Alcide didn't want to think about Trick, though.

"They're two inches in front of your left hand," Captain Palmer, just behind Microphone murmured, his lighter lighting up the darkness and causing the faces of the cramped men to materialize like they were specters that had been long buried beneath the earth.

Retrieving his spectacles, Microphone positioned them back on his face at the same time that there was some kind of commotion back the way they had come. Alcide had traversed the gap easily enough, but it sounded like the cook was having difficulty.

"I'd better go back and check on him," Palmer said. "You men keep moving."

Palmer's lighter went out and Alcide was crawling forward again, shutting his eyes to protect himself from the dirt clods Pike was kicking up in front of him. The air was hot and cloying, the taste of sweat dripping into his mouth and scent of earth heavy as he crawled.

Behind him, Microphone was trying to hide it, but Alcide could hear his breath quickening. The fifteen minutes of crawling was already doing a number on him. Gunny Webb had always been on his ass even to stay inside his foxhole, but the man didn't like tight spaces. In front of him Pike seemed to be as cool as a cucumber. He supposed you had to be that way to be a good sniper.

The tunnel opened up into what looked like a reinforced bunker and behind him Alcide could hear Microphone's sigh of relief. One solitary string of lights illuminated the hallway in harsh orange glow. When he stuck his head through, he noticed that theirs wasn't the only hole carved into the dirt and rock. A dozen more stretched out of the light's sight and into the gloom.

Alcide tumbled out into the floor and was immediately picked up by Preach and Basher. He and Pike turned back to help Microphone claw his own way out as well. The five men braced to start helping the others out, but no one came. Preacher turned to Microphone.

"Isn't the Skipper back yet?"

"I…I don't know," the radioman stuttered.

"Well, he was right behind you!" Preach said.

"The skipper went to help out the cook," Boudin said, "It been a minute now, though."

They all jumped back as a surprised scream came echoing out of the opening.

Every man stood frozen, staring at the hole as panicked shouts sounded, followed by the crack of a rifle being shot, and then another…

Microphone began shouting questions down the tunnel,

trying to reason out what was happening and hearing nothing but the panicked gunfire. Then another sound came over the screams, loud enough to nearly silence them, each new noise overlapping and echoing off the tunnel walls.

Click-click-click-click-CLICK-CLICK

Alcide saw the blood drain from Preach's face. He started shedding his gear.

"I'm going back for them!"

Pike brought a hand down on Preach's shoulder. The man didn't even seem to be flustered. And though he didn't say it, he had one stripe more than anyone else there.

"Don't be an idiot, Corporal Cantor. Has anybody got a flare?"

Microphone nodded and broke a flare, then tossed it back into the tunnel, and though it was now lighted, the situation of the rear detachment was no clearer. Pike knelt down, and though there was nothing like wind down in the tunnels, licked his thumb and held it up as he positioned his sniper rifle at the hole.

Boudin's mind immediately flashed to Trick.

"Wait, you're not going to…"

"No," Pike said calmly, "I'm just going to cover their escape."

"You, with the flamethrower. What's your name?"

"Basher, Sergeant."

"Get behind me, Basher. If I jump out of the way and call for you, you know what to do. The rest of you, shake a leg. I'll buy you some time."

Despite the rather clear orders, Microphone, Preacher, and Alcide didn't take a step. Grimly, Alcide stepped up to the tunnel entrance and felt around the opening, cursing under his breath when he realized that it wasn't soft earth but hardened stone on all sides.

Sliding his knife out of its sheathe, he cut onto his upper arm, deep enough that a dark red stream of blood came flowing out. Dabbing his hand into the cut, he stepped up and began drawing the guarding symbols on the stones.

"What are you doing?" Preach asked, stepping up next to him.

Alcide didn't look at him, his eyes dancing across as he drew the interconnected lines and symbols. "Making sure that whatever is chasing them isn't going to come boiling out of that tunnel."

43. AUGUST, 1942

Jake panted, scooting backwards as fast as he could, occasionally stopping to fire back into the gloom. He heard one of the things hiss as the bullet hit it, but in the dark Jake could only guess at its wounds.

He'd struck a match when he'd reached the head of the tunnel, cursing at Doodles to get his ass moving. Without the light he didn't know if he would have been able to see them. As soon as the cook had shoved himself into the hole, they'd come surging over the edge of the crevasse. Most of the Clickers were no bigger than his hand, but there were a shitload of them.

"Son of a..." he didn't have time to finish his curse before the first ones reached him, stingers stabbing at his boots, unable to penetrate the soles. They must have been juveniles. Jake stamped, crushing four of the monsters beneath his boot, firing with his Thompson, the blow knocking a few more back.

He threw himself to his belly and began to crawl backwards through the tunnel, barely keeping ahead of the little fuckers as they stopped to feast on the flesh of their dead siblings. The last thing he saw was the sight of more coming up over the edge of the crevasse.

When he'd been a kid, he'd seen his uncle throw out bait into the dirty brown pond behind his house. The water had roiled as the fish fought each other for the food, scales gleaming and churning up the mud so much that Jake was sure that the entire pond had come to life.

"A nest! The dumb fuck tripped a damn nest!" he shouted to the tunnel. "Martino, I'm going to kill you, you asshole!"

"Sorry, XO!" Martino's voice echoed back, so matter of fact

that Jake could barely even stay mad. Besides, he had more pressing worries.

Jake scooted on his hands and knees backwards through the tunnel towards Ezekiel and the rest, his breath coming quick, occasionally firing back the way he came, the panic building as his heart beat like the thrum of a battleship's engine.

The ping of his Thompson running empty seemed to echo louder than monsters' pincers and his heart froze as he began to dig through his jacket, looking for an extra magazine. Clicking echoed off the chambers, loud enough that Jake was sure that the darkness before his eyes concealed a veritable city of Clickers, just coming at him in the dark.

He felt something brush against the edge of his fingers, and in the murk he wasn't sure if he had imagined it, or if a baby Clicker had just misjudged its mark.

"Fuck this," he whispered to himself, slinging the Thompson and thrusting his hands into the dirt. Shoving himself as far back as he could go, crawling fast enough that he imagined he was like a worm slithering its way through the dirt.

The clicking began to fade and Jake smiled, his heart slowing just a beat. He was going to make it. The things were practically mindless, stopping to eat the flesh of their comrades instead of dealing with him. He'd reach the tunnel exit and chuck a few frags up back the way they had come and bury the fuckers.

He was already digging for the pineapple in his jacket when his head bashed into the back of the cook's feet.

"What the fuck are you doing!?" Jake hollered, slapping at the cook and trying to usher him to move. His slaps became more and more frantic as he heard the creatures' sounds growing louder.

Through the muffled dirt, he heard the cook say, "Pinchy is stuck!"

Jake gritted his teeth, a small whine escaping as he dug deep not to just shout or get violent. The tunnel had suddenly become very well lit. Someone must have tossed a flare in. He could see the white Clicker with the distinctive cartoon inked on its back pinned under a piece of rock which had shaken loose from the ceiling.

"Doodles. Christopher. Listen to me. You need to go. I will get your friend."

"No you won't. You all hate him."

"You get your ass out of here you dumb squid!" Jake shouted, shocked at his own command voice peeking through, which in that moment could have cowed Gunny Webb. "The United States Marine Corps does not leave any man…or beast… behind. I said I will get your friend out and I will. Now move!"

He almost cheered when he felt the cook begin to move again. With the way cleared, he glared at Pinchy.

"I ought to leave you. But I gave my word as an officer and a gentleman."

He jammed his Thompson under the rock. It was a terrible thing to do to a weapon, but he was out of options if he wanted to live. Lever formed, he put his full body weight on it, and dislodged the hard black rock long enough for Pinchy to scuttle out.

It was at that moment Jake felt the barest hints of claws begin to touch his boots. Panic seized his chest as stingers began falling. None could pierce his boots, but a moment later he began to feel tiny stings, like his sister pinching his legs when they were kids.

He didn't squeal like he did when they were children, but this was worse. The burning started and it took everything he had not to wrap himself up and bawl. He moved forward and every inch came with a new stab.

Jake vomited, then had to crawl through the puddle of hot bile in the dark, his chest seizing as he struggled to breathe. He was aware of vague movement ahead of him. Doodles was struggling just like he was in the cramped space between rock and earth.

Through blurred eyes he saw something that looked like light. Ezekiel and all the others were calling to him. He brought the grenade into his hands, pulled the pin, and let it drop behind him as he kept crawling forward.

A few seconds passed before the explosion sounded. There was a mass of hissing and then the rumbling of disturbed earth. He had halfway made it out of the tunnel when the ceiling came crashing down on his lower half.

44. AUGUST, 1942

Ota Hanshiro screamed into the void. Briny saltwater filled his lungs. The *Umibozu* creation had hollowed him out, every pump of fetid venom shutting down more and more of himself until only his mind was active.

This creature was infinitely more advanced than anything he had been able to create in the laboratory. As a scientist, he didn't believe in magic, but whatever its nature, the dark power of the *Umibozu* could create far more complex things than he could.

The water went above his head. He desperately willed himself to stay above the sea, shouting into the void of his mind that the brain *Kurikka* had created to take a breath of air and turn back towards the land.

But his head sank beneath the waves and the darkness of the ocean overtook him. His lungs were no longer working, but his tongue could taste the salt as the seawater flowed down his throat.

He was slower than the rest, the Dark Ones whose forms had become murky silhouettes as they dove deeper. He felt the water sliding through his hands, thin bits of flesh already beginning to grow between the gaps in his fingers.

Webbing, like a lizard or frog.

This new revelation only led to more mental screaming as he tried everything that he had to will his hand to move a different direction to head back to the surface. His hands moved under his control again and he laughed in triumph before more pain shot through his shoulders. The brain *Kurikka* tightened its grip until his mind was subsumed again.

Ota wasn't sure if "subsumed" was the right word. No alien mind was replacing his own, but his thoughts, morals, and emotions were transforming into something new. He was Ota Hanshiro, colonel in the Emperor's Army, but he also would not rest until all humans, his beloved wife and unborn child included, drowned before the never-ending water.

Emperor... Chieftainess... Tokyo...R'lyeh...

The thoughts ebbed and flowed like the tide itself and with every hot sting of venom injected into his spine, his body, like his mind, transformed further.

"How long will you be useless for?" the bio-vizier asked him, working on a mighty and ancient device of arcane provenance.

"I...wish to be of use," something that was not Ota replied.

She grabbed one of his hands and looked at it, turning it over.

"Until your hands have developed, you will only be able to do crude work. Go, aid the little brothers in defending our city."

The waters were thick with *Kurikk*...with Clickers, hard carapaces brushing against Ota's arms as he floated in the abyss. He could feel his new brethren speaking in his head, simple, animal ideas. There was a patrol boat above, with fourteen juicy humans on board. The Clickers were curious, black eyes staring upwards, tails quivering as they sensed the presence of new meat. It was when the splashing began that the creatures angrily swarmed towards the surface.

The Ameri...the humans had just dropped the second of the oddly shaped objects when the first pack of Clickers came scuttling over the side of the hull. Through the water he could hear the dull sounds of panic, the gunfire, Clicker corpses sinking through the murk and trailing blood behind them.

The Ota-thing watched all of it, his mind torn between joy, pride, hunger, and terror.

A body floated past him, eyes wide and clawing at his throat as he tried to breathe, Ota floated closer to him, reaching out a hand to the dying American's face. His mind flickered away into the monster he was becoming and he dug his fist into the man's dissolving flesh. The meat came away easy and even as he screamed inside his head, he shoveled the sweet tasting slurry into his mouth, feeling the warmth wash down his throat. The human had time to stare in abject terror before his lungs gave out and he sucked in a deep lungful of sea water.

The Clickers came, five of them digging into the soft slush of liquefied blood and bone. One of the survivors on the PT boat decided that this was it and detonated the fuel. A chorus of high-pitched wails of agony sounded and a brilliant ball of fire lit the night sky. And below the waves, the thing that had been Ota Hanshiro was knocked dizzy, the force of the explosion knocking him into a reef. The brain Clicker on his back was stunned from the impact against the hard coral.

For a moment the ways of the deep were gone, the dark voices of the *Kurikka* and *Umibozu* no longer whispered in his head, and Ota summoned his will. He could move his arms and legs again. He began to swim. The ocean was dark, and the abyss seemed to go on forever. There was nowhere to go, really. The home islands were too far and even if he could make that journey, the *Umibozu* would still have their hold on him.

His lab, his studies, if he could make it there… he might have a chance.

So Ota swam up through the underwater passages to the caves he and the rest of the Unit 731 men had taken shelter in for the past few years, where he had bred and studied his albino and *Kamikaze Kurikka*.

The brain *Kurikka* was beginning to come around. Its claws beginning to tighten, sending pain racing up and down his spine. Liquid heat began to pump from the thing's tail again. He emerged from the pool inside the cavern at the same time that he lost control of one of his arms.

It wasn't much more than twenty feet from the opening to the underwater river to the metal grate that he had installed to keep his experiments from rampaging across the island. The distance seemed impossible. He felt a hot pinch of pain as the nerves in his left leg were commandeered. He limped along with just the right, desperate to reach the door and save himself. The new personality the brain *Kurikka* was injecting him with obviously other ideas.

In the end, before he could even reach the lever, Ota

Hanshiro found himself gibbering to himself, fighting the thing on his back, but no longer able to move.

And so, he sat there in the dark until the iron grate began to lift, exposing the dim light of the cave.

45. AUGUST, 1942

Ezekiel stared with wide eyes at his best friend. He'd heard the screams, the explosion, saw the flash of light and plume of dust that came shooting from the tunnel mouth. But it hadn't prepared him for the sight of Jake. He'd immediately tried to pull him out of tunnel only for Boudin and Martino to hold him back, but even they couldn't stop him from reaching out a hand, a motion that Jake mimicked.

His face was pale white. He'd only managed to get one arm free before the tunnel had come crashing down on him, the same arm that was now beginning to swell up larger than the hot dogs that his father had made for everyone on Independence Day.

"Ez-ek-iel…" Jake rasped, his tongue like a fat worm on a hook, chest coated in his own filth.

He struggled out of the men's grasp and when he gripped Jake's hand, the skin popped like a bubble in a pool, liquid flesh and bone melting into a slush on the floor, one that Ezekiel didn't care that he was squatting in.

"Jake, Jake, stay with me," Ezekiel murmured, desperately trying to pick up the glop off the floor and shove it back into the stump of his friend's arm.

"Go… go…" Jake gargled the words, stretching his neck out, pained breathing escaping his lungs.

Ezekiel shook his head, even as out of the corner of his eye he saw flickers of movement in the other tunnels.

"Come on, Skipper. There's more coming," he heard Preach say as more hands were laid on him.

Ezekiel shook his head desperately and they had to pull him

along. Jake strained his neck out, eyes bulging, and before they dragged him away, Ezekiel watched as the flesh sloughed off his bones.

46. AUGUST, 2020

Cam inserted the nozzle into the fuel tank of the beat-up windowless van he had managed to get after taking out a payday loan in Wichita. He didn't have a paycheck, but that hadn't seemed to matter to the payday loan guy.

He sighed. Not loudly, he'd thought, but then Jade had those super-hearing ears of hers. She said she could hear almost two miles off underwater. On land it was less, but still amazing.

"What's up?" she asked, her voice muffled behind the mask.

Cam glanced around. A truck stop on I-70 wasn't exactly Times Square, but it was a damn sight more crowded than the deserts of New Mexico. Luckily, the Dark One dressed up like Dark Man wasn't even the craziest looking thing on this side of the gas pumps. The truckers with their thousand-yard stares didn't seem to be eavesdropping on the conversation of the marine biologist and what could have been the Elephant Man for all they knew.

Cam turned out his empty pocket. "That's the last of it."

"Bah," she said, "Come on, Doctor C. You've been saying that since I met you."

"Well, this is officially the last dollar of the last loan anyone will ever give me, and I got it from a particularly dimwitted loan shark in Wichita. But knowing my luck he'll probably be at the front of the line of people who want to break my kneecaps."

They clambered into the van. Cam glanced backward to check on the white Clicker, in his miniature, refrigerated tank. The creature had been miserable being cooped up, and ultimately Cam had jacked the refrigeration unit up to maximum, putting it in a state of near hibernation. Every day they checked it and fed it a bit, but it barely moved any more, and Cam hoped that he wasn't causing the creature irreparable harm. The smiling caricature on its back didn't make clear one way or another how the actual beast felt.

Jade thankfully waited until they were back on the highway before unwrapping the raw, slightly rotting fish they had picked up in St. Louis. Boy, did it stink. She devoured it completely, eyes, bones, and all.

Davis had never let her eat the way her own kind did. He'd insisted on human behavior from her in every sense. She had to eat, sleep, walk, talk, everything like a homo sapiens. In a guarded moment she had admitted to Cam that the only time in her life she'd felt like her taste buds were really alive had been ripping the nose off her "father's" face. It seemed Dark Ones thrived on hot blood and flesh still warm from body temperature rather than cooked.

But, failing that, she could tolerate some seafoods, and actually seemed to prefer them a bit rotted. That was probably evolutionary, Cam reflected. Her kind could only have subsisted on living sealife or refuse. Noodles and cheese and sandwiches were all strange and foreign to her metabolism.

In another moment of rare candor, she had admitted that for the first time in her life, outside Olathe, she had taken a proper, dry, pellet-like dook. For twenty years she'd suffered near endless diarrhea, and had only been able to identify it as strange after returning to a semi-ordinary diet for her species. With some embarrassment he'd asked her permission to take the spoor as it would be immensely valuable to his research. For a while she'd called him "Peter Peter Pooper Scooper" and the like, but he hadn't minded. She was fun and energetic, and her presence revivified him.

"Are we going to make it?" she asked, tossing the fish packaging out the window. "Yeah, we're going to be just fine."

He reached out and clasped her shoulder genially. He realized with a start that this was the first time he'd touched Jade since the moment they met, when he'd tried to examine her like a specimen and in a rage she'd nearly torn his head off. He snatched his hand back.

"I'm so sorry," he said, "I forgot for a moment."

She reached out and took his hand in her own. Her skin felt rough, like an alligator's, not smooth, like a snake's. Her eyes were soft, almost too soft for the alien monstrosity she was. "It's all right, Doctor C.," she said, "It's all right. I've come to trust you. Although…sorry, never mind."

"What?" he asked.

A beeping horn drew his attention back to the road. He'd been spending so much time looking at Jade, thinking about Jade, fawning over Jade, that he had nearly swerved into the other lane. He hadn't come real close to a collision, but he had made a real ass of himself as the driver of the red pickup truck made quite clear by flipping Cam off as they pulled up alongside.

"Fuck you, libtard!" the man hollered, honking his horn loudly, causing it to play "Dixie" while the pipes on the top of his pickup began blowing huge clouds of black, coal-like smoke.

"Ah, let me do it," Jade hissed.

Cam shook his head, keeping his hands at ten and two and not taking his eyes off the road. He was doing his damnedest to pretend he couldn't see the redneck and would have rolled up the window to avoid hearing him if the window rollers on the 1985 POS he had bought still worked.

"I said, 'Fuuuuuuck you, you fucking cuck!'" the pickup driver yelled.

Cam gritted his teeth, insisting on the path of least resistance, although it now seemed that being passive was leading to more resistance. Out of his peripheral vision he could see that the pickup's passenger was now mooning him. Cars were lining up behind them in the passing lane, but they seemed quite dedicated right now to making a row on the highway.

"What's it going to hurt to let me do it just once?" Jade asked. "How many times are you going to be on the highway in a car with the real-life Creature from the Black Lagoon?"

He turned back to her, shrugged, and decided to throw caution to the wind for five goddamned seconds. He nodded. Jade ripped off all her face coverings and shoved her lithe body into the hole between Cam and the wheel. She bared her teeth and roared ravenously at the couple rolling coal. Cam didn't get the chance to see her monstrous visage, but could tell from the way she was quivering in his lap that she was giving them a real show. Such a show, in fact, that the pickup swerved and went flying right into the concrete median.

Jade slunk back into her seat, an impossibly shit-eating grin on her toothy lips. She quickly pulled her disguise back on as the cars the coal rollers had been holding back started passing Cam, signaling their apparent pleasure with honks. Cam glanced in the rearview mirror.

"I think those fuckers are dead," he said. "Shit, we're leaving the scene of an accident."

"I wouldn't worry about it, Doctor C. Between us we're already guilty of kidnapping, murder, and breaking like, a million federal privacy laws and shit. Leaving the scene of an accident is going to be way down the list on your rap sheet."

Cam closed his eyes in horror for just a second, then remembered he was driving and re-opened them. He knew there might be repercussions for his actions, but he'd never really thought of it all at once like that. Hearing their crimes strung together in a single paragraph, they surely did sound like Bonnie and Clyde.

But, Cam reflected, they were setting out on a quest to save the world. If he could prove to this administration beyond a shadow of a doubt that climate change was real, they might actually take some action to arrest it. And if that meant finding a bunch of imaginary cryptids revealed by all of the catastrophic harm people were doing to the environment with their ignorance, then, by God, he was going to hunt down a bunch of imaginary cryptids and rub them in everybody's fucking faces in Washington D.C.

"I didn't realize you thought of me that way," he said.

"What way?"

"As your kidnapper."

She lowered her disguise so she could blink her eyes in that way he had described earlier in their road trip as "that Betty Boop way," resulting in an hours long tirade of her calling him "Oldy McOldington" and "The Oldsmaster General" and the like.

"You know I don't, Doctor C. In fact…" She trailed off.

"What?"

"Well, I was going to ask you for something, but it's kind of personal, and I'm worried you're going to think I'm an asshole and a crazy person for asking."

"Jade," he said, letting his glasses slip down over his nose, "after everything you've been through in your life, I wouldn't blame you if you were the biggest asshole and/or crazy person on the planet. But somehow, in spite of everything, you are a surprisingly well-adjusted kid."

"You mean that?" she clapped her hands together, sounding thrilled. "Nah, you're just saying that."

"I do mean that. If the feds don't lock you away or autopsy you, you should meet my niece and nephew sometime. They are some deranged little teenagers. You're good. Now what were you going to ask me?"

"Well…I guess my name was always Jade Davis. Like, people at Los Alamos just called me Jade. But my father—I mean, my kidnapper, he was my real kidnapper, not you, Doctor C, you're my liberator—his name was Davis. So I always figured my name was Jade Davis. But I don't want it to be anymore."

"Done," Cam agreed, "You shall be Jade…whatever you want to be. Except Davis. I'd prefer Jade Bieber to Jade Davis."

"Well, that's just it, Doctor C. Would it be all right if I called myself Jade Custer?"

He looked at her. "I…I'd be honored."

She clapped her long, thin, fingers on her bony knees. "Done! Now don't go getting all mushy on me. It's just a way to honor the greatest person I've met in my life."

"I won't let it go to my head," he agreed.

"Eyes on the road, pervert."

47. AUGUST, 1942

The Marines retreated swiftly, a cacophony of clicking trailing behind them as the monstrous crustaceans found themselves stopped by Dempsey's sacrifice and Alcide's impromptu magic.

But Alcide's work wasn't permanent. As soon as his blood dried they'd be on them like flies on a carcass. They'd probably already cleared away the rubble from Dempsey's grenade and were just waiting for the blood to dry. He wasn't sure exactly what the Tojos had been up to here in the dark, but they'd certainly been playing Frankenstein.

Maybe the Tojos and the Dark Ones have been stirring the gumbo pot together.

A bitter chuckle escaped his lips. Clickers were dumb animals, and for the most part he could handle that. He could get the creatures back into the sea, but if enough Dark Ones were around they'd tear through his workings and magics and send them marching back up onto the shore.

But then, he still hadn't seen any Dark Ones, just the occasional gore-drenched indicators of their presence.

They'd moved at an uncomfortable crouch, some places barely big enough for them to squeeze through, dirt falling across their shoulders when Basher accidentally scraped his head against the ceiling. He heard Microphone breathing faster when the walls started closing in again.

Panic kept them moving, even as the sounds of the Clickers *petits* died away as they fled. Alcide was sure that his company—well, squad now, really—looked like little more than rats, scurrying from hole to hole, squeaking down in the guts of the Earth.

The group emerged from the dark, and in the dim glow of what few lights the Japanese had running through the labyrinth, he saw Preach holding up his hand, gesturing for them to stop.

Every man turned to look at the skipper, but Ezekiel was lost in his grief, staring out into the looming dark with eyes as empty as the void. Alcide's father had talked about men going hollow in war. When they filled back up again they were never quite the same. The damage had been done. The cracks in the glass weren't going away. He'd heard about it, but hadn't expected to see it happen to the skipper.

"Skip? Skipper!" Preach grabbed the captain's arm, trying to elicit a response and getting nothing but silence. He grunted, shaking his head as he joined Doodles and Pike at the mouth of the tunnel. Alcide crouched next to them.

The silence was deafening. All Alcide could hear was their steady breathing and grunts from Doodles who was holding Pinchy tight. The creature wriggled in the cook's grasp, no doubt eager to race back down the tunnel and join its brethren.

Pike was nominally the ranking man, but knew better than to try to throw his weight around in another man's close-knit unit. He merely polished his rifle and nodded his deference to Preach. Preach, for his part, didn't much seem to want the button.

"What do you think, Boudin? Can you work some witchcraft or whatever here? I'd feel a lot safer knowing I wasn't going to have to be watching my rear in here." Preach asked.

Alcide had just finished bandaging his arm with a piece of fabric he'd ripped from his pant leg. He eyed the rock face. "Just near gave too much putting those workings on the other tunnels. I'm liable to bleed out if I give any more."

Preach nodded and glanced at Doodles. "You know the way, Doodles?"

Doodles shook his head. "Can't say I ever made it this far."

"We'll just have to use our wits," Pike said, blowing on the barrel of his rifle. "Do we follow those bodies or not?"

The tunnel forked, one path leading down further into the dark and the other back up at a slight incline. Two bodies lay at the entrance to the path that led up, their backs savagely torn open, innards thrown around the tunnel like a dog who'd found a doll's stuffing.

They'd been trying to run away.

Basher and Martino knelt over the bodies. Reluctantly, Alcide joined them. Martino glanced up before whispering, "Never thought I'd feel sorry for a fucking Tojo." Alcide agreed, but what had been done to them wasn't war. It was slaughter.

"This the work one of your fish-things, Boudin?" Basher asked, nudging his foot at the dead Japanese soldier's arm. Fresh claw marks wove their way down the dead man's flesh, almost degloving the arm.

Alcide nodded, squatting down next to the dead man and covering his face to protect from the stench. His eyes naturally drifted back the way the dead men had obviously come from.

The tunnel sloped down and over the coppery tang of blood and the heavy scent of earth, he could smell the sweet salt of the ocean.

"You guys smell that?" Alcide asked, moving to the edge of the other fork and staring down the incline, taking a deep inhale to confirm that he wasn't just smelling what he hoped was down there.

Preach whispered something to Pike. The lean sniper nodded and aimed his rifle at the mouth of the tunnel while Preach ushered Doodles and Microphone to join the other three men at the fork, leaving the skipper still standing stiff by himself in the middle of the room.

"Something putting a bee in your bonnet?" Preach asked when he drew up next to Alcide.

"I have a feeling my pack is down there; the rest of our stolen supplies too. Sounds like it might be a cave leading out to the sea," Alcide said. Every word was true, but more than likely that just meant more Clickers or Dark Ones were waiting at the bottom.

Alcide had experience with it, back home in the bayou. The piscine creatures' minds weighed heavy on a man's ability to think, crushing sanity altogether if you encountered them.

He could feel that same heaviness bearing on his mind now, brushing against his thoughts like a fly buzzing just close enough that it was uncomfortable. Every step he took towards the yawning tunnel, the pressure increased.

"Is this your magic, Robichaude?" Pike asked, the corners of his mouth quirking up with amusement.

"No," Alcide replied, "just my wits."

"Can't be any worse down there than up here." Preach said with a sigh. He gestured at Microphone. "Basher, take Microphone up the tunnel and radio in our position. Make sure you let Gunny know that most of us are still kicking."

Basher and Martino looked at each other and a wordless agreement passed between them. "Preach, no fucking offense to you and Harry Fucking Boudini here, but don't you think this whole fucking thing has gone tits up? The skipper has lost it, the lieutenant just melted into the fucking floor like he was my mama's Minestrone. We're in over our fucking heads."

Pike was listening quietly but intently. Alcide glanced at the skipper. He was still shell-shocked, just stared at them from where they had left him standing in the tunnel.

"You know what Gunny Webb would say if he was here, Martino: this isn't a democracy."

"Yeah, well fuck you, Preach. You only got two fucking stripes, which I figure puts it up to the fastest gun in the Far Fucking East here. What about it, Sergeant Pike?" Both Alcide and Preach looked at the quiet sergeant, his eyes focused on the two of them before going back to Martino and Basher. "I've seen more horror today than the whole rest of the war. But I don't think our mission's changed. And while it's strange, we've lost a lot of good men to get here. Let's not dishonor their memories."

Alcide never thought he'd see the day when Martino shut up.

Pike rested one hand against his rifle strap and with the other he pointed at the tunnel heading towards the surface. "Go and radio your people, like the corporal asked."

Microphone looked uneasy as Basher ushered him forward, both men heading up the tunnel.

"Thanks, Sergeant," Preach breathed, and looked ready to say more.

Pike held up a hand. "I don't like to talk much, Corporal

Cantor. That's why I got into this line of work. I don't much like people, either. But I like monsters even less. This is your show."

He fished a cigarette from his pocket, holding his hand out wordlessly for a light from Alcide.

Preach nodded. "Martino, look after the Skipper."

Martino glared at Alcide as he walked past. Alcide dropped his gaze away, the unspoken accusation lingering in the air: *Trick's dead, Dempsey's dead, and the rest of us are next. All on your say-so.*

Preach shook his head and shouldered his own weapon, looking at Boudin and the tunnel behind him. "You ready to go down there?" The tremble in his voice stoked the flicker of guilt that Alcide was already feeling.

He was too proud to say it, but Preach's face said it all. *I don't want to die down here in the dark.*

Alcide's chest twisted. He wished he could promise to get Preach home, that everything he was afraid of wouldn't come to pass, that he would see his sweetheart again. But he couldn't. He sighed wistfully as he imagined his own home, the muddy waters and the sweet smell of honeysuckle in the heat of summer.

He wondered what his mother was doing now, probably gathering up crawdads out of their towers of mud and whispering concerns about her sons. While his two younger brothers, Barthelme and Remy, were still too young to enlist, Alcide and Jean Phillipe had signed up a few days after Pearl.

Alcide could practically see his father sitting on the porch out in the back lake, staring at the water and listening for the Deep Folk to talk back, smoking his pipe and whispering prayers of protection over his sons.

He doubted that his father's wisdom could reach this far over the ocean, especially when it was split in two directions, with his brother somewhere in North Africa and he deep in a cave in this Pacific hellhole.

The memory of the sharp spices his mother used in her food cut across his tongue and for a few seconds he could almost imagine the fireflies. "I wish I was home too, Preach, I really do."

Preach smiled at him, wiping his eyes. "Maybe when we get home, I'll bring the missus and come visit the bayou."

Alcide smiled. "Think I'd like that."

Their conversation ceased when Basher and Microphone returned. Pike looked up from his solitary cigarette as Microphone adjusted his gear and gave a thumbs-up. "Gunnery Sergeant Webb said to hurry our asses up. Admiral Fletcher is pulling everybody out. He said they've got some weapon to take care of these things."

Alcide frowned. He'd thought his solution was the only way. Maybe the Navy really did have some kind of miracle weapon. But he doubted it. "I still think the only way..."

Martino abandoned the skipper to join the conversation. "Hey, there, you heard the man, Boudin. The fucking Navy's got a solution. We can get the fuck out of here. That's what they said, right, Microphone?"

Microphone adjusted his glasses and shrugged. "I'm just relaying the message, but if my opinion counts for anything, I'd rather take my chances back at the beach."

"I'm with pisspants there. This op is FUBAR, so let's cut our losses."

A tension settled over the cave. Alcide felt that the time for words had passed. He would use his rifle if he had to. Or even black magic, though he feared that greatly.

Preach raised his hands. "Guys, I know this isn't ideal, but the original plan..."

"Shut the fuck up, Preach. This is fucked, and everyone knows it!" Martino aimed his Springfield at Preach.

"Martino," Alcide warned.

Pike immediately had his rifle in his hand aiming at the private, but Basher raised the flamethrower in the sergeant's direction.

"That's my battle buddy," Basher said.

Pike didn't blink. Alcide was fairly sure that his eyes didn't even flick towards the other private as he whispered, "Get your weapon out of my face, Basher."

Basher shook his head. "Didn't you hear what he said? We don't have to die down here. I've got a wife and kid back home.

Maybe you guys don't care about getting back, but I do."

"Every one of you put your weapons down."

Every eye snapped to Ezekiel Palmer, who stood up straighter, storm clouds parted, senses completely recovered.

Martino's mouth opened wide, his eyes springing around the inside of the cave for support and finding that he might as well have been alone on the island.

Basher lowered his weapon as Palmer pushed past him. Getting within spitting distance of Martino, Alcide could see the skipper's eyes, his pain transformed into righteous fury.

"Maybe the Navy will save this island. If so, great. I'll swallow my pride and wear blue. And if they don't? And we could have and just walked away? Then we'll all have to tell our grandchildren how during the great Battle of Guadalcanal we gave up because the going got tough. That's assuming we have any grandchildren who haven't been eaten by sea monsters.

"We are going down into the dark. We are going to kill any Tojo, oversized lobster, or fish-faced bastard we find. And if I see any of you raise a weapon against a fellow Marine again, I'll do worse than any of them to your sorry ass."

48. AUGUST, 1942

The tunnel's downward incline was sharp. Ezekiel gave Boudin his lighter to lead the way. He went feet first, the flickering flame barely illuminating the rock walls for those trailing in his wake. Ezekiel felt like he was descending into a tomb, which in a way was true.

After all, they hadn't seen any living Japanese soldier, just the shredded corpses that Boudin's supposed Dark Ones had left behind. A morbid curiosity had seized the captain, and as he slid down behind the Cajun private, he whispered, "Blessed be the Lord, my rock, who trains my hands for war, my fingers for battle."

"I didn't realize you were a praying man, sir."

Ezekiel looked back in shock at Preach. He hadn't realized anyone could hear him.

"I'm not," he said. "Well, no atheists in the foxholes and all that, I suppose."

"And all that," Preach agreed. He took a rosary from around his neck and handed it to Ezekiel, who wordlessly took it and put it around his own.

They reached the bottom of the tunnel, boots splashing into a shallow run of water. It was tall enough to stand, but the Japanese hadn't strung any lights. He wondered if each step they took was just one step closer to a bottomless pit leading out to the sea, monsters waiting for one misstep.

He moved to the side of the tunnel, dragging Boudin with him, the other man's face highlighted by the flickering lighter. Ezekiel would have thought that it was a fleshless skull from the way the man leered.

"I can feel them close now, Skipper. You can, too, if you concentrate hard enough," Boudin whispered, putting one finger to his lips and pointing another at the Thompson that Ezekiel had finally gotten back. "Keep it handy. You won't have long when they come for us."

Even with his anger that pushed him madly forward, he wanted to shrink back from the man's gaze and the certainty of what lay in the dark he saw there.

"Everyone here? Sound off," Ezekiel whispered behind him.

One by one, the men replied in a whisper, ending with the cook who said, "Doodles" quietly, and then in a loud falsetto "Pinchy!" His small laugh silenced immediately in a grunt of pain as Martino punched him in the gut.

Ezekiel's finger tensed against the trigger of his weapon, his breathing coming quick as he imagined wet footsteps racing through the gloom. His breath eased when nothing came.

Boudin sighed and waved a hand. "Come on, not long to go now."

They traveled as quietly as they could, a difficult task as each footfall echoed down the tunnel corridor. If any beast or Tojo was lying in wait, they would have plenty of warning that intruders had come to their domain.

Ezekiel followed behind Boudin, both men hugging the wall as they edged through the tunnel. The private stopped at one point and crouched down, waving the flame across the top of the water and grimacing. "It gets deep here. Be sure to hug the wall tight."

Ezekiel passed the word back, stepping around the dark water and sloshing after Boudin. He'd made it just past the pool when the wall fell away into blackness.

He wobbled on his feet, trying to keep his balance before falling into the water, wincing as his knees bounced off the hard stone.

"Skipper, you okay?" Preach whispered behind him as Ezekiel waved a hand to ward him off.

Boudin's meager light flickered across the alcove, illuminating what looked like a small barracks. Empty bundle bags were strewn across the floor, cast aside in what looked like a mad dash to get out. There were no bodies inside as far as they could see, but as Boudin swept his light back into the tunnel, it looked like this was just one of several small alcoves designed to house the Japanese soldiers.

There was a light coming from the end of the tunnel and Boudin pointed to indicate to the rest that their destination was only a dozen yards away.

They'd made it halfway when the shape flashed out of the darkness, dark green arms wrapping around Boudin and pulling him into another alcove, the lighter tumbling into the water.

Ezekiel's heart pounded in his chest, all thoughts of caution lost as the men took up his same cry, sloshing through the water. Mic began scrabbling for a flashlight from his pack.

The men crowded around the entrance to the alcove staring into the blackness, seeing nothing but vague shapes rolling around in the gloom, and hearing Boudin's screams. A few matches flickered, but the alcove beyond was deep.

"Can't get a shot, sir," Pike said coolly, his form nothing but a murky outline.

There was a throaty croaking, like a toad but bigger. Boudin shouted something in response that Ezekiel couldn't understand, but the thing paused in its attack, long enough for Microphone's flashlight to flare to life.

Now illuminated, Ezekiel saw Boudin lying on his back, a fist clenched against his cheek, blood pouring from the claw marks raked across his face and chest. But when he saw the thing standing over him, Ezekiel felt his mind crumble like a house of cards and go fluttering away into the wind.

It was hunched over, dark black eyes deeper than the night sky staring into the bright light shining on it, its green scales rippling over powerful muscle. It stood taller than any man by a head and change at least, and its teeth were bared in a hoarse hissing, its arms thrown up to block out Microphone's light.

The moment passed in the blink of an eye, but the Dark One recovered from its momentary blindness and roared as it leapt, crossing the few yards faster than Ezekiel could track. Its mouth closed around Martino's head, teeth sinking through his flesh and deep into his skull.

Martino screamed, a high pitch shrill that echoed everywhere. He pulled the trigger on his rifle and the shot ricocheted off the walls around them. Ezekiel saw his hands jet up to clutch at the thing's jaws, attempting to dislodge the teeth pushing through the private's eye sockets. Then the creature wrenched and Martino's whole head came away in its mouth.

Ezekiel saw the dead man's skull cave in as the monster chewed, the lump traveling down the Dark One's throat as it leered at Ezekiel.

None of the men could raise their weapons, like a heavy curtain hung over their minds, drowning their sense of self-preservation. They weren't men with wills anymore, but cattle waiting to be slaughtered.

The Dark One reached a hand for his head and Ezekiel closed his eyes, afraid and unable to move under the thing's mental assault. Then he heard a cry and opened his eyes to see Boudin on the thing's back, a nail clasped tightly between his fingers, driving it directly between the thing's shoulder blades.

The Dark One reared back, shrieking, and Boudin fell back into the water, managing to splutter out, "Shoot it!"

Ezekiel shook his head, the fog seeming to clear as he raised the Thompson and pulled the trigger. The gun chattered and he saw Boudin scurry across the water as the Dark One raised its hands to protect its eyes, small wounds opening in its chest. Its scales were hard, and even at close range, Ezekiel saw that he had barely wounded it.

It swiped at Ezekiel, the blow knocking him off his feet and sending him spinning into the brackish water. He sputtered and coughed, rolling over and gasping at the monster standing over him. The other men had regained their senses, but in the weak light cast over the tunnel more of their shots missed than not.

But John Pike didn't miss.

The Dark One screeched and clutched at its eye. Thick, syrup-like blood fountained from the gutted socket, dripping into the shallow water. It gave a warning hiss and backed away, roaring. Pike didn't hesitate and fired again.

The monster's brain splattered against the wall. It wobbled on its toes for a few seconds before toppling backwards, landing against the wall, its blood leaking out and staining the already murky water an inky black.

No one breathed any easier, focusing their weapons on the thing's body for fear that it was going to get back up and resume its rampage. Ezekiel managed to find his voice first as he hoarsely commanded Basher to retrieve Martino's dog tags.

Basher looked at Ezekiel, his face a mask of shock. He managed to whisper, "He doesn't have a head."

Ezekiel grew calm as he spoke the words that would no doubt stick with this young man for the rest of his life. "He'd do it or you."

They'd spoken of these situations at Annapolis, when the mission was going to come before the lives and humanity of his men. Basher looked at Ezekiel like he was the one whose head was torn off, standing completely frozen. Ezekiel softened his tone. "Go ahead, son."

The spell and shock broken, Basher closed his eyes tight and he felt around the bloodied stump of his dead friend, the tag coming away easily.

Ezekiel patted the private on the shoulder, then addressed everyone else, "Do a weapons check, reload, take a breath before we get moving."

Boudin still sat in the water staring at the dead Dark One, only looking up when Ezekiel offered him a hand. "That's a young one, barely a teenager by their standards."

Ezekiel glanced at the massive corpse, trying to fathom what an adult would look like. He helped the private to his feet, watching as Boudin winced in pain, his hand cupping the side of his chest as fresh blood ran down his face.

"Need to get that treated. You could catch an infection," Ezekiel said.

Boudin waved a hand, barely managing to pant out, "Just… just get me that nail out of its back."

Ezekiel nodded, turning to Basher and Preach. "Help me roll that thing over."

Basher nodded immediately, moving to one side of the carcass while Ezekiel and Preach moved to the other side. He looked at his man, the private who had just attempted mutiny, who hadn't been afraid of court martial or worse. Now he looked terrified.

"On three," Ezekiel said, "One, two, three!"

Ezekiel plunged his hands under the thing's skin. Even in death, its flesh was coated with mucous. It reminded him of the skin of the bullfrogs he and his brothers used to catch down at the pond. The thing was terribly heavy and each man groaned, gritting their teeth as they strained, finally managing to topple the thing, its head submerged beneath the deep water.

The three men panted as Boudin placed a foot on the dead monster's shoulder and gripped the head of the nail. It came free with a wet squirt of near-black blood that caused Ezekiel to close his eyes lest he be splattered.

Boudin wiped the blood from the nail, placed it in his pocket, and glanced at Ezekiel who was still staring down at the dead Dark One. A knowing smile touched his lips. "Always overwhelming the first time, especially with that working they put in your head, the one that makes you freeze up, strains the bedsprings of your mind."

Ezekiel nodded, licking his dry lips, his fingers playing across the rosary Preach had given him. He wondered how things would have turned out for him and his had Boudin not been with his unit.

They'd either be with the rest of the men pulling back to the beaches, or more likely would be dead just like the Tojos that had run into these things. Either way, they were dead if Boudin couldn't deliver on this grand spell he had promised.

The silence was broken by the distant echo of clicking claws. Boudin glanced back the way they had come. "Must've gotten through the working."

Ezekiel nodded and swept a hand towards the end of the tunnel. "Then we better get cracking."

49. AUGUST, 1942

Can't believe they live here like this.

The thought crossed Preach's mind as soon as they entered what looked like the nexus of Japanese operations on the entire island. It was a sparse affair; rows of tables through the center of the room with what looked like their stolen supplies. A massive flag with the Rising Sun dominated one wall, as though the Tojo emperor himself were watching over them with an all-seeing eye.

Preach briefly wondered if they bowed to it like it was some kind of altar or temple. He'd heard the enemy considered the emperor a god, but it was hard to imagine worshiping a living man.

Preach stifled the laugh he could hear coming. He'd had his own encounter with darkness, and he'd been struggling to hold on to his faith. Christ on high hadn't bothered to come save him then, just like the Tojo emperor hadn't come down from his palace in Tokyo to drive off the American invasion of this island.

Instead, these desperate men had turned to the foul denizens of the ocean, castoffs from Noah's Ark, things that shouldn't have been, to accomplish their bloody crusade. Further proof the world was full of darkness and very little light. He'd always sworn to be part of that light, but lately it had been difficult.

The skipper look around the room, taking in the same sights, his eyes settling on an alcove that had a smaller flag and what looked like a bank of radios and maps. He turned around.

"Basher and Doodles, you two help Boudin sift through those packs until you find his. Preach, you check that metal slab over in the corner. We don't want any surprises coming out at us. Sergeant Pike, you keep an eye at the entrance. Microphone, let's see if the Japanese set up a relay in here. Maybe we can contact Gunny Webb without having to go outside."

Each man set to his task, with the insane cook and his pet diving into the massive pile of packs like they were a spring of fresh water on a hot summer day. Preach stared at the massive iron gate with what looked like another cave beyond it.

He could hear the water sloshing in the alcove beyond when he got close enough, the scent of the ocean drifting through the rusted hinges. He thought about the picture he'd seen nearly ten years ago, King Kong and his lost island, filled with monsters and prehistoric nightmares. Not much different from what they were seeing now on their own island, and just like the giant gorilla had existed behind his own gate of wood and bone, Preach wondered what was behind this door of iron.

He pressed an ear to the metal, jumping at the feel of the cool iron. There was no clicking, but he could feel that weight behind his eyes, less than when the Dark One in the alcove had attacked, but intense enough that he was sure that one was on the other side. But he could hear nothing but the distant thunder of crashing waves from the sea.

Preach shook his head. Seemed more likely than not that another one of the gigantic fish-men was just waiting for one of them to open the gate and drag them screaming down into the murky depths. Reluctantly, he began to pull away from the cool metal when he heard a voice, weak and pleading and barely distinguishable above the sound of the distant waves.

"Skipper! We've got a live one over here!" Preach hollered, shouldering his Springfield, and grasping the rope that ran into the apparatus for raising the gateway.

The skipper and Boudin both responded, jogging the short length of the room. The Cajun witchdoctor put his hand on Preach's shoulder. "Easy, you feel that?"

Preach could feel it all right. The heavy weight in his head was increasing, like the monster on the other side of the metal door had sensed their efforts to free it and had increased its pull on their minds.

The skipper eyed the door and called for Sergeant Pike and Basher. Both men joined them, their eyes fixed on the door like the monster would burst through the thick iron plate any second and disembowel them all.

"Get ready to shoot it." Pike nodded. Basher and Boudin joined the captain at the other rope opposite Preach.

"Be careful, Sergeant. These things are devil fast," Boudin said, though Pike didn't look like he needed any persuading.

The skipper held up three fingers, counting down, and then pulling, Boudin and Preach mimicking him. Rusted gears squealed as each man strained, pulling as hard as they could. The metal gate quivered for a moment, resisting their pull. Preach thought for a moment that the gate wouldn't rise at all, that it was, perhaps, too rusted. Then the metal shuddered and the slab began to rise.

There was a moan and a strange form came stumbling out, clutching its side, babbling in a tongue that Preach didn't understand. It was the thing's diminutive height that saved it. Pike fired as soon as he saw that it wasn't human, but the bullet went over its head, ricocheting around the interior of the small cave.

In passable English the thing croaked, "Help me."

He realized that it was no Dark One, at least, not entirely. It was something else, something in between man and Dark One. It looked like someone had taken a human and stretched the skin back, eyes widening and darkening into the soulless black of a fish, but the skull was only now beginning to catch up. Three slits cut through the thing's neck, half formed gills that fluttered, trying to draw breath.

It was clad in a tattered uniform, the pants the only thing that were more or less still intact. Its shirt had ripped down the center, golden lapels destroyed to make room for an expanding chest of sickly grey flesh and hardened patches of green scale like massive scabs covering the skin.

The thing's mouth opened and it again spoke. "Please help me. I'm not in control." Then it leapt towards Preach, the jumbled mix of human teeth and sharp, predatory teeth in its mouth rushing for his throat.

Boudin caught it halfway through, tackling the beast to the ground and rolling away, the wounds in his face bleeding as he rolled.

"No, no, I can't stop!" the thing gibbered before it opened its mouth and drank in the blood that ran down Boudin's face.

Preach saw Boudin recoil away as the thing's tongue lapped out and licked the blood from its lips, hoarsely whispering, "Emperor save me, it tastes good."

It tried to reach up and take more of the hoodoo man, but Basher and Captain Palmer appeared, holding the thing down as the skipper shouted for Pike to shoot the thing.

Boudin spoke up, "Hold off! I think I can restrain it!" He called for Preach to hold the thing's legs steady. Preach barely wanted to touch the thing with the rough skin weeping some kind of fluid that dripped over his hands.

Boudin crouched over the half-formed Dark One, gripping one of the nails he'd used to kill the other Dark One firmly between his knuckles. Then he drove it straight into the thing's chest.

Deep black blood welled up from the wound and the Dark One hybrid warbled something as it twisted its head, trying to take a bite from Basher's arm.

Boudin held out his hands, palms up and chanted, "As I have penetrated your flesh, so I have penetrated your power. Be still."

Preach had believed Boudin's power, had seen him trap the Clicker in the circle of the same nails, but when he saw the creature's limbs stiffen and thud against the dirt like two fallen logs, he stared at the man in a whole new light. This wasn't parlor tricks, sleight of hand, or cheap spectacle. This was power, real power. Whether proof of God's love for Boudin or the Devil's influence on him, Preach still wasn't sure.

The men breathed easier. The thing on the floor croaked, "Thank you" over and over again, sending chills racing down Preach's skin.

"Boudin," he said, "what the hell is this thing?"

Boudin looked up from where he crouched over the monster and shook his head. "I have no idea. I call on you to speak the truth, thing of evil. By what name are you called?"

"Ota," it croaked

"You're an Ota?" the skipper repeated, "Christ, how many of these monsters are there?"

"No," the thing said, "I'm a man. My name is Ota Hanshiro."

50. AUGUST, 1942

"This the one, Boudin?" Doodles asked as he pulled another pack from the floor and Alcide smiled when he saw the markings and talismans that he had adorned the fabric with. All powerful, and all designed to keep prying eyes from taking a peek.

"That's the one. Careful with the flap; boil your eyes in their sockets."

Alcide had to suppress a chuckle as Doodles handed the pack to him like he was handing off a hooker with the clap. Nevertheless, he was eager to make sure that the Tojos hadn't pilfered any of his supplies. Because now it was time for some real magic, from his side of the fence.

He glanced over at Pinchy. He'd noticed that Doodles's pet clicker had somehow lost its rubber bands, though so far it hadn't seen fit to attack them and he hadn't felt compelled to draw anyone else's attention to it. He was wondering, though, if the half-Dark One Hanshiro could commune with the Clicker the way a purebred could.

Alcide had spent plenty of years learning Darkish, the warbling tones and guttural words that took a lifetime to master, and even now they had to speak at a slower pace for even his father to understand, much less the rest of his family.

But Hanshiro spoke like a natural, or more accurately, like a man possessed. He insisted when he could, in his excellent English, that he was not in control most of the time. Then he would chatter in the Dark One language, aimed at the Clicker held tight in Doodles arms, who was slowly growing more and more agitated but seemed forever loyal to Doodles. If Hanshiro was telling the truth, Alcide had a suspicion about what was going on, because of the terrifying thing he'd found latched to his back.

They'd found it when Sergeant Pike had tied the monster to a spare chair (easier now that Alcide had bound him with his power), and when stripping off the tattered remains of the man's uniform, they'd found the disgusting creature.

It was a Clicker, but like the rest of the breeds he'd seen rampaging across the island, this was one that he had never seen before. The thing's claws were dug deep into the flesh of the shoulders, chitinous legs stabbing deep into the back, hard scales beginning to grow over the legs. The Clicker's tail had embedded itself deep into the base of the spine. The same growths of skin were growing over it as well, but unlike the legs and claws that seemed to just secure the creature to the half-Dark One's back, this was depositing liquid inside the abomination's body.

The shell on the monstrous crustacean was transparent; Alcide could see its organs producing the venom that was slowly being injected into its prey's back. It looked like squid ink or road tar, thick and viscous like syrup.

He'd find it fascinating if he wasn't so repulsed by this perversion of nature. Whatever this Clicker was, it had been crafted, made for a purpose, a purpose that Alcide was dreadfully certain was the conversion of men into monsters. Every pump of the translucent Clicker's venom caused more scales to blossom, more skin to darken and stretch, and more of Hanshiro's mind to be lost to the warbling madness.

Grasping his pack, Alcide joined the skipper in the radio room, his arms crossed as he watched Microphone work to try and establish contact with Gunny Webb and the rest of the men.

"We can move out whenever you're ready, Skipper," Alcide said quietly, not wishing to intrude on the man's thoughts more than necessary.

"Ever seen something like that in there, Boudin?" the captain asked quietly.

Alcide shook his head.

"Seen a lot of things wonderful to tell, plenty more give me shivers in the dead of night, but that creature isn't one of them. That's the thing about magic, Skipper. Once you grab a taste, it takes a mighty will to keep out the dark."

It was a sentiment that had served him and his time and time again. Alcide had seen plenty of men engaging in dark perversions of what magic could do. Maybe he couldn't speak for all the beliefs of the world, but more than most seemed to let it consume them. He had more than a feeling that the same drive had consumed the man slowly transforming before them.

"What about you, Boudin?" The skipper asked. "Are you down in the dark too? Or are you trying to claw your way back to a life like the rest of us?"

Alcide chuckled. "This is the only life I've ever known, sir. Sometimes you get used to the night."

The words seemed to be good enough for Palmer, who encouraged Microphone to continue working at making contact before motioning to Alcide that their prisoner needed attending to.

Preach and Basher stood over the thing and Pike watched the entrance, while Doodles struggled to keep Pinchy under control, the animal becoming more violent with every croaking torrent erupting from the half-Dark One's mouth and the friendly cartoon face inked on its back seeming to become a scowling demonic visage.

Alcide stepped up beside Preach, who shook his head. "It's like God blinked when he made it. It hurts to look at."

The monster wrenched its head, screaming profanities in the Dark Ones' tongue, then silencing as the human intelligence took control again. "Pl-eas-se, before it returns, help me."

The skipper crouched, locking eyes with his captive. "Tell me how you got these damn Clickers to march to your tune, and what your command plans on doing next."

A hiss escaped the prisoner's mouth. Alcide had heard and caused enough pain to recognize the sound, the struggle to maintain presence of mind as the agony drew closer than a lover.

"I lead a science division. We created new breeds of *Kurikka*." Hanshiro struggled to speak, his tongue beginning to narrow, excess flesh rotting and falling out between his distorted gums. Preach turned away, his hand covering his mouth.

"Hel…help me…I'm chan…changing. Can't hold it long. It's mind…too strong."

"This man here," the skipper said, pointing at Alcide, "knows how to help you. He'll pry that lobster off of you, and you'll spend the rest of this war in a nice camp, but I'm not letting him do a damn thing until you give us something."

It was a lie, plain and simple. Alcide didn't have any working or spell that could turn back the clock or give him some sense of himself inside the Dark One. Ota Hanshiro's mind would be devoured by the Dark One, like a dog overrun by parasites, and that would be the end of the man.

Hanshiro nodded, his mouth lolling open, bits of saliva splattering against the floor. "The *Umibozu* found us, here on this island, made contact with us." His eyes jumped between the Americans staring at him. "The Navy knows that the Empire can't sustain a protracted war with America. We don't have the resources. When I saw the killing power of the *Kurikka*, I knew they were the divine weapon we were…"

Ota's head wrenched, small beads of sweat spiraling down his distorted forehead, and then the Dark One took over again, spewing obscenities and doing its damnedest to force its mind onto the men in the room.

Captain Palmer looked at Alcide. "Any of this making sense to you?"

Alcide nodded. "Dark Ones make dark pacts."

"I guess you could say they flew too close to that Rising Sun of theirs," Pike said, casually smoking a cigarette.

One of Hanshiro's pupils dilated, drowning the white of his eye until there was nothing but the infinite black. The Dark One smiled and hissed at Alcide, both eyes glancing down at the nail sticking from its chest. Gooseflesh began to prickle on his arms as one of its hands began to twitch.

Then another spasm rocked its body and Ota Hanshiro's mind returned.

"They're dying. They don't know why. More of theirs are born deformed, or dead to begin with." A rueful smile stretched across his monstrous lips. "And with all their magic, they could not solve the problem. In their desperation, they turned to me, stroked my ego, made all the promises their inhuman kind can offer."

Alcide squatted next to Ezekiel, making sure that he was eye level with Hanshiro. "That is something I can answer for you. They shattered their civilization pursuing more and more power, so the legends say, and while their blood is strong, it is remarkably susceptible to what it touches."

All the heads in the room were looking at Alcide as he talked, a natural reaction, he supposed, to hearing of a lost and secret fallen empire. "Leaking fuel, oil, we're dumping an awful many things in the waters, and it's poisoning them. Won't be too long until they aren't around anymore."

Hanshiro nodded. "If what you say is true about their blood, it is the opposite with the *Kurikka*. They are marvels of evolution, adaptable like no other animal. It is no wonder they can be changed so easily."

"Changed?" Alcide whispered, "How?"

"The obsidian ones were created by the Dark Ones, as was this translucent one on my back. The white ones you've seen... my own creation." Ota smiled, his one human eye rolling back into his skull, his tongue lapping at his lips in pleasure.

Basher roared in rage, his face a mask of pain. Alcide and Palmer both shouted, but his fist was faster, lashing out and hitting the once-man square in the deep black of his piscine eye.

"You bastard! Do you know how many of my friends those things killed?"

A thin trail of stodgy blood ran from Ota's eye, his lips curled into a pained grimace. "You would have done the same, American. In defense of your people, you would have done the same."

Basher roared something primal, like a lion that had been injured, and lunged to attack the monstrous colonel. Palmer hollered for help, and between him, Preach, and Pike they managed to wrestle the burly private to the ground as he begged them to let him kill the monster.

"I was worthy, worthy to be counted among them, to be...

ey'ah, chthun, chu-ahzlrazee!" He lapsed back into the Dark One tongue, the Clicker on his back injecting more of its venom, his one remaining human eye dilating black.

Palmer looked at Alcide. "Any of that mean anything to you?"

Alcide reached a hesitant hand towards the translucent Clicker on Ota's back. The Dark One continued to rave as Alcide whispered more words, the pressure behind his eyes increasing as the thing attempted to press its will against his, to worm its way off the hook on which Alcide had him skewered. He wasn't afraid of losing quite yet, but at the end of the day, Alcide was only a man. He could grow tired, he could be overcome, and this soon-to-be Dark One's hands were twitching too much for his liking.

"World-over, they're dying out, struggling to continue their existence here." Alcide pointed at the brain Clicker on Ota Hanshiro's back. "So that's their plan to increase their numbers."

Alcide watched as the Dark Ones' design settled in the skipper's mind, his face going pale as he tried to chew the thoughts. Alcide thought to spare him the trouble of saying it out loud.

"He gave them an army of Clickers to break down our defenses. Then they'll kidnap as many of us as they can and make us like them. Like him."

Each man took a moment to process it. Alcide knew it was a hard thing to realize that this wasn't some war that was going to be fought over resources, or revenge, but for the continuation of their race. It wasn't the Dark Ones' world anymore, and the dominion of men was not going to be so easily overturned.

Hanshiro had come back to himself, nodding his head vigorously and grimacing as his cheeks and skin distorted, fresh blossoms of scales beginning to form in the folds beneath his eyes. "Yes, yes, American. Our war with you will be nothing when compared to the wholesale carnage they will loose on your shores."

A whoop of joy interrupted them. Microphone began to chatter the countersigns to Gunny Webb. Alcide looked at the tunnel, sure that he had heard a faint splash.

"Preach? Sergeant?" Alcide whispered, nodding towards the room's entrance. Both men looked down at Basher who glared back.

"Going to kill the oversized cod?" Preach asked, making sure that his grip on the bigger man was tight. Basher shook his head sullenly.

"Good," Pike said, offering the private a hand and helping him to his feet. Basher avoided eye contact with the rest of the men as he shuffled towards the entrance.

The group lapsed into a silence, only interspersed by the ranting of their mad prisoner and Microphone's half conversation with Gunny. Alcide rifled through his pack, breathing easier when he saw the ingredients were still there. At least they still had a chance.

He glanced up at Doodles and his pet, held tightly in his hands. The cook cooed at the thing, whispering sweet words. Alcide sighed, knowing that he was going to break the man's heart. To get the monsters off this island, Pinchy would have to die.

51. AUGUST, 1942

There wasn't much left of Ota Hanshiro now, just a sense of who he once was. He couldn't even remember who these men were that were standing in front of him, other than he wanted to tear their throats out and bathe in the sweet offal.

No, that wasn't who he was. Was it?

"Ota Hanshiro, Colonel, Unit 731, Imperial Japanese..." His speech slid away from him. The filthy human tongue he had speaking was something from another life. His life now was committed to the deep.

He could feel Clickers coming, a massive horde that the humans had cultivated with his help when he was still one of them. The juveniles had almost reached the mouth of the tunnel, the paltry workings of the human magus finally failing. The little brothers would rescue him, wash over these sea worms who dared to try to stop the resurrection of the Dark Empire. He would feast on their innards with them, then return to the deep city and his brethren.

All it would take was to dislodge the accursed metal that they had placed in his chest. The infernal working was keeping him as still as a fish left behind by the tide. All of his mental focus was on removing the spell the man had put on him, and little by little he could feel the magic beginning to ebb.

The workings of men had little effect on his kind. Magic was part of his kind. The landbound primates had to learn their craft from scratch and from long research.

With a start he realized that he had been an *Umibozu* again and hadn't realized it.

The American *tsukimono-suji* squatted in front of him.

"Hanshiro? Colonel Hanshiro? Are you still with us?"

The man had an odd accent, different from the formal English Ota had studied at university.

Ota nodded. He was still here, still him, at least for these next few moments. The American captain had promised that this man could save him. He looked at Ota with a look of immense pity, and Ota could only imagine what he looked like.

"Colonel, I need to know, where is their city? The Dark Ones done brought what we be bringing down on them. Otherwise, they'll take your home, just like they plan to be taking ours."

Despite his odd dialect, the man's words made sense. The *Umibozu* had betrayed him and taken everything from him, even his own body.

"You don't have long to make any kind of decision, Colonel. Soon the Dark One inside of you will take over."

"Past the farthest islands, in the open sea…I can see it in my head, down in the dark…thirty knots…"

The Dark One's mind reasserted itself and cursed inwardly that it had been weak enough to give these humans the location of its brethren. It spoke in its own tongue, knowing that the human magus would know what he was saying.

"Your workings are pathetic. You cannot harm us or our city."

The magus smiled, like all of their kind did when they were plotting something. "Oh, I thought that maybe too, at first. I could have driven the Clickers off the island with just my hoodoo. Your kind was a wrinkle. But apparently we've got something new, not a working either. Going to send every one of you off to hell." The magus waved at the big human that stood next to the door, who jogged over, raising his primitive weapon. "Course, I'm happy to send you there first."

He turned to the big human and spoke. "There ain't no saving him, Basher. Figured you wouldn't mind doing the honors, for Martino. Quick now, that working I put on him isn't going to last much longer."

The Dark One desperately began to try unraveling the working laid on him, fear and desperation washing over him, hastening the effort. He could feel his arms, twitching, raising slowly.

The large human raised his weapon, a small flame at the end, shaking his head back and forth and whispering something that the Dark One thought was a name.

"For Martino," the man whispered.

Whatever was left of Ota Hanshiro was grateful for it.

52. AUGUST, 1942

"Incoming, gentlemen," Pike said by the entrance, as cool as though he were giving the weather report. He fired twice down the tunnel.

Preach felt a familiar rush of fear. It was almost becoming like an old friend.

He'd thought that he'd seen it all. He'd lost family, friends, thought that he'd seen the worst of the world's inhumanity. Then he'd discovered a whole new definition of inhumanity.

Aside from a few patches of pale skin and human-shaped hands, despite webbing and scales, the Tojo had been almost fully transformed into a fish-man by the time Basher had unleashed the flamethrower on him.

When it was finished, Basher had hurried back to help Pike at the entrance to the tunnel as Microphone hastily gathered up his communication equipment, and the skipper was shouting orders. Everything was chaos.

Boudin ran past him, digging through his pack, barely glancing back up as he ran past Doodles, who was struggling with the Clicker in his hands. "Don't let him lose that thing, Preach!"

Preach nodded as hard as he could, trying to keep his hands from trembling as he joined Doodles in making sure that Pinchy didn't squirm out and rejoin its brethren.

The skipper had joined Pike in firing down the hall and neither seemed to be conserving their bullets. Preach could hear barely perceptible hisses as their targets felt the sting of the bullets. He wrapped his hands around Doodles' own, trying to control the trembling and bracing them to keep them from shaking. Apparently he'd flown halfway around the world to help a man hug his favorite lobster.

"Getting mighty close," Palmer said. "Basher!"

The two men jumped aside as Basher fired the flamethrower down the hall.

"You weren't kidding that was close, Skip," the farmboy said, wiping the sweat from his brow for more than one reason.

Pike and Palmer retook their places. "No chance we're getting back out the way we came."

Boudin came running, holding the remaining two coffin nails that he had retrieved from his destroyed mojo bag, unwavering as he drove one into the dirt on either side of the opening.

"This isn't going to hold them long, Skip."

Palmer hissed between his teeth and glanced around the room. The only way out was through the iron gate Hanshiro had been hidden behind.

"I guess we're going to be swimming out!"

Preach's stomach dropped as he looked at the tunnel and the lapping water of the ocean, like fingers beckoning him to dive in and drown. He had never been a good swimmer.

Boudin was drawing in the dirt, finger flying as fast as he could to draw the designs necessary for his witchcraft. Preach was amazed that he could remember whatever power he knew under the stress of everything.

"We've got one of those white ones coming," Pike said.

"Move!" Basher hollered, not bothering with military courtesies.

Pike and Palmer dove out of the way.

Preach saw the pale carapace of an albino Clicker rumbling down the hallway. A stream of flame from Basher's backpack caught it and held it back for a moment. Its flesh blackened and it collapsed to the ground. Then, like a massive campfire marshmallow, its black exterior began to flake and a wave of poisonous white innards began to flood out.

Boudin was so focused on his spell he didn't see what was about to befall him. He looked up just as the massive creature detonated. Releasing Doodles, Preach dove, hands outstretched, and shoved Boudin out of the way.

He felt something warm splatter against his body, but didn't immediately feel pain as he fell to the ground and rolled through the dirt. His breathing came machine gun fast, but he thought he had avoided the worst of it.

Then the pain began.

It was the most intense burning he'd ever felt. He could see that he was covered from his shoulders down in white goop that was already beginning to eat into his flesh. Blisters rose on his skin, popped away.

Melting. I'm melting.

It was the last coherent thought that Preach had before he began screaming. The Skipper and Pike appeared in his vision, yelling something that he couldn't comprehend over the pain. He saw Boudin, tears in his eyes, cutting into his wrist and dribbling blood onto the sandy floor of the cave, stopping a juvenile Clicker that was halfway across the threshold in its tracks.

Preach tried to wipe the goop off of his legs and took the upper layer of muscle off. Preach had never felt such pain. He saw something white and hard.

He realized it was his bone.

I'm going to die. I'm not going home.

His heart beat faster, but he barely noticed over the sheer agony as the last layer of muscle bubbled away, exposing his chest cavity. His internal organs came spilling out. Preach tried to shove his guts back into himself, only to find that his hand had melted down to the wrist.

Words like, "Do we have time?" echoed in Preach's ears as the world spun around him.

Boudin shook his head and pointed. The Clickers were pawing at the sand beyond his spell. It wasn't holding them back.

Arms grasped his shoulder and he was vaguely aware of faces he recognized, some streaming with tears. Basher was saying something and Microphone smiling weakly. Boudin seemed to be making an earnest promise of some sort. Pike just tipped his hat. And the skipper was kissing his rosary and no doubt giving a hell of a speech.

And then they were gone and he was alone, consumed by pain.

"Why have you forsaken me?" he whispered, a tear trailing down his cheek.

Panic and fear joined with the agony to transform Preach's last moments in life into unashamed terror as he pathetically whined for them not to leave him there.

He couldn't turn over to beg; the bones in his legs, as well as guts were now nothing more than sizzling slop.

Suddenly a hand wrapped around his remaining one. His focus returned just enough to recognize…Doodles.

"Hey, buddy," the mad cook said. "They call you Prayer Guy or something, right?"

Doodles pulled him into an embrace, though Preach knew there was distressingly little of his body left to hold. Glancing down he saw Pinchy nuzzling into his thigh, assiduously avoiding slurping up his melted remains. He guessed that was the highest form of affection a Clicker could show.

"Don't worry," Doodles said, "We'll be right here 'til the end. Then your God guy will have you."

It didn't take long for Doodles's promise to come true.

53. AUGUST, 1942

Alcide was sure that if he lived through this war, that he would never be able to get the image of Willie Cantor melting on the floor out of his head. The only thing left of him that was still mostly solid had been his shoulders and head. Everything else had slowly but surely liquefied under the damn albino Clicker's venom.

He couldn't have saved him. Even if he had been surrounded by the most powerful healing ingredients in the world, he couldn't have saved him. But it felt wrong to Alcide, looking into Preach's eyes as he pleaded to save him, mindless agony behind his pupils as he tried to form the words only to find his lungs beginning to dissolve as the deadly venom worked on him.

Microphone was shouting next to the sea tunnel, urging the rest of them to hurry, that the Clickers were getting through. One glance could confirm that. The nails he'd driven into the dirt were quivering.

The Clickers writhed over each other, carapaces undulating as they tried to get past the invisible barrier of will that he had erected. Their primitive animal intelligences couldn't understand why it was impossible to pass the spot that he had marked.

But it wouldn't last long. Workings always functioned better when done in secret, out-of-the-way places unseen by any eyes other than the caster. There were too many tiny eyes watching, too many spirits opposing. Alcide thought that his working might as well have been unraveling to match his breathing. The Clickers were already drawing closer, that infernal noise drawing Alcide's unmatched rage.

There were plenty of things he could do, but they wouldn't avenge Preach and at best would just lead to his death. He looked back down into the dying man's eyes and whispered, "I'm sorry."

He placed his hand across Preach's forehead, a motion of comfort, as if it could do anything to comfort the man who desperately wanted to live. Then he left, running as Pike shouted beside him, "Move your ass, Private!"

They regrouped inside the tunnel. Doodles, holding Pinchy tight, was the last to arrive. He'd been dawdling for some reason. There was no way the group could swim out and hold the maimed Clicker at the same time. The skipper let off a blast from the Thompson as the Clickers broke through.

Alcide wrangled his pack from his shoulders and opened the flap, looking directly at Doodles. "Hurry and put your crawdad in here. No time to argue."

The cook only glanced down once before he deposited his companion into Alcide's pack.

"A little haste would seem to be in order," Sergeant Pike mentioned casually as he fired a round. The Clicker he struck squealed as the bullet pierced its brain, segmented legs twitching as they scrabbled against the floor.

Alcide waded into the water until he was up to his waist. He could feel Pinchy fighting inside his pack, but he couldn't be worried about his ingredients or prepared workings now.

Now it was time to swim.

"Take a deep breath and pray that the Lord gives our lungs strength and our legs swiftness," Alcide prayed.

He took a deep breath and dove. The current flowed out and dully he heard the splashes behind him as the rest of the men followed. His rifle was lost in the water, but he left it behind gladly, his pack already weighing him down more than anything else as he was swept along through the tunnel. He kicked and stroked as hard as he could, trying only to breathe out a little at a time.

He had spent more time than most in the water. Back home in the bayou he'd learned to hold his breath while digging his hand under old logs and inside waterlogged stumps for the catfish that would nest there.

The current spit him out, the control of the tunnel traded for the wild waves of the open ocean. Alcide floated up and broke the surface with a mighty gasp of air. He floundered to the shore, the waves dumping him on the beach like he had just been spat out of a whale's belly.

His eyes were shut as he gasped for breath, feeling the coarseness of the sand under him, vaguely aware of the gasping breaths from the other men. He was too grateful for his own life, that he didn't bother counting those that came behind him.

There was a dull thump next to him. He opened his salt-caked eyes and saw Microphone staring blankly, face as pale as the frosting on a vanilla cake.

"Microphone?" he croaked.

The radioman didn't respond, his eyes wide and dull, mouth slackened. He'd taken a long drink of the ocean, and had passed out of all thought and life.

Alcide wearily stretched his hand over to the radioman and patted his arm, trying to find his voice over the dreadful soreness that still seized his throat. "Thank you, Microphone. I'm sorry it ended this way. When your soul gets to the crossroads, tell the keeper I'm good for the gunpowder and rum, then tell the Good Lord we could use his help now."

He hoped his words carried across the divide that separated the living and the dead. Either way, they needed to get off this beach.

The skipper groaned as he crawled to his hands and knees, coughs wracking his body as he spat out the sea water. Alcide walked over to him, managing to hack out, "Come on, Skipper. We need to be moving."

Palmer nodded, bent over and coughing, but Alcide was glad to see that he was at least on his feet.

The rest weren't far behind. Doodles came crawling towards him, still spitting water, but with his eyes focused firmly on the sack carrying his maimed pet. "Is he okay? Did he make it?" The cook reached for the pack and Alcide maneuvered it to avoid his grasp.

"Should be okay. Clickers breathe underwater. More than likely he's chewing on a few of my soaked ingredients."

His words didn't seem to dissuade the cook as he tried to snatch the pack back from Alcide's grasp. "Let me hold him. We aren't swimming now."

The skipper laid a hand on the cook's shoulder and shook his head. "Not now, Doodles. It'll be better if Boudin keeps Pinchy for now."

They didn't have time to waste. Already Alcide could see wavering tails appearing in the churning surf.

The Clicker army had followed them.

"Let's get a move on!"

The survivors followed his gaze, and didn't take much to get them moving after the first crustacean emerged from spray.

None of them had managed to keep their weapons except for Pike and even he ended up tossing his rifle after two misfires. Alcide didn't bother to wait for the sniper to catch up and neither did the others.

They looked like rats fleeing a sinking ship.

54. AUGUST, 2020

Jay Wilburn's glasses had slid halfway down his nose and come to a halt. A vigorous shake of the head would've sent them flying, but for the moment they were perfectly balanced for the trademark Wilburn staredown.

"What do you want me to say, Cam?"

"I want you to say what's in your heart, Jay. Or, more importantly, what's in your head. You're the second finest marine biologist in America."

Wilburn snorted and rolled his eyes. "The day you're better than me at this job is the day you stop peddling these ridiculous Atlantis stories."

Cam rolled his own eyes and dropped down into a chair opposite his old friend. "My God, Jay, how can you say that when you're looking at proof right now?"

"Proof?" Wilburn shook the glass encased box. "What I'm looking at is some prehistoric throwback, I will give you that. It is both like and unlike any other species of crustacean I have seen before."

"It's a goddamned monstrosity! Do you know how these things were used by the Dark Ones? As food, as pets, as beasts of labor."

"Let me stop you right there, Cam. I'm not even going to question your claim, because there is no way to prove a negative. I am merely going to walk you down the rest of this logical road. If you found a dog on the moon, would you consider that proof that there had once been a mighty human civilization there?"

"No," Cam grumbled. Wilburn closed his eyes and pressed his fists together in something akin to a Zen acknowledgement of Cam's defeat. "Look, all I need you to do is certify that this thingy is the weirdest dang crawdad you ever did see. Then I'll get out of your hair."

Wilburn folded his arms. "I'm not going to do that, Cam."

Cam gestured expansively around Wilburn's garage. It wasn't quite the same as meeting at the man's office at the National Aquarium in Baltimore, where he had a suite of top-tier equipment. The problem was that legally they shouldn't even have been meeting in Wilburn's garage. It was a testament to their many decades of friendship that Wilburn had even allowed him that.

"Rosamilia and Edler already gave me their votes of confidence." He dug into his satchel and pulled out the reports from the other marine biologists he'd managed to catch up with since leaving Los Alamos.

"Good for them. Let them stake their professional reputations on it. See, you don't even need me. Rosamilia and Edler have got you covered."

Cam waved the reports in Wilburn's face. "Look. Just look at their reports. They did everything but slobber on my knob and say I get to call it *metacarcinus custer*."

Wilburn slapped his arm down. "I don't need to read their reports. I don't need anybody to tell me how to think. I've already drawn my conclusions."

"I don't get it, Jay. What do you want? You want more DNA? You want more time to examine it?"

"You're not listening, Cam. And I think we both know why you're not listening."

Cam slammed himself down in the plush leather couch Wilburn kept in the garage. "Because you think I'm a quack. A sellout. A has-been. And maybe a never-was. Worse than Bill Nye, Doctor Wizard, and Neil deGrasse Tyson combined for vulgarizing science."

"Well, okay, Captain Self-Pity. Can you debark the S.S. Self-Pity, or will all the guests at your floating self-pity party feel too pitiful and have to slink off to some self-pity bar somewhere?"

"I don't even know what you're accusing me of anymore."

"Nothing. I'm saying there's nothing wrong with your

methodology. Or Rosamilia's or Edler's or anybody's. This is a new species you've found, Cam. You should be very proud. I don't see how it would make a big splash in the newspapers, or even the peer-reviewed journals, but you've always been better at publicity than me. I'm sure you'll make a movie called *The Prehistoric Terror* and make a mint."

"I was thinking *The Antediluvian Horror*."

"See? You've always been better at that crap than me. However I am not going to be putting my name or the implicit weight of the National Aquarium on any documents for you."

"Why not?"

Wilburn made a face like he was sucking on an entire halved lemon. "Let me guess, Cam. You've been on the road the last two, three weeks, picking up all of these scintillating testimonials from Frank and Armand and whoever else you could rope in with your last shred of old-timey celebrity?"

"I can't tell if you're trying to insult me or explain something to me."

Wilburn picked up the TV remote. They kept an old black and white TV in the garage, presumably to watch whenever Wilburn remembered how much he hated color and definition. It didn't have the rabbit ears Cam had long associated with such archaic devices, though. Wilburn had actually gone to the trouble to install a digital receiver on a television that probably still ran on vacuum tubes.

The TV sprang, much slower than it should have, to life. And there, in the upper right corner, was Cam's picture. Wilburn muted the television, and began flipping through channels, but it was clear that he had become the latest media obsession. Apparently he had gone on a murderous rampage through New Mexico and police in every corner of the country were working around the clock to catch him. It was 1977 all over again, except now they were calling it the Summer of Cam.

"What the fuck?" Cam asked, his hand going to his face.

Wilburn put a sympathetic arm around his shoulder. "Let me guess. You haven't been watching TV?"

"I've been sleeping in the van and only stopping for gas. And the fucking radio's broken."

"Well, Cam, I promise I won't report you. Frank Edler and Armand Rosamilia, on the other hand, have been saying that you forced them to sign some kooky testimonials. They've been raking in interviews like they're candy, or maybe I should say like they're ballpark brats."

Edler was famous for downing bratwurst and Rosamilia's love of baseball was legendary. He often said if he hadn't been a marine biologist he would've been a baseball announcer.

Cam's hand went through his hair, suddenly wet with sweat. "What are they saying I did?"

"I don't know. Did you break into a federal facility and pull off some guy's nose?"

"Oh, sort of." Wilburn took a step backward. "It wasn't me," Cam protested, "and the person who did it, did it in self-defense."

"Yeah. Well, I don't know if the stand-your-ground law quite covers biting a dude's face off, but good luck with that in court, Cam."

"This doesn't change your promise, does it?"

"No, I am not going to call the police after you leave. But I can't make that same promise for anybody else that you see. Cam, you want some friendly advice?

"Not really."

"You need to turn yourself in. The FBI is offering a twenty-six-million-dollar reward for you."

"Twenty-six million?"

"Yeah. It's the biggest bounty in U.S. history. A million more than bin Laden. Look, you don't have to tell me what really happened in New Mexico if you don't want. But whatever it was, you pissed the feds off bad. They're carpet bombing the airwaves trying to run you down. I mean, you think CNN and Fox News really want to be covering your dumb ass in the middle of an election season? Somebody's dropping millions into pushing this."

"All that rather than just admit climate change is real."

"That's your takeaway? Sure, that, or you gave the government a black eye in Los Alamos."

Cam stalked sullenly toward the side door of the garage. Aware now of his newly minted Most Wanted in History status, he didn't want to risk opening the sliding door he had come in.

"All right, thanks, Jay. For your forthrightness. And for being my friend."

Wilburn walked up and rubbed a little warmth back into his upper back.

"Hey, Cam. Do you need anything? A couple bucks? Some food? Clothes?"

Wilburn opened the garage fridge and pulled out half a hoagie. Cam waved him off.

"No. I'm not a lawyer but from what I remember from old Law and Order episodes, that would make you an accessory after the fact."

Wilburn shrugged. "It's just a sandwich. What are they going to do, send me to Gitmo?"

"I'm worth twenty-six million dollars to them, Jay. I'm sure they'd be happy to throw the book at you over a sandwich."

"All right. I mean, I'd at least let you stay in the house but..."

"No, no. Accessory after the fact."

"At least park your van down by the river back there. It's off my property. And nobody will bother you. Get a good night's sleep and..."

He trailed off. Normally the sentiment was to get a fresh start tomorrow, but really Cam didn't have that option. Tomorrow he'd be back to being a fugitive.

Feeling like a drunk in the middle of a bender, he made his way clumsily down Wilburn's driveway, now with the added disability of seeing eyes in every shrub and binoculars behind every window. He clambered into the van and slammed his head onto the steering wheel.

"Hey!"

He jumped up, beeping the horn, which set an alarm off in a nearby car, drawing exactly the kind of attention he didn't want. Half the lights in the houses of the little suburban cul-de-sac Wilburn lived in sprang to life.

He breathlessly drove the car down the dirt fishing trail Wilburn had indicated and parked behind a stand of bushes by a lake. Then he turned to look at Jade, who was grinning that massive, foot-high grin of hers.

"Sorry," she said, "I didn't mean to startle you. How did it go with Dr. Wilburn? You said he's the best, right? Is he in your corner?"

"He's a far superior scientist. I am merely more famous, which is and always has been a point of great contention in the academic community."

"You're throwing a lot of fifty cent words at me there, Doctor C. Want to tell me what happened?"

Cam glanced up the path to see Wilburn talking with a few neighbors in bathrobes. Wilburn was acting just as irritated and confused as the rest of them.

Cam held up a finger to Jade so that she would wait. Dutifully, for once, the reptilian cheerleader obeyed. The impromptu block party broke up and Wilburn, of course, gave a gaze down the fishing path that would have flattened a tiger before returning to his garage.

Sighing, Cam clambered into the back of the van. The place was littered with candy wrappers and empty sardine cans. Mostly, though, it was just an impromptu sleeping quarters for the both of them. And shoved into the back, strapped down with bungee cords, was the doodled Clicker, still in a state of near-catatonia since he had started setting the refrigerated tank to its coldest setting.

Jade had built a cocoon for herself out of sheets and blankets, which she wetted down every night. He just had some cushions and pillows for himself since it was still summer and the earth was slowly baking itself into a cinder thanks to all of the carbon his species was haphazardly dumping into the air.

She came and lay down, putting her head on her arm and sticking her knee up into the air like any teenage girl. He almost laughed. She truly continued to surprise him every day.

"We are the most wanted people in America."

"We are?" Jade asked, her fringe lifting off her neck slightly, a sign, he noted, of excitement.

"We are. And the other two scientists I dragged you around to get opinions on our white friend here called the cops to let them know we had stopped by. And Wilburn is probably inside right now doing the same thing."

"You mean we're like Mickey and Mallory?"

Her eyes, black, empty pits whenever he looked at them, shone now with an infinite excitement.

"I guess. But, Jade, I don't think you..."

She was kissing him. It was the first time it had happened in real life, at least. Disturbingly, it had been happening in his dreams every night since they had met. In a way, that made sense. All his life he had fetishized the Dark Ones and their civilization. It only made sense that he would have confused feelings upon meeting a real one.

And this girl was truly extraordinary, independent of being a mythical undersea monster. She was witty and charming and innocent and...well, that just made him feel like Humbert Humbert because he could just as well have been describing any teenage girl. Well, technically she was twenty, and not even human, so maybe those rules didn't even apply. It seemed strange to attribute all of these feelings to such a clearly alien creature. It also didn't help that he hadn't been on a date since college.

As for the kiss itself...it was strange, but not unpleasant. Her tongue was long, sharp, pointed at the end, and seemingly prehensile. There were several times he worried he was about to straight out choke on it, but somehow he didn't.

Kissing a creature who, with a snap of her jaws could have ripped his face off, or split his tongue in two, carried infatuation perverse and dangerous attraction. She was so physically potent, so overwhelmingly powerful, that his human body could have been nothing more than a plaything to her, like a monkey ripping the head off a frog to masturbate with.

She didn't break his body for fun, though. Instead she climbed up on him and fumbled to unbuckle his pants. She did pretty well considering she'd probably never used a belt buckle before.

"Is it...is it easier with me on top?"

His mouth fluttered. "Is this your first time?"

Her tongue slithered out of her mouth, and, without her head moving, it danced all over his face and neck, slipped deep into first one ear, then the other.

"Of course."

He felt embarrassed to have asked. Of course it was her first time. She'd been monitored and videotaped 24/7 at Los Alamos. This was the first time she'd been free in her life.

"I shouldn't," he said. "It's not right."

She quirked her head, looking more human than reptilian monster.

"What's not right, Doctor C., is letting me die or get tossed back into a cell for the rest of my life a virgin. I like you. You like me. It doesn't have to be capital 'L' love. It doesn't have to be marriage. But I would deeply, truly like to have this experience."

"As would I," he blurted out.

"Then show me what to do."

He put his hands around her hips. He really didn't have to do anything. After seeing her tongue at play, he was as hard as a rock. He shimmied out of his pants and tighty-whities. She looked down at him, fascinated.

"Take a good look," he said. He wasn't sure if that was the scientist in him, or the father figure, or the lover. Or maybe just the decent human being. He wanted this to be good for her, even if it felt so deeply wrong on about seventeen different levels. "You can touch it if you want to," he said when she looked to him a moment later for guidance.

She gently stroked his penis, causing it to throb. God, he didn't want to ejaculate prematurely in front of her. He never wanted to, of course, but in front of this emissary from another world would have been particularly embarrassing. Christ, why hadn't he just jerked off in the last few days?

"With your size," he said, "I think you need to be underneath. So you don't crush me."

"Just what every girl loves to hear."

"Or…" he said, taking firm hold of her wrists, strangely reminding him of the first time he had ever touched her. From the look on her face he saw she remembered that time, too, and showing him her bestial nature. This time was thoroughly different for them both, though. "You can put your hands and knees flat. And I can…well, I'll show you."

He had never been so intimidated in his life. At seven feet

tall, the girl was bigger than anyone he'd ever slept with, not that he had a ton of experience in that department.

All things considered, though, she wasn't too anatomically different from a human. He was worried he would have trouble entering her, but mostly her cloaca lined up with his penis. He fingered her briefly, snatching her breath away. He couldn't identify any clitoris or other outside genitalia. He would just have to hope penetration was pleasurable for her kind.

"You tell me," he said, "if anything feels uncomfortable or hurts. Sex means communicating openly with your partner."

"I understand," she replied.

Nodding, he entered her.

Immediately his mind was swept up in a nightmare haze. As he thrust, instead of seeing a beautiful, albeit alien young girl in front of him, he saw ancient cities with runic inscriptions on towering steeples complicated enough to put Babel to shame. He shook his head, trying to clear it, unsure if Jade was connecting with him psychically somehow or he was merely growing detached from reality, but still, the images flooded his mind.

Ten million years of civilization flew by as he evolved from something akin to a shrimp into a master of the undersea domain. Clickers swam through his vision, beloved pets, nipping at his knees even as he tried to inseminate his wife's egg sac, and both of them laughing at it. There were Stygian temples filled with chanting Dark Ones. Wars broke out, and they ate their captives. They came ashore and the shore was dry and brutal to be on, but still, they came ashore. And then there were his kind, and he remembered that he hadn't always been a Dark One.

Their species had interbred many times. This was far from the first mingling. Fully half of the Dark Ones had human stock in them. There were so many orgies by bonfires on the beaches of every ocean in all the land. For a moment, it seemed like all human and Dark One did together was fuck. And they were. And Jade was screaming.

He opened his eyes. Her frill was fully engorged. And tugging at his own scrotum he could feel the telltale last few moments before orgasm. She turned her face to the roof of the van and let out an inaudible scream, so potent that he thought, perhaps, no woman had ever truly climaxed before tonight.

Then, he, too, was caught up in the wave of it, and all was one. He was just a tiny pink creature, overthinking the spurting of semen into a mate. But he was also the master of the ocean floor, king of ten thousand generations of the inky depths. He was cumming, but he was also ascending into a higher form of consciousness. Not orgasm. Apotheosis.

His tiny penis slipped out of her and he fell over, spent, onto his bedroll. Imaginary birds fluttered in a little circle around his head.

"Was I any good?" she asked.

He nodded, unable to say more.

Twenty minutes later, arms wrapped around each other, Cam felt himself craving a cigarette, a dirty habit he'd given up nearly forty years prior. No word had been exchanged in all that time. No questionable replay. No professions of love or promises to call in the morning. They'd simply sat, both enjoying each other's presence.

"Should we turn ourselves in now," she asked, "or run for a couple of more days?"

He shook his head. "I'm out of gas money. I should've taken something from Wilburn, but I couldn't bear to do that to him."

"It's too bad," she said. "What'd you say we were worth now? A million dollars?"

"I didn't. But it's twenty-six million. The largest bounty in history."

She whistled in appreciation. "Too bad we couldn't have your friend take the bounty and give us half."

Cam sat straight upward, his back going from post-coital loosey-goosey to ramrod straight. He looked her in the eyes, and gently stroked her cheek.

"Come with me," he said.

"All right," she agreed with a toothy smile, "just let me put on my disguise."

"No. Don't bother."

He led her up the dirt path, not nearly fast enough to avoid tripping. He pounded on Wilburn's garage door. It had to be solidly three in the morning at this point. But, unsurprisingly, Wilburn was still awake. He answered the door and his eyes went wide at Jade's appearance. Jade tried to play the blushing debutante, wrapping her arms behind her back.

"Wilburn, how would you like to make thirteen million dollars?"

Wilburn shrugged. "I could take it or leave it."

Cam dug a finger into his friend's sternum. "Call the hotline or...whatever it is. Tell them we'll turn ourselves in. All we want to do is give our presentation. Oh, and I'll still want that peer review from you."

Wilburn shrugged. "Fair enough."

55. AUGUST, 1942

Sergeant John Pike's lungs burned as he ran. Every time he stopped to catch his breath for even a second the telltale *click-click click-click* not even a hundred yards behind him surged forward.

It sounded like the jungle was swarming with them, their twisted claws clacking out a symphony. With every turn of a palm frond or dodge behind a tree, he was afraid that he would plunge headlong into the waiting pincers, and no matter what color they came in, they'd make short work of his flesh. In a way, he was surprised by his survival instinct. He'd been courting death since the day he'd joined up.

To die in the mud and surf of some distant Pacific speck seemed preferable than going back to the empty life he'd left behind.

He'd had a child on the way. His wife had been so excited making up the house and crib down by the old Wolf River. She'd been out one early March morning, combing her hair on the dock in the crisp chill air.

A bad winter had sent runoff into the churning waters. Logs and other flotsam got lost in the strong currents and carried down the river until it would eventually dump into the sea unless they sunk straight to the bottom.

This had not been one of those times.

An accident, a twist of fate, an act of God…those were the terms that Pike had heard after the log had come barreling down the river, carried along as swiftly as an underwater rocket. It had annihilated the dock and turned him into a widower.

He'd enlisted a few weeks later, tired of the never-ending

parade of food trays from his neighbors and assurances that God still had a plan.

Now Pike found himself wondering what sort of a God would allow these monstrosities to exist.

A shallow river split the jungle in two. Pike barely paused before plunging in. The water wasn't deep, barely up to his knees, but it was slow going as he waded to the other shore.

The foliage on the shore behind him rustled. He looked back to see the white shells of a pack of *Kamikaze* Clickers plunging straight into the river after him, moving through the water like the log that had killed his wife, barreling straight towards him. They weren't wearing the explosives their kin had been equipped with during the fight at the airfield, but what he knew about this breed was that they did not stop, could not be distracted, would neither feed nor pause until they reached their target.

He was tempted to spread his hands, close his eyes, and wait for the end. Let death come on the end of claw and stinger. Instead, he turned and fled into the jungle, once more racing away from Death.

56. AUGUST, 1942

Basher crested a hill. He'd lost sight of the skipper and Boudin. The insane cook had been left behind in his sprint, and who the hell knew where Sergeant Pike had disappeared to.

The Clickers were swarming the jungle now. He'd only thought there were a few hundred underground, but now they were boiling out of every Tojo hole and stream along the way back to Lunga Point.

The closest he'd come so far had been when one of the obsidian-shelled monsters had come crawling out of a Tojo tunnel right as Basher was running over the thatch covering.

He wouldn't even have tripped if not for the Clicker emerging. It had sent him tumbling into the dirt. He'd scrambled to his feet even as the angry Clicker had begun to spray the venom from the tip of its stinger. Basher had screamed and rolled to his feet, hearing the sizzle and wilting of the foliage as the venom began to burn into the ground. He ran, hearing the monster's pursuit, sprinting as fast as he could, but losing his bearings in the process.

It was suicide to keep running with no sense of direction. He was just as liable to run past the gun sights of some Tojo holdout as to be caught by a Clicker, or, God forbid, a Dark One. It hadn't taken him long to find a hill after that. He'd climbed like an animal, all four limbs digging deep into the soil as he hauled himself to the top.

When he summited, the dull roars of a distant cannonade came rushing across the ocean. The strait was filled with ships. Admiral Fletcher had arrived in full force, distant rumblings and flashes of light illuminating the steel hulks as they fired at the island.

Lights dotted the shoreline and the staccato beat of machine guns dispensing death reached his ears. He could see scurrying shapes in the surf, more Clickers emerging to do battle with the Marines on shore.

Basher had initially thought that the sea was rough, the ships bouncing on the waves as they fired. But now he could see that the ocean was churning with Clickers darting in and out of the waves, crawling up the sides of destroyers and the aircraft carrier that dominated the center of the fleet. Men screamed and small arms fire raced up and down the decks as they desperately tried to repel the creatures.

Basher felt very small standing on the top of that hill, listening to the sounds of men screaming and the hissing of the creatures in the sea. Gunshots and cannons thundered in every direction imaginable.

He felt like a witness to Armageddon. He also thought of his wife and daughter. He knew in his heart he wouldn't see them again.

He thought of Martino, left decapitated at the bottom of the cave, and he wondered how long it would be until he joined him as just another body in the uncaring jungle. The dead private's dog tags were still in his pocket. He wondered if Boudin's hoodoo was beginning to get to him. He could practically hear his friend begging him not to be forgotten, to carry the memory of him as something other than a headless corpse left to rot in a dark tunnel.

He didn't know if he would make it off the island, but at least he could salute his friend's memory before he became nothing more than a ghost in someone else's.

Basher walked to a young palm tree, just barely bigger than himself, and draped Martino's dog tags across the leaf. It bent slightly under the weight, but ultimately held. A slight breeze brought the smell of smoke, oil, and blood to his nose.

The metal proclaimed Martino's name and service number, the only thing anyone would know if they managed to find it. Basher took a moment to salute the dog tags. "See you around, Martino."

Clicking sounded from the jungle again, close enough that

Basher could see the fern fronds pushed aside by big meaty claws.

He turned and ran down the hill, making a beeline for Lunga Point and the fight.

57. AUGUST, 1942

Doodles stumbled out onto the beach, the Florida Islands illuminated against the clear night moon. He thought it sounded like the Fourth of July with so many explosions and bright lights out in the sea tonight.

Pinchy's big brothers had made it a rough go. They seemed to be everywhere, but Doodles didn't mind dodging them too much. He was more worried about the Cajun. He'd taken Pinchy and disappeared into the jungle. They'd gotten split up, and now Doodles didn't know where his friend was.

Off to his left was a carrier that seemed somehow bigger than the one he had served on a lifetime ago. They were shooting at the water. It seemed silly to waste ammunition on the water. Everyone knew the Tojos were up in the hills.

Doodles didn't know what to do. Pinchy could be anywhere. They'd been separated once and he'd nearly gone mad with grief. He didn't know what he'd do if they never saw each other again.

Pinchy could have been struggling to free himself from the bag because the Cajun was dead! His chest twisted and a harrowing sob escaped his breath as he began to run up the beach towards the lights and explosions, screaming, *"Pinchy! Pinchy"*

The sand sucked at his feet, the ocean waves nearly knocking him from his feet as he sprinted through the wet tide pools. He fell more than once.

He barely noticed the swathes of corpses that littered the beach. Clickers that had been blown in two, their legs still scrabbling as primitive nerves tried to devour the cook as he ran past. The remains of American and Japanese soldiers floated in the tide, and if Doodles would have paused to look, he would have seen missing limbs, guts bouncing on the waves before they splattered against the sand, a feast for the small crabs enjoying the bounty of war.

The cook ran until his lungs burned, and the battle that had already seemed like an eternity away didn't appear to be growing any closer. His legs felt heavy, muscles screaming at him to stop. But he defied his muscles.

Can't stop. Pinchy needs me. He's alone, without a friend in the world!

A large piece of driftwood lay on the shore and Doodles stumbled over to it, collapsing and leaning against the hard bark, listening to the sounds of battle. He licked his lips. The Marines had given him some water, but his thirst had returned with a vengeance and he'd barely eaten anything all day.

He clenched the bark of the driftwood and felt it give way, rough but permeable, like fish scale. When he opened his eyes and looked at his hand, he realized that it was covered in black blood. What he'd thought had been driftwood was the heavily mangled corpse of a Dark One. The slack jawed mouth of the creature was dripping blood, its chest a painting of bullet holes from a machine gun emplacement.

The current had carried it down from the battle and it looked like the sharks had enjoyed their meal as so much death washed down the channel. The fish-man's body was missing feet and large chunks had been taken out of its center, exposing the bone and muscle.

Doodles scrambled off of the dead creature, staring into its eye sockets. The creature stared back at him, black eyes gnawed away by eels or crabs, but the cook's gaze was drawn to the thing's clenched hand.

It may have been missing its other limbs, but its one remaining hand tightly clutched a trident of unknowable metal. A weapon! Doodles scrambled forward. "None of Pinchy's cousins are going to send me into the clambake!"

He was already digging at the thing's stiffened flesh as his words echoed off the shore. Pulling the webbed hand apart didn't take much effort. Freshly dead, rigor mortis hadn't set in, assuming fish-men suffered from rigor mortis.

Doodles cackled madly as he raised the trident in the air. Larger than any weapon made for a man, he needed both hands to handle it. His whoops carried up and down the beach.

A dozen Clickers emerged from the forest, drawn by his victorious cries, but Doodles wasn't afraid. They were all bigger than Pinchy, but none of them carried his vivaciousness. The zest for life that had caused the monster to befriend the man.

"Come on, wee beasties! Pinchy and I are going to have a nice supper tonight! Come on you sons of guns! If three months on this island couldn't kill me, you boil bugs don't stand a chance!"

The Clickers didn't pause at his challenge, even as he beat his bare chest, screaming at the top of his lungs. He waved the trident wildly, but the Clickers all simply stared at him, their eyes flickering back and forth on their stalks. He stopped waving the trident and their eyes stopped. Then he slowly moved it and they followed.

It took Doodles a solid five more minutes of experimenting before he realized that the Clickers were obeying the trident, like a lion bowing before a tamer's whip.

Well, now he knew how to forage for himself, avoid the Japanese patrols, and keep the Clickers from bothering him. Suddenly, the sounds of battle didn't seem so compelling. Maybe he'd just stay here. All he needed to do was meet back up with Pinchy.

Well, those Marines had promised to let him go when they were done with him, and jarheads were big on stuff like keeping their word. Whistling a jaunty tune, he headed back for his encampment, calling occasionally for Pinchy along the way. All the Clickers he encountered along the way gave him a wide berth.

58. AUGUST, 1942

The bullets chewed through the undergrowth as Alcide ran, hollering the password at the top of his lungs. He emerged from the jungle with a Clicker at his heels. A quick glance on either side of him confirmed that it wasn't the only one.

Corpses littered the area, and what few trees had managed to find purchase in the sand had been reduced to bits of wiry pulp. He tried not to think about what he was stepping in when his feet passed through something wet and warm.

Incoming fire chattered and Alcide threw himself to the sand, covering his pack with his body and trying to prevent the maimed Clicker from escaping. Freed from the rubber bands the cook had managed to wrangle around the crustacean's pincers, the animal was doing its best to punch holes through the cloth pack.

Even now, Alcide could feel the chitinous legs pushing against his chest, tearing at his uniform and leaving long scratches where they raked against his skin. He mumbled a working to quiet Pinchy down and only now realized how exhausted he was from using so much magic so fast. Still, Pinchy stopped pinching.

He heard a hiss and rolled to his left without thinking, narrowly avoiding the jab of a stinger as it embedded in the sand next to him. The force of the blow sent sand flying and the massive, couch-sized Clicker hissed again, pincers reaching for him. Alcide began praying and trying to summon up some semblance of a working when the sharp burst of a Thompson submachine gun sounded.

Small bits of carapace flew and the maddened animal hissed

in displeasure as it backed up, snapping its claws at the group of men who'd broken cover to save him.

"Is that goddamned Robichaude?"

Alcide never thought he'd be thankful to hear Sergeant Arthur Webb's booming voice. He glanced up and saw the large man wading through pulped Clicker corpses like it was just another day at the beach.

A squad of marines flanked him, boys from the 2nd and 3rd by the looks of them, but a few from the old company. Their trigger fingers twitched as they glanced all around them, eyes scanning the darkness for anymore monsters eager to make a meal from them.

Alcide looked up at the big sergeant whose face was impassive. "Where's your rifle, Robichaude? Can't you see it's Judgment Day?"

There was a round of panicked calls from the men who had accompanied Webb. It was a somewhat subtle change, but Webb seemed to be yelling more than usual. He practically had to order each man to put one foot in front of the other. Five Clickers emerged from the trees and scuttled over the sand. Harsh squealing hisses split the air as they raised their stingers.

The bullets found them and Gunny gestured down at Alcide as he fired. "Get him on his feet and behind the firing line!" The men quick at the big man's orders, grabbing Alcide roughly by the arms. They weren't stupid, but they were acting lethargic, and seemed to only be able to function thanks to Webb's overpowering will.

They can feel it, that weight like an anchor dragging them down to murky waters. The Dark Ones working.

The sea was roiling with desperate fire from the carrier and destroyers in the strait. Masses of Dark Ones were attempting to sink the vessels and storm the shore. Their minds linked together were like a tidal wave, drowning every man on this island in the hopeless riptide of fear. Even Alcide, who'd been brought up to resist these kinds of attacks, could feel the pull nipping at his mind and senses like the sea biting away at the shore. One glance around the hastily built fortifications told Alcide all he needed to know. The men were fighting a battle they were sure would be their last. Perhaps the Dark Ones had made a mistake, then, Alcide supposed, to take away any hope of escape. To deny a man escape forced him to fight harder. The result was a force of Marines on the brink of insanity, eager to kill everything that drug itself from the sea or jungle. And no force on Earth could stand up to that.

Webb's men deposited Alcide against a sandy embankment, immediately firing over it at a Dark One that had rushed up the beach. Alcide heard its death gurgle as it flopped down onto the sand. A few Clickers that had been following in its trail diverted from their course to feast on the unexpected meal.

Webb had been right, perhaps. It looked like the end of the world, some dark rendition of Hell by a mad painter. Except here, the fires were waves and the demons had scales.

Distracted by the slaughter, it took Alcide a moment to realize that the Marines had left him in a makeshift casualty collection point. The battle dead lay in various states of demise: throats slashed, innards pulled and left strewn on the ground, blood pooling into the sand. The coagulated blood seemed to ooze through the sand toward him, so he could almost reach out and touch it.

Alcide stared at a dead Marine, but he couldn't see the man's real face. All he saw was Trick, confused, the unspoken question lingering on his dead lips.

Why didn't you save me?

"Robichaude!"

Alcide snapped back to reality and realized that Webb was snapping his fingers in his face, and probably had been for a little while.

"Christ, everyone's acting like this today. What happened down in those tunnels, Robichaude? Where's the skipper?" Webb stared at him, his eyes never blinking while Alcide recapped the tale.

He related the story of Dempsey's death, then Martino's, then Preach's. With each confession, another face was added to the pile of dead marines, worn like funeral masks and each one staring daggers at Alcide.

"And then we got separated in the jungle," he concluded.

Webb looked over at Alcide's pack. "You've really got the cook's pet in there?"

He nodded, steeling his heart. "It's about time I get this working underway. Enough men have died to get me here. After this is through, they'll be on me like flies on a dead horse. Going to need transport away from here. Going to head out to the open sea, get them to follow as far as I can."

Silence passed between the two men, both of them struggling with Alcide's apparent suicide pact. Alcide was thinking of his family, his brother over in Africa, and his ma, waiting for her boys to come home. She'd wonder why he'd stopped whispering to her from across the sea.

The dragonflies would whisper it to her, he supposed. They'd let her know that he wouldn't be coming home to see the bright dawn or taste the sweet honeysuckle when it bloomed.

It was a tough thing, consigning yourself to death, but Alcide couldn't see any other recourse. These were the cards he'd been dealt. Perhaps he'd spent all his life training as a hoodoo man just to be positioned for this day and hour.

Gunny broke the silence first. He had been staring out at the sea, at the battleship and the small flashes of light coming from its deck, the crew attempting to fight off the Clickers swarming up and over the sides. "Admiral Fletcher is getting desperate. We were supposed to clear the beach so they could bring their miracle bomb here, to level this whole damn island. That was before the damn fish heads decided to send fuck-all at us. Last radio call we got, the admiral was getting desperate, trying to decide if he should detonate it right out there in the strait."

Alcide immediately looked at the carrier, unsure of what he expected to see. A bomb that could destroy a whole island didn't seem possible, but then again, after fighting off wave after wave of prehistoric nightmares…helped to keep an open mind.

But if such a thing was real, it could reverse their fortunes and place a pain on the Dark Ones they'd be remembering for generations. He'd have to warn the future generations, though, lest the Dark Ones took their revenge.

He grabbed his pack, hoisting it up and immediately reaching for the trapped Clicker writhing within. Pinchy was still lethargic from his most recent working, but twitched like a rattlesnake.

He retrieved a battered leather journal, dull pencil wrapped in the leather strap keeping it closed.

He began to furiously write in the journal, uncaring if he got a few words wrong as long as he got them down.

"Get on the horn with the admiral, Gunny. Tell him to load his bomb into a PT boat and get it here to shore. I'll take care of the rest." He went back to scribbling. He was aware that the gunnery sergeant was still staring at him, and he didn't bother looking up from his work as he spoke. "I know you don't believe in my craft, Gunny. You can die on this beach, you and all these men, or you can listen to me, and possibly save the world for your grandchildren. Your choice."

Webb plodded off through the sand, shouting orders to groups of men as he passed. Alcide continued to write. He had a hell of a story to pass on.

59. AUGUST, 1942

Ezekiel Palmer was lost, there was no two ways about it. They had lost their weapons in the swim from the caverns and then they had lost each other. He thought that he could hear distant screams, but was unable to discern if they were friend or foe. He felt weary, his head a thousand times heavier than it should have been, and all he wanted to do was lay down, curl into a ball, and give up.

Jake's voice rang in his ear, an imaginary voice now, but one that he could remember like his friend was still standing there.

You're going to have to regroup and reassess, Zeke. You have to rely on the men to do the same. We just have to get Robichaude what he needs.

It was a fine sentiment, but one that he was beginning to doubt as time went on. After all, what had their actions led to so far but just more death? Jake was a pile of goo in a dark cave, Martino and Preach not much better. It didn't seem like there would be any of his boys left by the time they were ready to leave the island.

You've never been one for giving up, Zeke. This isn't you. It's them, messing with your mind. You heard Boudin, they drown you in fear. Get up, you son of a bitch. Get up!

Ezekiel thought that he might have been going insane. He knew that Jake couldn't be speaking to him, that this was nothing but his own mind running wild under the strain and stress of everything he had endured.

He forced himself to his feet and pushed through palms and ferns toward the noise. A myriad of sounds echoed through the jungle all around him. He breathed deep and kept walking.

Images faded in and out as he walked. He thought he saw Jake leaning against a tree, smiling the same cocky smile that he'd worn until their arrival at this place.

Hey Zeke? Aren't we overdue for drinks in Sydney?

Ezekiel ignored the mocking laughter from his friend, the image melting into red goo even as Preach loomed out of the bushes.

Skipper! Great of you to join us!

He held a severed, flaming Tojo head in his hands, the same man he'd seen burning on the hill. Sightless eyes followed him as he passed, their dead skin warping into ugly scales as their pupils widened until there was no color, only the swallowing darkness like a fish.

Get to the beach, just ignore everything you see, they're playing hell on your head. I'm not real, what you see isn't real, just push forward!

He was no longer sure if anything he saw was real. His feet hurt terribly and he was sure he was bleeding inside his boots.

Before he knew it, the trees began to thin, the jungle relinquishing its grip on his body and his soul. His boots crunched and squelched on the sand, and a quick glance down confirmed that he was stepping on the shells of freshly killed Clickers.

Ezekiel heard shouts of alarm and looked up to see men rushing from the beach toward him. A few of them fired, but he didn't flinch, just putting one foot in front of the other.

They were around him and shouting. He wondered how many of them were trying to see if he was real. If the Dark Ones were playing with his mind, then surely they were doing it with these poor survivors huddled behind their guns.

There was a face he recognized among them, big and bald, older than him, looking like he'd eaten nothing but nails his whole life.

He'd expected never to see Arthur Webb again.

"I hope you're here to take your command back, sir."

Ezekiel smiled. "Is there anything left of it, Gunny?"

"You're looking at it, sir. There's maybe twenty men left, including survivors from 2nd and 3rd."

"Lieutenant Colonel Puller?"

"Still fighting, sir, but we've lost contact."

"Have any of the men I left with turned up?"

Webb nodded. "Yes, sir. Robichaude. And he's still talking his magic nonsense."

"Did you…"

"I gave him everything he asked for, sir."

Ezekiel nodded. He looked down at the beach. Sporadic batches of Clickers emerged from the waves to head towards their lines, encountering a barrage of bullets and either retreating or dying where they stood.

Each line of corpses was closer than the last one.

He placed a hand on Preach's rosary, hanging beneath his dog tags. He looked up into the sky at the multitude of stars. "If there was a time for a miracle, it's now."

60. AUGUST, 1942

Vice Admiral Frank Fletcher had sailed into a nightmare. There was no simple way to describe it as anything else. Turner had given him the briefing, warned about the Tokyo Express dropping Japanese reinforcements, but he hadn't mentioned the damn fish-men.

After the small skirmish on the *Saratoga's* deck, he'd been prepared to tackle the freak lobsters whether Washington delivered on their lofty promises or not. Lord knew he'd boiled plenty of them back in Annapolis. Nimitz's courier had contacted them shortly afterward to let them know their superweapon was giftwrapped and ready for delivery.

The Gato-Class submarine *Bonefish* had surfaced nearly a half hour later. The hatch had opened and a steady stream of submariners had emerged with load after load of components under tarps. Combined together they would sink the entire island, or so the story went.

A small man clad in a tweed jacket and an overlarge pair of spectacles was last to board, quietly directing his sailors to be careful with a few of the tarps. This was Quince, the academic they'd shipped out from some hush-hush think tank in New Mexico. Supposedly he was the one that was going to be building this miracle bomb.

As soon as the last tarp had been stowed, Fletcher had ordered his task force to head into the strait. His radiomen had begun to fervently contact his bomber wing, while Quince had co-opted fifty of his sailors to start assembling the bomb in the hanger.

Fletcher had thought it prudent to keep the submarine in his pocket until Quince had given him the thumbs up. He wasn't about to lose his command over some vital firing pin or timer or damn washer that the egghead had forgotten to bring aboard. So he'd ordered the *Bonefish* to stay in the area and check in hourly. Not even two hours later they'd lost contact.

Fletcher would have preferred the silence to what came next. The radio had crackled to life, chilling the blood of every man on the bridge. There had been screams, frantic shouting that something had pried open the hatch and was killing everyone. The voice had hollered something else, a pained and panicked gibberish that had left Fletcher about to order the radioman to move the call to headphones and hopefully preserve some morale, but the sounds that had come spilling out of the speaker had frozen him in his tracks.

It had been a guttural groaning, sounds that Fletcher thought were like words formed in the deepest part of a frog's throat. A chill had raced up the admiral's spine as he had imagined something like a long tongue reaching through the radio, sucking his mind from him to take him down with the *Bonefish*. Every man who had heard it had been rooted to the spot.

The radioman had ended their psychic torture, plugging in the headphones through some amazing force of will, and noticeably not putting them over his ears. Fletcher had relaxed, feeling the tongue of power that had lain slick over his mind withdraw. His will had come back with it and he had turned back to his command crew.

"All ahead full, please, Mr. Warren," Captain Ramsey had said.

The helmsman had barely hesitated before pushing the throttle forward, the deep thrum of engines vibrating the hull, screws turning, massive propellers pushing them through the sea.

Fletcher had looked down at the deck, at the ocean below it, and had a vision of merciless, piscine eyes staring up at barnacle-encrusted hulls, plotting their slaughter.

This is a premonition. I've been given a glimpse of the future.

It was the only thought that he had been focusing on as his

crew and the crews of his entire task force fought for their lives.

A deck swab, a boy barely out of his schooling named Anthony, had been the first to spot the signal mirror frantically flashing from shore. Fletcher found himself standing on the observation deck of the bridge listening to his communications officer hastily relay the information.

They had two hundred or so men camped out on the beach, survivors from three different Marine divisions. No ranking officers were organizing the rag tag band, just a few non-commissioned officers led by a gunnery sergeant called Webb.

The next signal of lights from shore rapidly spread through his crew: *Here There Be Monsters*, the old mapmaker's warning. Webb clearly knew how to get through to sailors, who were a superstitious lot and fond of their traditions and stories.

Fletcher had his orders from Washington and his premonition from some monstrous evil in the deep. No one would have faulted him if he had turned around and sailed back to the open ocean, then let his bomber wing fly over and annihilate the island. In fact, he was risking court martial to do it, but his conscience wouldn't let him abandon the men on that island, boots on the ground who just wanted to get back to their families.

They'd readied launches and he'd ordered the dozen or so Patrol Boats to start ferrying the men on shore to the ships when they'd reported their first loss. One of his boats that hadn't been on evacuation duty had been laying mines to prevent Tojo subs from sneaking up and ramming a torpedo right up their keels. They'd gone dark abruptly and then his spotter had seen the dull orange explosion light up the night, the distant boom like a starting pistol for some undersea race.

The water began to churn, dozens of different radios calling into the *Saratoga* to report they were under attack. He'd immediately walked out to observe from the bridge, get a glimpse of whatever ships had managed to sneak into the strait. Anthony, the swabbie, took a trident directly through the chest, a dark form raising him up and letting him slide down the shaft of the weapon.

A trilling war cry came, followed by screams and gunfire.

Fletcher felt his heart stop. Ramsey immediately took charge, barking orders to his bridge crew, with a not subtle look to Fletcher for guidance. Fletcher could hear the screams from the deck crew, see the men running across towards the lower deck entry. All of them had seen Anthony's demise, and his killer had been joined by a dozen others.

Ramsey's executive officer, Lieutenant Commander Charlie Cole, hollered from the conn, "Captain! Mr. Blake from engineering is reporting the hull has ruptured! They're getting in!"

Fletcher's eyes unconsciously tracked down to the edge of the deck. He couldn't see the reported damage, but he could feel it in the depth of his being. His ship was damaged and the water was spilling through.

So were the monsters.

Fletcher was aware that his men were asking for orders, for guidance, but he felt drunk, like he'd had five bottles of bourbon.

"Damage report, Charlie," Ramsey said.

Focus, Fletcher, focus. The damn Tojo fish monsters are tearing your task force apart.

He put a hand to his head, pinching the bridge of his nose, rubbing at his hair like he could push the heavy weight out of his hand by sheer force of will.

"Mr. Cole," he said, allowing years of military training to turn him into a beacon of stability, "would you kindly get that damned scientist on the horn. I need to know if his bomb is ready."

The XO nodded and picked up the telephone. The first of his onboard complement of marines had assembled next to the lower hatch, already firing at the monsters that were overrunning his ship.

It was the gunshots that seemed to push back the sudden weight in his mind, every injury the fish-headed demons took disrupting whatever hold they'd placed over his mind. He saw one clutch at its throat, blood spilling out of its gills as its webbed hands tried to hold in the leaking life, before it toppled to the deck.

Fletcher felt his head lighten, like he had just taken a handful of aspirin, and he gripped the railing, letting the anger build. This was his command, and he would be damned if they were going down without a fight.

He glanced around the room at his officers, each one paled and scared. Even the grizzled master of the watch, Mr. Darly, was trembling.

"Any word, Mr. Cole?"

The XO looked up at him, head shaking. "It's chaos down there, sir."

Fletcher glanced at the radio. "What about the rest of the fleet?"

"I've got reports coming in from the *Advance, Prudent,* and *George Harrison.* They're experiencing boarding too, in greater numbers; their decks are lower in the water."

Fletcher gritted his teeth. It was time for every good man to do or die. He just hoped it was the former and not the latter.

"Tell the destroyers to open up with depth charges. Let's give them everything we've got. Mr. Darly, you're with me."

The spell of their dark adversaries was finally broken by the chorus of resounding, "Aye sirs." Cole and Ramsey had their plates full, and Fletcher needed someone he could trust to dig that tick from Los Alamos out of the below decks.

The first cannonade from their accompanying destroyer shook the water as massive shells exploded, sending enormous plumes of water swamping over the decks and bringing Clickers down on the unfortunate men below.

Darly was not a man who pulled his punches just because someone outranked him. "This is untenable, sir. We could drop every ship's complement of depth charges and I don't think we'd scratch these things' numbers."

Fletcher agreed. By his rough estimates, it wouldn't be three hours before the Clickers and their masters overtook them.

But looking at the five ships fighting for their existence, the dozen or so patrol boats whizzing through the white caps and dropping mines, and the twinkling lights of the encamped marines vainly trying to hold out, he'd be damned if he wouldn't fight to the last.

"How long have you been putting to sea, Mr. Darly?"

"This is my second war, sir."

"Mine, too. Third, if you count Mexico. Most guys on this ship, they've signed up since Pearl. The whole damn country signed up. None of us expected this, we demonized the Tojos, hated them, cursed them, saw them as monsters…but we've seen real monsters now, haven't we?"

Darly nodded. "Aye sir."

"We felt the call of the sea, you and I, Darly. And now, now the sea might call us back home, at the end of tooth and fang."

He sighed deeply. "Get a fire team organized and get that egghead and his bomb up on deck. Tell the boats to try to save as many of the boys as they can, but if we can't load that thing onto a bomber, we are detonating it here."

61. AUGUST, 1942

Professor Anton Quince, stood behind the mostly-intact bomb casing, checking measurements. The welders and riveters kept to their task despite the screams and war cries resonating through the metal womb surrounding them.

The regular running lights of the aircraft carrier had disappeared, replaced by a deep and baleful red. Bellowing warning claxons echoed throughout the ship, like some leviathan was letting its presence be known to the poor souls trapped inside this giant metal coffin.

Quince felt the smooth metal casing under his finger, smooth and elegant in a way. Hard to believe that such destructive power was contained in something that was maybe twice the mass of a man.

He had opposed this course of action before the military command. They were looking for ways to quickly and decisively end the war, but the power of the atom was not a toy, would not lead to a cessation of bloodshed or a halcyon age for America. This potential and danger wrapped up in things smaller than the eye could possibly see would change the world, and not for the better.

More than that, it wasn't ready. The device before him was a simulacrum, a dirty likeness of the actual weapons being designed back in Los Alamos. It had much less power than what was still being created, but he supposed it didn't matter. The destructive ability of this weapon would still be greater than anything that had been seen by the nations of men.

In spite of all of his misgivings, when his nation had demanded great sacrifices of him, the greatest being perhaps his conscience, he had answered the call.

Big Mama. That was what the boys around the base had called his creation. The others that had yet to be completed had names like *Little Boy* and *Fat Man*, epithets that sounded silly or non-threatening. It was a bit of ironic gallows humor, considering their intended purpose.

The sailors assigned to him hadn't so much as given him the time of day until their admiral, in a preternaturally calm voice, had ordered them to complete the bomb with absolute expediency. Then the hold had turned into a beehive of activity, such that Quince barely had anything to do himself except coordinate.

The admiral's words had been the last thing they'd heard before the internal radios had cut out, replaced by distant, echoing screaming and the sounds of fighting. Then it had just been a multitude of terrified sailors alone under the dull red light, working feverishly to complete something not a single one of them, Quince, perhaps included, could possibly understand.

Finish your work. Even if you die, the work will be done.

Quince didn't want to die, but neither did he think that *Big Mama* should lay unfinished at the bottom of the sea, surrounded by drowned corpses and monsters who didn't know just what it was that they possessed.

So, when the sailors had put down their tools to pick up weapons, Quince had quietly, but confidently corrected them. The admiral's orders hadn't been to defend themselves, but for them to complete this magnificent terror of knowledge. They were professionals, and understood that success in battle only came from doing one's job and relying on others to do theirs.

They had labored, a silence overtaking them except for the death taking place in the corridors and decks around them, the few sailors who had not been assigned to finish the bomb sweating profusely as they aimed their guns down dark corridors, looking for any sign of intrusion.

He walked around the device, making sure that each segment was done to instruction. A loud, unearthly scream, a million times more defined than any of the previous static, cut through the hangar, causing every man to pause. Quince briefly thought that no man could have made that noise, but he was a man of science, and quickly pushed down any foolish flights of superstitious fancy. There were no mermaids or sea serpents, even on the other side of the world.

"Ignore the noise," Quince said, trying to sound braver than he felt. "If we make one mistake, we either go up right here or when it comes time to detonate, we might as well be tossing rocks."

It was advice that Quince was having trouble following; the occasional thunder of a ship firing its cannons and the screams that echoed off the metal bulkheads inside were making it nearly impossible for him to concentrate.

Quince thought that his hands trembled harder with each new wail that came rebounding through the metal hallways. He tried to focus as best he could. He was allowing his dread and nerves to overwhelm his intellect. There was no such thing as monsters. Besides, if monsters existed, they had been rendered irrelevant when man had created this unholy device.

The only monsters on Guadalcanal are the Japanese.

But if that were true, why did some sounds resemble nothing that human or a machine should have been able to make? It was a question he couldn't answer as he continued to work.

The sounds and red lights and stress were making it impossible for him to focus. The weight of the world pressed in on his head. It ebbed from time to time, but always seemed to come flowing back, like his thoughts were wading through thick muck at the bottom of some lake.

Quince looked at the few remaining components on the steel floor of the hangar. The sailors assigned to these last few parts seemed to suffer from the same affliction laying siege to his wits.

How did these last few parts link together? He should have known. He'd studied this device's designs non-stop for nearly a year. There was a time he'd known it like the back of his hand.

Quince gritted his teeth and tried to shove through the delirium. His concentration broke when gunshots began to ring from the hangar entry, the half dozen or so sailors on guard detail firing down the hall. They were backing up. A few had already used up their rifle ammunition and resorted to automatic pistols. Quince could hear pained roaring from the ship corridor and dreaded seeing any living being that could make such a noise.

There was another sound, barely perceptible over the roaring and croaking; a series of clicks that now drowned out the shouts of alarm and gunfire. Panic seized Quince, the thought that he could die at any moment rocketing his mind through the mess of his thoughts.

He reached for one of the last two components on the floor, shaking the arm of a trembling sailor to help with the other. The sailor nodded his head and picked up the casing, struggling under the metal's weight. Quince angled the casing into position and, out of the corner of his eye, saw something large and red skewer the security detail near the door. The sailor next to him appeared, ready to drive in the rivets, sweat on his brow, but otherwise showing none of the terror he should have been feeling.

"Hurry, hurry," Quince whispered, listening to the sounds of driving metal as the rivets were driven into place.

Men were running in all directions now, trying to escape. Quince couldn't be sure how many men were still defending the hangar. Four? Fewer?

The sailor assisting him moved to run, but Quince shot his hand out, fingers firmly grasping the man's forearm. "I still need you. Please."

The man looked like he wanted to argue, but one glance around the hangar was all it took for both men to realize they weren't getting out of the room alive.

Growing up in Kansas, Quince had never even seen a lobster, and that had changed little during his stint in the middle of the New Mexico desert. Now he hoped to never see another one again.

Things that looked like lobsters spawned from the deepest circle of Hell were swarming around them. They were various sizes, some no bigger than his foot, others nearly as large as a horse. For a moment, he was amazed by the creatures, wondering where they could have possibly fit in the fossil record.

Then he saw three of them overtake a fleeing sailor. The man screamed in pure fear as he fired his pistol towards the incoming mass of chitin and claw. Quince watched as a stinger embedded itself in the man's leg, eliciting a high-pitched wail as he tumbled to the deck. The heinous creatures immediately swarmed over him, claws shearing away his flesh.

Quince heard the man's panicked curses and then a long, keening screech as one of the creatures dipped its claw into his eye socket. The white orb came away impaled on the point of its claw, optic nerve trailing after it as the monstrosity brought the organ to its mouth, lapping up the fluid as it ran from the popped sphere.

The man was already dead, but his body still underwent the effects of whatever venom the creatures had pumped into him. Before he forced himself to look away, Quince observed in grim fascination as the man's body slowly inflated, then popped, turning to a steaming liquid mire running across the deck.

The sailor beside him looked into his eyes. Quince wished he could offer some token of hope, but instead only managed to hoarsely grunt, "Almost finished."

He received a nod and both of them leaned down to retrieve the last piece of casing. It snapped into place perfectly, like the final piece of a jigsaw puzzle. He held it in place while the sailor drove the rivets into the casing, the normally loud sounds of riveting suddenly seeming so small compared to the cacophony of slaughter taking place all around them. In a perfect world, the sounds might even have gone unnoticed by the antediluvian horrors around them.

But this was no perfect world.

The sailor stepped back after the last rivet had been driven in and turned around in time to catch a glimpse of the instrument of his doom. What looked like a man crossed with a fish ran a black, coral-studded trident through the sailor's mid-section, pinning him against the fission bomb. The sailor grasped the shaft of the trident, airless coughs bubbling up with a great gout of blood that ran down his chin and onto the deck. The sailor's eyes rolled up in his head and the fish-man wrenched back its trident, dislodging the sailor's corpse from the prongs and sending him tumbling across the deck. Quince had never even known his name, never even stopped to check.

The fish-man's jet-black eyes swiveled and locked onto him, its mouth widening to expose needle-sharp teeth. Quince held his hands up, wondering briefly whether this creature was intelligent enough to understand a concept like surrender. Likely not, but if so, his own was refused, and the creature shoved the trident through his guts.

When he was thrown to the deck, the lobster-things immediately began to swarm him. The venom was ice cold in his veins, but even as his belly and face distended, his whole body beginning to inflate like a balloon, he was oblivious to his pain. Instead, he felt only wonder, and almost felt shocked that only minutes ago he had felt ambivalence, even anxiety about *Big Mama*, his completed masterpiece.

As new sailors began to enter the hanger, firing at the monsters surrounding the bomb, Quince whispered his dying words.

"Beautiful. It's beautiful."

62. SEPTEMBER, 2020

Cam rocked back and forth in the waiting room chair. This was it. There was no more money, no more top cover, no friends, no unestranged relations. There was just him, the vanful of evidence a few NOAA underlings had grudgingly helped him wheel inside, and destiny staring him down.

A hand came down on his shoulder. He stiffened, then felt it squeeze. He looked to Jade, or, what had become of Jade. She was still wrapped tightly in her ridiculous disguise. The NOAA people hadn't even frisked them, apparently accepting that once the dog and pony show was over, they would peaceably surrender themselves to a deep, dank, unmarked cell somewhere.

"You got this, Cam," the cheerleader's muffled voice said through her mask.

He smiled weakly, and she patted her massive hand on his shoulder. "I wish I had your confidence."

"What do you need confidence for? You've got me."

The door opened. Tammy, the secretary who had secretly been in his corner all along, stepped out, straightening her frighteningly severe pencil skirt. Cam rose, but Tammy didn't motion him in. Instead, she motioned backwards to somebody already inside the conference room. Wilburn stepped out, followed shortly by Edler and Rosamilia, who seemed to be trying to hide their faces under Wilburn's skirts.

"Bastards," Cam hissed, barely aware the words had left his lips. "Traitors."

"Whoa, whoa," Wilburn said, holding up his hands, "Relax, Cam. Frank and Armand went to bat for you."

The other two were scratching the backs of their necks.

"Yeah, I mean," Edler said, "what the news was saying was scary, Cam, and we kind of had to drop the dime on you. But when it comes down to it, at a certain point you've got to tell the truth."

"The truth came out," Rosamilia agreed. "We can't do any more than we've done, Cam. The bases are loaded but it's up to you to hit the grand slam."

Cam nodded as his three colleagues shuffled out. Finally Tammy nodded for them to enter. He and Jade wheeled their supplies into the conference room. Cam's breath caught in his throat. The Under Secretary of NOAA was there, of course, but he was not sitting at the head of the table.

"I'm not here," the man at the head of the table said in his weirdly confident yet stuttering public speaking voice, then stretched an imaginary piece of taffy between his fingers, "and this had better be damned entertaining, Custer. The last few seasons of your show had some of the crummiest ratings of all time. Of all time."

Cam cleared his throat. "Thank you, uh, sir. Climate change is real."

"Hoax," the man at the head of the table interrupted.

"It's as real as the nose on my face," Cam replied, unfazed, "and I could roll out a hundred thousand studies and facts and figures but that's not fun. That's not photogenic."

He'd already noticed the cameras rolling in the back of the room. They were being recorded, though whether for evidence at his upcoming trial or for broadcast later to an adoring public, he didn't know.

"So, here," Cam said, "Here's something exciting. Something that can grip the news cycle for twenty-four hours, if not a few more."

He whipped the cover away from the Clicker's cage. The man at the head of the table leaned in. "What the heck is that?"

"*Homarus Tyrannous.* Also known as a Chazzwozzer. But most commonly known in the vulgar parlance as a Clicker."

Click-click.

The various gray-suited, power-tied men at the table

jumped. So, maybe they weren't as dumb on this subject as they pretended.

The noise hadn't been the sluggish Clicker in the tank, though, of course. That had been Jade, sitting unobtrusively by. He'd bought a dog training toy at one of their stops, he couldn't even remember which one anymore, since they all tended to run together now. But it replicated the Clicker's signature noise nearly perfectly.

"Why's it got one of them comic book characters on its back?" the man at the head of the table asked.

"The creature's distinctive marking was made by the man who first discovered it, a brilliant Navy scientist during the Second World War. The incursions of these creatures have occurred throughout history. Sometimes directed, sometimes accidental. But when they're not directed, they're usually due to warming waters in their hunting grounds. And let me tell you something, gentlemen, the waters in their hunting grounds are warming all over. We are overdue for these monstrosities to come up on land, *en masse*."

"What kind of a hokey fairy tale is this?" the man at the head of the table asked, "You know you're going out live, Custer. This is what you want the American people to hear? Your ratings are going to be terrible, terrible. They'll practically beg me to lock you up."

"Lock him up," the men around the table agreed in near unison.

The cameras around the room were staring implacably at him, red lights nearly burning a triple hole in his retinas. So this was being broadcast live. It would be better than the trial of the century. It would be the madman being allowed a defense in front of the whole country. The people would either bay for his blood or give him the proverbial Roman thumbs up. Okay, then. He was ready. He'd made his bones on television before the man at the head of the table had survived his first bankruptcy.

"1999," Cam said, unperturbed, "Phillipsport, Maine. It was very nearly a disaster for the United States. One can imagine a world where three, maybe even four books of terror could have been written about that incursion and its follow-ons. But in our world a nuclear bomb was dropped to end the threat forever."

"Good. We should nuke more of our enemies."

"Before that," Cam said, gritting his teeth, "was Guadalcanal, 1942."

He triumphantly tossed a sheaf of papers onto the table. He pointed to each of the cameras in turn, not sure which one was showing him to the American public currently.

"Ask your grandparents," he said, "the ones who were there. The ones who still wake up in the middle of the night screaming. But they're a quiet generation, aren't they? Stoic. Nearly eighty years ago Uncle Sam told them to button their lips, and button their lips they did. But I'm calling on you, you remaining vets of Guadalcanal, to tell the truth now. Tell the truth about the *Kamikaze* creatures that looked like that."

He pointed a damning finger at the sluggish Clicker in the box.

"What they did to you and your friends. And their overseers, who looked like this."

Without waiting for his signal, Jade had already cast back her disguise and stepped forward into full view of the cameras. The under secretary looked like he was going to shit a brick. The man at the head of the table was, for once in his goddamned life, at a loss for words.

"Tell them who you are, please," Cam said, stepping back.

Jade's frill rose, making her seem even bigger than her natural basketball player height. Good. She'd left the cheerleader persona behind in the waiting room. Here was the alien monstrosity on full display.

"I was brought up," Jade croaked, as though she could barely speak English, "to be called Jade. I know this name was given to me as a joke, a light insult, by the people who raised me. But I reclaim it as my own. I am *Draco Acerbus*. Dark One in your tongue." She uttered a guttural obscenity and added, "in my own."

That was a delightful touch. Jade didn't know a word of Darkese, of course, and Cam barely had a passing familiarity with the written version. Whatever she had just said had been gibberish, but he could tell by the mesmerized eyes around the room that it had worked perfectly. Jade raised her hand and pointed a damning talon at the viewers on the other side of the cameras.

"Your people have driven mine near extinction. We held back the Clickers. Now you will be subject to their full wrath. They will boil up over your shores and devour you all. Your only hope is to restore the oceans. Stop dumping in them. Let the fish and other prey multiply. And the Clickers might, might leave you alone."

"And, cut," the man at the head of the table said.

The three red lights of the cameras went out. The room suddenly became much more relaxed, as no one was performing for the live audience anymore. Even Cam felt some of the tension bleeding out of his shoulders.

Tammy jumped up and embraced Cam, much to his surprise. She stepped back and, as though realizing she'd jumped the gun, pumped his hand wildly instead.

"Hell of a job, Dr. Custer. Hell of a job."

"Well, thank you," he agreed.

"You did good this time, Custer," the man at the head of the table said. "That will make for some compelling viewing. The Greatest Generation stuff? Mmm!" He kissed his fingers as though he were an Italian chef.

"Yeah, not bad, Dr. Custer," the under secretary said. "We should be able to up the Pentagon's budget by a few trillion for this. Maybe we'll even make up a new agency. Department of, I don't know, Dry Land Affairs or something."

"Pentagon?" Cam asked. "What do you mean? They're going to lead the climate change fight?"

"Ooh," the under secretary hissed, "you must have forgotten. This administration's official position is that there is no such thing as climate change."

Cam did a double take. Jade's frill sank into a depressed neck ruffle.

"What?"

"We're not going to do any of that pinko libtard save the whales shit, is what he's saying, Custer," the man at the head of the table said, "but we can probably drum up some fundraising based on this. Consider yourself pardoned for all of those murders or whatever. You're going to be a national hero."

"For…stopping…global…"

"I wouldn't say that next word if I were you," Tammy said.

Cam looked to his one friend in the room with disbelief, but the look on her face, the smile of petty triumph, made clear that she had betrayed him as much as anyone else. Perhaps more, even, for pretending to be on his side. He closed his mouth. The men, all men, universally, except for Tammy, reduced to a secretary by this administration despite her obvious, if ruthless competence, were shaking hands and whispering in one another's ears.

So. He'd been a pawn for them. This wasn't his triumph at all. He'd accomplished nothing. Not his goal, not some secondary goal, somebody else's goal entirely. He'd helped to fleece the useful idiots of America, who would demand a nuclear attack on the ocean rather than simply work on fixing the damage they'd already done.

He turned to Jade, that one, unexpected positive outcome of this whole mess. The unexpected, surprise love of his life. She wasn't looking at him. She seemed to be meditating. He sank into his chair. His life, his fortune, his good name. All pissed away. And for what? To line the pockets of these…jackals.

Click-click.

He turned to Jade, but she was smiling. The dog toy was sitting next to her in the next chair, untouched. None of the other government officials had noticed. He immediately whirled to look at the white-hued Clicker in its box. The refrigeration unit, he saw, was off. The water in the tank was near room temperature.

He stared at the animal for what felt like a lifetime. Then its claws came together. Its back shuddered, seeming to make the cartoon face laugh.

Click-click.

"What was that?" the under secretary asked.

"That was me asking for a Diet Coke," the man at the head of the table said, slamming his fist down. "Somebody get me a goddamned Diet Coke."

An explosion sheared through the NOAA conference room, as a million particles of glass tinkled to the floor. Pinchy, the white Clicker who had once been the lone companion of a stranded ship's cook, had easily ripped apart the tank that held it.

All eyes locked on the Clicker. Though at least eighty, Cam knew that would not necessarily make the crustacean a dotard. Sea turtles lived to be two hundred. Unchecked, some primitive species could reach prodigious ages. Had its tail not long since been sheared off, it likely would have started spraying acidic venom all over the room. Instead, it merely began clicking its massive, chitinous claws threateningly in the air.

A hail of bullets flew through the room, as innocuous, black-clad secret service agents began firing at the living fossil and finding its shell, as the men on Guadalcanal had all those years ago, nearly impervious to small arms fire. With lightning speed, Jade leaped up and ripped the throat out of the nearest secret service agent. The one on the other side of the room leveled his pistol at her, but in an astonishing display of athleticism, she seemed to throw herself completely under the table, knocking chairs and low-level government functionaries to the ground, before grasping the secret service man by the legs and ripping out both of his Achilles tendons simultaneously.

The man screamed as his unsupported body toppled over. Pinchy, meanwhile, was clattering up onto the huge conference table, as NOAA personnel and the administration functionaries flung themselves backwards. It hardly mattered. Pinchy, in an unreasonable display of focus for a mindless crustacean, seemed to be making a beeline for the man at the head of the table.

It was possible, Cam reflected, that Pinchy was attracted to the color of the man's tie, or some other inexplicable odor or noise or behavior. But glancing at Jade he saw an unusual level of concentration in her face. Though he didn't understand it entirely, these two species were in some way connected, perhaps through pheromones or something deeper. A layman would call it a psychic bond, and for lack of a better explanation, Cam guessed that was what was really driving Pinchy's murderous rampage right now.

Tammy rushed for the door. Cam looked up. Hmm. His leg shot out and Tammy tripped, her head smashing unceremoniously into the glass of the door. She went down like a lead weight, bleeding from her ears, and blocking the door from the other functionaries, who were now eyeing it.

Jade, her mouth full of secret service agent drumstick, returned to his side. She dropped two pistols, the only two weapons in the room, at Cam's feet.

"All right, now, stop," the man at the head of the table said to Pinchy.

Pinchy, to everyone's surprise, paused, its claws raised in the air, ready to strike.

"Listen, I get it. The whole climate change thing. It's huge. But it's not real. You're not really here because of…"

"Pinchy," Cam said, causing every eye in the room to rivet on him, "put us out of our misery, would you?"

Probably not understanding, but maybe, considering the amount of time it had spent in the company of Doodles Enterline, Pinchy slammed its claws into the president. Lacking tail venom, the Clicker had been forced to learn to pulverize its prey the old-fashioned way, rending muscle from bone and slicing, slicing, always slicing. It tore into the man's collarbones, ripped his skin into tiny slices, gouged his eyes, pinched his tongue and cheeks. Again and again the Clicker ripped into the man, devastating what little flesh clung to his tendons, demolishing the tendons, ripping, and ripping, and ripping. All the while, the man clung improbably to life, bemoaning his misfortune, and utterly confused that anyone could not like him.

Everyone in the room watched on in terror as Pinchy made a living meal out of what had, mere moments before, been the most powerful man in the world. Then it turned on them. Jade bashed heads together as they ran for the exit, until finally everyone in the room was in the war path of either the Clicker or the Dark One. By mid-afternoon, only Cam, Jade, and Pinchy remained breathing.

Jade, her mouth covered with gore, somehow still looked sexy as she dropped down into the spot between Cam's knees, encouraging him to rub her tensed shoulders.

"What do you think, Cam?" she asked.

"I think it's a shame they turned the cameras off so early."

63. AUGUST, 1942

Ammo was running low and morale even lower. The Dark Ones had slowed their attacks on the beach, but Ezekiel saw that defeat was just a matter of time, minutes if the progression of events was anything to go by.

The battle out in the strait wasn't going much better. The *Advance* was now a silent wreck, metal groaning with each new wave that buffeted against it. A few patrol boats still zoomed through the surf, never pausing for a moment.

Most men were slow to respond when the order came to fire. Even Ezekiel found himself raising his rifle just a few seconds slower than he should have. The will to live and to fight was slowly seeping from his mind and though he was aware of it, fighting it was like pushing through fog.

He walked up and down the defensive perimeter, trying to encourage the men, but few seemed receptive. The psychic assault was overwhelming, and some men were unable to act even to save their own lives.

More than one had been dragged over the sandy embankment to their deaths by a few Clickers that had managed to stealthily make their way through the shadows of the beach right up to the foxholes.

Only Boudin seemed unaffected and he had been scribbling furiously into a journal since Ezekiel had arrived, pausing only briefly to acknowledge his presence.

Ezekiel approached the communications shack. Webb seemed to be arguing with whatever disinterested flunky Admiral Fletcher had assigned to deal with the men actually in the fight.

Things didn't sound like they were going well.

"Listen, you pencil-necked...Yes, sir, I know who I'm talking to. Gunnery Sergeant Arthur Webb. I don't have an officer to... sir, I have more ass than you can chew and I will reach through this goddamned radio and..."

A stream of explosions drowned out the rest of Webb's tirade and most of the *Saratoga's* response, but it sounded like Fletcher had no intention of giving up his miracle weapon. He could hardly blame the man. In his place, he wouldn't have trusted a strange voice on the other side of the radio, either.

Ezekiel made a motion for the receiver and keyed the mic as Webb handed it over. "This is Captain Ezekiel Palmer, 1stMarines. That's right, Ensign, there's still an officer on this beach, but maybe you'd better clean the shit out of your ears and start listening to what the men on the ground are telling you, regardless of rank. We have a real shot to win this thing if you get us this wonder bomb of yours."

There was a hiss of static, a long moment passing. Ezekiel glanced up to make sure that the dark hulk out in the strait was still there.

I'm sorry, sir, but it's not up to me. The situation is untenable. We're going to detonate it on deck. I suggest you get out of there. And if you're a believing man, pray. This is the *Saratoga*, out."

He and Webb exchanged a grim look. Webb, who he'd never seen smoke before, shook a cigarette from his pocket, lit it, and passed it to each of the radiomen and then to Ezekiel.

"Keep trying," Ezekiel said to the radioman, though he knew there was little hope.

The radioman nodded, his gaze a mask of hopelessness, his eyes glancing out to the ship. "Yes, sir."

Ezekiel stepped out of the shack, and whether from genuine despair or the psychic influence of the Dark Ones, sank against a dirt embankment and closed his eyes. Alone with his thoughts, he wished an explosion would just take this cup away from him.

He didn't have more than a few minutes to wallow before a hand came down on his shoulder. Boudin was standing above him. "Not time to rest, Skipper. Long way to go yet, hear?" He reached down and pulled Ezekiel to his feet.

He handed him a journal. "What's this?"

"Full accounting of what we've been through, plus a bit of writing to my family that I'd appreciate be delivered once this is all said and done," Boudin replied.

Ezekiel nodded and gestured to Webb, who approached.

"Can you see to it that Robichaude's last will and testament makes it back to his family?"

"If I'm breathing at the end of this I will," Webb said. "If not, I'll at least make sure it's safe."

"Thank you, Gunny," Boudin said.

The big man gave a curt nod before he took another drag of the cigarette. "I don't think it really matters. The Navy isn't bringing your bomb to shore. They plan on detonating it in the strait."

Boudin's face harden, a mild curse escaping his lips as he looked out at the *Saratoga.*

He began to dig through his pack, producing a small glass mason jar. A few holes had been poked through the lid and Ezekiel could see what looked like grey moss and a few brittle leaves resting at the bottom. Resting on the leaves was a small insect that Ezekiel at first thought was an oversized fly until its thorax blazed with a calming yellow light.

"A lightning bug? I swear to Christ, Robichaude," Webb said, incredulously flicking the cherry of his cigarette into the sea.

Boudin smiled as he popped open the lid a crack. "I don't normally make working on men, but in Admiral Fletcher's case I'll make an exception."

Boudin whispered to the insect in the jar, low words that he couldn't hear and knew that if he did, he would not understand. Then he popped the lid off and the firefly buzzed into the night. Ezekiel watched it go, a small yellow light blinking every few seconds until it was swallowed by the darkness.

"You honestly think this will work?"

"Jesus Christ, sir," said Webb, "after everything we've seen, *this* is the thing you don't believe?"

The Cajun smiled. "See if you can get in touch with one of the PT boats, Gunny. If the chain of command isn't listening, maybe one of them will."

64. AUGUST, 1942

John Pike couldn't go on anymore, hopelessly lost amongst the never-ending green. Every time he'd thought he was headed in the direction of the battle, he'd been turned around.

In the dark of the night, surrounded by trees and the occasional corpse, he had followed the noise only to divert when he'd heard the nearby sounds of Clickers in fetid pools or the thick underbrush close to the rivers.

The monsters were not stealthy in their hunt. Every time a potential meal got close, it seemed to set off whatever ravenous instinct drove them, their claws making that unmistakable staccato beat.

It didn't seem possible that the creatures could be herding him, but every time he made to head in a certain direction it wouldn't be long before the clicks would begin anew and he found himself stumbling through the river.

He didn't have much energy left. He staggered slowly now, and if he fell, knew that he wouldn't be getting back up.

The humidity in this place was exhausting. Everything felt wet. Every breath he took felt like it was through a wet towel. There was no relief, just more sweat and the ever-continuing thump of his feet as he plodded forward.

He wasn't sure what distance he had covered when he finally fell, landing on his side in the stream and gasping for air in between sips of the cool water running past him.

The clicking came and his eyes wearily opened to see the white shells come peeking out of the foliage. Pike closed his eyes and waited for his death to come. He felt the barest tips of claws against his pants and drew in a deep breath, bracing himself. Soon he'd be with his wife and their baby.

Crack!

The Clicker's steaming orange blood fell over him as the bullet shattered its shell. The night came alive, bright rifle flashes illuminating the further shore and the men standing there.

There had been no more than a dozen of the monsters chasing him, and in the face of greater opposition, they fled into the jungle and the deeper waters of the stream.

A Clicker corpse a little bigger than his hand floated past him and he reached towards it, curious to see what it felt like, or if its stinger could still mete out death. But before he could pierce his own palm, hands slid under his arm and hoisted him roughly to his feet. He was staring into the grim faces of the Japanese soldiers who had saved him.

Pike felt his insides twirl, anger flooding through him. Fucking Tojo had saved him. He'd wanted to die, and he'd been saved by fucking Tojo.

There were two dozen or more, fanned out across the stream, aiming deep into the brush, their heads cocked, listening for any sign of another attack. The two that held him tight stood at rapt attention, their gazes rooted to the shore they had come from. Something sharp jabbed him and he craned his head to see a third Tojo pressing a bayonet lightly into his back.

Just in case I don't realize they're the enemy.

One of the men shouted something in Japanese. A man with a hard glare in his eyes moved from the brush with the telltale sword of an officer strapped to his thigh. The officer splashed into the water, tan uniform dampening as he waded. He paused for a moment at the foot of a wounded, twitching Clicker.

The man stared at the dying creature, the edge of his mouth just barely furrowing into a light sneer before he removed his sword and impaled it on the end of the blade.

"What is your name, Yankee Doodle?" he asked.

His English was good, but Pike thought that his voice sounded like a skipping record with a bad horn, hollow and choppy.

"John Pike, Sergeant, United States Marine Corps," he said, then rattled off his service number. He parroted the words he had been taught to repeat in the event of becoming a prisoner, already planning his strategy to resist whatever questions these men had for him.

"Oh, *Johnny Got His Gun,*" the Japanese officer said, eliciting chuckles from his men.

He took a few steps toward Pike, waving the impaled Clicker in his field of view.

"The *Kurikka*. You would say…?"

"Clicker," Pike said. He didn't guess it violated the Geneva Convention to give Tojo a grammar school vocab lesson.

"Clicker, yes, this makes sense. Our old commander was a good man, but this man from Manchukuo who took over for him, he was not right in the head, I guess you would say. The white Clickers were his."

"Hanshiro," Pike said, immediately wishing he hadn't.

The officer seemed surprised. "Yes. Colonel Hanshiro. He made a pact with the *Umibozu*."

This time the officer mimicked something tall and ape-like, but Pike had already heard Hanshiro use the word when they were interrogating him.

"Dark Ones," he supplied again.

"Dark One. Okay. This makes less sense, but okay. The Dark Ones betrayed us, killed many. My men and I barely escaped."

When he saw that Pike would not respond, the Japanese man held the dead Clicker closer to his face. "Colonel Hanshiro was a fool, too enraptured by spirits and their promises. These things are a threat to my people and yours. To…all people, I think."

Pike maintained his silence and stare. The Tojo spoke truth, but he didn't give a good damn. A bunch of good men had died because another smart Tojo had decided to play Frankenstein.

The Japanese officer leaned close. "You will take us to your commanders. We will work together to rid our land of these dark spirits. Then we can get back to killing each other if that is still your wish. This is an agreement you can accept, yes?"

Pike tried to search the other man's eyes for deceit and ultimately decided that there was none. At the end of the day, men were men, and men could always be trusted to fight a common enemy. But he had questions. He'd always been told Japanese soldiers would rather die than betray their country or work with the enemy. They had been raised from the cradle for war and expected to die.

Finally, Pike spoke. "What about your Emperor? The Land of your Ancestors?

Sergeant Pike, I am doing this for my Emperor. And the Land of my Ancestors. And my family, back home."

65. AUGUST, 1942

Admiral Fletcher tapped his hands against the railing, watching the bastion of light on shore, distant pops the only indication of hundreds of men fighting for their lives.

The miracle weapon was secure and on its way to the deck. Once it was there…the end would come for all of them.

His task force was on its last legs. Another ship had fallen dark, their hails going unanswered. Surprisingly, it was the patrol boats that were still most active. Only one from the half dozen still active had been sunk, the crew slaughtered by Clickers. He supposed that it must've been because the ships never stopped, zipping fast across the water, but the carrier and its escorts had presented nothing but a fat floating smorgasbord for the monstrous tribe from the sea.

He had seen a warband of them up close, sprinting across the deck with wet slapping footsteps that echoed far louder than they should have. He'd watched with morbid fascination as they'd thrown their tridents like Olympic-level athletes, impaling the security crew guarding the open hatch.

Fletcher felt the pain in his chest as he watched a man pinned to the bulkhead paw at his chest, feebly trying to dislodge the weapon from his ribcage. Fletcher wanted to look away but forced himself to watch his man's death. In a way it would help prepare him for what was to come.

He felt more than saw Charlie Cole's arrival on the observation deck and he barely managed to choke out a whisper. "Report, Mr. Cole."

"Invaders have been repelled, sir. The weapon is secure. I have a few teams sweeping the lower decks, killing off anything with skin tougher than a barnacle. They're bringing it up on deck now."

The man paused and Fletcher knew that this could not bode well.

"Something else, Charlie?"

"Dr. Quince is dead, sir. Enemy breached the hold. We've taken it back, but these monsters aren't stopping. Master-at-Arms is reporting shortages in ammunition and these things just keep coming."

Fletcher bowed his head and stared down at the ocean and the teeming forms he could see bouncing in and out of the waves. He supposed they didn't need the scientist to detonate the weapon, but if he hadn't finished it…

"What about the bomb?" he asked.

"Seems that our scientist delivered the last full measure. It's finished."

Fletcher glanced at the younger officer, watching the nervous trepidation as the realization of what was coming next filled his face. Eternal oblivion was about to take everyone on this island and Charlie Cole now knew he'd be standing before the throne of God sooner than he probably expected.

He didn't think that the young officer had anything to worry about. After all, he wasn't the one consigning everyone to death.

Fletcher sighed. The point of no return had come. His next order would send the bomb onto the flight deck, and if they couldn't load it in a bomber then they'd simply detonate it.

All he had to do was give the order.

There was a dreadful silence, the deep breath before the jump, and Fletcher opened his mouth to give the order but paused when he saw it. At first he thought it was something signaling at the top of the mountain, some Tojo patrol or the like, but as it blinked in and out of existence shedding its warm yellow light, he realized that it was bobbing closer to him.

He stretched out a finger and the firefly deftly landed on it. He smiled as the warm light played over him and he murmured, "A firefly way out here. Hell of a thing."

Even Cole seemed enraptured by the insect, wandering

close. "Didn't think they had those here."

Fletcher felt the weight on his mind melt away, like the small but strong light that the bug emitted had driven away whatever hopelessness and fear the Dark Ones had inflicted on him. All of it was transmuted into anger and a certainty that killing himself and his men was the wrong decision, that he could save his men if he just charted a new course.

"Mr. Cole, radio one of the patrol boats to dock with us and get that bomb loaded in it. Then contact that sergeant on shore."

He almost felt the firefly grin at him as it fluttered its wings and wheeled away into the night, blinking its light of hope onto a sea of hopeless men.

"Sir?" Cole inquired, his own eyes watching the insect's flight.

"Tell them to ready their man who can lead these things away. We're bringing him his weapon."

66. AUGUST, 1942

Webb wore a wordless expression of surprise, like a mule had taken to using his head as a kicking spot. He radioed in his affirmative to the *Saratoga* then turned to look at Alcide and Palmer. "Sir, I'd like permission to confiscate all the mops before Robichaude starts making them walk."

Palmer smiled. "That's the way I've been feeling all day."

"I guess your carrier firefly worked, Robichaude. The Admiral has approved this mess. The bomb's on the way."

Alcide nodded, trying to keep a serene expression like he was in control despite the incessant pounding of his heart. First rule according to his Grand-pap: folks tended to go along with the work when it seemed like you knew what was going to happen next and had an answer to anything that could arise.

"Thank you, Gunny. Any luck with our transport? I feel we're running out of time here."

It was an understatement if ever he'd given one. The Dark Ones seemed to track down his workings like bloodhounds. The psychic assaults of the Dark Ones were increasing, leaving half the men in a state of near-catatonia, Soon every man on this beach would lay down his arms or retreat into the jungle, their minds reduced to the primitive tree climbers their ancestors had been, doing anything they could to escape from the monsters that prowled the waterways.

Worse, the Clickers had begun to swarm and more than just the garden-variety.

An obsidian-backed monster hoisted itself from the surf and sprayed its putrid venom over a machine gun nest. The men inside boiled away but kept to their post even as the flesh fell from their bones and dealt death to their killer in kind. The obsidian Clicker twitched, orange gore mixing with the surf as its legs feebly clawed at the sand, the last nerves still not realizing that the creature was dead.

Webb returned to the radio himself, his last radioman having been filleted by a Dark One trident an hour or so before. Palmer grabbed Boudin and began to shore up the defenses.

"You're intending on going up with that bomb, aren't you?" the skipper asked quietly.

Alcide stared at the stars, trying to trace the designs of the constellations in the heavens over the plumes of smoke. He'd always enjoyed sitting on the river back home at night, checking his trotlines for bites out in the humidity of nature. Amongst the cypress was the closest he'd ever felt to God.

Here, amongst the blood and salt, he wasn't sure God was even still watching.

"Yeah, the working I have is going to bring all of these Clickers running after Pinchy. It'll look like a damn bee swarm if you've ever seen that. The Dark Ones aren't going to let me hijack their pets, they're going to come after us like we just burned their house down." Alcide trailed off and shrugged his shoulders. "Sorry for jawing sir, but, yes, it'll be a one-way ticket."

"I'll take one, too, then."

Alcide immediately shook his head, still trying to project that serene confidence he didn't really feel. "There are enough dead boys on this beach, Skip. You don't have to be among them."

Palmer's expression said more than his words."I know. And I remember every one of them. Microphone Holt. Preach Cantor. Allen Martino. Jake Dempsey."

Every name struck harder than a bullet. But he saw by Palmer's face that it was even harder for him. "Trick," Alcide added.

"I want to make the fuckers bleed."

Alcide could have put a spell on his commanding officer. It wouldn't take much just to plant a working in his mind to send him off to sleep, or simply change his mind. But he respected the man too damn much.

"Well, if them's your orders, sir, I'm just this many." Alcide held up three fingers, indicated his status on the enlisted pay scale.

Palmer smiled wanly. "Yeah, me too." As a captain, he was an O-3 on the officer's pay scale. "Now if you'll excuse me, it's been a while but I think I'm going to pray. Better get my sins squared away."

"Yes, sir."

Palmer never did get that chance to pray, though. John Pike appeared at the tree line, waving a white flag, followed by two dozen Tojos.

67. AUGUST, 1942

Lieutenant (Junior Grade) Bruce Stanley couldn't believe the request coming over the radio. He asked his operator to repeat it one more time but Duckwall, the green-behind-the-ears ensign from some Podunk stop in Illinois, stepped between the two men. "They're wanting us to pick up a contingent on shore to run escort for some wonder weapon."

Bruce wanted to lean back against the railing of PT-1228 and laugh his head off, daring the blue to strip sanity just like it had for countless other sailors tonight. The Brownings and Oerlikon were chattering away, the men not bothering to aim much. The Clickers darted in and out of the water and every bullet more than likely found a mark, making their problem more one of ammunition husbandry than aim.

The hull banged as the creatures flung themselves against it, trying to gain purchase. He'd ordered his helmsman Houghton not to slow down or change course. They'd been speeding by when the minelayer had gone up, the orange fireball brightening the ocean and illuminating the innumerable dark spots floating in the waves.

They'd started their voyage with a crew of seventeen, and the night had already seen them lose five. Robbie, a boatswain's mate from Cleveland, was snatched over the side when a Clicker had managed to latch onto the hull. He'd disappeared into the waves before he'd even had a chance to cry for help.

When they'd skimmed closer to the shore, a Dark One had leapt from the surf, caving in the head of another young sailor with one blow from its fist. Bruce didn't think he'd ever be able to get the image out of his mind of the man's skin imploding, teeth and eyes spilling out onto the deck as his corpse flailed, hands spasming like they were trying desperately to put his head right. Ensign Dillard, his second officer, had leapt onto one of the Brownings and blasted the monster to Hell, but not before their unfortunate crewmate's corpse had bounced into the sea. Bruce caught a quick flash of sinew and flesh stretching and tearing in gouts of red as five different creatures pulled the remains into their waiting jaws.

The harrowing attacks had continued for hours, to the point that Bruce had honestly thought about giving the order to retreat and make for the open ocean to get away from this nightmare. Pride more than honor prevented him from choosing the sensible, albeit cowardly course.

Then the radio had crackled to life and was asking him and his men to give more.

Back home in Youngstown, Ohio, he and his poker buddies had all volunteered together after Pearl Harbor. Only Parish, a small runt of a man with fluid in his lungs, had been found unfit for duty even in the Army. Bidding the others farewell, Parish had bitterly spoken about life being unfair, about how he wanted to do his part, his duty, same as any other man.

Bruce would never have spoken it, would stand his post to the end, but he would have given anything in that moment to switch places with his childhood friend. Maybe it was foolish. The last he'd heard from the rest of the gang, one had been killed in North Africa and another was presumed lost during an Atlantic passage. Maybe Parish had lucked out.

Bruce sighed and looked over at the helmsman Houghton with a shrug. "You have your orders. Let's get this boat shoreside."

Houghton grimaced. Occasionally they'd toed the line of insubordination before, blaming the loss of particularly foolhardy or suicidal orders on radio trouble. Clearly he'd been hoping Bruce would allow it again after receiving this, their most foolhardy order ever.

As a child, Bruce had listened to adventure stories on the radio every day after school and read only the silliest of boys magazines stories. He'd always imagined himself a soldier like his father, who hadn't come back from the Great War. He'd even practiced speeches in the mirror for a moment just such as this. He always imagined he'd say something heroic, then lead a valiant charge, saving the day just like his heroes.

Faced with it, though, no speech was worth the breath. No howling battle cry of courage accompanied them, no trumpets or thunderous fire signaled their glorious advance. The men just focused grimly and silently as they wheeled about and motored at full speed towards the shoreline.

Bruce braced himself, shouting for his men to fire on anything that blocked their passage to the shore. They were only a half-mile or so away from the beach, but with the number of creatures churning up the waters it might as well have been half a world away.

He saw brief flashes of orange in their wake. Coleman was bouncing in the seat on the 40mm as he pumped deadly fire into the water, pulverizing three Clickers that had been swimming directly behind their motor.

His forward gunners plowed the road, a Dark One's head disintegrating as a 37mm from the M4 punched a hole through its sockets. A grim smile spread over Bruce's face when the monster's corpse bumped and ground under the keel until it hit the propeller and was churned into a red mist that stained the sea.

Bruce could only imagine how they looked as they approached the shore, guns blazing. Probably looked like some sea monster come to join the rest of its kind in the slaughter of the surface dwellers.

"Two minutes to shore, sir. Should we reduce speed?" Houghton asked hesitantly, crouching as if the shore was going to suddenly spring out of a closet to surprise them.

"Maintain your speed, Houghton," Bruce replied grimly.

They lapsed into silence as the shore approached and Bruce shut his eyes. He waited in the darkness and braced himself against the railing.

"One minute!" Houghton shouted.

"One minute," Duckwall repeated when Bruce made no reply.

"Lieutenant Stanley," Houghton cried out sharply, "we're going to run aground!"

"No, we're not," he said, "but in this frenzy there's no way we get aground unless we time this perfectly. Wait for my…"

He felt the crash and he tumbled to the deck, bouncing off the metal covering isolating the helm from the rest of the boat. A collective shout echoed around him and the temporary halt in the constant fire from his ship resumed.

Bruce forced himself to stand, trying to clear his vision. Everything was a swirl of colors and darkness, and when he finally managed to clear his head, he saw that they had run up on a sandbar maybe twenty yards from the shore.

And wading through the water was a mismatched band of Marines and Tojos.

Bruce chuckled at the sight, mumbling to himself, "It's a madhouse, a fucking madhouse."

68. AUGUST, 1942

Something about coming all this way today, seeing all that he had seen, had made Palmer forget about the Japanese. But they obviously hadn't forgotten about him. Seeing that they had captured Pike reignited his rage.

They shouted and Pike was shouting too, trying to defuse the situation. More than a few of the Marines on the beach had surrounded the Tojo detachment, ordering them to throw down their weapons.

In that instant, he could have ordered his men to open fire and gun down the Tojo bastards. But seeing them, face-to-face, changed his mind. They weren't rats or monkeys or monsters. They were just men.

"Captain Palmer," Pike said, "they just want a chance to talk to you. They could've killed me. I know you don't know me, but..."

"Don't know you, Sergeant Pike? You're my brother." Pike, who had never before shown a human emotion, looked weirdly touched. "What do you men want to talk to me about?"

The Japanese leader, a second lieutenant if Ezekiel remembered his rank identifications correctly, stepped forward. He was young enough he could have been Jake.

"Fukuda, Imperial Japanese Army," he said in careful English.

"Palmer," Ezekiel replied, "United States Marine Corps."

Fukuda reached for his sword and unsheathed it, which caused quite a lot of shouting among the men.

"We'll never get a better chance, sir," Webb growled.

"Will you relax, Gunny? It's a fucking sword."

Fukuda inclined his head. A bow. Something he would never normally do to an enemy.

"I apologize. A…cultural misunderstanding. I wish to offer you my sword. By this, I mean…"

"…a truce," Ezekiel realized.

"Exactly so," Fukuda agreed.

"Lower your weapons, men." Grudgingly, they obeyed. Pike relaxed and lowered his arms.

"I assume we can pool our resources during the immediate threat," Fukuda said, "and when that passes we can…reconsider our options."

A maddeningly familiar noise came from the foliage.

"*Kurikka*!" went up the cry among the Japanese.

"I guess we're about to get our chance to find out. Listen up, Marines, you don't kill anything that's got a human face, and I fucking mean it."

Fukuda said what Palmer assumed was something similar to his men.

Together, the IJA troops with their slow-firing Arisaka rifles and the Marines with their Springfields began to fire in the same direction.

A Japanese soldier screamed at the top of his lungs as one of the monsters impaled his leg, flesh beginning to swell as its claws went to work, tearing at the man's genitals. Ezekiel was unsure how the man maintained his composure.

He was sure that the soldier knew he was going to die, but when he realized that he couldn't pull the bolt to chamber another bullet, he began frantically stabbing the monster with the bayonet affixed to the end of the barrel. The blade bounced off the shell more often than not, but it did not seem to deter the man from his deathblows, and when he finally sagged into the things' grip, the Clicker bled from four separate wounds.

A slew of bullets from the man's comrades ended the monster's life. Ezekiel directed fire at the other creatures before they could draw close, with every man back towards the foxholes they'd carved onto the beach. They maintained fire until the creatures had joined the rest of their kind's corpses littering the scrub and brush close to the jungle.

There had been little talk about the intent of the Japanese after that. An unspoken understanding passed between them.

The truce almost broke when Basher came stumbling out of the tree line, but Pike was close at hand to calm the man down, and Basher had long since lost his flamethrower anyway.

Basher looked tired, haggard, but who didn't anymore?

"Private, glad to see you made it," Ezekiel said, clasping the man's hand.

Basher looked up at him and tried to smile. "Close going there for a minute, Skip."

He caught the private up on what had transpired since he had come into camp. Basher glanced over at the Japanese "reinforcements" who were watching the ocean, occasionally picking off Clickers that emerged from the surf.

"Can't believe Gunny is comfortable with a chicken coop's worth of Tojos behind his lines."

"He doesn't have to be comfortable," Ezekiel replied, "and neither do you. It was my decision."

"Oh, sorry, sir. I didn't mean…"

"I know you didn't. You need water? Food? There should be plenty of spare weapons and ammo around." It was a morbid thought, but Ezekiel was past worrying about it.

Basher stood and moved off to retrieve a new weapon. An errant thought struck Ezekiel and he called after him. "Basher, did you see the cook out there?"

The private shook his head and called back, "No, sir! Maybe Sergeant Pike did." Ezekiel looked to where the sniper had posted himself, a small dune covered in short beach grass, his dark uniform making him look just like another piece of the scenery. When he reached the man, he found that Pike had managed to acquire a new rifle. Where he'd found the scope to complement it, he had no idea, but he was surprised that the man wasn't staring at the water, but at the sky.

"Why is your gun pointed at the sky?"

"Oh, I figured it's the one place the Clickers haven't attacked us from yet." Ezekiel glanced up at the sky, afraid that he would see the stars obscured by some chitinous nightmare carried on the night by membranous wings.

Instead he just saw the heavens, still sparkling against the black.

"No right-thinking Creator would make those things fly."

A beat passed and the men shared a good laugh over the thought.

"Did you need something, sir?"

"Oh, yes. Did you see the cook out there in the jungle? Hate to leave a man to fend for himself."

Pike shook his head. "I didn't see any men until I ran into Lieutenant Fukuda there, sir. He's on his own, but we're all on our own, really."

As if to accentuate his words, a massive groan split the air, like a gigantic whale had breached the surface and trumpeted its death moan.

One of the destroyer escorts in the strait listed back, its prow lifting up into the air, metal grinding as its super structure tried desperately to keep itself together. A crack split the night and Ezekiel watched as the ship stood up and shattered down the middle, fires dotting the deck and steaming as oil and fuel spilled over the channel.

"A few of those white bastards that melted the tanks punched right through the hull," Pike said quietly.

Then he heard Webb's voice saying, "Everyone look alive, transport is coming in!"

It wasn't hard to spot what transport he was referring to. A PT boat was bearing down on the beach, guns blazing.

Pike raised himself up then followed Ezekiel as both of them scrambled down the dune and across the sand. The boat crashed on a sandbar, prow pointing towards the beach. Pike thought he could hear mad laughter coming from the deck as a man staggered to the edge, staring at the wading Japanese and Marines.

"Are these Tojos friendly?" the man shouted at the top of his lungs.

"Yes, they are!" Ezekiel shouted.

The sailor shrugged. "Not the strangest thing I've seen today. Did someone call for a ride?"

Clickers emerged from the surf, crawling across the sandbar and directly towards the beached ship.

69. AUGUST, 1942

Alcide opened his eyes. The time had come.

Basher was the only man strong enough (and willing) to handle Pinchy. Maybe the injured Clicker knew what was coming, because it struggled in Basher's grip. Alcide sat in a circle, drawn in blood from the dead men.

In one hand he held his combat knife, in the other the handful of teeth that he had pulled from the dead marines they had found on their first night there. Laid out in front of him were the three coffin nails from his mojo bag.

He turned to Basher. "Hand it to me."

The man looked relieved to hand over the creature. Alcide took the Clicker in hand and held it within the center of the circle. Placing his knife and the teeth to left and right of the struggling crustacean, he picked up one of the coffin nails and drove the first one through one of Pinchy's claws.

The Clicker squealed in pain. Alcide ignored it, driving the second one through its other claw, and finally the last went into the stub of the thing's tail. Orange blood bubbled up out of the wound along with the clear venom that sizzled as it dripped onto the sand.

The creature writhed as it tried to pull its claws away from the shore. Alcide dug into his pack until he produced the small pestle, scooping up the teeth and the venom still leaking from its wound.

He dripped the venom across the teeth and watched as they began to dissolve. A cut from his knife across his palm added his blood to the mixture and he began to whisper the incantation.

"As you have given death, so will death be given to you. I consign you to the same. The cup of oblivion has been poured out and until my power is removed…you shall know nothing but the same."

He flipped the pestle over, dumping the mixture over the creature. Its struggles slowed until it finally ceased moving altogether. If anyone had touched the animal, they would have felt a cool film covering it, like pinesap hardened over the shell. Until the nails were removed, it would stay in this state of preservation.

Alcide reached over and dabbed his hand in the blood of the dead Marines, drawing designs onto the creature's shell and whispering the next spell that would complete his plan.

"Your kin thirst for death and your bloodline has yearned for ruin. The hunger that has consumed you I pour out onto your brethren. So that in this hour, you and they shall fall prey. As the wicked run to destruction, they now run to you."

Anyone standing by would have felt the pressure of the working, like the world had taken a deep breath and exhaled, power radiating out from the beach, to the island, and over the waves.

Then came the response, a cacophony of angry clicking that echoed over the waves, so many that it drowned out the continuous sound of gunfire and artillery from the ships.

Alcide snatched up Pinchy, tucking him under his arm and leaving his pack where it lay, running towards the ocean and the beached patrol boat.

The deck crew fought admirably, Brownings and M2s chattering away at the water. The Tojos that Pike had picked up held a perimeter even if the water was up to their waists.

The Clickers were no longer teeming to kill the men that were seemingly easy prey in the oceans, but were now headed directly towards Alcide and the spell-frozen Pinchy.

"You still want that ticket, Skipper?"

Ezekiel Palmer turned from the tip of the sandbar and saw Alcide wading, trying to make it to the boat. Alcide thought he heard him shout something, but he couldn't hear it; his entire focus was on getting to the boat alive.

A Clicker burst from the water and lunged at him. Alcide threw himself into the waves, the deadened sounds of the undertow tossing him as another wave broke in the surf. He felt something under his arms and kicked out at his attacker, but not before he was pulled underwater. His lungs were near bursting when Lieutenant Fukuda pulled him out.

"*Hayaku, motto hayaku*!" the Japanese officer shouted, gesturing with his sword at the PT boat. A Marine waded over, pulling him along. One of the Japanese soldiers wrestled with the Clicker that had attacked him, eyes closed, letting it sting him repeatedly. In one hand, the man held what looked like a small black pineapple.

There was a small pop, then orange and red blood misted over the waters and the men, and something indescribable that the fish and gulls would feast on floated on the waves.

His comrades didn't pause to mourn him, barely even glanced, they just continued to usher Alcide along. Pumping his legs and fighting the tide, he made it to the sandbar even as the men around him began to scream.

The monsters were coming from all directions. Alcide saw the skipper helping what Marines had volunteered for this mission into the ship. Basher, still in the water, shouted for him to hurry.

Two Dark Ones rose out of the water, barking in their throaty tongue at the Clickers swimming past them without a second thought, no doubt wondering why their control over their pets had winnowed away to nothing. Then their large eyes fixed on the humans beached just fifty yards away and they raised their weapons in a war cry. They charged forward and Alcide saw them raise their tridents, ready to throw.

Fukuda noticed them first and Alcide watched his face twist into a specter of rage. He gestured with the sword towards the fish-men, "*Takibi*!"

Two of his men fumbled with their Arisakas and only one managed to fire, catching the Dark One in the arm. Black blood erupted as it leapt and stabbed the Japanese soldier through the sternum. Alcide heard the crunch of bones and saw the running blood of the man as he went limp on the end of the weapon, rifle dropping into the water.

The other Dark One went for the Japanese soldier's counterpart, batting aside the bayoneted rifle and grabbing the man by the neck, webbed hand squeezing. Alcide saw the man writhe for a few moments, the monster increasing the pressure until the man's tongue lolled out of his mouth and his eyes were squeezed from their sockets.

The two Marines who had waded out to help him wrenched him forward, firing with their Springfields at the two monsters. Fukuda pulled him up onto the sandbar.

He heard screams behind him, and a quick glance showed five Clickers of various sizes overwhelming the closest marine. His screams ceased as he fell beneath the waves.

"Portside, kill the bastards!" the captain of the PT boat cried.

A sailor swiveled the deck gun until the pair of Dark Ones were directly in the path of the barrel. The two creatures had killed the other Marine, at the cost of a few minor injuries, and both of them stared directly into the gun like it was just another of man's weapons that they could power their way through.

The first creature practically exploded, black gore raining down into the water as the mass of meat that had once been half of its chest and legs fell into the water. The other clutched at the stump where its arm had just been, crying pathetic whimpers as it tried to stem the tide of blood leaking into the water. It fell backward into the deeper water before the deck crew could bring the gun to bear, disappearing into the surf.

Then Alcide was hoisted up and found himself standing on the deck of the PT boat, Captain Palmer standing next to him.

"He's aboard!" Palmer shouted.

The man Alcide presumed was the boat's commanding officer began shouting orders. Alcide clutched Pinchy tightly and stumbled to the small nest where the helmsmen were already beginning to reverse, the boat groaning.

"All aboard that's coming aboard!" the Navy lieutenant shouted.

To Alcide's surprise, Basher climbed aboard. The surf was practically more crab than water, so he didn't blame him. Then, to Alcide's double surprise, Basher reached out a hand to help up Fukuda, who looked around at the carnage surrounding the vessel.

Fukuda paused, considering, then shook his head with finality.

"If you succeed, remember that we are men, too."

Then he batted the marine's hand aside and drew his sword into a guarding position, turning to face the ocean's hordes and screaming, "*Banzai*!"He charged through the water and slashed the tail off a large Clicker feeding off the remains of the Dark One killed by the deck gun. Then the man turned and slashed at another, and another, drawing blood each time.

Dozens of Clickers scuttled across the sandbar, either stopping to feast on their dead masters or pursuing the retreating boat, but the Japanese officer threw himself at every creature he could reach, and each one fought back, until he was ragged and bleeding.

A ghostly white form bigger than the largest gator Alcide had ever seen pitched itself out of the water, scuttling across the wet sand. It was an albino Clicker, heading straight for the PT boat.

The boat commander noticed the incoming monster, his face paling as he pointed and shouted for his gunners to kill it. Then Alcide saw Fukuda throw himself onto the ghostly creature's back, raising his sword and stabbing it in a downward blow. The Clicker collapsed on the sandbar, and for a split second, Alcide thought that if he ran the man might have made it back to shore. Then he saw the animal's shell begin to bubble and spasm.

The Clicker exploded. Steaming gore flew like a depth charge had been dropped on the dead animal. A human arm, still clutching the hilt of a sword, flew over the boat, melting as it twirled in an arc before it hit the ocean and was immediately dragged down by a passing Clicker.

70. AUGUST, 1942

Ezekiel stood on the foredeck of the PT boat. The commander, Bruce Stanley, joined him as they raced back towards the *Saratoga.* He seemed to have everything under control. His radioman was already relaying to the other PT boats still floating to rally at the aircraft carrier.

He almost felt superfluous, captain of nothing but the last two men that he had come ashore with two days ago. Ezekiel glanced at Basher, who was waving a Browning like it was a Garand, apparently preparing in case they were boarded.

And then there was Boudin, leaning against the metal canopy enclosing the helm, holding Pinchy tighter than a lover and muttering some incantation or other.

Adrift, listless, and bound on a trip to the end.

In this he found he was only similar to the five Japanese soldiers that had managed to board the ship before they'd left the sandbar. Most of the crew ignored them, huddled together on the middeck, checking their ammo and making sure that their weapons were in working order.

Ezekiel stared down the line at Pike. The sergeant had been the first aboard, driven by the strange death wish Ezekiel had still not asked him about. Pike was near the Bofors 40mm at the stern of the boat, an anti-aircraft cannon. He had his sniper rifle pointed at the water. Ezekiel checked to see what Pike was aiming at and wished he hadn't. His stomach clenched.

The water churned. Masses of Clickers, more than he could count, pursued them, weaving through the water faster than sharks. He saw countless red shells, hundreds of obsidian, and the odd flash of white against the dark of the ocean. And for every one that he could see, he wondered how many of their masters swam after them, unseen beneath.

Their one piece of luck was that all of the Clickers and Dark Ones had been swarming the island and had to chase them. Otherwise they might have been attacking from all directions instead of wildly pursuing them.

Pike took a few potshots but it seemed more than hopeless.

"How's it looking?" Ezekiel asked.

"I'm hitting what I'm aiming for, but I can hardly miss in this. We don't have enough bullets.

"The whole damn fleet doesn't have enough bullets. But we've got a witch doctor."

"How comforting," Pike replied drily.

"We'll take the bomb, lead them out, then blow them all to hell. Every single one of them," Ezekiel replied, hoping it was true. It seemed unbelievable, but the unbelievable also pursued them, jumping and clawing to be the first to feast on their flesh.

The man at the radio, Ensign Duckwall, hollered, "PT-790 has got the bomb. They're angling out to meet us with all the remaining boats."

A flurry of activity seized every man, making sure their weapons were loaded, and all of them keeping an eye at the splashing mass coming up from the depths behind them.

Stanley joined him, eyes wide as he stared at the innumerable horde. "We… we need a destination or else they're going to cut us…" He paused for a second and stared at the masses. "My God."

Ezekiel glanced at the foredeck and his man sitting there. "I think it's time we ask our witch doctor for his heading."

71. JUNE, 2021

Cameron Custer downed the whiskey. It was cheap stuff. Though he wasn't as bad off as he'd been during his road days, he was still living off a tiny government stipend rather than the fortune he'd expected to rake in for his earth-shattering discoveries.

He had been reduced to little more than a side note in the new reality of the world. Monsters existed, and they were fascinating. Too many cameras had been rolling for the feds to deny Jade or Pinchy's existence, though since the live feed had cut off before their rampage, the administration had been forced into a sort of *Weekend at Bernie's* scenario to explain the missing personnel in the middle of an election season.

The feds had grilled Cam at length, particularly about what had happened to Pinchy, who had disappeared in the aftermath of the NOAA rampage. He'd asked Jade if she'd "suggested" the Clicker disappear, but she had remained mysteriously quiet about the matter. Since he had no information to give them, they'd eventually given up.

As a carrot, the feds had offered Cam some money to disappear. As a stick, they'd threatened him with the bottom of the deepest hole in Gitmo if he revealed anything other than what the official story claimed as a stick. As the only other witness to what had happened at NOAA, Cam's cooperation had effectively shut down everything but conjecture in the media. "Other" was the operative word here. Jade had agreed to no such disappearing act.

The Dark One had become an overnight celebrity. Hollywood was rushing out an epic film of her life story. He'd even heard she was writing a tell-all book about her time as a captive of the US government and her rescue by the dashing Cameron Custer. Not that he had been contacted by anyone for his side of the story, or interviewed, or consulted. Jade was doing the talking for both of them it seemed and the media was eating it up.

He'd expected TV deals, a new rise for his star, whole species named after him, his legacy assured. Instead, after satisfying the G-men that he wasn't going to talk, he'd found he had nowhere to go and nothing to do. When they'd offered him a bus ticket to get the fuck out of Washington, the only place he could think of to go was Alcide Robichaude's hometown.

He'd found Alcide's journal and effects in Sergeant Arthur Webb's trunk, when both Robichaude and Webb's own words in the journal bore out that the Cajun had wanted the journal returned to his family. Custer had gone looking for information about what had become of Arthur Webb and had discovered that the sergeant had died leaving Guadalcanal, his troop carrier sunk by a Japanese sub that had snuck into the strait. That was how he'd found himself washed up and out on the shore of some no-name bar in Texas, asking after Robichaudes and finding none of the locals willing to talk about them.

He downed the last of the shots he had ordered. With no money to pay for more and no direction for where to go next, he had decided just to sit in this bar until someone tossed him out.

The TV crackled overhead and he looked up and saw Jade sitting comfortably on what looked like Jimmy Fallon's couch, cracking jokes about her appearance and putting on the appropriate airs of a star.

Custer snarled in anger, throwing the empty shot glass and shattering it against the TV screen.

"Hey, hey! What the fuck are you doing?" the portly bartender hollered, waddling down the bar, eyes squinted together like a too-fat dog's.

Cam anticipated getting thrown out on the street, would probably welcome the shit-kicking he'd earned, if only because then he could feel something. He was surprised when he heard a voice behind him say, "Easy, Gavin. He's just a little too into his rotgut, yeah?"

Cam made a halfhearted wave of his hand, not apologizing in the slightest, nor even looking at the man who was apparently acting as his advocate in keeping his ass from being kicked.

"Bring us another round, Gavin? Good stuff, not that swill we serve the out-of-towners."

The bartender glowered at the mess of broken glass, but the stranger slapped a bill on the counter that would obviously more than cover the trouble and the bartender nodded. "Sure thing, Luc."

Cam swiveled in his stool, looking at the man sitting next to him. He was young, barely half his age, a head of messy brown hair over piercing green eyes. Cam grinned broadly, reaching his hands out. "Thank you, young man! If you keep me drunk, I'll…I'll tell you all about your favorite fish."

It was all he could think of and all he was good at anymore. He had to giggle at the last bit, lest he start sobbing, and immediately slammed back the newest shot as it was delivered to him.

The green-eyed man shook his head. "You're not doing so good, are you, Dr. Custer?"

He tried to compose himself, realizing that whatever dignity he had left was wrapped up in the opinions of the fans, who were dwindling away as time went on. This kid looked the right age, had the look of someone who was eager to ask for an autograph. He'd seen it before.

"Where are my fucking manners? Sorry, you obviously know who I am. What's your name, son?" Cam smiled, eyes lidded, already fumbling in his pocket to see if he even had a pen.

The man offered his hand. "Luc Robichaude. A pleasure, sir."

Cam felt his mouth go dry. Even through the haze of alcohol, he knew the name. He squinted, realizing belatedly that the man had a thick Cajun accent. It couldn't be a coincidence.

"I- I read about your…" Cam realized that he had no clue what the deceased Alcide was to this man.

Robichaude answered for him. "My great uncle. Heard through the grapevine you'd found his journal. Found yourself a Clicker too, didn't ya?"

Cam nodded, his mood darkening as he reached for his drink. "Fat lot of good it did me too." He held his drink out. "Oh well. Here's to your uncle and his saving the world."

Robichaude returned the toast, wincing after he finished. "My grandfather wasn't a well-liked man. War changes men, yeah? Still, he taught the art of root work to my father and the rest, always talked about Uncle 'Cide, the bravest man. The Deep Folk heard the stories from their kin, passed it along to us..." His eyes settled on the journal sitting comfortably in Cam's pocket. "Long have I had a desire to read his account."

Cam felt his hand reflexively curl around his pocket. From what he read about this man's relations, he wasn't sure that he couldn't charm the book right out of his pocket. As a scientist, he didn't believe in magic, but as the discoverer of an ancient civilization of merfolk, he didn't discount it either.

"You're not going to...take it from me, are you?" he asked, as diplomatically as possible in his current state.

"No, nothing like that, Dr. Custer. I've come to offer you a deal."

Cam smiled, raising his glass again. He hadn't meant to sell the journal back to its rightful owners, but wasn't going to turn down perfectly good money, especially not in his current state. "Now you're speaking my language. Don't know if you've noticed," he said, gesturing grandly at the empty bar, "but I've reached the bottom of the barrel."

Robichaude chuckled. "Trust me, Doc. There is always further to fall."

Cam looked down at his tattered shirt, stained pants, and old sports coat that redefined the word shabby. "Maybe. How much cash are we talking about here exactly?"

Robichaude shook his head. "No, no, Doc. What I'm offering isn't something of this world, like money. Nah, nah, this is something more, something you been searching your whole life for but haven't found."

Cam knew a pitch when he heard one but found that he didn't care. It wasn't like any other opportunities were going to come knocking. "All right, I'll bite."

Luc Robichaude smiled like he had just reeled in the biggest fish of his life. "Then how would you like to experience undersea worlds?"

72. AUGUST, 1942

Alcide looked up from his fugue when Palmer laid a light hand on his shoulder. He'd been lost, aware of where he was, but doing his best to push back the psychic might of the Dark Ones.

He was muttering powerful magic, incantations that his father had taught him were only to be used in the most dire of circumstances.

Alcide chuckled bitterly. Too many people had seen his spells. Secrecy gave hoodoo its potency. Even if he lived he'd return home effectively powerless.

But he'd driven back the smothering blanket that the Dark Ones had laid on the men. They went to their duties swiftly and without hesitation.

He felt empty now, hoodoo and everything else had been part of his upbringing since he had been just about old enough to even crawl. His Pa had taught him everything. And even if he knew that he wasn't going home when this was over, he wondered if his Pa and brothers knew what he had given away.

"Sorry, Skipper. Lost in my own thoughts." His words were accentuated by the sound of one of the Brownings dislodging an unwanted passenger. A Dark One had stabbed a trident into the hull and was being dragged as they turned in a wide arc to avoid a small school of Clickers.

"They're going to roll us if we don't get a heading, Boudin," Palmer stated calmly.

Alcide stood and nodded, reminding himself of all the men had given their lives for this moment. He reached the helmsman and repeated the directions Ota Hanshiro had given him. Neither of them had been Navy, but Lieutenant Stanley was able to quickly turn the directions into coordinates, and the radioman transmitted the information to the other boats.

Alcide took a deep sigh and looked out at the flotilla. It was quite a thrilling sight, the eight remaining PT boats swerving into formation. If there had been any kind of ship before them, they could have sunk it with the torpedoes they were hauling.

And behind them were the monsters of the deep.

He was sure that the entire line extended over a mile, all of them swimming as fast as they could and beginning to gain ground. The radio crackled and he heard Admiral Fletcher's voice. "Godspeed, everyone."

Gunny Webb's voice came next. "I'll expect you Marines to be in formation at 0600 tomorrow. None of your goddamned excuses."

Chuckling, Stanley handed Palmer the handset. "We'll be there with bells on, Gunny." He tried to hand the mic back to Stanley, but he waved him off.

"No, no, no. This is your operation now, Major Palmer."

"Major?" Basher asked, snorting. "Can't you squids read rank?"

"A boat can only have one captain," Palmer replied. Marine O-3s always got a courtesy promotion when shipboard. He glanced around at the motley collection of Marines, sailors, and Japanese soldiers, all working in tandem. He keyed the mic. "This is Major Palmer aboard PT-1228 to the most…unusual task force in history. This is it, men. We're on our own from here out. Follow us."

73. AUGUST, 1942

Savo Island passed to their right, their heading taking them North out of the strait, leaving behind the lights of shore and the relative safety of the fleet. There was no cover coming now, no more reinforcements, just the men on the boats and the bomb.

Ezekiel could see the weapon, like a giant steel egg, sitting on the nearest boat on their starboard side. Four men were positioned around it. While large, he had expected something far grander, something that would have taken up the entire length of the boat. It was almost comical that such power was contained in something so innocuous. But he knew that it was the last chance he was going to have to ruminate on the situation. The Clickers had just caught up to them.

The Japanese soldiers took position on either side of the Bofors, along with Pike, who was laying down on the deck to steady his aim. Ezekiel readied the Thompson he'd "inherited" from the PT boat's arms locker. The nearest Clickers jumped in and out of the surf, inches from the deck.

He tapped the shoulder of the Bofors gunner and he didn't hesitate. The gun roared and a section of water exploded in orange pulp, again and again. The rest of their ragtag armada did the same, not really bothering to pick their targets. The whole ocean had become a target.

The anti-aircraft cannon couldn't aim low enough to hit the creatures closest to the deck, and Ezekiel steadied himself, aiming at the trio of different monsters that had crawled aboard.

The Japanese soldiers fired with precision, their rifles splitting chitin and spilling blood. The Clicker they had killed flopped to the deck, and then slid back into the waves. Another had reached the base of the Bofors and Ezekiel fired, ten bullets chewing through the creature's skin.

The last Clicker that had made it aboard stabbed its stinger at the gun mount, trying to get at the gunner's feet. Ezekiel fired again, listening to the thing's pained squeals. Kicking with his foot, he sent the corpse tumbling across the deck, hitting another as it crawled from the surf. He hastily tried to reload as one of the Japanese soldiers took up his flank, firing his rifle.

A Clicker exploded from the surf on their port side. Ezekiel barely had time to duck and the Japanese soldier wasn't as lucky. The Clicker wrapped around his head, tail stabbing into his face. The man fell to the deck, body twitching and inflating like some kind of demented party balloon.

The Clicker feasted, its eyestalks wavering as it shoveled the man's brain matter into its craw, blood and venom sizzling as it spilled out onto the deck. Ezekiel felt his stomach hitch, bile rising as he aimed and shot, killing the Clicker.

The Bofors went silent, steam rising out of the end of its barrels as the gunner cried, "Reload!"

Ezekiel wrestled to get his feet under him. Pike fired next to him and another boiling roil split the sea; he'd managed to kill one of the white Clickers. As if they had a sense of retribution, a dark-shelled obsidian Clicker latched onto their hull. Ezekiel saw the tail stiffen, venom dripping from the tip, and the Bofors gunner had a moment of wide-eyed realization of what was coming.

The venom sprayed and the gun began to melt along with the man sitting in the gunner's seat, metal blending into flesh. Ezekiel would have given anything to silence the high shriek as he watched the vaguely human-like blob bounce around under the straps securing it to the seat. Fingers fumbled and dissolved in small globs that splattered against the deck and then the man's head flopped back, falling away and rolling into the sea, a trail of dark blood behind it.

The four remaining Japanese soldiers lost it, all of them dry heaving. Pike rolled away to avoid the steaming heap of what once could have been called a man.

The obsidian Clicker scuttled closer, heaving the rest of its bulk onto the boat, one claw reaching out to shovel the bloody slush into its craw.

"*Basher!*" Ezekiel hollered and pointed at the dark creature. The private immediately swiveled the Browning around and fired. He aimed at the center of the thing's body and its eyestalks and claws both popped, mangled by .30 cal bullets until it was nothing but bleeding meat.

Ezekiel grabbed Pike, hollering into his ear, "Keep them busy! Don't let them board!"

A myriad of screams split the air. A *Kamikaze* Clicker with an apparently functional bomb had rammed into the side of the PT boat two positions from their port. He saw men spiral into the water as the boat floundered, barely surfacing before they were left behind in the dark.

Ezekiel stumbled to the helm where Boudin clutched Pinchy. To his surprise, the Cajun was rocking back and forth, whispering to the petrified Clicker. He grabbed him by the scruff.

"You're not going nutso like that cook, are you, Boudin?"

Boudin seemed to realize what he was doing, and looked shocked.

"Sorry, sir."

Ezekiel turned and addressed the boat's commander, Bruce Stanley. "We're losing too many! How long until we get to the coordinates?"

Stanley glanced up at him. "Ten minutes at best possible speed, sir! PT-808 just went down, seven boats still floating!"

"Keep us as close to the bomb as possible. The Bofors is done for. Have our deck guns keep pressure on their crowd."

The lieutenant nodded and relayed orders to his men. He returned to Boudin and squatted until he was eye level with him."I know you've got a lot going on, Boudin, but we could use any help you can spare."

The Cajun smiled at him. "What do you think I'm doing, Skipper? Don't it feel clear moving around the deck? Don't it feel nice without having to wade through their mojo?"

Ezekiel did notice that the pressure he'd felt all night was gone. He hadn't been aware until told, but felt grateful for whatever Boudin was doing to keep it from coming back.

He was about to leave the man to his hoodoo when Boudin's head snapped towards the prow, and in a small voice that only Ezekiel could hear, whimpered, "Oh no…"

Ezekiel straightened and looked out at the ocean. So he'd been wrong about the Clickers only approaching from one direction. The waves surged as something moved under the surface. Something large.

"Guns forward, guns forward!" Ezekiel shouted.

"Forward?" Basher shouted incredulously. The men in the rear more than had their hands full.

The water exploded and a massive Clicker breached. It was easily the size of a sperm whale. Astride its shell, holding its trident aloft, was a Dark One. Obviously an important member of their tribe, its body was adorned with piercings and coral regalia. It managed to shout a croaking war cry before the Oerlikon cannon opened up, the gunner doing his damned best to kill the creature and its master.

The Clicker moved its claws, shielding its master from the incoming fire. Its claws popped and shuddered, spilling blood and chunks of ravaged meat. It uttered a high-pitched squeal and Ezekiel saw the creature's tail waver in position.

"The tail! Shoot the stinger!" He knew that the gunner couldn't hear him over the sound of the deck gun, but he kept shouting anyway as he waded forward, firing the Thompson and watching the bullets barely make an impact.

The other Browning gunner swiveled around, hearing Ezekiel's warning, and fired, chewing through its body and sending the creature's tail flopping down to the deck, nearly flipping the boat.

The Dark One roared and raised its trident. Ezekiel tried to cry out another warning before the creature threw the weapon. It lanced through the air, impaling the gunner through the chest.

The man spasmed for a moment, blood running from his mouth and around the dark metal before he fell still. The Dark One laughed, a loathsome sound that sent Ezekiel into a fit of rage.

The Browning finally ran dry and the Dark One leapt off the Clicker as it finally succumbed to death, even as two more emerged from the sea, both just as large and both carrying Dark Ones.

A few of the deck crew hustled forward, rifles firing. Ezekiel heard a scream and turned to see another of the Japanese soldiers pulled off the boat in the claw of a massive Clicker.

The Dark One leapt across the deck, a massive hand caving in the chest of one of the deck crew. Ezekiel turned the Thompson and fired. The gun ran dry but the Dark One seemed unaffected, as though its scales were too hard for bullets to pierce.

The Dark One was so large it was able to snatch Ezekiel off the deck and squeeze his head in a single hand. Only now, in its grip, did he realize it was female.

"Why do the little brothers ignore our commands and follow you? Where is your magus?" the Dark One croaked in flawless English.

"No magus here," Ezekiel grunted as the thing's claws dug into his scalp. "What's your name, doll?"

A grotesque smile split the thing's face.

"I am the greatest bio-vizier who ever lived. Your magus is a child compared to me, but an irksome child still. What spell is he casting? You'll cost us time, but that's all. We'll sink your petty fleet and then take your mates and your broodlings for our own."

Boudin was on his feet, hurrying forward. Ezekiel knew he was coming to rescue him, but he couldn't risk that happening now.

"All right, all right," Ezekiel said with a cough, "Our magus isn't here. But he gave us a…working. A spell…thingy. To call the Clickers. I'll give it to you. Here, it's in my pocket."

He reached into his pocket and pulled out a grenade, surreptitiously pulling the pin.

"He said this egg was precious and that as long as…"

He didn't even have to finish his story, which was a shame because he'd come up with a whole thing in his head. But the bio-vizier snatched the grenade out of his hand and swallowed it whole, laughing. She dropped him to the deck.

"Your magic is weak, primate. We will topple your whole..."

She also sounded like she might have had a whole speech prepared, too, but it didn't matter much because her stomach exploded in all directions like a poorly baked muffin collapsing. Her top half and bottom half separated and were quickly swallowed by the sea.

Boudin reached him, looking shocked that he'd solved the problem himself.

"Well, that was something, sir."

"Yeah," Ezekiel coughed, fighting to see through his splitting headache, "some of us don't need magic to solve all our problems."

"Speaking of problems," Boudin pointed at the bio-vizier's two companions.

"Well, grenades seem to work," he muttered.

"You better be fucking sure of that throw, Palmer!" Stanley shouted behind him.

"He's sure, sir!" Boudin called out.

"Just call me Tiny Bonham," Ezekiel said. He pulled the pin and watched as another of the deck crew was impaled by a Clicker's tail, wrenched from his place and thrown screaming into the sea.

Ezekiel lobbed the grenade, watching it make its slow arc and then explode. Parts of the Clicker's shell went flying as a large gush of blood and one dead Dark One went flopping into the sea.

"Not a bad throw," he said to Boudin.

"Yeah, you did that all on your lonesome, sir," Boudin replied.

The creature seemed almost confused by its handler's demise, its mangled claw waving through the air like it would ward off the crew's unceasing fire. The other Dark One roared, turning its mount around, the Clicker swiping at the men surrounding the deck gun.

There was a sharp crack and then a short splash of black blood. The Dark One toppled off, a hole clear through his forehead. Clearly its companions had not been as impervious as the chieftainess. Ezekiel glanced behind him and saw Pike give a small curt nod, chambering another round.

He felt a hand on his shoulder and turned to look at Boudin, who pointed at the boat with the bomb. "We have to get there, Skipper. This boat isn't long for this world."

"You know something?"

Boudin nodded, his face pale. After all they'd been through, that was enough to convince Ezekiel.

He looked over at the speeding boat carrying the bomb and pointed emphatically, hollering at the top of his lungs. "Can we change rides, Lieutenant Stanley?"

Stanley looked like he'd just asked to punch his mother.

"You can try, sir. I'll pull you alongside."

The helmsman swung sharply right, sending them towards the other PT boat. The radio came alive as PT-790 asked what was happening. Then they were right alongside them and Boudin was clutching Pinchy, bracing himself against the deck.

Ezekiel began shouting for everyone to prepare to abandon ship. Most of the men looked confused, but Basher and Pike both had seen him talking to Boudin before he began issuing the order. They knew better than to question.

A *Kamikaze* Clicker hit them midship, the impact rocking them up. Men bounced off the deck, screaming, falling into the abyss where the Clickers swarmed them.

Tearing them to pieces.

The PT boat came flopping back down onto the water. Ezekiel looked around, dazed. They were gaining water, their port side listing into the drink. He saw Boudin take a running leap and cleared the gap, barely making it onto the deck of the other ship. Had he missed by inches the boats would have shot past and he would have fallen into that churning drink.

Stanley had pulled on a lifejacket, shouting at what remained of his crew to abandon ship. Ezekiel tried to do the same for his own, turning to see Pike dangling from a railing with one hand, the other attempting to save one of the Japanese soldiers from sliding into the water.

"Sergeant, let him go!"

Pike shook his head, hollering for the other man to hold on. The Japanese man hollered something that Ezekiel couldn't understand and then slid into the water and the waiting Clickers.

The seawater had flooded into the stern and the deck was already below an ankle-deep swell. Pike looked at Ezekiel helplessly and then his eyes deadened. Ezekiel knew what was coming before the man even committed the action and he was already shouting for him to stop, to jump the gap to what little dry deck remained.

But John Pike threw his rifle into the sea and retrieved two grenades from his jacket, pulling the pins. He locked eyes with Ezekiel and gave a two-fingered salute before he threw himself into the sea. The Clickers found him instantly, but he didn't suffer. Two gouts of water split the sea and chummed the waves.

The PT boat had begun to slow, water finding the engines. Basher leapt behind him, making it onto the deck of the other boat. It was only him and Stanley left.

Ezekiel turned and took a running leap, feeling the salt spray on his cheek as he cleared the void. For a split second he thought he had misjudged his jumping point and that he would tumble into the sea only to roll across the opposite deck near the PT-790's Bofors gun.

A few hands reached out to grab him, and when he was back on his feet, he heard the men clamoring for Stanley to jump. The man looked terrified. The PT boat was slowing. It was now or never.

Stanley jumped and the propeller finally gave out. He missed the jump and fell into the sea. The entire crew let out a scream, a few of Stanley's surviving deck crew crying to the commander of the boat to slow, to turn, to save the man.

Ezekiel saw the man bob back to the surface, arms flailing, then he heard the keening wail as the Clickers found him. The last he saw of Bruce Stanley was a pincer slicing his head from his body.

He tore his gaze away. "Launch a torpedo into that boat. Blow it to Hell!"

The commander of PT-790 nodded, relaying his order. A quiet settled over the men, all of them staring back at the blackened sea. A brilliant orange fireball illuminated the sky and a noise like distant thunder sounded.

"Hope it killed the bastards," Basher said.

Ezekiel looked up. "There are more. There are always more."

"I'll fix it," Boudin promised.

"You'd better," Ezekiel said grimly.

"Two minutes!" the helmsman called.

Ezekiel staggered over to the bomb, reaching out a hand and placing it across the casing. The name *Big Mama* was painted on the side.

Boudin was next to him, staring at the weapon. "Beautiful. Such power here. I can feel it."

"How did you know that they would come for that boat?" Ezekiel asked quietly. "Can you see the future now? Do we succeed?"

"Their working, the one that drains men of their wills, holding it back as I have sometimes gives me flashes of intent, of instinct." Boudin shrugged. "Might've just been luck. Hard to tell anymore. But, no, I can't see what will be."

Both of them lapsed into silence, waiting for their destination and the end.

74. AUGUST, 1942

The boat slowed to a crawl and Alcide heard a man call out, "Water is shallow here, looks like an atoll."

It made sense. The Dark Ones could build in the deepest trenches, but a place like this offered some protection.

Well, nothing could protect them from him.

Sighing, he turned to Pinchy. The face inked on the poor thing's back seemed to be scared. The poor little creature had turned out to be a friend. At least he could save one friend today. He whispered a working over it, ordering it to flee as far and as fast as it could. Then he pulled the nails out of its claws and chest. Pinchy shook himself like a wet dog coming out of the rain, then promptly scuttled over the side and disappeared. He spotted its white back appearing over the waves once as he disappeared into the horizon.

"We can set it to go off once it hits the seabed or we can get it on a timer. Either way, we need to set it and head for the hills!" The new lieutenant's voice rose a few pitches, his eyes darting around as he explained the bomb to the skipper. The remaining PT boats had formed a perimeter.

Palmer looked at him. "What do you think, do we have a chance? Maybe set it to remote, get home in time for Christmas?"

Alcide shook his head. "They'll tear it apart as soon as we leave it unattended. Someone's got to make sure it goes off."

He looked around at each man, feeling the terror, the longing, the desire to live more powerful than any magic. And the urge came one last time to offer them a way home.

"I'm not leaving this boat. The last I see of this world is going to be this violent sea and beautiful stars. I suggest the rest of you hitch a ride out with our escort now."

The nearly eighteen men on the boat looked at each other, more than one looking sorely tempted to take his offer. A silence reigned except for the trolling motors of the circling boats and then Basher spoke quietly. "I'm not going anywhere, Boudin. You're not going to be alone and when we get to that bar where Martino's waiting to share a drink with us."

It seemed he spoke for everyone as they went to their stations, preparing to hold off the incoming swarm.

Alcide turned back to the bomb and was presented with a small timer. He looked up at Palmer and tried to force a smile. "You still want to make peace with your Creator, Skipper? How much time do you need?"

Palmer clasped Preach's rosary between his hands. "A minute should be plenty."

Alcide nodded and set the timer. Basher called, "Here they come!"

Ezekiel pulled his Colt, the only weapon he had left, and fired at the left side as a mass of Clickers came swarming over the side. Maybe one in every three shots pierced their hides. His gun clicked empty and he threw it into the mob, drawing his knife.

Basher's Browning swiveled and launched a barrage into the clawing horde. He only stopped firing when five Dark Ones came riding out of the waves, the lead's Clicker wrapping its claw around the mounting, silencing the private's war cry and turning it into a gurgle of pain. The pincer squeezed and Basher was snapped in two, his legs' nerve endings keeping them kicking while his torso landed in a heap of blood on the deck, mouth hanging open and staring directly at Alcide.

At the same time, Alcide caught movement in the mass of dead Clickers on the deck. A small transparent form scuttled forward, tail and pincers raised, hissing in eager anticipation. It was a brain Clicker, like the one that had transformed Hanshiro. It made a beeline directly for Palmer, who was staring at the top half of what used to be Basher.

"Skipper, move!" Alcide cried just as the transparent Clicker shot forward. Its claws dug into Palmer's shoulder and Alcide heard him snarl as he realized just what had landed on his chest. He gripped the animal hard, his hands cut by the scrabbling legs trying to gain purchase in his flesh. He crushed it, killing it before it could make its way to his neck. But, in a final spasm, the brain Clicker's tail dug deep into his stomach, just above his navel, and his arms went limp. Ezekiel wobbled on his legs, like they were trying to carry him in two directions at once, his head craning back, a small sliver of saliva running down his chin. "Boudin…Robichaude…" His body pitched itself over the side and the waves swallowed him.

Alcide closed his eyes, swallowed the lump in his throat, and committed to his course. The timer began to tick away immediately.

"All boats retreat! I repeat, all boats retreat and get—" The radioman was killed by a Clicker tail through the skull, impaling his head to the glass. The beast's smaller brethren immediately began to feast on his softening body. The countdown continued.

0:50

Every man was dead except for Alcide. He reached across Basher's corpse, dabbing his fingers in the man's blood and drawing the protective sigils around himself, hoping that he had just enough power left to keep them at bay for another few seconds.

0:40

An obsidian Clicker the size of a city block, carrying a Dark One came to a stop on the other side of the canopy, it and its brethren tipping the boat forward under their combined weight. Its rider, a massive twelve-foot monster, dismounted and limped towards Alcide.

0:33

Alcide was sure that this was their chieftainess. There was an air about it of a time long passed, a primordial savagery, the nets and fishhooks adorning it looking like trophies of long-ago battles, and the coral growing out of the left side of its face a battle scar rather than a sign of age.

It limped towards Alcide, its eyes glancing down at the small warding he had drawn onto the deck, and gave a derisive snort, speaking in its own language. "Pathetic. Thousands of tides I've swam through this world. Did you think your meager spells would turn me aside, magus?"

0:21

Alcide shook his head. A sad smile playing across his lips, then he spoke back in the beast's own language, or at least the dialect he had learned from the tribe back home. "No, old fish, but it got you to pause your rampage. And this is the last tide you will see of this world."

0:15

The Dark One roared like it had been slapped and raised its trident. Alcide closed his eyes. He felt the impact and was lifted off his knees, wrenching to a stop with a sudden jerk, pinned to the bomb.

0:10

Sweet agony racked his body and every attempt to draw breath was just another sting. The Dark One's anger melted away, satisfaction replacing it as it growled, "Die, human."

0:05

Alcide spat blood directly into the thing's face, the action taking what little strength he had left as he whispered, "You… first…"

0:01

There was an all-annihilating white and Alcide was dead before he felt any of it.

75. AUGUST, 1942

GySgt Webb looked up in wide-eyed wonder. Out in the distant sea, there was a second sun. They had been in the process of burning the dead monsters, piling them in giant piles that had already begun to smell of rot, like dead fish left out under a hot sun.

Then the horizon had brightened, like the drill sergeant up in the sky had shone His flashlight in the entire world's bunk. Every man on land and sea stared and wondered what it was they were seeing. Then t

he shockwave hit them. Webb was torn from his feet, landing on his ass. The man nearest him was thrown into a foxhole.

"My God," Webb whispered as the light faded.

He took off his helmet, thinking about CAPT Palmer and Robichaude. The childlike wonder was now mixed with a vague unease, verging on existential terror. His people had done that, not the Dark Ones or the Clickers.

The monsters had disappeared. Whatever hoodoo Robichaude had worked had done the trick. The sea was quiet, but for the occasional shark breaking the surface to feast on the innumerable dead.

The war ahead would be long, brutal and full of heartache, but at least they'd be fighting men. Sure, there would be dark times ahead, and no doubt more deployments of the horrifying new weapon that had just been deployed. But, in the end, through sacrifice and hardship, the fighting men of the USMC would persevere and...

A chill shot up his back as some horrible, multi-legged thing scuttled across his boot. For a moment he was terrified to look down.

Fucking sand crab. He crushed it under his heel.

76. JUNE, 2021

Luc Robichaude's truck was an old beater, the seats worn and battered, tears in the fabric revealing the interior stuffing. They traveled down Texas Highway 77, their destination uncertain until, to Cam's disbelief, they turned at a sign that read Uncertain.

The small town of Uncertain sat on the bayou system that the Robichaude's had called home for generations beyond count. And, according to Luc Robichaude, a colony of Dark Ones lived underneath its muddy water.

"Colonies of them all over the world, Doc. And with them comes Clickers, leftovers from when the oceans reached a lot further than they do now. Occasionally get one of their saltwater kin swimming up the Mississippi. Quite a difference. Like city folk coming down to visit their redneck cousins, see?"

Cam listened, enraptured, as the cypress trees and their Spanish moss reached out and closed around them. Robichaude made a turn onto a dirt road.

"You keep saying Deep Folk, Robichaude. Your great uncle called them Dark Ones. And the way you've described them is…different. Is this a separate subspecies?"

Robichaude shrugged his shoulders. "I suppose. They've been called all manner of things: Dark Ones, Deep Ones, Deep Folk. You'll see for yourself shortly the difference between them and your…lady friend. But whatever you call them, always be wary around them."

They emerged from the road into a small clearing. He saw two houses separated by thirty yards or so, and two boathouses that stretched out into the jutting trees and muddy water of the swamp.

Robichaude got out of the car. A large white dog appeared from behind the house on the right, happily trotting up and pushing his head under the man's hand, then turning to stare at Cam.

"He's a guest, Mojo. Don't go biting now," Robichaude said, barely glancing at the dog as he walked down toward the shore. "Don't mind him none. He's not overly friendly."

Cam hurried after him, sliding down the surprisingly slick hill, his shoes leaving tracks of mud in the soft grass. Robichaude walked out to the edge of the boathouse dock, waiting for Cam to catch up and gesturing out at the impenetrable forest. "Last chance, Doc. You want this, want to live and study them Deep Folk up close?"

Cam nodded, his hand reaching into his pocket to feel the old journal. "Yeah, I do."

Robichaude nodded, and reached out an expectant hand. Cam took a deep breath and placed the book into the Cajun's waiting grip. He saw Robichaude grin broadly. "Don't know how much that means to me. My folks are dead, brother and sister too, any words from kin are a comfort. Now sit back and get ready to see something powerful."

Cam did as he was told, sitting in an old plastic chair that looked like it had been on the dock for a few decades, watching as Robichaude produced a small harmonica in his hand. He played a haunting Cajun melody. Cam had never been one for any music other than the classics, and this didn't change his mind on the subject, but the tune intrigued him. He wondered if Robichaude had trained them somehow or if they had simply worked out an arrangement. Either way didn't seem in line with the inhuman creatures he'd read about.

When he finished, Robichaude sat on the edge of the dock, watching the water intently. They didn't have to wait long.

After maybe half an hour of silence, Robichaude stood and gestured for Cam to do the same. Beyond the witch doctor's shoulder, he saw the water slosh, disturbed by something massive moving beneath it.

Then it rose, dripping with mud and algae, twelve feet or more of muscle and scale. Its jaw was long, with an inner row of sharp tips. He recognized this as the same kind of Dark One that Alcide had described in his journal: primordial, untouched by whatever cataclysm had corrupted the Dark Ones' genetics, resulting in Jade's distinctive phenotype. It wore a crown made of dark mussel shells. In its left hand it held a trident and in its right a large bag that looked like it was made from some kind of alligator skin. But the most striking part of its appearance was the eyes, not completely black like Jade's, but brown and surprisingly human.

Robichaude bowed slightly and Cam followed suit. The monster inclined its head back. It said Robichaude's name, pronouncing each syllable slowly, and Cam was surprised to find that it spoke relatively clearly. "Ro-bi-chaude."

Moreso than he ever had in Jade's presence, Cam recognized almost palpably that, if it wanted to, the thing could reach over and snap him in two. Robichaude glanced back at Cam.

"Doc, meet Lincoln, chief of the Deep Folk."

Cam raised a hand in greeting, something that the creature mimicked. He looked at the Cajun and mouthed, *Lincoln?*

Robichaude ignored his disbelief and addressed the monster again. "He's read about my kin, studied the Clickers live, and knows about the rare breeds. If there is anyone who can help get you what you want, it's him."

The Dark One, Lincoln, turned its large eyes to him and croaked out something that he didn't understand, but he got the intent all the same.

You will come with me.

Cam nodded, fear and wonder mixing together. This had been the agreement, to live and learn amongst the Dark Ones themselves, help advance their knowledge from what he knew, from what he'd read.

The monstrous fish-man reached out and gingerly wrapped its hand around his body, leaning its trident against the boathouse and opening the sack wide, the yawning dark opening to receive him.

"If you don't go mad, you tell me what you learn when you come back above water. If you decide you ever want to come back," Robichaude called after him.

As he was placed into the sack and the string made of sinews drawn tight, he heard Robichaude call to the monster."Tell your grandpa I said hello. If anyone can make a brain Clicker to help him, it's that man you've got there."

The creature said something in its own language before Cam was wrenched downwards as it dove back into the river. The sack began to fill with water and he laughed as he left the world behind.

77. OCTOBER, 2020

Bubbles appeared in the water off the coast of a Pacific island. A few moments later a dog-sized, white Clicker with a distinctive, non-natural black marking on its back clambered up onto the sand.

Pinchy scuttled across the beach, stopping only to dig up a nest of seagull eggs. She was famished from almost three solid weeks of scrabbling along the ocean floor. Although she had no concept of terrestrial time, she knew she had been away from home for much too long.

First she'd been caught in that damn cage. She'd managed to kill a few humans after they had pulled her up out of the water and onto the boat. But then they'd subdued her with weights and chains. For a while after that she'd been kept in a largeish tank in the center of that warehouse, being gawked at by humans all day and snapping at them fruitlessly.

Then the next while was a blur. All she remembered was being cold and insensate. Ultimately, she'd been drawn out of her cold slumber by the calming appearance of a wise presence, an immature but kind Dark One who calmed Pinchy's nerves with her emotions.

A delightful slaughter and feeding had ensued, and in the chaos that had followed, the young Dark One had encouraged her to run and avoid any humans she saw. She'd scrabbled to the nearest waterway and followed it to the ocean, and from there her natural compass had kicked in.

Now, finally, after a long trek, Pinchy was home. She scuttled up to the human village first. The place was a cheerful, colorful place, painted in all sorts of colors. Four generations of artists, all descended from her first human friend, had turned the place into something of an artistic Mecca. The village children cheered and waved as she entered, and she tolerated them all running up and rubbing her carapace for good luck. She sat and endured it in place for a few minutes, her tail flicking back and forth like a metronome until they finally let her have her space again.

She made her way to the village shrine, where a bowl of mashed up fish and crab always waited for her, day or night. Part of the reason she tolerated the kids harassing her was that they were so devoted to chasing away the rats and other animals who sometimes tried to take her offering. Given a choice between a rough petting session from an overzealous infant and an empty food bowl, she would choose the former any day of the week.

She managed to slip out the back of the shrine without too much further kerfuffle. From there she headed down to the cliff faces on the west side of the island. Long ago she'd had a cluster of eggs here, and it had since become the designated breeding ground for her brood and her brood's broods and so forth. At this point dozens, if not hundreds of her kind were prowling the area, all showing varying shades of her own white carapace.

None yet approached her dog-like size. Given time, they would all grow larger, but so would she, ensuring that generations could always be identified. One of Pinchy's great… no, great-great grandchildren came rushing up, all atwitter.

Together they conducted an elaborate dance of legs and snapping claws, gradually communicating what was on the other's mind. Pinchy expressed her happiness to be home and some portion of what had gone past, though the broodling was too excited to pay much attention to the old matron's thoughts.

Pinchy gathered from her great-grandchild that new mates had appeared in the area. No longer would incest have to be the norm amongst her nest. A veritable army of bright green glowing Clickers had appeared and soon the ocean bed would be churning with eggs and spermatophores.

Pinchy danced with other favorite offspring and a few new additions to the nest since her disappearance before growing tired and begging off. All of her business for the day attended to, she knew she could finally relax. She climbed up to the highest point on the island, a small hillock rarely frequented by the humans of the village below.

The humans stayed away for superstitious reasons. The site was a cairn, marked in an unusual style for the graves of the island by a crossed pair of sticks. Pinchy had long ago unburied the body, though.

The unearthed skeleton lay nearby, lounging in a manner similar to how Doodles had lain in life. Pinchy cuddled up against his ribcage and draped his arm over his carapace with her claw. She settled down to rest for the evening in the same way she always did. While she'd been away she had missed her friend.

EPILOGUE

SEAFOOD FOR THOUGHT

Philadelphia Post (Opinion)
August 12, 2020

It's a hoax.

Yes, yes, yes. We've all seen the video. Those of us who didn't watch it live have waggled our YouTube cursors back and forth over it a hundred times by now.

"Dark Ones."

"Clickers."

I can't believe I even have to write this piece. You do know about Hollywood magic, don't you? You do know Luke didn't really blow up the Death Star and Bruce Willis wasn't really a ghost, right?

Yes, yes, yes. We've all heard from the so-called film "experts" insisting that what happened couldn't have been faked. And there is the ongoing mystery of what really happened to the director of NOAA and the other government officials in that room. But do I really have to be the one to tell you, especially in this political climate, that the Democrats would happily execute such a coup? And that they would make up as preposterous an explanation for it as possible?

"Dark Ones."

"Clickers."

Anyone who believes that probably also believed masks would protect them from the kung flu two years ago.

National Journal of Oceanographic and Oceanological Studies
December 7, 2020
Wildasin, Canon, Thomas, San Giovanni, et al.

Abstract: The discovery of the Clicker this past year, much like the coelacanth in the 1930s, has led to a boom in "living fossils." But should every odd new cancerine species be considered an individual? There is, for instance, great doubt about whether the bioluminescent "glowing Clicker" discovered off the coast of Guadalcanal in the Pacific constitutes a distinct subspecies or is merely a regular Clicker which has been exposed to some unknown natural phenomenon, perhaps radiation from the Fukushima event.

RADIOACTIVE TERROR

Transcript, *Deadlier Catch: Fishing for Monsters*
February 6, 2021

Glenn: It was the middle of the night when they came up, brilliant green like the auroras we have up here.

Ware: Captain Glenn, you were the first man to begin deep-sea Clicker fishing and the only survivor of your crew. Were you aware of this breed before you attempted to fish off Guadalcanal?

Glenn: You mother<censored>, of course I didn't know! We came loaded for the regular red ones. I didn't know a god<censored> school of glowing green bas<censored> was going to shoot fire from their god<censored> tails and sink my god<censored> boat!

WEDDING ANNOUNCEMENT

Humans Magazine
May 17, 2021

Wedding bells are in the air…or under the water? That's right, it's a May wedding for the now world famous Dark One

Jade Custer and her fiancée, Kanye West. Recently divorced, Kanye was born…

MY COUSIN SAW THE GILLMAN IN HIS GARAGE

Robert Fontenaux "Snorkel" et al.
Transcript, *Finding Gillman*
June 24, 2021

Snorkel: We are here in middle of nowhere Fouke, Arkansas, location of the infamous Boggy Creek and its monster. But all of that has been thrown out the window by a Dark One sighting.

Dee Dee: Starting from the Wright Patman Dam, the Sulphur River flows for miles and miles before meeting the Red River, an area commonly referred to as the Sulphur River Bottoms.

Shay: People have always said that there were undiscovered species in the Bottoms, and that appears to have been proven true, now that local resident Dustin Pickens has spotted a real life Dark One. We here at the GFRO take every sighting seriously and we cannot wait to hear his account.

Pickens: Yeah, so I've got a big stream behind my house, like big, big, crazy big. <spits> Anyway, I was heading out to get my cousin Bradley a beer, Coors, cause he's dirt poor and can't afford any good <censored>. So, there I was opening the door, and this seven-foot-tall son of a <censored> was using the belt sander!

…AND A PRAYER

Tucker, Williams, et al.
Transcript, "Good Morrow"
September 19, 2021

Ollie: …and that hippopotamus went wee wee wee…all the way home.

Tom: <chuckles> Quite a scoop, Ollie. Of ice cream!

Ollie: Oh, you're just joshing me.

Tom: That's right, I am. Now, Ollie, you're on location in… where is it, exactly?

Ollie: Folgefonna Glacier, Norway. Now all the talk around town has been about how much the glacier has diminished recently. In fact, today is the warmest day on reco…holy shit!

Tom: Bleep…did we bleep him in time?

Ollie: What the fuck?

Tom: Ollie, please, we are broadcasting live. Please remember that a big portion of our audience is children of poor people who can't afford streaming services.

Ollie: They're in my hair! They're in my hair!

Tom: Ollie? Ollie? Greg, is the camera still running? Are you guys okay out there? Sorry, folks, I think we're having technical…oh, there it goes. Greg, our cameraman, is capturing footage of…what is that? Are those Clickers?

Diane: I think they are Clickers, Tom. I mean, the silhouettes…

Greg: Jesus Christ!

Tom: Greg, are you okay?

Greg: Motherfuckers have grown wings. They're flying!

END

Thank you for reading CLICKERS NEVER DIE. Whether you liked it or not we hope you'll take a moment to leave a review on Amazon or your favorite book review site. Reviews are vitally important to us as authors, both to help us market our book and to improve our writing in the future. Thank you!
- Kozeniewski and Young

ACKNOWLEDGEMENTS

Stephen would like to thank Brian Keene, who didn't poop those items, Amy Lower, for her unwavering support in all things, and Wile E. Young, whose devilish handsomeness during the book tour will be his main contribution to this text.

Wile E. would like to also thank Brian Keene, who offers up the wisest advice when he is boycotting pants. He would also like to thank Emily Rice for her patience, strength, and ability to provide a needed kick in the rear. Finally, he would like to thank Stephen Kozeniewski, who continued to cheer as Wile E. carried the entire project on his shoulders.

ABOUT THE AUTHORS

Stephen Kozeniewski (pronounced "causin' ooze key") is a two-time winner of the World Horror Grossout Contest. His published work includes the Splatterpunk Award-nominated THE HEMATOPHAGES and its Indie Horror Book Award-nominated prequel SKINWRAPPER. He lives in Pennsylvania, the birthplace of the modern zombie, with his girlfriend and their two cats.

Wile E. Young is from Texas, where he grew up surrounded by stories of ghosts and monsters. During his writing career he has managed to both have a price put on his head and publish his southern themed horror stories. He obtained his bachelor's degree in History, which provided no advantage or benefit during his years as an aviation specialist and I.T. guru.

His longer works include *Catfish in the Cradle* (2019), *The Perfectly Fine House* (2020), *The Magpie Coffin* (2020), and *Shades of the Black Stone* (2022). His short stories have been featured in various anthologies including the *Clickers Forever* (2018), *Behind the Mask—Tales From the Id* (2018), *Corporate Cthulhu* (2018), *And Hell Followed* (2019), and *Bludgeon Tools: A Splatterpunk Anthology* (2021).

CROSSROAD
PRESS

Printed in Great Britain
by Amazon